Bantam Books by Thomas William Simpson

THE CARETAKER
THE HANCOCK BOYS

THE
HANCOCK BOYS

A NOVEL OF SUSPENSE

Thomas William Simpson

BANTAM BOOKS
New York   Toronto   London   Sydney   Auckland

THE HANCOCK BOYS

A Bantam Book / March 2000

ISBN 0-7394-0923-9

Published simultaneously in the United States and Canada

Bantam Books are published by Bantam Books, a division of Random
House, Inc. Its trademark, consisting of the words "Bantam Books" and
the portrayal of a rooster, is Registered in U.S. Patent and Trademark
Office and in other countries. Marca Registrada. Bantam Books, 1540
Broadway, New York, New York 10036.

WARNING

Herein lies a tale of love and lust, clarity
and confusion, greed and infidelity, homicide and possibly even fratricide.

Not for the squeamish or the delicate
of nature.

IMPORTANT PERSONS
(MORE OR LESS IN ORDER OF APPEARANCE)

John Hancock. . . . . author
Will Hancock. . . . . author
Frank Hagstrom. . . . . attorney
Nicky Pegg. . . . . nanny
Sylvia Gierek. . . . . housekeeper
Clara Dare Hancock. . . . . art dealer
Sir Rodney Byrnes. . . . . suitor
Thomas Young. . . . . world traveler
Babe Overton. . . . . actress
Gerdy MacDaniel. . . . . psychiatrist
Leland Fisher. . . . . publisher
Rafe Paquita. . . . . fisherman
William Hancock. . . . . father
Lenore Hancock. . . . . mother
Headmaster Masters. . . . . headmaster
Linda Carson. . . . . family friend
Zelda Cosgrove. . . . . professor
Charles Dare. . . . . art dealer
Anita Dare. . . . . art dealer
Al-the-Gumshoe Brown. . . . . private eye
Hillary Fisher. . . . . vamp
Dicky Cosgrove. . . . . psychopath
Florence Baker. . . . . professional student
Maxwell Edison. . . . . attorney

And the Lord said unto Cain, "Where is Abel thy brother?" And Cain said, "I know not. Am I my brother's keeper?"

—GENESIS 4:9

PROLOGUE
APRIL 27, 1984

Hancock had a problem with Hagstrom. A big problem. For months, Hancock had been searching for a way to solve his problem. Now, finally, after many excuses and much lollygagging, the time had come to take action.

He left his seedy motel room just off Sunset Boulevard and climbed aboard his used ten-speed Schwinn. He had on shorts, sneakers, a gray T-shirt, and close-fitting nylon gloves. He also had a small leather pack slung over his shoulders. Inside the pack was a ball peen hammer, an ice pick, and a .38-caliber Saturday night special wrapped in one of those small thin motel room towels.

Hancock's own mother, Lenore, had she still been alive, would not have recognized her son. His light brown hair was tinted dirty blond, a process he'd done himself in his motel bathroom sink. A false mustache of the same color was pasted to his upper lip. Mirrored sunglasses hid his deep blue eyes. But even in disguise, Hancock certainly didn't look like a young man with murder on his mind.

Hancock crossed Hollywood Boulevard, downshifted, and started into the hills. His route was a tricky one, winding along such modern thoroughfares as Achilles, Hercules, and Apollo. But Hancock knew the turns without even glancing at the road signs. And a good thing, too, because the uninitiated could easily find himself lost up in those Hollywood Hills. And once lost, an officer of the law out on neighborhood patrol might be called upon to help extricate that person from the endless loops and switchbacks and cul-de-sacs.

A policeman was exactly what Hancock did not need.

His thighs and calves were like bands of steel from all the bike riding he had been doing since arriving in California. He had no problem on even the steepest ascents. He made his way up Laurel Canyon Boulevard until he reached Mulholland Drive. A sharp left on Mulholland, and suddenly he had less than a mile to go. Traffic was light. Dusk was just beginning to fall. Perfect timing. Right on schedule.

Below, he could see Beverly Hills and the city of Los Angeles covered with a slightly orange and toxic haze. The smog prevented him from seeing Santa Monica and the great green Pacific beyond. But he had no time for sightseeing. He kept pedaling, his powerful legs working like a pair of pistons, his heart pumping wildly to keep up with his homicidal desires.

Tough to imagine Hancock as a killer. This clean-cut, middle-class white kid from back East. Harvard-educated, his whole life stretching out before him like one big happy Hollywood movie. What, you might wonder, is going on here? Why the .38 special and the ice pick and ball peen hammer?

Just past the Fryman Canyon Overlook, Hancock swung left off Mulholland onto Allenwood. Then another quick left onto Edwin Drive. Edwin Drive dead-ended after just a few hundred yards. Hancock pulled into the last driveway on the right. The Schwinn bumped across a section of decorative cobblestones. But the cobblestones soon gave way to smooth macadam. Maybe a hundred feet from the house, he pulled off the drive into a landscaped area of small trees and shrubs. He ditched the bike behind a rhododendron and on foot moved closer to the house.

The house was a long, low-slung contemporary made of

redwood and glass. It commanded panoramic views of the valley below. Hancock watched and waited as night fell and millions of lights snapped on across the valley.

There were no cars in the driveway. Once dusk had faded to darkness, he peered into the garage. He spotted his father's vintage T-bird and Hagstrom's mile-long Lincoln. No sign of Babe Overton's Mustang. That meant there was a good chance Hagstrom was inside. Alone.

Slowly, Hancock made his way around the house. When he reached the window of Hagstrom's office in the back right corner, he took special care to shield himself from view. The desk lamp was lit, papers were strewn across the desk, the attorney's briefcase lay open on the carpet, but there was no sign of Hagstrom.

Nor was Hagstrom in the master bedroom or the den or the kitchen or the dining room. Dammit. Maybe Hagstrom had gone out with his young squeeze after all. But months of reconnaissance had taught Hancock and his brother that rarely, if ever, did Hagstrom leave the house without taking either the T-Bird or the Lincoln.

Made almost entirely of glass, the front of the house overlooked the Valley of Angels far below. For over a year now, Hancock and his brother had been discussing and contemplating their attack. There had been numerous delays and setbacks. Murder, after all, was an awfully big step, a major commitment, not exactly something the Hancock boys did on a whim. Now, suddenly, Hancock's heart felt as if it might explode at any second right out of his chest. He suddenly feared he could not go through with this.

He stood there, wondering what to do, thinking he might have to retreat, feeling the sweat under his arms even though the night had turned chill. He decided he'd have to call his brother back East, tell his brother the responsibility once again rested on his shoulders. He could not do the job. He could not go through with it.

But then something rather extraordinary happened. Some might say Fate intervened in the lives of John and Will Hancock.

When he looked through the tall, floor-to-ceiling windows, Hancock spotted Big Frank Hagstrom standing on a wooden chair that had been placed on top of the glass coffee table in front of the living room sofa.

Earlier in the evening Frank Hagstrom had thrown a length of heavy-duty half-inch hemp over one of the exposed beams that crossed the fifteen-foot-high ceiling, tied off one end, then fashioned a hangman's noose on the other end. He had then taken one of the dining room chairs, placed it on the coffee table, and climbed skyward. A few minutes later, rope in hand but unable to finish himself off, he had climbed back down.

Distraught over various emotional, financial, and legal matters, Frank, normally an extremely strong and decisive individual, had been climbing up and down off his makeshift gallows for a couple of hours. He had just climbed up for maybe the tenth time when Hancock arrived unannounced at his parents' old house to put a bullet between the attorney's eyes.

This was a twist of fortune Hancock had not anticipated. He just wished his brother could be here to bear witness.

He watched as Hagstrom climbed down, then up again, then down again. Hancock had no idea why Hagstrom was contemplating suicide. If he had been a reader of the metro section of the L.A. *Times,* he might have had some small inkling. Over the past several weeks there had been quite a few stories mentioning Frank Hagstrom as possibly being involved in various sordid activities with a wide range of unsavory characters. But the newspaper had only brushed the surface. Frank Hagstrom, civic leader and one of the most sought-after attorneys in Los Angeles County, was in trouble. Major trouble. He had been stealing from the wrong clients, losing the wrong cases, associating with the wrong lot.

Hancock and his brother were just two of the many folks hot on Frank's trail.

Hancock watched for at least half an hour. He finally concluded that Frank Hagstrom did not have the guts to hang himself. So he decided to go inside and pay the lawyer a visit, maybe give him a hand with his suicidal desires.

But first Hancock had to get into the house. Then he could see about taking care of a little unfinished business. Family business . . .

PART ONE
JUNE 6, 1999

SUNDAY MORNING—
BOSTON, MASSACHUSETTS

So these two police detectives show up at the John Hancock house on Louisburg Square in the Beacon Hill section of Boston. They want to talk to Mr. Hancock.

Nicky, the teenage nanny from Yorkshire, answers the front door. She sneers at the two detectives after they identify themselves. "I'm afraid Mr. Hancock's working, and when he's working I'm not permitted to disturb him."

The cops exchange expressions of annoyance. One of them says, "It won't take long, miss. Why don't you just tell Mr. Hancock the police are here?"

Nicky has her orders: no interruptions. She's been with the Hancocks eight months now and she learned that one on her first day.

"It would be better," she tells them, "if you came back this afternoon. Or maybe if you called first and made an appointment."

"Sorry, honey," says the other detective, "but we ain't comin' back dis afternoon, and we definitely ain't makin' no phone calls or no appointments. We got urgent police business here. Now you run along and tell Hancock we wanna see him before I haul you in for hamperin' an investigation."

Nineteen-year-old Nicky glares at the detective. "I'll see if he's available." Then she slams the door in their faces.

The detectives look at each other and shake their heads.

"Brassy little bitch, huh?"

"Yeah, real bitchy. But from here on out, Joey, I want you to let me do the talking. Don't take no offense, but you sound like a freaking low-life hoodlum. Telling her we *ain't* coming back and we *ain't* making no phone calls or no appointments. Jesus. We want to get ahead, we got to do better than that."

"Hey, Moe, listen, I felt like I had ta get tough wit' her. Didn't you go for my hamperin'-the-investigation bit?"

"Yeah, Joey, I went for it. You're my ace in the hole. So when Hancock gets here you just stand there and look like a cop."

Nicky retreats to the kitchen where she activates the intercom for the third floor.

John Hancock, lost in some fictional maelstrom, practically jumps out of his leather desk chair when the intercom buzzes. He has been a long way off, buried in the depraved psyche of his twisted protagonist.

The intercom hangs on the wall beside the door. He pushes the button. "This better be good, Nick. Fire in the hole. Floods on the Charles. Barbarians at the gate."

"It's the police, sir."

"Police? That's worse than barbarians. What do they want?"

"They want to talk to you, sir."

"Probably they want money. For their widows-and-orphans fund. It's a subtle, and I suppose legal, kind of shakedown."

"Shakedown, sir?"

"Never mind, Nick. Tell them I'll be down in a few minutes."

John Hancock crosses his office to the large front window and draws back the sheer cotton curtain. No sign of a patrol car out on the Square. They must have come in an unmarked. Maybe that dark blue Chevy Caprice parked over on Pinckney.

Hancock returns to his desk. He glances at his morning's output: four and a half hastily scribbled pages on a yellow legal pad. Unlike his brother, who prefers to work directly on the keyboard, Hancock has always written his first drafts in longhand. He enjoys the frenzied spontaneity of the pen slashing and dashing across the page. But he knows there will be no more slashing and dashing this morning. His concentration has been zapped.

On his way downstairs Hancock stops off at the master bedroom, a cozy suite on the second floor furnished in antique cherry. A quick glance in the mirror and he decides boxer shorts and T-shirt might not make the right impression. He pulls on fresh chinos and a cotton sweater.

Hancock stands a hair under six feet. His brother stands six feet exactly. Next year they will both turn forty, but in a pinch they could probably do thirty-five, maybe even thirty-three. They weigh one seventy and one seventy-one respectively, lean and solid.

A man who likes to keep grooming time to a minimum, Hancock wears his light brown hair closely cropped. Wash, towel dry, and go. Out of necessity, brother Will wears his hair precisely the same way.

Hancock heads downstairs. He pulls open his front door. The two Boston police detectives look slightly miffed. Probably a result of being made to wait. Hancock smiles and invites them inside.

They stand in the foyer, an expansive and affluent space occupied by a crystal chandelier and several original oil paintings, including a small Monet of a boy fishing from a bridge. The detectives do not notice. They are not art connoisseurs.

Joey and Moe flash their badges. Hancock takes a quick and disinterested look. No reason for him to think these guys aren't who they say they are.

"This is Detective Connor," says Moe. "I'm Detective Raymond."

Hancock shakes hands all around. He loves to shake. "What can I do for a couple of Boston's finest on this lovely spring morning?"

Moe makes a small production out of studying his note pad. "You are Mr. John Hancock. Is that correct, sir?"

"Yes, it is."

Moe flips through the pages of his pad. "Mr. Hancock," he says, "we're here this morning on a missing person report."

"Missing person report? Who's missing?" John's eyes narrow. He grows instantly alarmed. "Not the boys? The boys aren't missing."

"Boys, sir?"

"My sons? They're not missing, are they? I walked them down to the Church of the Advent just an hour or so ago for Sunday school. Should have stayed myself for service, but, well, I had work to do."

"This is not about your sons, sir."

"Well, that's a relief. Then who are we talking about?"

Moe checks his pad again. "Do you have a brother, sir? A Mr. William Larson Hancock?"

Hancock regroups. Then, "Well, yes . . . but he . . ." John takes a deep breath. "Excuse me, detective, but who, exactly, is missing?"

"We have a report your brother Will is missing."

Hancock studies the two officers. "You're kidding me. I mean, this is some kind of joke. Right? Lee Fisher sent you?"

"This is not a joke, sir. And I'm afraid I don't know any Lee Fisher."

"Leland Fisher. He's my publisher. A pretty fair practical joker. Sometimes—"

"This is not a practical joke, sir."

Hancock sees that now. He takes a second to square up his thoughts, then asks, "Can you tell me who filed the report?"

Joey, despite Moe's earlier warning, takes a step forward and demands, "Let's not play games, Mr. Hancock.

You got any knowledge concerning your brother's where-abouts or not?"

Hancock rubs his forehead. He does not wish to sound impatient. "I have plenty of knowledge," he tells Detective Connor. And then, again, to Detective Raymond, "I would like to know who filed the report."

Moe goes back to his note pad. "I believe your wife did, sir."

"My wife?"

"Is your wife Clara Dare Hancock?"

"Yes."

"Is Mrs. Hancock home, sir? Perhaps we could talk to her, also."

"She's in London." Hancock can feel his brain begin-ning to churn. He does his best to keep calm. "On busi-ness. She left yesterday."

"I see."

"I have no idea," says Hancock, "why my wife would have filed a missing person report on my brother. Do you know when she filed the report?"

Moe returns to his pad. There's not really anything on the pad, at least nothing about this Hancock business. Just some directions to the house on Louisburg Square, and a short list of stuff his bossy girlfriend ordered him to pick up at the grocery on his way home: Bologna, for chris-sakes, and Cheese Nips. If she serves bologna sandwiches again for dinner, he'll kill her.

"The report's dated Friday, sir. It could have been filed then or maybe the day before. I didn't take the call, so I have no way of knowing. Our job is to come out and follow up. See what we can find out."

Hancock, his normally smooth and trouble-free face suddenly lined with confusion and a fair amount of anxi-ety, nods. "I understand."

"So," asks Joey, tired of his bit part, "you gonna help us out with this or what? If you know where your brother's at we can clear this up quick."

Hancock takes another deep breath, then says, "I hate

to tell you this, Detective, but my brother Will has been dead almost twenty years. He died in a skin diving accident off the coast of Belize back in 1982.''

Joey and Moe did not hang around long after learning of Will Hancock's tragic and premature demise. They were not instructed to hang around. So they mumble some subdued apologies, then beat a hasty retreat.

A retreat, Hancock notices while standing on his front stoop, not to that dark blue Caprice, but to a fire-engine-red Ford Mustang parked up the street. Not your typical cop car, he thinks, but then maybe detectives drive their own cars these days. No reason why they shouldn't. Still, he finds a pen in his pocket and a scrap of paper on the hall table. The one guy's name, he's pretty sure, was Raymond. The other guy, he can't quite remember, Connolly or Carver, something Irish like that. Though he sounded more like an Italian. From Brooklyn.

Hancock scribbles down their names, then stuffs the paper into his pocket and heads toward the rear of the house in search of Nicky. He finds the nanny in the kitchen sipping tea with Sylvia, the cook and housekeeper.

"Ah," he says, "two of my favorite women in the world." And then, as is his habit, he quotes a bit of the Bard, " 'That man that hath a tongue, I say, is no man, if with his tongue he cannot win a woman.' "

Nicky, uncertain, blushes. Sylvia scowls. But only on the outside. On the inside she succumbs to Mr. Hancock's charms. It is a game they play: he the carefree American with the wagging tongue and devilish smile; she the repressed eastern European, dour, silent, and disapproving. Still, Hancock often wonders if Sylvia knows the truth, if she has this massive deception all figured out.

"Have we heard from the boss?" he asks. "Has she called?"

Nicky shakes her head. "I haven't spoken with Mrs. Hancock, sir."

Sylvia scowls again. She does not actually answer the question. The question, in her mind, is an insult. "I would never not inform you of a personal call." Her English is slow and formal, but perfectly enunciated. "A call from Mrs. Hancock especially."

Hancock smiles at the Polish cook. "Ah, Sylvia, you would have made one hell of a general. Had you been in charge of the border, the Nazis never would have crossed the Oder." He bows formally to the ladies. "And now, if you will excuse me, I will attempt to get some work done so that we might get the bills paid, keep the wolves from the door."

Hancock heads for the back stairway, but stops on the bottom step. "Are you going to get the boys, Nick? Or shall I?"

"I'll fetch them, sir."

Hancock nods. "Send them up when you get back, would you? The three of us have places to go, things to do, games to play."

John retreats to his third-floor office. He tries to go back to work on the latest Hancock novel, but the unexpected arrival of those two Beantown detectives has sucked all the creative juices right out of his brain.

So he paces. Back and forth across that large office. Surrounded by the necessities and indulgences of the writer's life: pens, pencils, computers, printers, encyclopedias, maps, dart board on the back of the door, putter and a slew of golf balls, fax machine, oak filing cabinet, thick dictionary on a wheeled stand (opened, though Hancock pays no attention to it, to the page defining the word *fratricide),* Post-It notes posted everywhere, and paper, reams of paper, blank white paper, lined yellow paper, paper filled with words and sentences and stories. And the books, shelves of books, all variety of books: novels, biographies, histories, science books, travel books, books on politics and war, books on farming and animal husbandry. Books from floor to ceiling. Books containing all the knowledge in the world.

Amongst all this stuff, Hancock paces. And wonders why his wife would have called the police to report his brother missing. Strange. Very strange. He wants to call her and ask her, seek out an explanation. Several times he picks up the phone. A couple of times he even begins to dial. Once he actually rings up her hotel in London. The Savoy, of course. Only the best for Clara. She never settles for less. A silver spoon in her mouth. Not born with one, but earned, through hard work, diligence, and deception.

Hancock hangs up before the front desk clerk answers.

For Hancock has learned over the years to reign in his instincts, control his emotions, pull back and assess the situation. If his wife did call the cops, she's probably expecting him to call and demand an explanation. Better not to call, to wait her out, see how things develop. Of course, he could phone her up and say nothing at all about his little chat with the two detectives. Just ignore the subject altogether. See how she handles herself under those conditions.

Perfectly, that's how she'll handle it. Just like she handles everything. Besides, Hancock knows once he has her on the line, he'll blurt out the whole bit about the cops stopping by to inquire about brother Will.

The boys put his dithering on hold. They came roaring up the stairs, a couple of firemen responding to a five-alarm blaze. Choking from the smoke, but fearless in the face of flames, they press forward without concern for their own lives.

"Up here!" shouts John junior, the older of the two, age six. "A victim!"

"Let's get him out!" hollers young Willy, age five. "Before he fries!"

They charge into the office, wrestle the victim to the carpet, resuscitate him with their make-believe oxygen tanks, then hustle him down the stairs and into the master bedroom where the air is fresh, the coast clear.

Hancock gives them both bear hugs, then thanks them

for saving his hide. He hands them each a buck for their courage and heroism in the face of peril. Of course, what the old man is really paying them for is their burst of creativity. He thinks creativity, above all else, is man's greatest gift, the one thing that ultimately sets him apart from the other beasts roaming the planet in search of food and shelter. Hancock encourages its daily practice in his offspring.

John junior and young Willy take their money and run. They go straight to their bedroom where they rip off their Sunday school duds and pull on dungarees and sweat-shirts.

John junior and Willy share a room, just the way their father and their uncle shared a room in the old days. These two might not be identical twins, but they are clearly brothers. A blind man could see that. And Hancock believes brothers, especially when still youngsters, should bunk together so they can build that all-important frater-nal bond.

They put away their Sunday school clothes, then race from their room to find their father, easily the greatest and coolest guy in their little universe. He's still lying on his bed, his thoughts retreating to those questions concerning his wife and his brother and those two detectives.

"Let's go, Dad! Time to go!"

More bear hugs. "Where are we going?"

"Over to the Common. You said we could fly the kite after Sunday school. Maybe play hide and seek."

"Fly the kite?" Dad wonders aloud. "When did I say that?"

"The other day. A couple days ago."

Hancock thinks it over. Figures out what must have happened. "You're right," he says. "I did say we'd fly the kite after Sunday school. So let's roll. What are we hanging around here for?"

The boys shrug. They do not waste another second. Off they go. An energetic and happy trio.

Before John Hancock became a father, he was not at all

sure he even wanted to have kids. Now his two boys mean more to him than anything else in the world.

On his way out the back door, John grabs the cell phone and stuffs it in the pocket of his windbreaker. Just in case he suddenly becomes overwhelmed with the desire to call Clara.

SUNDAY AFTERNOON—
LONDON, ENGLAND

Clara Dare Hancock frightens most men. Her beauty. Her height. Her confidence. Her charm. Her intellect. Her money. And maybe most of all, her drive, her undaunted ambition. She even gave John Hancock a pretty good run some years back before finally succumbing to his considerable talents. Of course, Hancock had some help seducing Ms. Dare. Two against one can hardly be construed as a fair fight.

Right now Clara glides around her suite at the Savoy: large bedroom, lavish bath, sitting room complete with bar and gas fireplace. Clara, all five feet ten of her, glides around that five-hundred-pounds-per-night suite with style and grace: left hand on left hip, right hand pressed to right ear, a tiny cellular flip phone handling the business end of things.

"I don't care if it *is* Sunday, Joanne. I don't care if it's Easter Sunday. I want you to get over to the gallery, get the lights on, get the heat up, get the floor swept, and get the dust off the furniture."

Clara pauses to listen to her gallery manager, Ms. Joanne Smith, but she does not listen for long. "So this was supposed to happen tomorrow. So what? We have to be flexible in life, Joanne." Clara takes a moment to sweep a few strands of her short blond hair from her forehead. "If our Arab friend wants to see the paintings today instead of tomorrow, I think we should accommodate the man. After all, he is interested in spending a considerable amount of money in our modest little shop."

Clara Dare Hancock has been stroking—figuratively, not physically—this particular Arab, for months, almost a year. He fancies himself a man of culture, what with his two years at an Oxford boarding school and his ten zillion dollars in Swiss banks. Clara just wants a minuscule slice of his fortune, and in return she will give him a large Toulouse-Lautrec of Paris show girls and a dark, gloomy little Manet that the Met craves, but they want it for a song and Clara is certainly not in the charity business. Maybe someday, when she's old and gray and wrinkled, Clara will recreate herself as a philanthropist, but not now, not today.

So she gives Joanne, very knowledgeable when it comes to Impressionist and Post-Impressionist art, but rather dull otherwise, her marching orders, then she closes her cell phone and tosses it on the sofa. Clara is long and very lean with never-ending legs and clear, sky blue eyes. One thinks of a mindless runway model, not a tough and savvy businesswoman brokering expensive pieces of art, when one catches a glimpse of Ms. Clara Dare Hancock.

She runs her hands down the sides of her ankle-length silk robe and sighs. Clara is all alone in that suite, but she hates to be alone. And so she does what she has always done, done since just a little girl left home alone while her mother went out and scrubbed floors for a living: She pretends in some psychologically warped part of her brain that she is up on stage, that an audience, hushed and captivated, watches her every move, her every gesture. She does not disappoint. She loosens the waistband of her robe and lets it fall from her shoulders. And beneath the robe, nothing at all; no bra, no panties, just smooth white skin. Her breasts are small, but firm, and very nicely shaped. She still, at thirty-six, has a tiny waist, but hips a bit wider than she would like, the result of two births, neither a piece of cake, both virtual wars within her womb. But ask her and she will tell you she would not hesitate to fight those wars again. Those wars gave her the greatest victories of her life: John Jr. and little Willy.

She crosses now to the bed and picks up the room phone. She gets an outside line and dials up the Beacon Hill town house. Just to say hello. Just to tell her boys she loves them and misses them and can't wait to see them. It's only been a day, but the separation makes it feel like a month.

Too bad Sylvia answers and explains they've all just left to fly the kite.

Another sigh, this one filled with disappointment, then, "Please tell them I called, Sylvia. And that I will call again later."

Sylvia assures Mrs. Hancock she will relay the message. Clara sighs again. She wanted to hear their little voices, so full of wonder and enthusiasm.

Half an hour later the phone rings as Clara luxuriates in the deep tub topped with velvety soft Savoy bubble bath. She thinks about not answering it, but decides it might be her Arab friend. So she reaches out through the bubbles and grabs the phone off the marble ledge. "Hello?"

"Clare?"

"Yes."

"It's Rodney."

As if she didn't know. That snooty upper-class English prattle. Nearly as stuffy as the Prince of Wales. Whom Rodney knows, by the way. Just one of the reasons why Clara finds Sir Rodney amusing. "So it is."

"You've arrived?"

"Just," lies Clara. Actually, she's been in town almost twenty-four hours. An eternity in Rodney-time. Usually he sniffs her out anywhere in Europe within minutes of her clearing Customs.

"Settling in?"

It fascinates her how he rarely speaks in complete sentences. "Yes," she answers. "I'm having a warm bath." Never hot. It would scorch that fine white skin.

"Ah, how delightful."

Sir Rodney Byrnes: the title goes back some generations, back to Britain's early days in Africa. One of Rodney's ancestors joyously killed large numbers of Bantu heathens in the name of the Crown, killed them with cannon and rifle and various poisons when all the heathens had were sticks. And maybe a few stones. But they also had gold and diamonds in their unspoiled hills and the Hanovers certainly coveted those. So Byrnes the Elder helped the residents of Buckingham get the goods. And for his efforts, Queen Victoria granted him knighthood by touching some silly ornamental sword to his shoulder and declaring his atrocities great and wondrous deeds for the Empire.

So here we have Rodney, a number of generations removed from all that Dark Continent loot, pressing past forty now, and not really a single accomplishment under his belt. He once dabbled in the dramatic arts, fancied himself, for a time, a Shakespearean in both intellect and temperament. Too bad he couldn't act worth a cat's ear, though he did once demonstrate an uncanny ability to mimic women, both in voice and in movement.

But lack of talent and ambition have been the least of Rodney's problems. His biggest curse has always been his romantic heart. Unlike most members of his family, who ruthlessly married for the dough, Rodney has long wanted true love. Sure, he wants the money, too, but not without the romance. Over the years he has had his share of lusty entanglements, a dozen or more heart-wrenching affairs, but the combination of pounds sterling and breathtaking love has never quite happened for Byrnes the Younger.

Until that is, his introduction one artsy afternoon a year and a half or so ago to Ms. Clara Dare Hancock of Boston, Massachusetts. His love for her proved instant and enduring, especially after he found out she owned successful art galleries in Boston, London, and Paris. A beautiful and intelligent woman with her own money. Only from America.

Rodney has been pursuing Clara ever since. And so what if she's married? That merely makes the chase more tantalizing.

Clara lolls beneath the bubbles. "Yes," she tells him, "it is rather delightful."

A low moan falls from Rodney's mouth. "Perhaps I could come up and join you?"

"Come up? Where are you?"

"Down in the lobby, actually," admits Rodney. "Just thought I'd pop around."

Clara is not surprised that Rodney is downstairs. In fact, she is surprised he took so long to call. And even more surprised he's not out in the bedroom, chatting her up through the bathroom door. A quick smile and a gentle hand on an elbow, and Rodney could easily charm one of the Latvian room maids into producing her passkey.

"Sorry," she tells him, "it's not a good time. I have a meeting in less than an hour."

"At the gallery?"

"Yes."

"With this sheik fellow?" Rodney's tone is ripe with sarcasm. Like all Englishmen in his social class, Rodney envies and loathes all well-heeled foreigners. In particular, the superrich Arab oil tycoons. After all, not so many years ago, the English controlled all that sandy real estate covering the black gold. Now a bunch of unshaven camel herders control the oil, control everything, dammit, including most of downtown London.

"I think," says Clara, "he's ready to buy the Toulouse-Lautrec. And hopefully the Manet."

Rodney suppresses a sarcastic retort by thinking about the profits Clara will soon reap. Profits that, if he plays his cards right, could one day flow his way. "That," he tells her, "would put you in the pink."

Clara is no fool. She knows what Rodney Byrnes wants. She knows he wants her to leave her husband, move to London, become his lover, maybe, eventually, marry him.

But none of that is going to happen. Ever. She enjoys Rodney, at least as a social creature. He can be charming and entertaining. He knows everyone and is invited to all the best parties. Last July he even took her to the semifinals at Wimbledon. They sat together in the Royal Box, just two rows behind the Duke and Duchess of Kent. They had strawberries and cream with lords and ladies. Yes, it had all been dreadfully boring, but it proved to Clara that she had come a long, long way from her humble boarding-house beginnings in the low-rent district of Greater Boston.

But domestic life with Rodney? Not a chance. Clara loves her family.

Thomas Young takes a cab from Heathrow Airport to London. Thomas just flew in from Edinburgh. He has been up in the Highlands, near Balmoral, fly-fishing for shad and salmon. In two and a half days he caught almost forty fish. Thomas can catch fish like few men on earth. He uses his fly rod like a magician uses his wand. The man has a very delicate touch. Extremely soft hands. And exceptional powers of concentration.

Late afternoon in London now. Gray and dreary. Occasional drizzle. But Thomas wears sunglasses. Ray-Bans. And a suede-brimmed baseball cap. And a false mustache. He does not have any baggage. Not even a small overnight bag. He left everything in his hotel room back near Heathrow: his suitcase, his duffel bag, his fishing gear. Thomas does not plan on being in London for long. Just a few hours. Then back to the hotel. And up early for his morning flight to Miami. Unless he changes his mind and goes to Boston. There's always that possibility.

In the pockets of his oilskin jacket, Thomas carries his cellular phone and his pager and his U.S. passport. They go everywhere he goes. He has to stay in touch.

In another pocket, he carries a length of strong, thin wire typically used to hang paintings. Also in that pocket is a tin of waterproof blackface. And a small jar of white makeup. And a pair of fine leather gloves, unlined and very soft.

In the pockets of his trousers, Thomas carries the usual stuff: wallet, keys, spare change, a thin folding Swiss Army knife. Only really one item a bit out of the ordinary: a plastic sandwich bag partially filled with a very fine white powder. Not quite as fine as talcum powder. And not really white either. Kind of off-white. Beige. Dirty brown.

The cab crawls through Piccadilly Circus. Traffic's bumper-to-bumper even on a rainy Sunday.

"That was South Street you wanted, right, mate?" asks the driver.

"Yes," answers Thomas. "Berkeley Square will be fine."

"Right-o, mate. Have you there in a jiff."

Ten minutes later, Thomas pays the driver and steps out of the black cab. He turns up the collar of his oilskin against the drizzle. He heads west along Hill Street. As he walks, he reaches into his pocket and gets his brand-new leather gloves. He pulls them on, a nice tight fit. He flexes his fingers a few times, then picks up the pace.

At the corner of South and Waverton he finds number 34, an old and ornate apartment building with a marble facade. A dozen mailboxes line the left-hand wall of the vestibule. Thomas studies the names above each box. There, over number 402: BYRNES, R.

The glass door between the vestibule and the front hall is locked. Thomas goes back outside. The drizzle has slowed to a mist. He goes along Waverton until he reaches the first back alley on his right. Halfway down the alley he locates the service entrance to 34 South Street. No locked doors back here. Everything wide open. And no one around either. He walks right in.

Back among the trash cans and the electrical boxes and the cleaning equipment, Thomas finds the freight elevator. He steps inside and pulls closed the sliding door. While the elevator slowly rises, Thomas takes out his cellular phone and dials up the number of the Byrnes flat. No answer. Just a clipped message: *"Rodney here. Leave word or ring me back later."*

Thomas hangs up and puts the phone back in the pocket of his oilskin. The elevator stops at the fourth floor, at the rear of a long hallway. Just two large flats up here on the fourth. One on the left and one on the right. The one on Thomas's right is 402.

Like a man who has done this kind of thing before, Thomas approaches 402 while he pulls out his Swiss Army knife. He unfolds one of the several available tools; a thin, flat blade with a slight hook at the tip. Thomas slips the blade into the lock of the doorknob of 402. He holds the knob steady with his left hand while he delicately stirs the locking mechanism with the hook on the end of the blade. His soft hands and responsive fingers make the job a cinch. Through his fingertips he can feel the lock beginning to retreat, to slide out of place.

Seconds later and he's inside Byrnes's flat with the door once again closed and locked. Thomas has a leisurely look around in the fast-fading, early evening light. It's a spacious and well-furnished flat. Lots of nineteenth-century antiques from the days when Rodney's ancestors were plundering the Dark Continent.

Thomas removes his oilskin jacket and drapes it over the back of a carved chair in the living room. His leather gloves he keeps on.

He heads for the kitchen to make himself a cup of tea. No telling how long he will have to wait for Sir Rodney to return home.

SUNDAY MORNING—
LOS ANGELES, CALIFORNIA

The time difference between London and Los Angeles approaches that of the average work day, but the difference in hours only begins to suggest just how dissimilar two cities occupied predominantly by English-speaking white Christians can be.

Babe Overton, for example. Babe is, and always has been, an L.A. Girl. At twenty-five, Babe had it all: great good southern California looks, a knockout body, a hot Hollywood agent, and a long list of successful TV commercials for such trendy products as Pampers, Tums, and Summer's Eve. Babe also had a rich sugar daddy who treated her like a princess. The future, so goes the cliché, looked bright.

But now, a decade and a half later, Babe no longer looks quite so fresh, quite so chic. These last fifteen years have been rough on Babe. Life has not turned out as she had hoped.

It would be safe to say Babe's life has been an uphill battle since the day her lover, the powerful L.A. attorney Frank Hagstrom, committed suicide back in the heyday of the Reagan presidency. After Frank's death, depression, stress, failure, and far too much of that southern California sun, turned Babe old before her time. Her once smooth and lovely skin now has the look and feel of dried-out leather. Crow's-feet at the corners of her eyes and mouth flair out like the blades of an Oriental fan. Look closely, however, and you can still find the youthful beauty that once existed there: the emerald eyes, the full lips, the high cheekbones. Babe had a face the camera loved. She looked wholesome and sexy at the same time.

So, one bad turn and Babe's life turned to stone. Tragedy struck and Babe sank to the bottom of the emotional pool.

But this, after all, is L.A. The City of Angels. And in L.A. you can seek guidance for your physical and mental ills any time of the day or night. Sure, it's Sunday, five o'clock in the morning, eight full hours behind Greenwich Mean Time, but so what? Babe's shrink is on call. Gerdy MacDaniel is ready and willing to listen and counsel twenty-four hours a day, three hundred and sixty-five days a year. Gerdy does not believe in the Gregorian calendar. She finds the relentless cycle of days and weeks and months both stifling and anally retentive. The calendar, along with the clock, are, in Gerdy's philosophy, the two most suffocating illustrations of man's need to exert control over nature. Gerdy prefers to go with the flow. And so she catches an hour of sleep here and an hour there, whenever the parade of psychologically ailing takes a break. Gerdy sleeps right on her patients' sofa. Orders take-out from that sofa also. Mostly herbal teas and whole-wheat pita stuffed with sprouts and hummus and fresh Tabouli.

Gerdy rarely leaves her office. She no longer even keeps an apartment. Hers is, Gerdy believes, a very centered and satisfying life. She enjoys helping people. Primarily because of her weird office hours and domestic eccentricities, she has become the shrink of choice for many of Hollywood's movers and shakers.

Babe has been Gerdy's patient for years. This morning Babe is reflecting for the millionth time on her long-lost lover Frank. Gerdy pretends to listen, but she has trained herself to doze when her patients go into return mode.

Gerdy knows people in L.A. love reruns. They will replay the same episodes from their lives, à la *Leave It To Beaver* or *Happy Days* or *Seinfeld,* over and over. It's as though they dream of going into syndication. One day Gerdy intends to write a book about this phenomenon.

". . . but honestly, Dr. Gerdy," says Babe, "I don't think Frank committed suicide. I don't think he hung himself at all."

"We have been through this many times before, Babe. Why, suddenly, are we going over it again?"

"Because," Babe answers, "the man simply had too much to live for. He had his work. He had his kids. And he had me. He loved me. He worshipped me."

"Yes, Babe, I know," replies Gerdy, hard at work to keep the exasperation out of her voice. This is why she makes the big bucks: one fifty for fifty minutes, and don't think she doesn't watch the clock when the sofa's occupied. New Age gobbledygook has its limits. "Frank loved you. He cared about you very much. But we cannot deny that he had problems. Massive problems. The kind of problems that drive people over the brink. Frank had legal problems, marital problems, financial problems, problems with—"

"Yes," interrupts Babe, "I know all this. But he loved me. He loved me. After he got his divorce he was going to marry me. He was going to make me a star. We had our whole future planned out."

"I know, Babe," Gerdy says patiently, even though she would like to thump this woman on the head for living so desperately in the past for all these years. "And I know how you feel. But we have discussed this many times, and concluded just as many times, that Frank was at wit's end with his mounting troubles. He was looking for a way out. He chose to escape by taking his own life."

"No!" shouts Babe. "I don't buy it. Not anymore. He might have wanted to escape, but he wouldn't have killed himself. He would've picked me up and we would've fled to Mexico or the south of France. He never would've left me. Not like this."

Gerdy cannot help herself; she sighs. "I really don't like
hearing you talk this way, Babe. Not after all the time
we've spent together. I thought we had made some progress. I thought—"

"What about the camera?" Babe blurts out.

"The camera?"

"Yes, Frank's camera. His Minolta."

"What about it?"

"It was missing. The camera was missing. And what
about the vomit?"

"The vomit?"

"Yes," Babe insists, "the vomit. The vomit on the floor.
Don't you remember the police found signs of vomit on the
rug under where Frank supposedly hung himself?"

"Yes, but—"

"It was not consistent with what Frank had in his stomach. It was someone else's vomit, Dr. Gerdy. I think it was
the vomit of the person who killed—"

"Babe!" Gerdy shouts her patient's name in an effort to
bring some semblance of calm back to the situation.

Babe, startled, apologizes. "I'm sorry. I didn't mean to
get so carried away."

"That's okay, Babe. I just don't like seeing you so distraught."

"I know you don't, Dr. Gerdy. But I've been thinking
about the camera and the vomit for days. And I think I
know whose vomit was on that rug. I think I know who
killed Frank."

Gerdy thinks she needs a long holiday in Bali. "Who,
Babe? Tell me who killed Frank." Over the years there has
been quite a parade of suspects.

"The Hancocks."

"The Hancocks?"

Babe nods her head. "The boys who lost their parents in
the car wreck out on the freeway. Frank was representing
their estate."

Gerdy sighs again. She cannot believe how far into the
woods her patient has strayed. "Yes," she says, "I remember the Hancocks. You told me all about them years ago.

There were two of them, as I recall. Twins. They were upset with Frank because he had to tell them there was no money left in their parents' estate."

"Yes," says Babe, "exactly."

"And so for that," asks Gerdy, "you think they *killed* him?"

"I'm sure they did. I remember once when they came to the house and threatened Frank."

"Threatened him?"

"Yes, Dr. Gerdy, threatened. With physical harm. And even death. God, I'm sure the Hancocks murdered Frank. Or at least one of them did. My memory's a little fuzzy, but I think one of them might've died in some kind of accident. Drowned or something. I can't remember. But the one who's still alive lives in Boston. He's a writer, a novelist. I know. I checked. I checked it all out."

Gerdy does not read novels. Or go to the movies. She hears enough fantasies all day long. "Boston?"

"Yes, Boston."

Gerdy is only mildly alarmed by Babe's outburst. Seventeen years in the business, she has seen and heard it all. Right there in her office she has seen patients turn into Jesus of Nazareth, Adolf Hitler, Barney Rubble, Claus von Bulow, the Jolly Green Giant. She has seen patients kick furniture and punch walls, scream till they lose their voices, cry till they run out of tears. A hysterical woman ranting about the improbable killers of her long-dead lover pretty much goes in one of Gerdy's ears and out the other. Someday, she knows, it will all be in the book.

She glances slyly over Babe's shoulder at the small clock half hidden between a couple of books on the bookshelf. Thank goodness, she thinks, just seven minutes to go.

SUNDAY MORNING—
BOSTON, MASSACHUSETTS

Rarely does one find Leland Bernard Fisher in Boston on the weekends, but last night Leland had a black-tie affair at his offices over on Beacon Street. What with The Boston Press one hundred years old this year, there have been parties galore. Give Leland a reason to party and the man will surely give it his all. He's been a party animal for over three decades now. Many who know Leland find it quite extraordinary that life still runs through his veins and arteries. Mainly these days it's booze and a little weed, but the past is littered with pills, coke, psychedelics. Leland has been an abuser since just a teenager.

Last night Leland started out with just a glass or two of Chablis, but as the social swirl of the party grew more heated, so, too, did Leland's need for a full-blown buzz. So he turned to Jägermeister. Half a dozen shots of that sweet, gluey, licorice-tasting concoction and probably more. Many more. That dull throb now echoing across his forehead, that sour taste upon his swollen tongue, that nauseous rumbling from the back of his throat to his stomach—all of these signs point to the consumption of far too much Meister. Leland knows well the cruel symptoms of overindulgence.

But for chrissakes, why not overindulge? Just a few days ago he found out that that bastard John Hancock was screwing his wife. Tooling her right in the back seat of Leland's very own vintage Bentley. At least that's the way it looked in the photos. Admittedly, those eight-by-ten blowups, shot by Al-the-Gumshoe Brown, looked fuzzy and out of focus, but son of a gun, it sure looked to Leland like the old in-and-out. Of course, Al was two blocks away when he snapped the shots through his telephoto. And yes, that Bentley does have smoked glass in the rear for the express purpose of privatizing what goes on inside that spacious cabin. But in one photo the winsome duo is perched upon the smooth leather seat, and in the very next shot they've disappeared, down onto the voluminous and richly carpeted floor. And a few frames later, here comes Hancock, out through the door, grinning like a Cheshire cat, hand on his zipper. At least that's the way it looked to Leland when he did his inspections through Al's magnifying glass.

And there was Hancock again last night, looking handsome and trim, as always, dressed to kill in his light wool-and-silk tux, coming through the door of The Boston Press, some fine-looking chickadee, not his wife, on his arm, smiling easily, sharing a moment of intimacy with all who crossed his path. Like some goddamn politician.

"Leland! How you doing, good buddy?" Five bestsellers under his belt, and another one undoubtedly on the way. Unless, Leland the publisher and editor thought, I do something nasty and underhanded to mess it up for the SOB.

And then Leland spotted Hancock's big hand coming at him. Hancock wanted to shake. Hancock loves to shake hands. And always a big, firm, manly shake. Okay, not bone-crushing or anything, that would be a sign of insecurity, but always firm. And solid. And strong. His eyes squarely focused on your eyes.

And while they shook with the right, Hancock gripped Leland's shoulder with his left. Another annoying habit— shoulder gripping, neck massaging, all this touchy-feely

stuff. It drives Leland nuts. Mainly because he doesn't have
the guts to reciprocate. The Fishers have always kept their
hands to themselves.

And then, of course, Hancock had to give the flab surrounding Leland's waist a squeeze. A little pinch. Just so
they both knew it was there. Leland has flab everywhere.
Hancock has not an ounce of flab anywhere. Leland is
short and thick. Hancock tall and lean. Hancock towers
over Leland, a good five or six inches. And Hancock writes
like a dream, turns even the dullest transitionary sentence
into an eye-opening frolic. Leland, even though he carries
the titles publisher and editor in chief, has a hard time
stringing two coherent sentences together. Plus, Hancock
is a blue-blooded WASP from one of Boston's oldest and
most distinguished families. The Boston Tea Party, the
Continental Congress, the Declaration of Independence,
all that Revolutionary War crap. At least Leland, and an
awful lot of other folks, think this is Hancock's heritage.

Despite all this, Leland likes Hancock. He's been the
guy's publisher, after all, for eighteen years. They've hung
out together, traveled together, driven around the Big Apple in a limousine together sucking on Dom Pérignon and
smoking thick stogies blended with Cuban tobacco and
Colombian Gold after Hancock first hit the *Times* best-
seller list with his hold-nothing-back sicko thriller *The
Killer*. But screwing your buddy's wife—that's a Com-
mandment thing: Thou shalt not hump your buddy's bride.
And if you do hump her, be prepared to pay the freight,
pal. Be prepared to meet your Maker. Leland's not a violent guy, but right now, given the opportunity, he could
definitely inflict some damage on said author.

He ingests half a dozen Bufferin with a glass of tomato
juice. He would like to draw the blinds, crawl back into
bed, and drag the sheets over his head for a few more
hours, but familial duty calls. A promise to one of his
kids . . . which kid? . . . from which marriage? . . .
Jägermeister stole that particular tidbit away. But one of
his offshoots, anyway, wanted to go sailing this afternoon.
And Leland, a pretty fair captain with the stick and the

string, as well as a conscientious and doting daddy, said if the wind swirled the Fishers would sail.

So Leland takes the elevator to the underground parking garage of his fancy Back Bay digs. He keeps three vehicles under there: the 1939 vintage Bentley, a fully-restored 1973 BMW 3.0csi, and a loaded Chevy Suburban. He selects the csi. A very sweet ride, and one of Leland's all-time favorite cars. Today he hopes it will make the trip out to the Cape tolerable. He expects to reach some excessive speeds once he escapes the urban sprawl south of Plymouth. Speed usually helps Leland clear his brain, drive away even the most hideous headaches.

And right now Leland needs a clear head. He needs to decide what to do about this business between Hillary and Hancock.

SUNDAY MORNING—
CAYE CAULKER, BELIZE

Rafe Paquita sits in his wooden shack at the edge of the cove. Rafe, right now, is a guy ripe with anger, depression, and desperation. Last month his wife left him. She said she was leaving because he was mean and irritable all the time. But Rafe knows that's a lie. Rafe knows the truth. Rafe knows there's another guy. Some guy his wife knew way back when. And now the guy's some slumlord over in Belize City. That's where Rafe's wife is. She took the kid and what little money they had and went to the mainland to live with her mother. But Rafe knows she's seeing the slumlord. The bitch. To hell with her. Of course, he misses her, would like nothing better than to win her back, bring her home. Or maybe not. He's not really sure.

Rafe (pronounced Ra-fee) is trying really hard not to think about his wife right now. He has other things on his mind. Big things. Important things. Things that will change everything.

But first Rafe has to catch up on his reading. Rafe learned to read right here at the small wooden schoolhouse on Caye Caulker. In the years since, he hasn't really spent much time practicing the art. Doubtful he's ever read an entire book cover to cover. A few fishing magazines, maybe. The occasional newspaper. Some Belize tourist board brochures trying to entice Americans to come on down and spend their gringo dollars. His marriage license. He read that. And signed it. Moron. And the letter from his wife. The one saying she didn't love him anymore. He read that. Then spit on it and tore it into a hundred pieces.

Yeah, Rafe's an angry guy. But he hasn't always been angry. Throughout his youth and most of his young adulthood, Rafe was an easygoing, happy-go-lucky, Caribbean Island kind of guy. No troubles, mon. Easy on the breeze.

Rafe made a decent living off the tourists seeking warm sunshine and crystal clear waters. He took them fishing and skin diving in his small boat. He drank beer and rum chasers with them at the local bars. Rafe knew what the white folks wanted: a cool, loose, laid-back island boy they could call their pal. He could get them ganga, if they wanted it, and even women for a while, back in the late seventies and early eighties, back when the Hancock boys came to visit. The Hancock boys didn't want women, though. They wanted something far wilder than a Caribbean whore.

But those days are long gone. Caye Caulker, once home to many a wandering hipster and expatriate loner, cleaned up its act long ago. The Americans who come now have little sense of adventure. They bring along all the comforts of home (hair dryers, facial scrubs, moisturizing sun blocks, an extra pair of Tevas), or they certainly expect to find these items within a block or two of their TV-and-telephone-equipped hotel room. "No fax services! Son of a bitch, what a dump," Rafe recently overheard while passing by the front desk of a local hotel. Oh, yeah, they all arrive on the island now with their vouchers for fishing and scuba diving. They might as well stay home and experience Belize on their cyberspace surfboards.

So what's left for Rafe? Not much. He tried a few years ago to sign on with a couple of the big outfitters, but they didn't like the cut of his jib. They prefer white boys from Pennsylvania and Minnesota taking a year or two to see the world before going to work for Daddy's accounting firm or construction business, boys with Ph.D.'s in fly-fishing and underwater photography.

Rafe's pissed off, all right. About the Global Village. About his wife. About his life. But he can't think about all that crap right now. It'll drive him nuts, make him want to do crazy stuff. He needs to focus, concentrate. He needs to get these books read. Check out these magazines. Get a feel for his old buddy, John Hancock. And his brother. What was his brother's name? Bill? Will? Wally? Something like that.

Until recently, Rafe probably had not thought about John Hancock, or his brother, for ten years. Or more. They were just distant memories, as lost and forgotten as his carefree youth, before he got married and had a daughter and couldn't make a living. But then, quite by chance, one of life's little twists of fate rolled up onto Rafe's lap. And the moment that twist settled, the Hancock boys rushed out of Rafe's past and into his present.

It must have been about three weeks ago now. Rafe sat in the lobby of the Tropical Paradise Hotel. He had his eye on a young American couple who'd looked kind of lost, like they didn't have any fun-in-the-sun vouchers and maybe could use the services of an island guy who knew his way around. They were upstairs, in room 29. Probably napping and fornicating and trying not to make that old iron bed squeak too loud.

While waiting for them to come downstairs, Rafe glanced through the magazines on the coffee table. Nothing very interesting. A two-month-old *Snoozeweek*. An even older *Sports Illustrated*. A *National Geographic* from 1989. But next to the ancient *National Geo* was a book. A pretty thick book. It had a purple dust jacket. And on the front, a picture of a dagger with blood dripping off it. That dagger definitely caught Rafe's eye. Something the art department up at The Boston Press would be giddy to hear. He took a closer look. Above the dagger it said, THE SETTLE-MENT. And below the dagger: A NOVEL BY JOHN HANCOCK.

Rafe picked it up. Not because he recognized the name, but just because he wanted to see how much a book like that might weigh. Not really as much as he thought. He turned to the last page, page 532. He wondered how long it would take to read a book that long. Too damn long, he decided. Probably the rest of his life.

But he didn't put the book down. No, Rafe figured it would look good if that American couple saw him reading when they waltzed into the lobby. Give him some credibility. Make him look like an island intellectual. So Rafe held onto the book. He pretended to read. When that got boring, he turned the book over. A full-color photograph of the author filled the back. Rafe recognized the face immediately. A bit older, no doubt about that, but still, Rafe was sure it was him. One of them anyway. A decade and a half had come and gone, but it was definitely him, one of the brothers, no question.

"Son of a bitch," Rafe muttered right out loud in the lobby of the Tropical Paradise Hotel. "I'll be goddamned." He opened to the inside rear flap and read, with no small amount of effort, the brief biography of the author:

John Hancock has penned several best-sellers, including *The Killer, Revenge, Alter Ego,* and *Brotherhood.* The great-great-great-great-grandson of the great American patriot, John Hancock, Mr. Hancock lives in Boston, Massachusetts with his wife, the fine-arts dealer Clara Dare, and their two young sons.

Boston, thought Rafe, his brain beginning to swirl. Well, well, well, well, well. His plan began to form that very second. Within minutes it began to take shape. And by the end of that afternoon, his thoughts had quickly turned to action.

Rafe now possesses quite an array of reading materials by and about the author John Hancock. To put together his little library took some time, effort, and money, but Rafe feels it was time, effort, and money well invested. He has a *People* magazine with pictures of John and Clara and John Jr. and little Willy, all smiling and relaxing in the living room of their posh Beacon Hill town house. The author at leisure. Look at that carpet: as thick and rich as a lion's mane.

Rafe also has book reviews from such periodicals as *Time, The Atlantic,* and the *New York Times Book Review.* He has a two-year-old copy of *Vanity Fair* with a scrawny and damn near naked supermodel on the cover, but with more pictures of John Hancock beginning on page 238. Rafe does his best to read the lengthy article. Mostly he skims. So much nonsense about novel writing, about plot and scope and character. Rafe does not have the power to concentrate on all that crud. He wants to get to the juicy parts, gnaw the meat off the bone.

Finally, near the bottom of page 241, right next to a huge Calvin Klein ad for a brand new asexual eau de cologne, Rafe spots what he's been looking for. The words jump right out and grab his eyes: *Caye Caulker.* And sure enough, right there in black and white, the story of John Hancock's brother Will drowning off the coast of Caulker in a diving accident when the boys were on vacation during Christmas break 1982, while graduate students in the creative writing program at Harvard University.

Rafe half expects to see his own name in print. He'd been there, after all, driving the damn boat, guiding the Hancocks from diving hole to diving hole. But quick enough he realizes Hancock's not about to mention him to the guy writing the article. That might cause some curious George to come to the island and start asking questions, start looking for some dude named Rafe. And that wouldn't do. That wouldn't do at all. This Rafe fellow might have a different tale to tell. Something not quite in synch with the J. Hancock version.

Interesting, thinks Rafe. Very interesting.

He leans back in his chair. For the first time in weeks a smile passes across his face. He imagines a pipeline, a financial pipeline, running from Boston to Belize, a never-ending source of fuel to feed his needs and desires. He could fix up his place. Maybe get a new place. A bigger and better place. Get his wife and daughter back. Start over.

A simple phone call might do the trick. *"How you*

doin', John? It's your old bud, Rafe Paquita from Caye Caulker. Remember me?" He already has Hancock's telephone number. Just called Boston information, and, much to his amazement, a few seconds later the operator gave him the number. Just like that. Nothing to it.

Okay, thinks Rafe, so call the guy up, remind him of their old acquaintance, and let him know, subtly, that they have a situation on their hands.

Or maybe a phone call's the wrong move. Too impersonal. Yeah, this demands a personal appearance. This is, let's face it, a very delicate matter.

Rafe ponders the situation for several minutes. Finally he decides he needs to take a business trip. To Boston.

BOSTON COMMON

The Regal Papillon, with its seven-foot wingspan, soars over Boston Common. It flies above the lush green tree-tops. The enormous butterfly with its nylon sail and graphite spars cruises back and forth across the sky. A single, almost invisible line of ninety-pound test keeps the enormous kite in precarious contact with the earth.

Down on the ground, on a gentle slope just across Beacon Street from the State House, John Hancock flies the single-line Regal Papillon with all the same concentration and finesse that he puts into the rest of his life. When the kids wanted a kite, John didn't settle for the cheapo plastic job from the local gypo shop down on Cambridge. No, he did some research. Found out some guy named Joel Scholz was building these handmade superkites that had won a bunch of competitions and awards. So Dad bought one of those. Only the best for his boys. Except the kite was too big and too strong for them to fly. Until just recently, Dad had to fly it for them. They could only stand by and watch.

The enormous kite must be close to three hundred feet in the air. The drag is tremendous. John can feel his forearms and shoulders beginning to ache.

Young Willy tugs on his father's windbreaker. "Come on, Dad, you're having all the fun."

"Yeah," says John junior, "give us a chance."

"Okay, okay," he tells them. "But you have to hang on tight. One slip and that baby will be out over the Atlantic."

"We'll hang on."

"Take turns," he lectures them. "When your arms get tired, hand the spool off to your brother. That's what brothers are for."

Hancock relinquishes control to his older son. The Regal Papillon practically lifts the six-year-old right off the ground. But not wanting to disappoint his father, young John junior fights back and gains control.

Hancock gives the boys a few pointers, then retreats to the base of a stately elm just a few yards away. Not only were his arms growing tired, but some other business has been gnawing at his brain ever since they reached the Common.

Satisfied the boys can handle the kite, he pulls his cell phone out of the pocket of his windbreaker. He dials up the Savoy in London, and when the switchboard operator answers, he asks for Mrs. Hancock's room.

John figures this is the perfect time to call his wife. He'll just tell her he's in the park with the boys, flying the kite, hanging out on a warm, breezy Sunday afternoon. He'll say he just felt like calling, saying hey, letting the boys say hey. They all wanted to know how Mom was doing over across the Atlantic. John has no intention of mentioning the visit this morning from those two Boston police detectives; oh, no, not a word about them. He'll just wait and see if Clara alludes to that particular event in even the subtlest of ways.

Too bad the phone in Clara's room rings and rings and rings. Six, eight, ten times it rings, and still no answer.

Clara left half an hour ago for her meeting with her Arab friend.

The switchboard operator returns to the line. "I'm afraid Mrs. Hancock is not answering, sir," she says, rather snippily. "May I take a message?"

Hancock declines and hangs up. He glances at his watch, calculates the time difference. Early evening in London. Maybe she's at dinner. More than likely with that pompous ass Rodney Byrnes. Hancock wouldn't mind a bit if that stuffed shirt fell off the Tower Bridge and drowned in the foul-smelling Thames. In fact, Hancock might, if no one was looking, give the SOB a shove.

John stuffs the cell phone back into his windbreaker and checks out the boys. They have the Regal Papillon zipping back and forth across the sky.

He knows he can always call Clara on her cell phone. But he hates to do that. It seems like such an intrusion, such an invasion of privacy.

"Dad!" shouts John junior "My arms are tired."

"Yeah," shouts Willy, "mine, too!"

Dad smiles and stands. He's glad to come to the rescue.

"I've had enough kite flying," says John junior.

"Me, too," says Willy. "Let's play hide-and-seek."

So that's what they do. After Dad hauls in the Regal Papillon.

LONDON

Clara's sheik wanted both the Toulouse-Lautrec and the small, gloomy Manet. But like all Arab men, he had to bicker over price before closing a deal. Psychologists call it the open-air-bazaar mentality. It's a genetic thing. That's why you see so many Arabs selling cars now down at your local Chevy and Toyota dealers.

Unfortunately for the sheik, his adversary in this particular transaction held all the good cards. Not only did Clara have what the sheik wanted, but her stunning beauty and great charm had the rich oil tycoon practically drooling on the lapel of his preposterously expensive Savile Row suit. They simply do not have women like Clara Dare Hancock back in the sheikdom. Back home the sheik has plenty of wives and mistresses, some of them even reasonably attractive, but because the male-dominated culture so successfully oppresses its women, all of the sheik's female companions are little more than human doormats. Oh, but to bed a woman like Clara. To bring her fulfillment and satisfaction. To hear her cry his name as he draws her near . . . "Abula! Abula!"

The sheik would spend millions for that.

Too bad the sheik does not understand that more than

petro dollars are needed to satisfy a woman's physical desires. Especially a woman like Clara.

Right now Clara feels like celebrating. And why not? She has the sheik's check in hand. One point two million pounds. She has already calculated her commission: nearly one hundred and twenty thousand dollars. Enough to pay the bill for the suite at the Savoy and perhaps do a bit of shopping along Piccadilly. Of course, most of the money will go right back into the business. Her mentor, the great art dealer Charles Dare, taught her the importance of reinvestment, of making acquisitions whenever you had spare change. That spare change is why she personally owns a Monet oil, a Picasso sketch, an unfinished Degas, and several other near-great works of art. They all hang in the Hancock town house up on Beacon Hill.

"So," she says to her gallery manager, Joanne Smith, "working Sundays does have its rewards."

Joanne smiles, even though the sale did not make her all that joyous. She loved that Manet, despite it's being somewhat dank and gloomy. She would have preferred to see it go to the Met for less money. At the Met the painting would have been seen by millions. But now, Joanne knows, it will hang in some airless palace owned by that ignorant sheik. Only a handful of people will ever see the painting again. Such a waste. The money means nothing to Joanne. Her small commission will go directly into her retirement mutual funds; funds that earn only a few percentage points per annum due to her insistence upon ethical, environmental, and humane investment.

Clara's cell phone rings. She digs into her large black Ferragamo handbag, digs out the phone, and flips it open. "Yes? Hello?"

"Was that a smiling Arab I just saw leaving your place of business?"

Clara laughs. "Did he actually have a smile on his face?"

"Indeed he did."

"He bought them both."

"For a tidy sum, I hope."

"I would've let them go a bit cheaper if he hadn't been visually undressing Joanne and me the entire time he was here."

"I'd like to do more than visually undress you, dear."

"Oh, I'm sure you would, Rodney," says Clara. "But then, English men are also pigs. They just have better manners."

"It's in the breeding."

Clara has the feeling they have had this conversation before. "Where are you anyway?" she asks. "You must be nearby?"

"Just across the street, actually," answers Byrnes. "The limousine is running and I'm at your service."

"Dinner reservations, I assume?"

"For eight o'clock. At the Oak Room."

"You read my mind."

"Of course I did, love. That's one of my finest traits."

"Yes."

"I just want to make your stay in London as enjoyable as possible, Ms. Dare."

"That's Mrs. Hancock to you, Mr. Byrnes."

"Please," replies Sir Rodney, "don't remind me."

Clara laughs again. The sale has made her downright giddy. "Do we have time to pop around to the hotel? I'd like to change clothes and freshen up before dinner."

"Plenty of time to freshen up," Rodney tells her. "All the time in the world. But hurry, the champagne is on ice."

Thomas Young continues to wait for Sir Rodney Byrnes at Rodney's Mayfair flat on South Street. Thomas has no problem waiting. Over the years he has developed tremendous patience. He has the patience of a Zen master, or a Buddhist monk. This evening, while waiting, he has consumed three cups of Rodney's fine English tea, a couple of raisin crumpets, and frozen yogurt bar he found in the ice box.

Now he feels the time has come to prepare for the evening's ritual. He grabs the tin of blackface and the small jar of white makeup out of the pocket of his oilskin jacket and goes into Sir Rodney's bathroom. Removing the false mustache, Thomas smears the blackface across his forehead and cheeks. In just a few minutes he has applied a fine coat over his entire face. While it dries, Thomas drops his drawers and squats on the toilet. It takes several minutes and no small amount of effort, but eventually he has a meager bowel movement.

Thomas returns to the sink and opens the jar of makeup. He scoops out a dab with the tip of his index finger. He carefully applies it to his right eyelid and his right eyebrow and the area under his right eye. Pretty soon he has made a nice white circle around his eye about the size of a silver dollar.

He applies the makeup to his left eye next. Exactly the same as his right eye. And finally, he paints his lips, wide and round.

Thomas checks himself in the mirror. Pitch-black face. Big white eyes. Huge white mouth. Very weird. And very spooky. Won't Sir Rodney be surprised?

Next comes the part Thomas does not really want to do, but knows he must if he wants to execute the ritual properly. He reaches into the toilet with a wad of paper towels and scoops out a small piece of his stool. Like virtually all Americans, Thomas has a real phobia about poop. Lots of cultures accept shit for what it is: waste reality. But Americans love to pretend the stuff does not exist. Pass it and flush it and don't look back.

Haitians worship it. And Thomas's little ritual this evening certainly has its origins in Haitian voodoo.

So he takes his scoop of scat, crosses Sir Rodney's inner sanctum, and pulls open the front door an inch or two. No one in the hallway, so he opens it further. He bends down and smears the waste across the bottom of the door. A strong desire to retch very nearly overcomes him, but, finished, Thomas closes the door, returns to the bathroom, and quickly flushes away the evidence. He washes his hands in hot water. Thoroughly. Twice.

The human dung on the doorway, according to the

houngan (voodoo priest) who sold Thomas the extremely potent zombie powder, will cause Sir Rodney great physical and emotional distress. Especially if Byrnes is having carnal thoughts about Clara. Which Thomas feels certain the Englishman is.

When Rodney approaches the door, his heart will begin to pound, his breathing will grow raspy, sweat will flow off his forehead, and his mouth will turn as dry as the Mojave Desert.

Satisfied all necessary preparations have been made, Thomas flips off the bathroom light and returns to the living room. He removes the loop of picture wire from his jacket and the bag of powder from his trousers. Then he settles back on the sofa to await Sir Rodney's arrival.

LOS ANGELES

When Babe Overton leaves Gerdy MacDaniel's office on Sunset Boulevard, she does not go home. Having not slept for almost twenty-four hours, Babe certainly should go home. Take a warm shower. Maybe have a bite to eat. Get some sleep.

But Babe chooses to do none of these things. And this being a free country, Babe is allowed to make her own choices. Even if the choice she makes might mean curtains for a fellow human being.

Home for Babe is a two-bedroom garden apartment in West Hollywood. She lives there with Mary Ann, a forty-something divorcee who works at a fancy nail-and-hair boutique over on Rodeo Drive. Babe and Mary Ann are friendly, but they are not really friends. Had their lives worked out better, they probably would not even know one another. They certainly would not be living together.

Babe has decided the time has come to confront the Hancock boys. Demand to know what they know about Frank's death. Dr. Gerdy may not agree, but Babe feels she must do this before she can get on with her life. And she feels she has to do it now, today, right this second, or else she will lose her nerve.

So instead of going home, Babe tells the cab driver to drive her to the Greyhound bus station out on Wilshire Boulevard. Babe has a car, but right now it's in the shop getting repaired. Not that Babe would drive all the way across the country by herself even if her little Nissan were working perfectly. Babe does not really like to drive. Especially long distances. Or at night.

She has everything she needs to make the trip: reading glasses, money, suitcase, a small black pistol. Babe carries the pistol everywhere. Frank Hagstrom gave it to her for protection more than fifteen years ago. Even then L.A. was a rough-and-tumble town. Now, of course, it's an urban hellhole riddled with ethnic and economic violence; a tinderbox ready to ignite between the blacks and the whites, between the Anglos and the Chicanos, between the haves and the have-nots.

Babe figures the pistol will help her convince the Hancock boys that she means business. It will force them to tell her what she wants to know. She will not shoot them, as long as they agree to tell her the truth about what happened to Frank.

And Babe knows how to use the gun. Frank took her to the shooting range several times after he gave it to her. He wanted her to have proper training in how to load, fire, and clean the weapon.

Mostly now the gun just rests in the bottom of her large leather handbag. Once a month or so she might take it out and hold it in her hand. Babe has small hands, and the small snub-nosed pistol fits very nicely in her palm. It is black and cold and quite heavy for something so small. The weight is a constant reminder that the gun lurks at the bottom of her handbag beneath her wallet, her compact, her eyeliner, and her lip gloss. Sometimes the added weight feels like a burden. Sometimes Babe thinks about taking the gun out of her purse and putting it in the drawer beside her bed, but she never does. Many years ago Frank told her to carry the pistol with her always. Babe knows how much Frank cared for her, how much he loved her, how much he wanted her safe and secure. This is why she needs to cross the continent and seek some answers. It may seem like a desperate and far-flung move to make, but even after all these years Babe feels the weight of Frank's tragic end heavy upon her heart.

Babe wishes she could drive out to LAX, get on a flight to Boston, knock on the Hancocks' door tomorrow morning, and just do what needs doing. Unfortunately, she has a very deep fear of flying. Once, years ago, she was on a flight from L.A. to Seattle to film a Zest commercial. A violent thunderstorm struck during the flight. The plane took a pounding. One of the engines quit working. Babe felt sure she was about to die. But the pilot made an emergency landing at an airstrip outside of Eugene, Oregon. No one was hurt, but Babe never flew again.

Also, Babe is no fool. She knows the metal detectors at LAX would find the gun in the bottom of her handbag. No metal detectors at the bus station.

So she will take the bus. No, it will not be quick getting to Boston. It will probably take several days to cross the country. But Babe has been waiting more than fifteen years. What's another few days? It will give her time to think, to work on the details of her plan, to mull over how best to confront the Hancock boys.

WOODS HOLE

Leland Fisher got lucky. When he arrived at the family compound in Woods Hole on the southwestern tip of Cape Cod, he found his daughter Jaguar sound asleep. That meant Leland did not have to sail. And a good thing because even on terra firma Leland felt like a sailor bobbing and weaving on heavy seas. Too much Jägermeister will do that to a man.

Jaguar was the Fisher offspring who, a few days ago, had requested a sail with Dad. Jaguar, just to cover a bit of Leland's fragmented family line, is the oldest of two children from Leland's second marriage. She's sixteen, very nearly seventeen, and at that age the young ladies frequently have a change of heart. Sailing sounded like something Jaguar really wanted to do with her daddy back on Thursday, but a whole lot can happen in a young life between Thursday and Sunday. In Jaguar's case she broke up with Gary on Friday, hung out with Conrad Saturday afternoon, then spent Saturday night making up and making out with Gary. She didn't get to bed until, like, three-thirty in the morning. So now it's the middle of the afternoon on Sunday and Miss Jaguar is still sound asleep.

Which suits Leland just fine. No way does he plan on

waking her up. She can sleep until Monday morning as far
as he's concerned. Let sleeping children and sleeping wives
lie has been Leland's motto through four brides and twice
that many kids. Leland likes to tell people he would be a
rich man if not for all the alimony and child support payments he has to make. But even with those payments Leland does okay. He has the snazzy apartment in the Back
Bay with its views overlooking the Charles. He has the
compound here on the Cape with its large main house and
two cabanas down at the edge of Vineyard Sound. And he
has the ski chalet out in Sun Valley. Leland hates to ski. He
says he hates it because of all the standing around in un-
comfortable boots, because of the freezing cold tempera-
tures and icy winds, but really Leland hates skiing because
he never quite got the hang of it.

Leland holds onto the ski chalet despite his attitudes
toward the local sport because of Bernard. Bernard is Leland's oldest child, one of three from his long-dead first
marriage. Bernard, who seems destined to be a ne'er-do-
well, lives in the ski chalet. He skis and fishes and farts
around. Leland envies his son. His son has no conscience.
He sucks off the family teat without suffering even minor
pangs of guilt. Of course, his mother was a goy, some kind
of Protestant, though not a practicing one.

Unlike his eldest, Leland has always been saddled with
enormous bags of guilt, good old-fashioned Jewish guilt.
And a good thing, too, because without guilt pulling him
back into line, he would have gone overboard years ago.
Booze and drugs probably would have done him in before
he ever hit thirty.

Leland sits now out on the back patio off the family
room. Nice and warm out here in the bright, late spring
sun. He can look out across the long sweep of grass to the
calm waters of Vineyard Sound. Not much wind out there.
No good for sailing. But incredibly clear. Visibility unlimited. He can easily see the white bluffs of Martha's Vineyard just south of West Chop.

In closer, just an arm's length away, on the glass coffee
table, Leland can see his Blood Mary, his Sunday *New*

York Times, and the note left by his wife; that would be wife number four, Hillary Vandemeer Fisher. Yes, another goy. His third. Call it his weakness. And this one of Dutch and German descent. Good looking, and, at least on the surface, of sound disposition. But scratch around a bit and you'll find one stubborn and steely babe. And, when cornered, as nasty as barbed wire. Still, Leland has hoped since the day they wed that she would be the end of the line. The last, best woman in his life. But now, out of the blue, this insane liaison with Hancock.

Dear B,

Out and about. Wasn't sure when you were coming. Or even if. Be back late afternoon. Kids with Lois.

Love and kisses,
H.

Out and about with whom? That's what Leland wants to know. Out and about with Hancock? Holed up in some Hyannis B&B? It makes Leland nuts thinking about it. Not that he has always been the most faithful husband in the world. He's done his share of marital damage over the years. But Christ, this is different. Or maybe it's not. Maybe it's karma. Bad karma. Coming back to haunt him. Giving him a taste of his own medicine.

Jesus, thinks Leland, I'll have to ponder this. Maybe it's not so simple as I first thought. Maybe this is payback time for all my transgressions.

The Lois in the note would be Lois the Fishers' nanny. Lois does most of the child rearing for the two youngest Fishers, Annie, age four, and Becky, age three. Hillary, the mother of these two lovely lasses, is far too busy to do much mothering. She has shopping to do and luncheons to attend and tennis matches to play. And parties, so many parties: tea parties, cocktail parties, fund-raising parties.

Hillary rarely has time for the kids and she never has time for her husband. But, thinks Leland, his mind admittedly preoccupied with infidelity, she does find the time to

screw that no-good thankless bastard Hancock. Leland
thinks about all the stuff he has done for Hancock over
the years. All the success he has brought to Hancock's
novels. All the money he has made the SOB. And this is
how he shows his gratitude?

Leland smacks himself in the side of the head. Hillary
and Hancock, Jesus! What a stinking mess. Does this mean
I'll have to get divorced again? For the fourth time? I don't
think I can take it. I think I'd rather die.

Leland wonders if he should retaliate. Maybe contact
that Mafia hit man whose autobiography he published last
year. Pay him fifty grand to break one of Hancock's legs,
maybe slice off his pecker. Hey, a man gets crazy when he
gets jealous. Jealousy has been the catalyst for many a
violent and vicious act.

But Leland's not about to hire a hit man. Not a chance.
He's basically a gentle and forgiving soul. Like all of us
groveling around on the planet, Leland is a mixture of
good and evil, black and white, sweetness and malice. Leland is capable of adopting stray and starving kittens. But
he's also capable of blackening his second wife's eye during
a spirited exchange following an evening of drinking and
illegal drug use.

Leland, those Al-the-Gumshoe Brown photographs of
Hillary and Hancock in the Bentley imprinted upon his
brain, sighs and sucks down the rest of his Bloody Mary.
He no longer has the shakes. In fact, he feels pretty good
now with several ounces of vodka circulating through his
bloodstream. One more little nip in a few minutes and he'll
be tip-top, good as gold.

He picks up the Sunday *Times*. All fifty pounds of it.
Finds and pulls out the *Book Review*. Tries to read the
cover story, a lengthy discourse on some new environmental book that recently hit the shelves. Tries, but fails. His
concentration keeps slipping away, mostly back to his
bride.

Leland doesn't really give a damn about the environment, anyway. When no one's looking, he throws glass
bottles and aluminum cans and all things plastic right in

with the rest of the trash. Leland knows, with six billion people on the planet, and millions more arriving by the end of the week, the environment, no matter how many books we write, cans we recycle, rules and regulations we pass, is screwed right up the wazoo.

So Leland turns to the back of the *Book Review,* to the best-seller lists, hard and soft, fiction and nonfiction. Only one Boston Press title: Number eleven on the hardcover fiction list is *The Settlement,* by John Hancock.

The book's existence further complicates Leland's already complicated emotional dilemma. If Hancock is having an affair with his wife, Leland will have no choice but to terminate their writer-editor relationship. Hancock's association with The Boston Press will have to end. No way around it. Twenty years down the tubes for twenty seconds in the back seat.

On the other hand, if he dumps Hancock, Leland knows it will play havoc with the balance sheets. Hancock makes more money for The Boston Press than any other author they have under contract. And don't think the top brass down in the Big Apple don't know it. They will be extremely irritable if Leland gives Hancock the ax. The top brass does not care about John Hancock's indiscretions or Leland Fisher's hurt feelings.

All they know is that Hancock's books bring home the bacon. *The Settlement* went as high as number six a few weeks after its publication. It would have gone even higher, sold even more copies, save that several of the megaauthors (King, Grisham, Steele) crowded the top spots.

Hancock, Leland knows, could have, years ago, gone for absolute super stardom, but he was unwilling to completely compromise his storytelling. Basically, he refused to keep telling the same story with a slightly different cast of characters. The top spots typically go to those scribblers willing to sell their souls to the Devil, write in a perfectly droll and gutless style, stick to the tried-and-true plot lines. Leland has always respected Hancock for not selling out, for hanging on to at least a smidgen of his literary dignity.

"But where the hell," he asks himself out loud, "is the dignity in slipping it to my wife? I thought the guy was my friend, my buddy. Of course, maybe it ain't so. Maybe it'll all turn out to be a misunderstanding. I mean, it's not like those photographs really prove anything."

Leland sighs and rubs his eyes. He does his best to assure himself this is all just his wild imagination spinning out of control. His wife has been loyal. His old buddy has been true-blue.

He decides to do another Bloody Mary. Maybe put in a call to Al Brown and tell the Gumshoe to double his efforts. Get the real story, and get it soon.

On his way to the kitchen Leland recalls a bit of advice his grandfather, Aaron Fisher, once gave him: "Never make the tough decisions on Sunday, Lee. Or any other day of the week."

CAYE CAULKER

Rafe does not suffer from guilt. Nor does he have a fear of flying. But he does have one small problem: money. Or in this case, a serious lack thereof. Rafe called Continental Airlines: eight hundred and forty-six bucks, Belize City to Boston. And that's with a two-week advance purchase, staying over Saturday night. Where, he wondered, would he stay? At the Hancock house?

Rafe doesn't want to wait two weeks. He wants to go now. But full coach fare, totally unrestricted, will cost him almost thirteen hundred big ones. A drop in the bucket, he figures, if he can get to Hancock. Put his extortion plan into action. Get those greenbacks flowing south.

But where and how to come up with the green? That's the big question. Rafe knows you sometimes have to spend money to make money. He understands the necessity of venture capital. But he's reluctant to take on a partner. He wants to keep this deal a one-man show.

He doubts he can put together three hundred dollars, much less thirteen hundred. He hasn't had thirteen hundred bucks at one time since the coke craze back in the eighties when he could buy a gram for fifty, double it with cornstarch, then sell both grams for a hundred apiece.

Rafe really only has one asset: his boat. Only trouble is, half of it belongs to his wife. He can't really sell it without her permission. And right now she's not even talking to him. Still, maybe he could sell it, get the cash flowing from Hancock, then buy it back. Or something like that.

It's all so damn complicated. But Rafe knows one thing for certain: to get the cash flowing he needs to get to Boston. And to get to Boston he needs cash. Call it Rafe's own personal catch-22.

He tosses aside his still-unread copy of John Hancock's *The Settlement,* throws open the door of his shack, and goes out into the bright Sunday afternoon sunlight. Hotter than jalapeños out here. Like stepping into a damn furnace. Sometimes Rafe thinks Caye Caulker must be the hottest place on earth. Rafe's tired of being hot all the time. Moving slow to keep from sweating. Constantly trying to stay clear of that infernal sun.

Rafe thinks maybe he'll buy a one-way ticket to Boston. Hang out up in New England for a while. Where it's cool. Where the snow falls. Rafe's never seen snow, never seen ice, except in a glass of whiskey on the rocks. He'll come back wearing a nice suit and new shoes. Make a good impression on his wife. Take her and their daughter back up to the States. Maybe get a job selling real estate. Or stocks and bonds. Live happily ever after.

But right now he darts from palm tree to palm tree in an effort to hide from the sun. The guy is desperate to get to Boston, pay Hancock a visit. To do so he has to sell his boat. No way around it. Sell the boat or sweat to death. Sell it or lose his family. Lose everything. But he has to stay cool. He has to sell it to the right buyer, someone who won't ask a million questions, won't announce to the whole damn island that Rafe just cashed in his last asset. And he also has to make sure his wife doesn't find out about the sale. No one can know about the sale. Just like no one can know he's heading for Boston.

But maybe, he thinks, he shouldn't go to Boston. Not directly. Maybe better to fly to, say, New York. Take the train or maybe the bus up to Boston. That way he doesn't leave a trail.

Rafe smiles. Pats himself on the back for staying cool, covering the details.

Oh yeah, Rafe knows if he can get to Hancock all his problems will vanish, disappear into thin air.

BOSTON & LONDON

John Hancock, oblivious to the many minds interested in altering his fate, glues the tiny balsa wood shingles onto the roof of the firehouse. The shingles are not much bigger than his fingernail. The firehouse is about the size of a washing machine. It has doors and windows that open and close. It has bunks up on the second floor where the firemen sleep between fires. It has a pole the firemen slide down when the fire alarm sounds. And it has fire trucks, several of them, parked in the garage on the first floor.

The firehouse is just about finished. The roof needs shingles and the exterior needs paint. Will, as John, started the firehouse back over the winter. But he quickly lost interest, leaving completion of the construction project to John. John doesn't mind. He enjoys working with his hands, building something for the boys. He especially likes it when he's writing and he hits a snag in a story, when the plot comes crashing down around him. He often retires here to the basement, picks up a hammer or a saw, and thinks through the problem. The tools occupy his hands, allowing some of his pent-up physical energy to dissipate while his brain works through characters and plot. But today he's not thinking about the new book; he's thinking about his brother and his wife and those two police detectives.

He decides he's glued on enough miniature shingles for one day. The desire to call Clara has returned. So he cleans up, turns off the lights, and goes upstairs. Passing by the family room he spots John Jr. and little Willy sitting in front of the TV playing video games. John just stands in the doorway and watches them. The mere sight of his boys brings him the most profound joy. John knows the most important job he has in the world is to keep those two youngsters happy and safe.

Eventually, John turns away. He goes down the hall and climbs the stairs to the third floor.

A little after four o'clock, according to the clock on the wall of the office. That would make it about nine o'clock London time. Hancock crosses to his desk, sits on the edge, picks up the phone, and dials direct.

"Good evening. Savoy Hotel. Alice speaking. How may I direct your call?"

"Mrs. Hancock, please."

"One moment, sir."

The phone in Mrs. Hancock's suite rings and rings. No answer. Hancock hangs up before Alice comes back on the line. He knows it's stupid and controlling and immature of him, but he hates it when his wife's not in her room. Especially at night.

And now he has the same question he faced earlier over on the Common. To call or not to call the cell phone?

He decides to call. Then he decides not to call. Normally, late Sunday afternoon, if he wanted to call, he'd just pick up the phone. No big deal. Just call and chat, maybe put the boys on the line. But this is not a normal call. Not after the visit from those police detectives. Showing up unannounced, telling him his wife filed a missing person's report on his brother. His long-dead brother. No, not your typical Sunday afternoon call by any stretch of the imagination.

Still, he takes a deep breath and dials the number of Clara's cell phone. The phone line makes a series of electronic noises while the satellites and the cellular towers do their digital dance. And then, in a moment of pure modern magic, Clara's phone begins to ring.

It rings inside Clara's black Ferragamo purse which sits on the empty chair between her and Rodney Byrnes. They sit at one of the prime tables of the Oak Room inside the posh Le Méridien Hotel on Piccadilly. Surrounded by crystal chandeliers and gilded carvings and Chinese vases overflowing with fresh spring flowers, they have just begun their appetizer: a shared plate of poached oysters in a delicate red wine sauce.

Fork zeroing in on his mouth, Rodney frowns at the sound of the telephone. "I hope that's not our Arab friend."

Clara, who doesn't really care for oysters but loves the chef's presentation, reaches for her purse. "It's surely Hancock in search of his wife's loving voice."

Rodney rolls his eyes and pops an oyster. He'd prefer the Arab.

Clara unfolds the phone, glances at the caller ID screen, and smiles. "Just as I suspected." She hits the receive button. "Hello, Mr. Hancock." She practically sings his name into the telephone.

"Hey, Mrs. Hancock."

"I was beginning to wonder if you'd ever call."

Rodney sighs and shoves a couple more oysters into his mouth. So dead suddenly are his taste buds that he might as well be eating frozen fish sticks lathered in lard.

"I tried the hotel a couple times," says Hancock, "but there was no answer."

"It's been a busy day."

"So where are you now?"

Now that, thinks Clara, is my guy. Always straight to the center.

"Dinnertime," she answers. "We're at the Oak Room."

"*We?* You and the well-heeled Arab?"

"Oh, no," says Clara. "I've finished with him."

"And how did that go?"

"He bought both the Manet and the Toulouse-Lautrec."

"You're kidding?"

Clara is all smiles. "Absolutely not."

"You finally reeled him in?"

"Yes, I did. After quite a battle."

"Congratulations, baby. You definitely earned that one." Hancock knows his wife has been working the Arab for a year or more. She has wined and dined him, shown him paintings in New York, London, Paris, even the Middle East. But that, after all, is Clara Dare: ambitious, persuasive, and incredibly tenacious. She does not give up.

"And I think," she tells him, "everyone in the deal walked away happy: the buyer, the seller, and yours truly, the intermediary."

"I wish I was there to celebrate with you."

"And you know I wish the same."

"If not me, birdie, then who? I know you detest celebrating alone."

"Sir Rodney, of course."

"Jesus, Clara. Doesn't that weasel have some hole to hide in?"

"Now, Hancock, be nice. He's being a perfect gentleman."

Rodney gobbles down those oysters at the speed most men reserve for salted nuts.

"So where," asks Hancock, "did you say you were?"

"The Oak Room. At Le Méridien."

"Champagne?" Hancock knows Clara loves champagne.

"Absolutely."

The agitation creeps along the small of Hancock's back. And what guy wouldn't be agitated if his wife was drinking champagne in one of London's ritziest restaurants with some trust-fund turd who has nothing better to do than run after married women?

"Well, love, I must say, I'm very excited about your arrangement."

"It's just dinner, Hancock. Now don't go off on one of your tantrums."

Of course, John knows it's not he who goes stark raving mad with jealousy; that distinction belongs to Will. But then, Will is John. Sometimes. Half the year. Every other month.

"Don't worry, baby. I just wish I was there instead of him."

"And so do I."

"So how is Sir Rodney?"

"He's just fine. Would you like to say hello?"

"No," Hancock shoots back, "I wouldn't." But then he thinks maybe he would. "Yeah, okay, put him on."

Clara covers the mouthpiece and says to Rodney. "He wants to say hi."

Rodney scowls. "To me? You must be joking?"

"Actually, no."

Reluctantly, Rodney takes the phone. "Yes, hello, Hancock, old sport. Is that you? Phoning up from the States, are you? Dreadfully long way away."

Clara rolls her eyes and pokes at one of the oysters. Too rubbery, she decides, and so sips her champagne instead.

Rodney babbles on. "So, old sport, how's the new book coming along?"

"Don't give me that old sport crap, pal," says Hancock. "If there's one thing I hate more than warm beer, it's a phony."

Rodney, not wanting Clara to get wind of this, smiles. "Now, Hancock, I really don't think—"

"Look, Byrnes," interrupts Hancock, "I trust my wife, but I sure as hell don't trust you. So do yourself a favor and keep your grubby little Limey hands off her. Touch her even once and I'll rearrange your face so that your own mother won't recognize you. Now go take a leak or something so I can talk to Clara in private."

Rodney, shocked and crimson from this attack, hands the phone back to Clara without raising even the mildest protest.

"What," she asks, once again covering the mouthpiece, "did he say?"

Rodney shakes his head, but then manages to mutter, "Using some quite colorful language, he told me to keep my hands off you."

Clara laughs a hearty laugh. "Hancock is rather proprietary. And," she adds, "he does occasionally offer some excellent advice."

Rodney sighs and nods. This was not the evening he had in mind. "I think I'll excuse myself for a few minutes. I have a phone call or two to make."

After he leaves the table Clara speaks into the phone. "There you go, Hancock. You drove him away."

"Good riddance."

"I just hope he comes back to pay the bill."

"I'll pay the damn bill."

"So what has you all bent out of shape? It's obviously more than just Rodney Byrnes."

"How do you know?"

"A woman's intuition. Plus seven years of marriage."

"Maybe it's the seven-year itch."

Clara laughs musically. "Don't worry, baby, I can still scratch your itch."

"Are you sleeping with Rodney Byrnes?"

"Is that what you think?"

"Just answer my question."

"Dammit, Hancock, you know the answer to that is a resounding no. Now tell me what you're so testy about."

"He's such a horse's ass. Running after a married woman like some damn dog who hasn't been fixed."

"Which reminds me," says Clara, ignoring her husband's petty jealousy, "our sons have indicated their desire for a puppy. I wondered how you felt about it?"

"We're going tomorrow after school to look at goldens."

"Golden retrievers?"

"Yup."

"Boy, those two sure know how to pull their daddy's strings. You won't make an acquisition until I get home?"

"Of course not. Now what about Byrnes?"

"What about him? He's harmless. And he knows the Prince of Wales. And a great many other rich and foolish snoots. Which is good for business. Now tell me, what's really bothering you?"

Hancock knew she would know. She always knows. She has a sixth sense. She often knows something is bugging him even before he does. So, should he tell her about the cops showing up, demand an explanation about this missing person report? Or should he play it cool, troll a little longer, see if he can get her to say something first?

"Nothing's wrong," he tells her. "I just miss you is all. So do the boys."

"And I miss you all, too. I called earlier. Did Sylvia tell you?"

"The second we walked in the door."

"John's cold is better?"

"He's fine. Nothing but a stuffed nose. You worry too much. Do you want to talk to them?"

"I thought I'd call when I got back to the hotel. Talk to them before bed. I'd rather just talk to you now." For this last remark Clara makes her voice softer and sexier.

And don't think Hancock doesn't notice.

"So tell me," she asks, "what else did you do today?"

Innocent question, wonders Hancock, or exploratory incision? "I did some work on the new book this morning."

"How did that go?"

Hancock chooses his words carefully. "My concentration wasn't that keen."

"No? Why not?"

He wants to tell her exactly why not. He wants to blurt it right out. But instead he says, "Too many interruptions."

"Really?" asks Clara. "Like what?"

"The usual stuff. The kids were kind of wound up."

"Didn't they go to Sunday school?"

"Sure, they did. I walked them over. Nicky brought them home."

"But you still couldn't get any work done?"

"Not much."

"So what was the matter? Why couldn't you concentrate?"

Hancock has played the game long enough. He's been waiting all day and now he needs to get at it. "I had a visit from the cops."

"The police?"

"That's right. The police."

"What did they want?"

"You know exactly what they wanted," he feels like saying, but manages to hold back. He just wants the cops' visit out on the table. The subject of their visit is another matter entirely.

"They wanted," he answers, "what they always want: money."

"Money?"

"They were looking for donations. It seems there is a plan afoot to put some of Boston's finest on mountain bikes. They're looking to the already overtaxed citizenry to help with the purchases."

"I see," says Clara. And then, "So nothing was wrong?"

"Wrong?" asks Hancock. "Like what?"

"I don't know. Usually the police show up when something is wrong."

"Yeah," agrees Hancock, "I guess they do."

"But everything is all right?"

"I think so."

"Why are you being so weird and evasive? Is everything all right or not?"

"Everything's swell." Hancock can see his wife is not about to broach the subject of the missing person report. At least not directly. Fine. Then he'll just leave it alone, too. For now. "So when are you coming home?"

The question elicits a long pause from Clara. Finally she sighs and says, "I could be back as early as Tuesday. Thursday at the latest. I really should pop over to Paris. Just to make sure things are running smoothly."

"So sometime between Tuesday and Thursday?"

"Right. But first I need to go to New York."

"New York? How come?"

"I might have some news on the new gallery. Everything might finally be falling into place. I'll let you know tomorrow. Maybe we could meet there and spend the night."

Hancock feels some of his suspicion drain away. "I like the sound of that plan."

"Me, too. So let's do it. Plan on meeting me in New York either Tuesday night or Wednesday night."

"I'm looking forward to it already."

They offer their affections and say good-bye, after Clara promises to call the boys in a few hours.

Hancock hangs up the phone. He takes several deep breaths while he tries to piece together the various threads of the conversation. Did Clara call the police or not? And if she did call them, why did she call them? What was her motive? Is the whole thing some kind of veiled threat? Some kind of warning? Of course, maybe Clara didn't make the call to the police at all. Maybe somebody else made the call. But who? And why? So many damn questions. Hancock likes a good mystery, but not at his own expense.

It might be wise to put together a list of possible suspects, with his wife's name at the top. At least for the time being.

But before he does that, Hancock thinks he needs to call the farmhouse out in the Berkshires north of Stockbridge. See if he can raise a voice on the line. And if not, he'll have to leave a message. There's no way he can just let this visit from the cops slide. It's a little too disturbing. And there's far too much at stake.

Rodney Byrnes returns to the table even before Clara has the cell phone back in her bag. He's been watching from the wings; too much the gentleman to return, but too much the guttersnipe not to do a bit of eavesdropping.

"So," he wants to know, "all sweetness and love between you and your covetous scribbler?"

"Are you being cynical, Mr. Byrnes?" asks Clara. "Or merely impolite?"

"Neither," insists Rodney. "Inquisitive is all."

"You are never simply inquisitive, Rodney. But the answer to your question is yes, all sweetness and love."

"No trouble on the home front then?" Rodney pulls out his chair, sweeps up his linen napkin, and sits.

Clara glances at her dining companion. "Why should there be any trouble?"

"No reason."

"Were you hoping for some trouble?"

"Of course not."

"I don't believe that for a second, Mr. Byrnes. I think you would love to see some trouble brewing on my domestic front."

"Now who's being cynical, Ms. Dare?"

Clara laughs while she pushes some garden greens around on her plate. "I'm not being cynical. I simply know you would find it quite to your liking if I dumped Hancock, moved to Europe, and cohabitated with you in various grand old hotels where we would play and have sex and generally do as we please."

"Sounds like an electrifying life-style to me."

"I'm sure it does. Pursued by the gossip press, photographed by Annie Leibowitz, interviewed by Dominick Dunne. Of course, in order to enhance my reputation as *the* art dealer of the new millennium, we would occasionally have to pull some rather daring stunts."

"Perhaps we could float naked down the Thames?"

"Too polluted."

"Maybe we could skydive off the Eiffel Tower?"

"I hate heights."

"A love-in then. Like John and Yoko."

"I hate copycats."

Rodney, not the most creative bloke in London town, needs a few seconds to pull another stunt out of his pocket. "I've got it! Everywhere we go we'll have a party. A grand party. Invite only the best and brightest people."

"I love parties."

"Of course you do. So when do we begin?"

Clara enjoys these exchanges. All her life she has been a dreamer. "Tonight," she answers. "Why not tonight?"

"Tonight indeed. Let's draw up the guest list."

Yes, Clara loves fantasies. Her love of fantasies, after all, is why she married John Hancock in the first place. There has never really been any greater fantasy than that. And she intends, very soon, in just a few days, to intensify that fantasy, make it burn even brighter.

Clara looks across the table at Rodney. She smiles and says, "A very nice idea, Sir Rodney, but, well, I have my boys to think about."

"Your boys?"

"Yes, my boys. I can't desert my boys. They need me. And, of course, I need them. I love them all madly."

"Well, maybe," says Rodney, thinking of that quaint American custom, "they could visit every other weekend."

Clara forks some garden greens into her mouth and chews slowly. She thinks about the scene in New York later in the week: the commotion and the surprise. She just has to make sure her best friend, Linda Carson, gets the boys out of Boston. Up to New Hampshire. Safe and sound.

"Clara?"

Clara hears her name. She looks up and sees Rodney. "Yes?"

"Did you hear what I said?"

"Oh, Rodney, I don't know if I did or not. I so hate to disappoint you. You are quite fun, you know, extremely amusing. But you really need to understand: You and I will only ever be friends. I have another whole life separate from you. My real life. A life I love. I don't mind making my husband a little bit jealous, but that's absolutely as far as I ever intend to go."

CALIFORNIA & BELIZE

Babe Overton has not really had a life she loves for a long, long time. She loved Frank. And she loved show business. She loved being an actress, even an actress in dopey soap commercials. Babe loved going to the set and going to the beach and going out for dinner and going dancing. She hardly ever does any of those things anymore. Now she mostly goes to work and goes to the movies and goes home to bed. She goes shopping and to the cleaners and to see Dr. Gerdy. She once in a while goes out for a drink if some man invites her. But the men are usually married and just looking for something on the side. Or recently divorced and pretty much unable to talk about anything but their ex-wife. Or groping at her after just one whiskey sour. Or asking her if she ever did it with another woman. Or just plain weird.

Babe feels like she had her chance at happiness. And through no fault of her own, it was snatched from her grasp. Look at her sitting there on that Greyhound bus. About halfway back on the right. A window seat. She may look a little weary from lack of sleep, but there's a sweetness, a shyness about her. And also something sad. You can see it in her eyes. Make eye contact with her as you pass along the aisle of the bus and she might not give you a great big grin, but neither will she scowl and drop her eyes.

She could easily be a forty-one-year-old woman traveling to Sacramento to see her ailing mother. But no, Babe's going a lot farther than the capital of the Golden State. She's going all the way, clear across the country on the one-hundred-and-sixty-nine-dollar special—L.A. to Boston in four and a half days. She still has that gun in her handbag, but not really murder on her mind.

As the bus heads east across the California desert, Babe tries to think of herself as a modern businesswoman at the outset of an East Coast business swing. Software. Maybe pharmaceuticals. Leisure apparel. Whatever her chosen vocation, she simply has a job to do in Boston. And before she gets there she has to formulate a plan of attack. What should she say? How should she act? Should she be straightforward and matter-of-fact? Or should she be subtle and pleasant about the whole thing, pretend this is merely an old wound she is trying to heal?

Hopefully, after all these years, they can just talk about what happened up there at the house in the Hollywood Hills off Mulholland Drive. Talk, like adults. Come to some kind of understanding, some kind of reconciliation.

Babe, really, is like many of us at various times in our lives: wounded, suffering, insecure, uncertain, ripped apart by a past gone bad. As trite as it may sound to the hard and the uninitiated, Babe needs closure.

The trouble is, if she doesn't get it, if she doesn't find some satisfaction, violence could result. Babe is not a violent person, probably about the least violent person in a very violent society, but even normally passive people on the verge of despair sometimes crack and kill. It happens all the time. Everyday. Read the paper. Watch the news. Look out the window.

Rafe would like to kill somebody.

"I'm sorry, sir," says the voice on the other end of the

telephone. "The earliest I'd be able to get you out of Belize City and into New York would be Wednesday."

"I want to go tomorrow."

"As I said before, sir, that flight is completely booked."

"Yeah, yeah," says Rafe, "I heard you. So Wednesday's the earliest?"

"Yes, sir." The voice is void of emotion. It could easily be computer-generated. "Would you like to make a reservation on the Wednesday flight?"

Rafe, impatient to hoof it north, thinks about what he should do, but not for very long. "Yeah," he says, "I wanna make a reservation."

"And how will you be paying, sir?"

"Cash," answers Rafe. As long as those two gringos he's supposed to meet with later come up with the green for his boat.

"I'll need a credit card to issue you a ticket, sir."

Rafe hasn't been called sir this many times in his entire life. "I don't have a damn credit card."

The voice does not quaver for even an instant. "We could make the reservation and you could go to the airport and pick up your ticket."

"It'd take me all day to get to the airport."

"Then perhaps a travel agent," suggests the voice.

There is, remembers Rafe, a travel agent on Caye Caulker now. Some Canadian broad who came down here on vacation a year or so ago to snorkel and sit in the sun and never went home. Matilda, her name is. First she opened a place to buy and sell seashells, then an ear-piercing shop, then the travel agency. Strange dame. Small and squat. As wide as she is tall. But friendly. *Happiness Is Being Alive* scrawled across her hats and T-shirts. She knows everybody. And she loves to talk. A big-time talker. Rafe knows if he buys the ticket to the States from Matilda, within an hour every person on Caye Caulker will know his itinerary. But if he wants to head north on Wednesday he doesn't have much choice.

After Rafe concludes his business with the airline agent, from his office inside the telephone booth in the back room of Jackie's Bar & Grill, he goes out onto the front porch to nurse a beer. He sits in the shade of the awning and tries not to sweat. Late afternoon, hottest time of the day. For hours now the sun has been beating down on the island, frying everything in sight.

Rafe finishes the beer and orders another. Jackie, the owner-bartender-waiter-cook, replaces the empty bottle with a full one. "So, mon," he says, "word out you sellin' yer floater."

"Christ," Rafe mutters, "someone ought to declare this island a goddamn gossip zone."

"So it's true then, mon?" Jackie has long dreadlocks and a scruffy Rastaman goatee. He's originally from Atlanta where he once had ambitions of doing the Five-Day Business Planner for the Weather Channel.

"No," says Rafe, "it's bullshit."

Jackie laughs. He has the best and brightest teeth on the island. The result of excellent dental hygiene as a youth. "What you gonna do wit the dough, Raff? Give it to the Missus?"

"Bugger off." Rafe sucks down the ice cold beer in one long swallow.

Jackie laughs some more. "Maybe you open a casino. Be the Dan Trump of Caye Caulker."

Rafe decides to remain mute. He goes down off the covered porch and out into that nauseatingly hot late afternoon heat. The sun scorches him immediately. While behind him, Jackie laughs and laughs.

Let 'em laugh, thinks Rafe, let 'em laugh all they want. I'll get the last laugh.

And who knows? Maybe he will. He's got the goods on a guy up in the States. A guy with plenty of jack. A guy with a situation.

LELAND & JAGUAR

After his third Bloody Mary, Leland Fisher calls John Hancock. Too bad the line's busy. Hancock has the phone tied up with an overseas call to London. Leland keeps trying anyway. It's taken him six ounces of vodka to fetch the nerve to make the call.

Leland hates busy signals. He finds them annoying, an impediment to instant gratification. He can't believe Hancock doesn't have call waiting. But he's already had this discussion with his best-selling author, and it seems Hancock finds call waiting a rude and obnoxious telephonic intrusion.

Leland hits redial for at least the tenth time. Still busy. Son of a bitch! Who, Leland wonders, can the philanderer be talking to?

Of course, the real question is this: Why does Leland want to talk to Hancock right now anyway? What good does he think it will do? Leland honestly believes that once he gets Hancock on the phone, he'll have the nerve to ask his all-star if he's screwing his wife. Chances are pretty good, though, that Leland will lose his nerve. He's not really a guy with a lot of gumption. Basically he's a jelly-fish, no backbone at all, especially when it comes to personal matters. Still, it's absolutely free to think tough. Leland is an old pro at thinking tough.

He once again hits redial. And once again he hears that damn busy signal. It might as well be Hancock's silky smooth voice repeating over and over, "Leland's a schmuck, Leland's a schmuck, Leland's a schmuck."

"Dammit!" Leland slams the receiver down onto the cradle.

"What's the issue, Dad?"

Leland looks up from his cushiony seat out on the verandah of his Woods Hole retreat. His daughter, Jaguar, the one he had expected to take sailing, stands in the open doorway looking pale and sleepy-eyed, and, thinks Pop, ever-so-slightly anorexic. Jaguar is about five feet six, maybe ninety pounds, dressed and loaded down with quarters for the cigarette machine. She wears nothing but a long white T-shirt that reaches halfway down her pencil-thin thighs. Across the chest, in red letters, the T-shirt says: DARE ME & I'LL DO IT.

Great, thinks Leland, staring at her. "You're too skinny. Do you ever eat?"

Jaguar yawns. "Eat less, live longer. That's my motto."

"Yeah," says Leland, who tries, but usually fails, to treat his kids like real people, "well, try this one: Eat nothing, look like death, die young."

"Are you saying I look like death?"

This, Leland knows, is a trap. "I'm saying you could use a little meat on your bones."

"I don't eat meat."

"So what *do* you eat?"

"This is boring, Dad."

Leland sighs, picks up the phone, hits redial, gets a busy signal, hangs up. "Are you just getting out of bed?" he asks his daughter, his tone clearly adversarial.

Jaguar thinks about turning on her heel and walking away, but one-on-one time with Dad happens only rarely. "Long night."

"It's four-thirty in the afternoon."

"Is it? . . . So what? Didn't you ever stay up all night, then sleep all day when you were my age?"

"No," Leland lies.

"Come off it, Dad. It's such bullshit how parents lie about their pasts."

"Do you have to say bullshit?" Leland asks this even while he repeats the redialing process. Still busy. "How the hell long is he going to talk?"

"Do you have to say hell?"

Kids, Leland thinks. It's amazing there's so many of them. If not for the powerful desire to copulate . . .

"Sorry."

"How long is who going to talk?"

"What?"

"Who are you trying to call?"

"No one." Leland dials again.

Jaguar sighs, pauses, puts her right hand on her right hip, sashays a bit, and says, "I'm pregnant."

"What?"

"You heard me. I'm with child."

Leland hangs up the phone. "You are not."

"Yes, I am."

"Don't talk trash."

"I'm pregnant, Dad. And I don't know who the father is. But I'm positive he's not Jewish. I think he's black. Or maybe Puerto Rican. Plus, I'm strung out on crack."

"Last week it was heroin."

"So this week it's crack."

Leland wonders if happiness might have slipped his way had he remained single and celibate. "Maybe," he tells his skinny daughter, "you need three sessions a week with that shrink instead of two."

Jaguar feels better now. "To deal with this family?" She sighs again. "I should probably go every day."

"What's wrong with this family? I take good care of this family. No one wants for anything."

"Except love and peace and understanding."

"Oh, Jesus."

"Dad, wake up. This family is, like, totally dysfunctional. I have a mother, a father, three stepmothers, two stepfathers, a brother, three stepsisters, threestep—"

Leland tries to follow the math. "Wait a second. Your mother's remarried again?"

"Christ, Dad, that happened last fall."

"Last fall?"

Jaguar sighs. "You're pitiful."

"Oh, right," says Leland without much confidence. "I almost forgot." Actually he has no recollection whatsoever of his second wife's third marriage. But nothing will be gained by admitting this to Jaguar. He takes another look at his daughter. She's come out onto the verandah now. She kind of swirls in half-pirouettes. As a kid she dreamed of being a ballerina. Leland dreamed of taking over for Yaz out in left field at Fenway Park, settling in under the Green Monster to haul in those towering fly balls, nothing but long outs. Too bad Leland was nearsighted and couldn't hit it out of the infield even when the other kids' dads pitched to him underhand. Jaguar never had the coordination or the drive for ballet. Still, dreams die hard. Leland owns a box right behind the Bosox dugout. Goes to twenty, thirty home games a year. Just sits there, drinks beer, and dreams.

Jaguar does her little pirouettes. Lately, Leland remembers, Jaguar has been talking about becoming a writer. Or no, maybe a psychoanalyst. But that might be one of the other kids. He sometimes gets confused. Which is understandable for a man with eight children.

"Come over here," he says to his daughter, his voice commanding and seductive.

Just a few months shy of seventeen, Jaguar has spent a good deal of her life pursuing attention. Her parents were already quarreling on a daily basis by the time she came along. By her third birthday a full-fledged marital holocaust had broken out. By five she had two houses, two bedrooms, two sets of toys, and too many strange adults using the bathroom. By nine she had two mothers, two fathers, and, in her mind anyway, some very weird step-siblings.

Leland pushes forward in his seat. Jaguar settles herself on his flabby lap. She weighs, he thinks, nothing at all, a mere feather. Anorexia pops into his head again. Or that other one. The one the dead princess had. Bulimia. He thinks it might be smart to talk it over with Jaguar's mother. Or aren't they on speaking terms right now? Another little detail Leland can't remember. Some of the exes talk to him; some don't. It mostly depends on whether or not they're satisfied with the size of the checks they receive from his accountant on the first of every month. They rarely are.

"So you think we're a pretty dysfunctional unit, hey, Jag?"

She looks at him and rolls her dark eyes. "Dysfunctional? Dad, be real. We're, like, way beyond dysfunctional. We could be the model for a Tolstoy epic. Or a Pat Conroy tell-all."

"Pat writes about southern angst. That's another whole can of worms."

"Okay, so we need a writer who can tackle the northeastern WASP-Jewish thing."

"Maybe John Updike."

"Updike's not a Jew, Dad."

"I know that, but—"

"And besides, Updike would have been better if he'd learned to deal with his sexual hangups."

Leland thinks his daughter makes a valid point, but he offers another view. "Maybe without his sexual hangups he wouldn't have written anything at all."

"So you think art is basically a way for troubled and tormented people to cast out their demons?"

Teenagers, thinks Leland. But says, "I think we all have our troubles and torments, Jag. Artists and writers get in touch with theirs, and then, if they're any good, they help us get in touch with ours."

"Is that a validation of the process?"

"I don't know. I don't think art needs validating."

"Everything needs validating. Nature, calculus, love."

Leland suddenly feels an incredible tug at his heart. It could be the first tweaks of a coronary, but it's not. It's this Dad-Daughter thing. Leland is really a very emotional and sentimental guy. And here he is with his teenage daughter who is almost a woman sitting in his lap, and he cannot believe how fast she has grown up. Seems only weeks ago he taught her how to walk. And talk. And spell banana. And now, out of the blue, she's discussing art, love, life. On a level that he probably cannot even get in touch with anymore. Hell, he knows he's made a mess of things. Like with Hillary. If he'd been more of a husband, more of a mate, she never would've been in the back of that Bentley with Hancock.

A few tears actually well up in Leland's puffy eyes. "I love you, Jag," he tells her, hoping she will not mind that he has so abruptly changed the subject. He gives her scrawny body a squeeze. "You know I love you, don't you?"

She does not mind that he changed the subject. Although, she is a teenager, and teenagers must, under all circumstances, remain cool and aloof.

"Sure, Dad," she tells him, "I know you love me." And then, in a moment of weakness, she says, "I love you, too." But before Dad can roll into a full-blown weep, she adds this brief postscript. "Of course, love is way overrated. The only thing that fucks life up more than love," suggests sixteen-year-old Jaguar Fisher, "is greed."

"Please don't use the 'f' word, Jag."

"Why? It's just a word. A four-letter word. No different than love or lust or luck."

"Oh," says the parent, who has probably used the word six or eight thousand times over the years, maybe more, "I think it's quite different. I think—"

The front doorbell rings. Jaguar jumps off her daddy's lap and starts back into the house. "That'll be Rob."

"Rob? Who's Rob?"

"Rob MacDonald . . . or Macomber . . . or Magoo," says Jaguar, heading for the front door. "Something like that. I met him last night."

"Last night?"

The doorbell rings again. Leland recognizes at once that this Rob fellow is an impatient sort, probably a premature ejaculator. Most teenage boys are.

Jaguar calls from the front hall. "We'll be up in my bedroom, Dad. Try real hard not to bother us, okay?"

Leland, flustered, and still overcome by the emotion of having his little girl on his lap, thinks about what goes on in a bedroom and blurts out, "No sex, Jaguar! Do you hear me? You're too young to be having sex!"

Jaguar just laughs.

Leland rubs his eyes and picks up his Bloody Mary. He stares at the glass, then challenges himself not to bring it to his lips. He's no idiot. He knows booze has screwed up his life, gone a long way to ruining his too many marriages. Maybe, he thinks, if he could get himself sober, once and for all, he could fix things with Hillary.

But first, he knows, he has to find out where Hillary stands with Hancock. He picks up the phone and hits redial. Still busy. "Christ!" grumbles Leland, and drains his glass.

Had he called two minutes ago the line would have been open. That would've been immediately after Hancock hung up with his wife and right before he dialed the number of the old stone farmhouse out in the Berkshires north of Stockbridge. By the time Leland called back, Hancock had a fresh connection, albeit a rather brief one.

But now Leland is sick of calling. He figures Hancock is probably gabbing with Hillary, setting up a time and a place for their next love fest. The thought, of course, makes Leland feel more than a little crazy. He has that sick, panicky feeling down in the pit of his stomach. He figures he better get Al-the-Gumshoe Brown back on the job. Tell the P.I. to get the goods, find out what's really going on.

Leland picks up the phone and dials Al Brown's number over in Brookline.

Al's line is open. Wide open. Al's just hanging out with a beer and watching the Bosox lose to Cleveland. He answers on the second ring.

Finally, thinks Leland. Progress.

*"You've reached the offices of Adventure Travel Enter-
prises. Sorry we're not here right now to take your call.
We're probably out seeking new and exciting destinations
for your next travel experience.*

*"Please leave your name and number if you would like a
real live human to call you back. Or, if you would like a
brochure about our company, please leave your name and
address and we'll get one out to you as quickly as possible.
Thanks for calling Adventure Travel."*

A little windy, thinks Hancock, even though he recorded the message himself, in a slightly disguised voice,
but it does the job.

After the beep, he leaves a message. "Jefferson. Adams.
I think it would be wise to parlay. Sooner than later. Not
that we have a full-blown crisis on our hands, but it does
deserve our attention. What did the Duke of Anjou say to
King Charles? 'Defer no time, sir. Delays have dangerous
ends.' My sentiments exactly."

Hancock hangs up the phone. He stands and begins to
pace back and forth across the third-floor office of the
Beacon Hill town house. All he can really do now is wait
for Jefferson to call back.

While he waits he would like to dig into that book he found last week at the library on the psychology of genocide, but this missing-person business has a stranglehold on his concentration. The new Hancock novel, the one in progress, as yet untitled, features a psychopathic blueblood WASP who has it in for various ethnic groups who he believes are destroying the fabric of American life.

For months Hancock has been reading any material he can get his hands on about murder on the grand scale. But no reading today. Today he's too preoccupied.

He does stop his pacing long enough to look up the word in the *Webster's New Universal Unabridged Dictionary*, resting on its own table along the wall in the middle of the office. The dictionary is open to page 729. In the left-hand column, at the top of the page, is another word: frat · ri · cide *n.* 1. The act of killing one's brother. 2. A person who kills his own brother. [Latin *Fratricida*, from *Frater*, (brother) and *cidium*, a killing, from *caedere*, to kill].

But Hancock does not stop to read the definition. He flips ahead to page 764. He skims the page and finds: gen · o · cide *n.* The systematic, planned annihilation of a racial, political, or cultural group. [Greek *Genos* (race) + cide].

He reads the definition over three or four times. He has read it a hundred times or more since beginning work on the new book. But tonight the words barely register. He has far more personal matters clogging his brain.

He goes back to pacing. He thinks about calling the cops. What precinct, he tries to remember, did those detectives say they were from? Or maybe they didn't say. He can't remember. Which ticks him off. Usually he remembers everything, every detail. The consummate observer.

Hancock thinks it would be wise to call the local precinct, see if he can get more information on this missing person report. Who took the call? Exactly when did the call come in? What, precisely, was said by the caller? Was it definitely a woman? Or could it have been a man?

No, better to talk to Jefferson first. Get his take on the situation.

Hancock returns to the desk, once again picks up the phone. He digs the beeper number out of his memory. It's an 800 number, reachable practically anywhere in the world. Which, in their line of work and with their rather delicate domestic circumstances, comes in pretty handy.

He dials the number, then follows the automated directions. He punches in the return number, followed by the pound key. Then he hangs up.

And continues pacing. No telling where that page might land. There had been talk of a trip to the Alps, but it had been wet and cold over on that side of the Atlantic. Banff up in the Canadian Rockies had also been a possibility. The late spring heli-skiing on the glaciers north of Lake Louise was supposedly still pretty good up on the high peaks. Not that Jefferson is really much of a deep-powder, back-country skier; he prefers gentler, groomed terrain. He leaves the crazy stuff to Adams.

Each month Adventure Travel Enterprises runs a six-to-sixteen day trip somewhere in the world. Sometimes these are guided trips, but more often they are solo journeys, taken alternately by Jefferson and Adams, which have no destination until the traveler goes to the airport and purchases a ticket. An account of the journey then finds its way into print via the monthly Adventure Travel Enterprises newsletter.

Hancock, creator and cofounder of A.T.E., continues to pace. He wants to talk to his partner, and he wants to talk to him ASAP. Hancock is not a patient man. Like Leland Fisher, he wants instant gratification. It's only been six or eight hours since those cops came to the door, but Hancock wants the mystery they brought to his home resolved. Now.

There is, he knows, one other way to contact Jefferson: the Adventure Travel Enterprises cell phone. But cell calls are too easily intercepted and traced. They are definitely not secure. So Adams and Jefferson long ago imposed strict limitations on the use of their A.T.E. cell phone: business only, no personal stuff. Unless, of course, there's an emergency; a real emergency. Something to do with Clara or the boys.

Hancock has to admit that presently the situation at hand cannot be classified as an emergency. A breach of security is not warranted. At least not yet.

VOODOO

Thomas Young, still sitting on Sir Rodney's sofa, hears his beeper go off inside his oilskin jacket resting on the wooden chair across the room. He makes no effort to retrieve the page. Only one other person in the world knows the number.

Downstairs, Sir Rodney Byrnes, staggering just a bit, pushes into the vestibule, fumbles with his keys, and unlocks the front door of #36 South Street. Rodney's had too much to drink, plus he's feeling pretty sorry for himself after Clara's rejection. Not that he intends to let her rejection slow down his advances, but it was still a cruel blow to his already fragile ego.

He stumbles into the elevator. His temples pound. The elevator ride up to the fourth floor makes him nauseous. All that champagne has his stomach churning, his mouth feeling stale and cottony.

The elevator door opens. He steps out into the corridor. The wicked smell of feces hits him immediately. He cannot help himself. He bends over and retches right on the fine wool carpet not five feet from his front door.

The door is painted red. In the dim light Rodney does not see the scat smeared across the bottom. All clammy and sweaty now, heart racing, he struggles again with his keys, finally finds the right one, jams it into the lock, opens the door, stumbles inside, and promptly throws up again. This time all over a priceless African wood carving brought back from the Dark Continent by some warring ancestor after the Boer War.

Rodney, nose running, eyes watering, breath smelling of champagne and vomit, sways into the living room and switches on the light. At first he cannot believe his eyes. He has no idea what it even is. Over there. Sitting calmly on the sofa. A man? A beast? A hallucination? Rodney thinks maybe he should scream, but nothing comes out but a faint squeak.

"For chrissakes, who the hell are you? What the hell do you want?"

Thomas Young, still in blackface, stands and crosses the room. Rodney is now too stunned and petrified to move. Thomas raises his left hand, palm turned up and slightly cupped. Resting in his palm is a pile of the dirty brown voodoo powder. Thomas holds the hand very close to Rodney's shocked face. He blows the powder into Rodney's mouth and nostrils. Rodney instantly recoils.

Thomas Young does not really know the exact ingredients of the powder he has in his possession. He has, on several occasions, inquired of the voodoo priests he knows in Haiti, but they provide only vague, mystifying answers. "Ground-up roots from sassafras trees." "Cemetery earth." "Dead men's bones."

Thomas knows there is also a chemical in the mix. Tetrodotoxin, or TTX. It is extracted from various species of puffer fish, and also from a variety of local Caribbean land newts. It is a powerful and potentially deadly agent. Thomas has no idea precisely how the powder works, but he has seen, up close and personal, what the powder does. The powder is the pharmacological reality behind the Haitian zombie, the living dead of that strange and mysterious island's peasant folklore.

Whatever the powder does, it does it now, in less than a minute, to Sir Rodney Byrnes.

Rodney, after sneezing four or five times, after trying to mumble an obscenity or two, after feeling himself start to go numb, after a series of convulsions, crashes to the floor.

Thomas drags him across the carpet and pulls him up onto the sofa. Rodney's head lolls over onto his right shoulder.

"Now, Sir Rodney," begins Thomas, "try not to struggle. You've been given some medicine to keep you calm. I didn't give you very much, but it should make these next few minutes a little more bearable."

Thomas tucks a small pillow between Rodney's head and shoulder so that Byrnes sits more upright. The Zombie powder has left Rodney pretty much paralyzed. His eyes are open. He can still see and breathe and hear, but he cannot move. The powder has rendered his nervous system virtually inoperable. Nevertheless, the man looks mighty scared. A thin line of vomit runs out of the corner of his mouth and down his chin.

"I'm not into torture, Rodney," says Thomas Young, "so don't worry too much about suffering. I really hate to see people suffer. I've done my share of suffering over the years and it's not really much fun. I don't like to inflict it on others. I'm actually a gentle soul, a man who tries to sort out the differences between right and wrong, between good and evil."

Rodney makes some deep guttural sounds, but the powder has stolen his ability to speak.

"Shh," says Thomas, and presses his index finger to Rodney's frozen lips. "You really have no need to speak. Seek peace. Turn inward. Say a prayer."

Thomas picks up that length of picture wire off the mahogany coffee table. He wraps the end of the wire around the palms of his hands. He gives the wire a little tug, pulls it taut.

"See, Rodney, some people believe it is a sin to covet another man's wife. I believe this myself. And I know that you are guilty of this sin. I doubt very seriously if you have actually possessed this woman, for I know, ultimately, this woman is good and virtuous and loves her husband and her children. But her essential goodness does not excuse your guilty and filthy mind."

Thomas snaps the wire in Rodney's ear. Then he bends down and presses his nose hard against Rodney's nose. Rodney groans. Thomas presses harder. Next he presses his whole face against Rodney's face: lips, cheeks, eyes, ears. Back and forth he rolls their faces together. Soon Rodney, too, is covered with the black-face.

Thomas pulls back six or eight inches. He gets his mouth nice and wet, then spits directly into Rodney's face. All part of the voodoo zombie ritual. All useful and necessary components to drive away the evil spirits that lurk within and around Rodney Byrnes, to kill the lust the man has fostered for Clara Dare Hancock.

"Sir Rodney," says Thomas, unwrapping the wire from his right palm, then gently rubbing his gloved hand over Rodney's damp, black face, "you are cleansed now. You are free. The man of the woman you covet has made you clean. You are pure and ready for transport into a less lustful world."

Thomas rubs Sir Rodney's neck and shoulders. He feels Clara's suitor relax. Then he takes up the wire again and wraps it around his right palm.

Not wasting a second, Thomas wraps the wire around Rodney's neck. He draws the wire tight. Not too tight. Just tight enough. Tight enough to cut off the flow of oxygen to the lungs. Tight enough to cut off the flow of blood to the brain. Tight enough and long enough to give Sir Rodney the fright of his useless life.

That task complete, Thomas spends the next few minutes cleaning up the evidence of his brief visit here to flat 402 of 36 South Street. He cleans up everything except for the scat on the door. The scat he leaves. The scat will keep intruders at bay.

Soon enough, Thomas is back out on the street, walking in the direction of Berkeley Square. Face clean, false mustache back in place. He has on his leather-brimmed cap and his oilskin jacket. No need for sunglasses. No need to turn up his collar. The drizzle has stopped. The night sky has started to clear.

He walks all the way to Piccadilly Circus before hailing a cab. It feels good to walk, to stretch his legs, to get the smell of Sir Rodney's fear out of his lungs.

So he walks, and soon enough his thoughts begin to wander. This time tomorrow he will be in the Bahamas, on Exuma, settled in the Hotel Peace and Plenty, preparing to do battle with the bonefish. Of course, sometime between now and then he will have to call his brother, find out what John has on his mind.

Yes, take a closer look at Thomas Young and you will surely think you see John Hancock. But you do not see John Hancock. You see Will Hancock. William Larson Hancock. Traveling, as they both do when on Adventure Travel Enterprises business, under the name Thomas Young.

There is no Will Hancock, not really, not anymore. There is only John; two of him, actually. They are absolutely and perfectly identical, the Hancock boys, physically the same right down to the size of their feet, the color of their eyes, the shape of their ears, the whiteness of their teeth.

Their mannerisms, too, are perfectly identical: the way they nod, laugh, sigh, gesture with their hands when telling a story. View them side by side (though finding them together in public has been a rare occurrence indeed for many, many years) and you might discern some minor variations on a very similar theme. But put some distance between them and they magically become the same person: John Hancock.

But do not be deceived, as so many have been; the Hancock boys, John and Will, could not possibly be more different.

SOME OLD BUSINESS

MERRY CHRISTMAS

In the late fall of 1982 the Hancock boys, both alive and well, were twenty-two-year-old graduate students in the creative writing program at Harvard University in Cambridge, Massachusetts. The holidays were fast approaching, and John and Will decided they needed a vacation. With Mom and Dad dead, and with no other family to visit, the brothers chose a warm weather port for their getaway.

They flew to Belize on Christmas Day. They spent Christmas night at a cheap and dirty hotel on Cockburn Street in Belize City. All night long cockroaches the size of mice marched in and out of the drain pipe in the filthy bathtub.

Then, as now, Belize City was basically a ramshackle, third-world city of about fifty thousand mostly poverty-stricken souls. Built originally as a temporary settlement for Euro-whites who had come to ransack the interior of its logwood and mahogany riches, the city kept growing and never quite gave up on itself. But the Hancock boys had just escaped urban life; they had no desire to hang around longer than necessary.

First thing in the morning they headed out to the off-shore islands. In those days, most of the tourist boats made a beeline for San Pedro on Ambergris Caye, about sixty miles northeast of Belize City. But San Pedro was full of grungy-looking Americans smoking weed and drinking cheap tequila and trying to grow dreadlocks. The Hancock boys could watch that action back up on Cambridge Common. So in the afternoon they caught a lobster boat bound for Caye Caulker.

The tiny island and its one run-down village did not offer much in the way of excitement, so the Hancocks brought along some thrills of their own. They passed just forty-eight hours on Caye Caulker, but their brief stay gave the islanders something to talk about for months. Years even.

The Hancock boys booked a second-floor room at the two-story Caye Caulker Guest House on the north edge of the village. That afternoon they went swimming in The Cut, a narrow channel that had been created by Hurricane Hattie back in '61. There they met, for the very first time, Rafe Paquita, just eighteen years old at the time, a smiling and still unmarried local who promised to take care of all their needs for one low fee. Rafe assured them he could lead them to all the best bars and restaurants on the island. (Not a major coup, considering the island had only a handful of either one.) But he could also take them sailing. And fishing. And skin diving.

"I tell you," he told the Hancock boys, "I have the most finest connections." And then, after smiling at them for a good thirty seconds, he added, "And even though I see two of you, because you look like one, I charge you only once. How is that for good deal?"

"I guess that depends," John, always the shrewder businessman, answered, "on how much you charge for one."

That night, after consuming a couple of small but tasty local lobsters each, the boys bought Rafe a few beers at the bar of the Paradise Hotel. He seemed harmless enough. And he claimed he had a boat. And some scuba gear.

"Tomorrow," he told them, "I take you brothers out to the reef. The famous Belize Barrier Reef. Longest reef in the world. I take you to the best dive sites: Sponge Avenue, Mackerel Hole, George's Cut. You have a very excellent time."

The boys watched Rafe's ever-smiling face with its stained yellow teeth, red eyes, and mottled brown skin.

"You brothers know how to dive, right? You know how to operate the gear?"

"Oh, yeah," John assured him, "we know how to operate the gear."

The Hancock boys were certified scuba divers. Back when their parents, William and Lenore, were still alive, the whole family had taken the certification course in preparation for a trip to the Florida keys. There they had all gone diving together at the John Pennekamp Coral Reef State Park. But a year later William and Lenore crashed their brand-new Cadillac Eldorado into the back of a tractor trailer. One of the consequences of that accident was an end to family holidays. The boys had not been diving since.

They were in the water by nine A.M. Sans Rafe. "Rafe don't dive," was all Rafe said to the brothers' inquiry. "Rafe stay topside. Take care of his boat."

Rafe couldn't have gone under even had he wanted to; he owned four oxygen tanks, but only two regulators, two masks, two weight belts, and two sets of flippers. And so, after reacquainting themselves with the scuba equipment, the Hancock boys slipped over the gunwale of Rafe's ancient Whaler into the warm, crystal-clear, blue-green water. The sun was hot, the water plenty warm; they had no need for wet suits or gloves or booties. The Caribbean felt like an enormous saltwater bathtub.

Rafe had his boat anchored on the edge of the reef about half a mile off the south shore of the island. The boys spent an hour in the shallow water watching a vast array of colored fish darting through the clumps of coral. Will rarely ventured more than a few feet below the surface. He swam in circles, fearing the large aquatic creatures that might lurk over his shoulder. John dove deeper and strayed farther. John had always been the wilder brother, the one who crossed boundaries and broke rules. Will followed, usually with reluctance.

When the air in their tanks ran low, the boys surfaced and swam back to the boat where Rafe sat smoking a thin reefer and waiting patiently. "Hey, brothers! Pretty cool below, huh? You see that big barracuda come up on you a while back?"

Will had not seen the barracuda. Had he seen the barracuda, he would have been back in the boat in seconds flat.

Rafe steered the boat around to the north side of the island so the boys could have a go at the North Cut. As they slowly made their way up the west coast of Caye Caulker, Rafe pointed out some of the other local dive sites.

"Below us," he told the brothers, "a whole maze of caves run through the coral. All kind of fish in those caves. Barracuda. Sometimes sharks. They go in after the fish. Very wild place to dive. But tricky with all the different ways in and ways out. Easy to get lost, run out of air, panic, drown. You need a guide, but that guide not be me."

John liked the idea of investigating the underwater caves. He could imagine his heart pounding against his chest as he slithered through a crack in the coral. Will said he preferred to stay clear of any caves. He suffered from claustrophobia.

On their second dive at North Cut, the boys had a pretty good scare.

Rafe had assured them that sharks were a rarity. "Morays and barracuda, yes, but sharks, not once in a blue moon I see one."

Well, the Hancock boys saw one. A big one.

"An eight-footer," John later insisted.

"Ten feet or better," corrected Will, once safely back aboard Rafe's little Whaler.

Both agreed the shark was a hammerhead, one of the scariest looking creatures in the sea with its huge, rectangular head and its two roving eyes posted out on the ends like a couple of searchlights.

Will could not have been more than twenty feet below the surface when the shark appeared. John, much to his brother's annoyance, had slipped down a sheer coral wall to check out some amberjacks. He was down fifty, maybe sixty feet. Will wanted to stay closer together, but no way was he going that deep. He claimed the depth made his ears hurt, but fear was the real culprit.

About halfway between the brothers there was a cut in the reef where a constant stream of larger fish swam in and out. Will could see the fish perfectly through the clear water: tile fish, grouper, snapper. He tried to get his brother's attention so they could share the sight together, but John had his eyes riveted on those amberjacks.

Suddenly, a school of snapper swam into view, making haste for the protection of the reef. Their flight caught John's attention. Both brothers soon found out why such a rush: A big hammerhead was out cruising for lunch. Too bad the shark couldn't fit through the cut. He came to a dead stop just inches before the coral. He swished his massive flukes and changed direction. In an instant he had his enormous and lethal body pointed straight down to where John watched with his eyes as big and round as baseballs.

Will screamed, but, of course, nothing came out, except his regulator, which caused him to swallow a bunch of sea water and begin to choke. His arms and legs began to flail. The sudden and unexpected movement must have distracted the predator, because a split second before slamming his broad and ugly head into John's skull, that shark veered away and headed for open water.

That night, still jittery and worked up from their encounter with the hammerhead, the Hancock boys powered down excessive quantities of alcohol at Syd's bar on the inlet. They talked about that shark for so long and in such obsessive detail that even Rafe, a great lover of free drinks and verbal verbosity, finally grew bored and went home. John and Will barely took notice of his absence. Midnight came and went and still they babbled on.

Then, around one, the combination of too much booze and a near-brush with death turned their chatter downright morose.

"Jesus," Will lamented, "what if that ugly son of a bitch had bitten your head off?"

"I would've been a bloody mess, bro. Food for the fishes."

They each poured down another shot.

"And where," Will asked, "would that leave me?"

"Bro, I believe that would leave you motherless, fatherless, *and* brotherless."

"We can't let that happen," announced Will. "Not now or ever."

John, at twenty-two utterly immortal, shrugged and said, "It never will."

Still, they brooded over the idea of death for several minutes, over the dismal reality that one of them could die at any moment. It was not a happy concept. Not only were these guys orphans and identical twins, but they had rarely been separated since conception. A few hours here, a day or two there, but all things considered, the Hancock boys, up until that moment, had more or less lived their lives as a single, harmonious unit.

They ordered another round of drinks—shots and beers. They did not often get soaked to the gills, especially Will, but this night would be exceptional on several fronts.

It must have been after the sixth or seventh shot of rum that John suddenly had a profound inspiration. Like most profound inspirations, he had no idea at the time that his simple declaration would change his life, and the life of his brother, forever.

"You know," he mumbled, his face half buried in his beer mug, "it definitely wouldn't be too cool if one of us died, but wouldn't it be the coolest if one of us pretended to be dead."

"Say again?"

"If one of us pretended to be dead . . . but was, you know, really still alive."

Will, pretty well snookered, rubbed his bloodshot eyes.
"I don't follow."

"It's, like, I die, but I don't die. Think of the possibilities."

"You're drunk," announced Will. "I have no idea what
the hell you're babbling about. And neither do you."

"I'm talking possibilities here, bro." John's brain had
powered into overdrive.

"What possibilities?"

"We're twins, right?"

"Last I heard."

"Identical twins?"

"In appearance only," said Will, just to get his brother's
goat.

"Fine," agreed John, "but absolutely physically identical?"

"Ninety-nine percent, yeah."

"Ninety-nine point nine percent."

"Okay, so?"

"So that's what I'm getting at."

"I'm still waiting to hear what you're getting at."

John took a long slow look around the bar. The few
remaining patrons were all well-oiled and heavily involved
in their own schemes. The barkeep had slipped out the
back to smoke a bone.

"Okay," said John, leaning over close to his twin
brother, "here's what I'm getting at. Let's just say that big
old ugly hammerhead had chomped me in two, but not
really."

"Not really?"

"Right."

"He doesn't chomp you in two?"

"No. He chomps me in two, but not really, and you
come up for air all panicky and upset and right away start
telling people that some big-ass shark just ate your
brother."

"Even though this big-ass shark hasn't eaten anybody?"

"Correct."

"Okay. So then what?"

"So then we pretend I'm dead."

"We pretend you're dead?"

"You're catching on now, bro."

Will could feel the booze playing with his brain cells, causing them no small amount of damage. "Okay, so you're dead. But not really. What good does that do us?"

John sighed and shook his head. "Jesus, bro, get with the program already. Think about the possibilities. Do I always have to be the one to provide the inspirational spark in this duo?"

"I wouldn't say always."

John sighed. "Okay," he explained, "so I'm dead and you're not."

"You're dead and I'm not."

"Right. I'm dead and you're not."

"So?"

"So you go back up to Cambridge. Study, mourn, cry on Zelda's shoulder, go to class, do what you usually do."

Will was starting to get a handle on his brother's fantasy. "While what?" he wanted to know. "While you hang around down here in Belize pretending to be dead and soaking up the sun and hunting for babes?"

John smiled. "Merely a few of the possibilities, brother."

"So maybe you better give me another. What's in this deal for me?"

"Hell, we take turns soaking up the sun and hunting for babes. That's what's in the deal for you. First you be the hardworking responsible one who pushes our academic and literary career forward. Then, after a month or two, we trade places. You get to be the hedonist or the shark hunter or whatever you wanna be. That's the beauty of this deal, Will: You do whatever the hell you want. No restraints. No restrictions. You're dead, after all."

"I thought you were the one who was dead?"

"We take *turns* being dead."

"Yeah, but John's the one who's supposed to be dead. Not Will."

"Whatever. You. Me. One of us."

"You."

"Okay," said John, "me."

Will nodded while struggling to get the scenario straight in his head. "You really think we could get away with it?"

"Sure as my name is John Hancock, I do. We have no other family. No one to mourn our passing. No one to raise a ruckus. It's just you and me."

"Sounds interesting."

"Shit, it sounds perfect. The best of both worlds. Plus, with one of us dead, we can write off half our debts, all those thousands of dollars in outstanding student loans inflicted upon us by that asshole Hagstrom. They can't collect money from a corpse."

Will nodded. His own inebriated thoughts had started to stir. "But what about the writing?"

John shrugged. "What about it?"

"We'd keep writing as a team?"

"Of course."

"We have to keep writing as a team."

"No question."

"I mean, that's where the future lies."

"Absolutely."

The booze had Will pretty riled up by this time. He finally had a firm handle on the possibilities. "We'll live out our fantasies even as we work to succeed and pursue our ambitions. . . ."

Brother John nodded enthusiastically, even though success and ambition were mere sideshows in his philosophical equation. John was primarily interested in having a good time. Now. Today. "You got it, brother. You're right on target."

To be dead and loose in the world at the tender and innocent age of twenty-two. The Hancock boys did not for one second bother to contemplate the consequences or the complexities of their wild fantasy. That would have been a downer. And they were far too intoxicated with booze and possibilities to deal with downers.

And John, of course, had one, a huge one, a monster one. It was easily the father of all possibilities. John had held the big one in reserve, just in case Will had balked at his pitch.

He leaned over even closer to his brother. "Hagstrom," he whispered in Will's ear.

"Hagstrom? What about him?"

"Think about it."

"I'm thinking."

"With one of us dead, but not really, where do you think that puts Big Frank Hagstrom?"

Will instantly caught the drift of his brother's thinking. His eyes and mouth broke into a devilish grin. "I think that puts Big Frank in harm's way."

"Indeed it does, bro. No way one of us can be in two places at once."

Early the next morning, after staying up most of the night plotting and scheming, the Hancock boys went looking for Rafe. No doubt about it: they needed an accomplice to make their plan work.

They found him sound asleep in his hammock hanging from the porch of his shack down by the harbor.

John gave him a shake. "Rafe. Wake up."

Rafe stirred but did not open his eyes.

John gave him another shake. "Rafe, you want to make five hundred bucks? Cash? For a couple hours' work?"

That brought Rafe wide awake. He rolled out of his hammock and listened to their plan; at least to the sketchy details they were willing to provide.

"So," he asked, "you brothers want to do this as a joke on someone, or what?"

"A joke," answered John, "right. A practical joke."

Rafe laughed. He loved practical jokes. And he loved the brothers' plan. Had they asked, he probably would have helped them pull this off for free. But the money sounded pretty good, too. "For five hundred cash," he told them, "I help *both* of you disappear."

"Not necessary," John told him. "One of us will do."

Rafe and Will went to get the boat ready while John hustled back to their room to fetch a few of his things. He settled for a pair of faded Levi's and two shirts, plus the swimsuit and T-shirt he already had on. The pants and shirts he tossed in a plastic bag. He figured he'd better leave his suitcase and the rest of his personal belongings behind, just in case anyone came around later to investigate.

On his way out the door, John spotted the two green U.S. passports lying on the bureau: one belonging to him, the other belonging to his brother. This, he suddenly realized, was a detail they had not discussed. Early in their parlay the night before, John had implied that he would be the one to die, to take the hit. But nothing definite had been decided on the matter of whose name would be permanently taken out of circulation.

So who, exactly, would be the one to perish?

John knew, standing there, a passport in each hand, that the decision was suddenly all his. He held the power. If he took his passport, Will would return to the States as William Larson Hancock, and that name would live on. But if John took Will's passport, Will would have no choice but to return to the States as John David Hancock.

John stood there for a good sixty seconds, mulling it over, weighing the pros and cons. The formidable moral dilemma pulled him to and fro. This, he knew instinctively, was one of those momentous decisions that could, and probably would, forever change the course of a man's life. Or in this case, two men's lives.

He could have, of course, taken both passports and discussed the situation with Will. But that would have necessitated a loss of control. And so, in the end, as much out of vanity as anything else, and perfectly aware that his decision might someday come back to haunt him, John tossed *his* passport back onto the bureau. He simply could not kill himself off. The name, he told himself, by way of justification, was an American classic: John Hancock. It would be a crime to throw it away.

And so to save his name, and his life, John threw Will's passport into the plastic bag along with his clothes. And then, the choice made, he turned and hurried out the door. He found Will and Rafe down at the harbor. They had refueled Rafe's small battered Whaler.

"All set?" John asked, his guilt overshadowed by his eagerness for the grand adventure ahead.

Will nodded, but without much enthusiasm. Doubt and reluctance had already started to drive away last night's semi-drunken ebullience.

The trio climbed aboard. They messed around with the scuba gear for a few minutes so it looked to those passing by like they were going out for another dive. Then they untied the lines and pulled away from the dock.

Once they reached open water, Rafe steered north for Ambergris Caye. The Hancock boys sat in the front of the boat amidst the scuba gear and the extra tank of fuel. They went over their plan one last time. John did most of the talking. The details were clear and simple. All they needed, he insisted, was a little luck, and plenty of guts.

The small boat swept past San Pedro without slowing. The boys had originally planned for John to go ashore at San Pedro and make his way back to Belize City, but Rafe had come up with a better idea.

"Somebody maybe see us at the San Pedro docks," he'd said. "That no good for you two to be seen together. That put the whole plan in trouble."

"So what do you think?" the brothers had asked.

"I think Mexico."

So now they continued north along the east coast of Ambergris Caye. Half an hour or so later, Rafe pointed off to the west and shouted above the whine of the outboard motor, "Over there! Mexico!"

"You're sure?" John wanted to know.

"Oh yeah, man! I sure!"

John turned to Will. "Almost time, bro. You ready for this?"

Will took a deep breath. He definitely was *not* ready.

The effects of last night's booze had long since worn off. He was right now as sober as he had ever been in his entire life. He wanted in the worst way to tell John that the scheme was stupid, insane, absurd. He wanted desperately to call the whole thing off. Only he didn't have the guts to say so to his brother. He didn't want his brother thinking he was weak and scared.

John squeezed his shoulder. "You're not getting cold feet on me, are you, bro?"

Fear and trepidation raced through Will's body. But at twenty-two, he was still too young and far too inexperienced to grasp the full, long-range consequences of what they were about to put into motion.

And so Will gathered his courage and said in the strongest voice he could muster, "I'm ready. No cold feet for me. What about you?"

"You know me, bro. Always primed for a little excitement."

Will suppressed a desire to throw up. "Right."

"The next several days," added John, "will demand a command performance."

"That's why you're going and I'm staying," Will replied. "I've always been the better actor."

John smiled. He would give his brother that much. No time or need to argue that point now. Will might be the better actor, but John knew he was the one with the *cojones* to cross Mexico and enter the United States on the lam. Will definitely did not have the stomach for that kind of duty. Which was the real reason why John was going and Will was staying.

"So," John asked, "we're all set?"

Will braced himself against the bulkhead as the boat bumped through the shallow surf. "All set."

Rafe took the boat in close to shore. There was nothing for as far as they could see but deserted beach and open sea. Rafe cut the motor.

"Mexico?" John asked again.

"Mexico," Rafe assured him. "Follow the beach north.

Go two, maybe three miles till you come to a village. Catch a ride up the coast to Majahual. From there go north to Cancún or west to Chetumal. Either place get you a bus to Mexico City. Or wherever you wanna go."

John stood up. The boat bobbed in the wash. John had to grab Will's arm to keep from losing his balance. He had on dark aviator sunglasses and a Boston Red Sox baseball cap pulled down low over his forehead. The time had come to deal with the passport. He had to let his brother know the score. He couldn't just leave it hanging. So he opened the plastic bag and sifted through the few things inside.

"Time to roll, brothers," Rafe announced. "This not a good spot to get caught by Mexican shore patrol."

John pulled out the passport and held it up for all to see. "That's a relief," he said, the approaching lie like verbal poison upon his lips. "I thought for a second I'd forgotten this little piece of business."

"Why do you need that?" asked Will. "The whole idea is to cross the border on the sly so there's no record of you entering the States."

"I know," answered John. "But just in case I get caught, I better have the goods."

Will nodded, reassured. "You're right. Just in case. Good thinking."

That's when John opened the passport and made a show of examining the contents. "Oh, shit," he mumbled, his face ripe with feigned annoyance.

"What's the matter?"

"Before," John lied, "back at the room, I grabbed my passport off the bureau on my way out the door. At least I thought it was mine."

"Yeah?"

"I must've grabbed yours by mistake."

Will did not immediately see the significance of this announcement. "So what?" he said. "Just give it back to me."

"But I can't," said John.

"Why not?"

"Like I said a second ago, I'll need it in case I get caught at the border."

Will, seeing the logic, nodded. But an instant later his eyes narrowed and then went cold. He got it now. It all came clear. It meant he would have to reenter the United States as John Hancock. Which meant he—Will Hancock—would be the dead brother.

"Can't wait any longer," he heard Rafe say. "Gotta roll. Out of the boat now or we all go back to Caulker together."

All his life Will had trusted his twin brother, had trusted him implicitly without question and without suspicion. And for good reason: They had always told one another the truth. They had always been a team; the Hancock boys against the world. But now Will suddenly found himself wondering if John had done this passport switch on purpose. A wave of fear and doubt washed over him.

But what could he say? What could he do? He had no proof. Of course he had no proof. There was no proof. John wouldn't lie to him. No way. They were brothers. It had happened just the way John said. It was a mistake. A goddamn stupid mistake. And so what? It's nothing but a name, after all, a silly name.

Maybe. But a crack, slight though it might have been at the time, had nevertheless opened in the solid granite wall that was the foundation of the Hancock brothers' relationship.

Will felt John's hand squeeze his shoulder. Then John's arms went around Will's chest. John hugged his brother close.

"Here we go, bro. Time to have ourselves a little fun."

Will swallowed hard, then nodded.

And with that, John stepped out of the Whaler into the warm, shallow water. He did not want to linger. The time had come to act, to make his escape.

Will wanted to say something, anything, but Rafe pulled the cord on the outboard and the engine growled to life.

"Houston!" John shouted to his brother. "The Airport Marriott! I'll be there in four or five days!"

Will started to respond, but the racing throttle drowned his words. The small boat spun around and battled its way back through the surf. Will turned and waved, but John had hit the beach running. Hard and fast. All Will saw was his brother's back.

DEATH, MARRIAGE & BIRTH

It may sound like a stretch, but the Watergate break-in and subsequent cover-up by Richard Milhous Nixon had a profound effect on the young brothers Hancock. Here's how it happened: Tricky Dick's team of Cuban burglars got caught in the act, Dick tried to sweep the whole mess under the Oval Office rug, and the rug got pulled out from under his phlebitis-inflamed feet. Dick, as every school kid knows, had to throw in the towel, thereby handing over all coaching duties to that old Wolverine workhorse, Gerald Rudolph Ford. Gerry soon pardoned Dick for his sins against the Constitution. It was this pardon that put into motion events which directly impacted the Hancock boys, John and Will, just teenagers at the time.

Remember Squeaky Fromme? The young Charles Manson groupie who tried to take Gerry Ford out of the game while Gerry was on a campaign sweep out in the great state of California?

Well, just minutes after Squeaky pulled the trigger on her heretofore concealed weapon (a weapon, by the way, very similar to the one in Babe Overton's handbag), the boys from the Associated Press had the story on the wire flying across the country. Initial reports were, of course, highly exaggerated. The scoop on Gerry's death, like Dewey's victory, was a bit premature. Squeaky's gun never went off. And even if it had gone off, Gerry would have lived to tell his grandkids about it. The firing chamber, authorities later discovered, was absolutely empty. Not a single bullet hiding anywhere. Nevertheless, assassinations constitute big news. The TV and radio guys, always seeking some reason to interrupt your regularly scheduled programming, had a field day.

The news interrupted a funky Dave Brubeck number playing in the brand-new 1975 Cadillac Eldorado belonging to William and Lenore Hancock. So brand-new that William and Lenore were actually on their way home from the showroom in Beverly Hills when the newscaster's solemn voice crackled through the speakers. "The President of the United States has been shot! Repeat: President Gerald R. Ford has been shot!"

William and Lenore exchanged glances of shock and dismay. Just a few nights earlier they had met the President and his lovely wife, Betty, at a one-thousand-dollar-per-plate Republican fund-raiser. William and Lenore were solid Republicans. News that their man had been shot disturbed them greatly.

So disturbed was William that he immediately reached down to crank up the volume on the radio of his brand-new Eldorado. Unfortunately, William was not yet familiar with the ergonomics of his big new cruiser. He had to take his eyes off the road for a split second or two to find the volume control. But a split second or two can equal eternity on the jam-packed northbound lane of the San Diego Freeway when even motorists in the slow lane zip along at eighty miles per hour.

No one knows for sure, but it seems likely that a whole slew of drivers out there on the San Diego Freeway reached for their radio knobs at precisely the same instant. All wanted to hear more about the first president since JFK to take a slug. This curiosity caused a general lapse of concentration that rocked that stretch of highway.

The next morning it made page one of the L.A. *Times*.

Just below the story about the attempted assassination of the President. Gerry was back on his feet, doing just fine, shrugging it off like a missed tackle. Too bad some quick-fingered photographer had caught the President on film just moments after Squeaky made her attack. Jerry looked pretty spooked in that photo, like he had just been crushed by the entire defensive unit of the Ohio State Buckeyes.

Unfortunately, William, searching for his radio knobs, wasn't as fortunate. He failed to see the bright red brake lights of the tractor trailer looming just a few feet ahead. To avoid the cars in front of him, the driver of that tractor trailer, a certified professional, had decelerated from sixty-five miles an hour to about fifteen miles an hour by pretty much locking up his huge set of air brakes. William should have done likewise. Still traveling at a quite rapid speed, eyes averted, he plowed straight into the back of that low-slung tractor trailer toting several tons of swimsuits and tank tops.

There was a picture of the flattened Cadillac in the newspaper. In the caption under the picture it explained what had happened to the occupants: decapitated. That's right. William and Lenore Hancock, beloved parents of John and Will Hancock: decapitated.

And to think that Tricky Dick, exiled off the coast of south Florida, out on the island of Key Biscayne, griping about the media liberals who had brought him down while throwing back some Kentucky mash with good buddy Bebe, had absolutely no idea what ruin he had indirectly wrought.

And to think also that there are still people bumbling along among us who do not believe in the interconnected karma of the universe.

Later that same day, the Hancock boys, age fifteen, back East at boarding school, received word, while dozing through an American history lecture on the causes of the War Between the States, to report to the headmaster's office. This order perked the boys up immediately. They had no idea, of course, that their parents had just been killed. They knew only that it was the third day of classes in a new school year and already they were bored and fidgety. But a showdown with Headmaster Masters, now, that could turn the day sweet.

The headmaster was a stodgy old triple-chinned thick-waisted gent who had not been caught smiling since the days of *Ozzie and Harriet*. Ancient, ornery, and as bitter as old chicory, Headmaster Masters did not like the Hancock boys. He preferred young men who studied hard and towed the line, who kept their mouths shut until ordered to speak. The Hancocks followed none of these mandates. Especially the brash John Hancock. Whichever one he was. Headmaster Masters could never tell the boys apart.

If not for a few indisputable facts, Headmaster Masters would have long ago sent the Hancock boys packing. These facts included the following: Both boys were straight-A honors students. Both boys had already skipped one entire academic grade, and could probably skip another one if they were so inclined. Both in fact, looked like shoo-ins for Harvard University's early admission plan. They cocaptained both the football team and the tennis team. Their quick tongues had last year earned the school's debating team first place among private schools in New England. And then there was their father, William Hancock. Not only did William pay his boys' room, board, and tuition on time and in full; he also made several very generous donations to the alumni fund each year. The funny part was: William Hancock was not an alumnus. William Hancock, or so went the rumors, was not even a high school graduate. William Hancock, with his heavily accented eastern European English, was clearly not American born or bred. As for where he'd acquired his Hancock appendage, no one knew for sure.

But now William Hancock was dead. So was his wife. And the job had fallen at the feet of Headmaster Masters to pass this tragic news along to their unruly offspring.

Question: Did the disagreeable and disgruntled headmaster take some perverse pleasure in telling the Hancock boys that their parents had been decapitated? Maybe so. Headmaster Masters, like many of us, had a cruel streak buried not very deep in his psyche. A man who had once dreamed of delivering great oratory to the fawning masses, Headmaster Masters loathed young people who had too good a time, or too much self-confidence. The Hancock boys had both. Masters silently looked forward to them growing old, and getting saddled with bad marriages and bad jobs and bad gums and bad bellies and bad debt. A good dose of failure would wipe the smiles off their smug faces.

The Hancock boys knocked on the door of Headmaster Masters's office on the first floor of Picton Hall. Actually, they didn't just knock. They tapped out the opening to the *Bonanza* theme music. And then, before the headmaster could respond, they entered, hoping, no doubt, to catch the headmaster engaged in some compromised activity; perhaps picking his nose or smelling his armpits or fondling his genitals. Thus they stepped into his office, came immediately to mock attention, and saluted. "J. and J. Hancock reporting as ordered, sir!"

Headmaster Masters sighed a mighty sigh. He sighed so boldly his jowls jiggled. Then he grabbed hold of his enormous oak desk and hefted his heavy frame out of his leather chair. "Have a seat, boys."

"We didn't do it, Headmaster Masters. Whatever it is, we didn't do it."

Normally, "Be quiet and sit down!" would have roared from the headmaster's mouth, but this day he took a more delicate approach. "You haven't done anything," he assured them.

"So this is just a social call?" asked John.

"Tea and scones?" added Will, always the wittier of the two, but also the quieter, and never first to offer up a wisecrack.

"Not today, boys. I'm afraid I have some bad news. I hate to be the one to bring it to you," he then announced, "but your parents have been in an accident."

"An accident?" Will asked.

"What kind of accident?" asked John.

"A car accident," answered the headmaster.

The two boys exchanged glances. Then John asked, "So, are they okay? They're okay, right?"

Headmaster Masters's thoughts and emotions spun wildly. He longed to be a strong and compassionate father figure at the very same moment he wanted to bring these two upstarts crashing to their knees.

"I'm afraid they're not okay," he told them. "They're dead. Your parents are dead."

So there it was. Laid bare. Out on a cold hard slab.

The Hancock boys, virtual strangers to bad or emotionally distressing news of any kind, did not immediately catch on to the profound significance of this announcement. A second or two had to pass before the terrible word took hold.

"What?" one of them mumbled.

"Dead?" asked the other. "What do you mean, dead?"

The headmaster had been rather brutal in his delivery, but after his cruel and crushing verbal blow, the ancient educator brought himself back under control. He hastily went on to handle the situation with the proper mix of sorrow and civility the monstrous tragedy demanded. He even managed to give each of the boys a reasonably heartfelt hug.

That primordial, two-headed beast, good and evil, on the loose again.

The Hancock boys, as even the most cold-hearted among us can surely imagine, were devastated. From wise guys to sad guys in the blink of an eye. One second on top of the world, joking and messing around, the next second buried beneath mounds of grief and confusion and sorrow. Life's first cruel blow. It had all been a lark up until then.

Will broke down first. The moment he realized this was not some sick practical joke, he began to weep. His mother? Dead? Killed in an automobile accident? Impossible. He had seen her just last week. She had brought him and John back to school. She had kissed him on both cheeks, run her fingers through his hair, told him she loved him, told him to be a good boy, told him he did not always need to follow his wild and riotous brother's bad example. Then she had kissed him again and walked back to the car. That was the last time he saw her. And now, tears streaming down his face, Will knew he would never see his mother again.

Will wept freely.

John did, too. But he also wanted answers. He wanted to know where and when and how come. "How come, dammit? How come this happened?"

The headmaster, feeling it now, feeling the pain and the intolerable depth of the loss these twins had just suffered, wanted in the worst way to provide them with some wise and comforting answers. But Headmaster Masters had been around a long time. He knew at times like this there were no answers. Only clichés. Followed by emotional chaos.

The Hancock boys flew home to Los Angeles for the double funeral. The caskets, of course, were closed. The undertaker had done his best to sew the heads back onto the bodies, but his best had not been anywhere near good enough. The thread job on the boys' mother was especially unflattering. The back bottom edge of that low-slung tractor trailer had made a pretty nasty cut.

John and Will, working to hold back the tears, stood around Gray's Funeral Home in Westwood receiving visitors and accepting condolences. A vast majority of the people who swept through the flower-strewn parlor had the look and the feel of complete strangers. And for good reason: the boys hardly knew a soul in all of Los Angeles County. Not only did they go to school back East, but they usually spent their summer vacations in various wilderness and athletic camps scattered across the country. They probably did not spend ten days a year at the redwood-and-glass contemporary up off Mulholland Drive.

As for extended family, there simply wasn't any. No Hancock siblings, no cousins, no aunts or uncles, no grandparents. Their mother hailed from Lorain, Ohio, but had been brought up in New Jersey by a maiden aunt after her parents joined some kind of pyramid cult that did not allow children. They, or so went the familial tale of woe, had dropped little Lenore off in Ho-ho-kus, N.J., then flown down to Guatemala or Nicaragua where they wore nothing but hemp loincloths and pyramid necklaces, never to be heard from again.

Lenore Larson, a bright and sweet but rather serious girl, had put herself through Rutgers University with an academic scholarship. She'd majored in international relations, and after graduating went to work for the Interior Department, Bureau of Immigration. She'd spent her days behind a desk expanding the population of the United States with peoples from such diverse places as Latvia, Chile, and Cameroon.

In 1957 she'd met with an East German man seeking political asylum. He spoke only a few broken phrases of English, learned, he told her, "from Hollywood feature films." He told her he loved movies and America. "In America," he insisted, "I have free opportunity to express myself and to earn dollars. Lots of dollars."

Lenore had heard this before. She heard it as often and with the same precision as one hears the cuckoo from a fine Swiss cuckoo clock. Everyone wanted to come to America and be free in the Land of Plenty. Free and rich. Lenore could not blame them for their desires. Just about every other place on the planet was rapidly being overrun by mass murderers and wild-eyed despots posing as socialist reformers and communist saviors.

The young East German man was tall and straight and, Lenore thought, exceptionally handsome. She also thought he looked a little lean, maybe even gaunt, but nothing that a few good meat-and-potato meals wouldn't fix. He said he had studied to be an actor, but that in the GDR (German Democratic Republic) actors were considered only slightly more appealing than sick dogs, so he worked to earn a few deutsche marks by laboring in an East Berlin umbrella factory.

Lenore smiled at the young man's joke about sick dogs and actors. He seemed like a pleasant man. He had a kind face. But his name raised a red flag. She had no choice but to bring his name to the attention of her superiors.

Right there on his papers, in all uppercase letters, it said: WILHELM FRANZ GOERING. The name jumped off the page.

"The name," he tried to reassure Lenore, "not to worry about name. For sure it is a bad no-good lousy name, but in no way am I relation to Hermann the Nazi psycho Luftwaffe Reichsmarschall responsible for so many murders during the war. Goering like Smith or Jones here in United States."

Maybe not quite.

"That's fine," murmured Lenore, pretty much believing him because he had honest eyes, clear and blue.

Nevertheless, Wilhelm Franz Goering was detained while the Bureau of Immigration checked out his story. The United States was not in the business of letting Nazi war criminals into the country.

Well, maybe every now and again.

They kept Wilhelm in jail, even though they called it a detention center, for six weeks. Lenore, for reasons she did not fully understand, went several times a week to visit him. One time when she arrived, Wilhelm had a copy of the Declaration of Independence in his hand. It was a reproduction of the original, printed on thick, heavy bond paper.

" 'We hold these truths to be self-evident,' " Wilhelm recited, his English improving daily, " 'that all men are created equal . . .' That's as much as I memorize so far," he told her, "but I have decided to memorize whole Declaration by heart. It will make me better American."

Lenore assured him he already knew more of the Declaration than most Americans.

"I have made more important decision also," he told her. "I need new name. The name I have of no good quality. I need good American name. After much thought, I have chosen this one." Wilhelm pointed proudly to the name scrolled boldly across the heavy paper of the Declaration of Independence. "I take this name as my American name," he informed her. "The one written the biggest. Here, the first name at the top. Hancock, they tell me it is pronounced. John Hancock."

That's the kind of thing you can do here in the Land of the Free. You can just step right up and take any old name you want. And within just a few days or weeks, everyone will believe that is your real name. Americans have very short memories.

By the time Wilhelm Franz Goering legally changed his name to Hancock, he had decided to go with William rather than John because everyone he knew in America called him Wilhelm or William anyway, including his fiancée, Lenore. The first name, he decided, did not really matter; he was just happy to finally rid himself of the Goering appendage. And absolutely elated that no one at Immigration had turned up the distant ancestral connection between himself and Hermann the Hatchet Man. William did not think he should suffer simply because the family tree had produced one bad apple.

Lenore married William at New York City Hall seven weeks after they'd met. Then, for four glorious days, they honeymooned on the Jersey shore, strolling the boardwalk and otherwise occupying themselves with getting physically acquainted.

After the honeymoon they moved into a tiny apartment in the East Village. Lenore continued her work with the Bureau of Immigration, while William pursued his dream of becoming an actor. He reached Broadway in just a few short months, when he landed a job as an usher at the old Majestic Theater on Forty-fourth Street. He got to hand out *Playbills* and sweep up cigarette butts and give directions to the gentlemen's and ladies' lounges. But he lost the job three weeks later when several well-heeled patrons, after overhearing William's thick German accent, complained to the theater manager about "the Aryan Nazi lurking in the lobby."

* • *

In the late summer of 1959 Lenore became pregnant. By this time William had turned to sales. He enjoyed his work. The job gave him plenty of autonomy, and every day he got to meet new people. And by being the tallest umbrella salesman in the entire Times Square area, he did very well. His height advantage allowed him to hold up the umbrellas that much higher than the other salesmen whenever the imminent threat of rain loomed over the Big Apple. On rainy days he sometimes sold as many as thirty umbrellas. As he sold the umbrellas for two bucks and bought them wholesale for a buck, he eked out a tiny livelihood. But William had not escaped from communist East Germany and come all the way to America to eke. He had come to America to be rich and famous and free. Plus he had his pride, and a baby on the way.

Sitting around the apartment one night with Lenore, fiddling with an umbrella that had refused to open in the middle of a downpour, William Hancock had a small but profound epiphany. He turned to his wife, who sat on the sofa knitting a pair of pink baby booties. Lenore felt certain the growing bulge in her belly contained a little girl, meek and mild-mannered.

"You know, Len," said William, whose English had made enormous strides, "in East Germany they make generally bad products. Pitiful products. Light bulbs that blow the first time you turn them on. Hammers that crack in half, the first nail you drive. Coat hangers from metal so weak and thin they collapse the second you try to hang up your coat."

"The workers in a Communist country," replied Lenore, knitting with a wild frenzy, "have little or no incentive to produce good products. Give them the opportunity to earn a profit and they could make the best coat hangers in the world."

"True," agreed William, who in this early stage of their marriage deferred to his wife in almost all matters. He worshipped her, considered her his savior. She had given him a safe and loving haven in America.

"It's the system," she added, her needles click click clicking, "not the workers. People are the same everywhere."

William nodded. He gave his wife's pronouncement several silent moments of respect before he related the true meaning of his epiphany. "More than two years now since I first land in this country, and only one product have I found that is better made in East Germany."

Lenore looked away from her booties, a small furrow upon her brow. This was the fifties, after all. Even in the East Village one did not often hear a positive word uttered about those dreaded Communists. "Oh? And what is that?"

"Umbrellas!" William exclaimed. "These umbrellas are junk. They are not made well at all. They are made to break, so the user will have to go and buy new one the very next time it rains."

"And do you mean to say," asked Lenore, "that the Communists make their umbrellas better?"

"Definitely better. But also more practical." William held up the umbrella he had just repaired. "Watch this." He held the handle in his left hand while he used the fingers of his right hand to depress the metal clasp and raise the hood of the umbrella. "You see?"

"See what?"

"You need *both* hands free to open hood!"

"So?"

"So this is nonsense!" William was all worked up. "In Germany, in the factory where they made me work for five long years, we made sturdy umbrellas you could hold and open with one hand. Press a button here, on the shaft, and presto, like magic, the hood snapped open! It freed up your other hand to carry a briefcase or a can of beer or a baby or whatever!"

Lenore's frown disappeared the moment her husband uttered the word *baby*. She immediately conjured up this sweet and lovely image of the Hancock family strolling

down Fifth Avenue in a light summer rain. They had their
umbrellas wide open and it did not matter a toot if those
umbrellas had been made in East Germany or East Lan-
sing, Michigan.

It turned out the umbrellas William Hancock sold on
Times Square were manufactured across the East River at a
small, brick, somewhat dilapidated factory in Queens. The
guy who owned the factory, Golan Rubinstein, was old
and arthritic and wanted in the worst way to move down
to Miami Beach. None of his children had any interest in
umbrellas. They had all gone into medicine or law or precious metals. For years Golan had been trying to sell his
umbrella business, but no one wanted to buy it. Until along
came William Wilhelm Goering Hancock. So the old Jew
and the young Kraut, after much haggling, cut a deal.

And soon thereafter, practically overnight, William
Hancock gave up his dream of becoming a famous thes-
pian and metamorphosed into a hardworking and intensely ambitious middle-class American businessman. He
suddenly liked Ike and loved the old Army general's plan
for lower taxes and less government. William had, of
course, always hated Communists, but now he added
Democrats, bleeding-heart liberals, and anyone on the dole
to his hate list. William Hancock had metastasized into a
true-blue Republican.

William spent so much time at his umbrella factory on
Newtown Creek that Lenore finally decided to give up the
apartment in the East Village and move to Queens. Not
only would it save money on rent, but it would give her a
chance to see her husband more than an hour or two a day.

They lived in two small rooms on the third floor of the
factory. It was in one of these rooms that William Hancock
designed his first one-handed, push-button umbrella. He
borrowed more money from the bank, hired a patent attorney, and made an application to the patent office in Washington, D.C. Another immigrant about to make good.

On the same day that William Hancock received preliminary patent approval for his one-handed, push-button umbrella, Lenore Hancock gave birth, not to one sweet little lass, but to two screeching laddies.

The identical twins were born late in the afternoon on May 9, 1960 at St. Vincent's hospital in Manhattan. Mom and Dad named the older boy John and the younger boy, who came along six or eight minutes later, William junior, though from the very beginning they called him Will.

The nurses in charge of the nursery did everything in their power to keep track of who was John and who was Will, but the absolute sameness of the boys made this task virtually impossible. Several times, in the week the twins spent at St. Vincent's, they were placed in the wrong bassinets. So as they left the hospital, one in the arms of their mother and one in the arms of their father, the likelihood that John was Will and Will was John loomed mighty high indeed.

Back on the third floor of the umbrella factory, William and Lenore did a thorough inspection of their two squirming infants. They lined those boys up on the bed and checked them out from head to toe, front to rear. Half a dozen times they studied their scalps, their faces, their arms, their backs, their chests, their tiny penises, their legs, their feet. They even took a close look through William's magnifying glass, the one he used to spot defects in his umbrellas. But try though they might, Mom and Dad could not find a single physical characteristic to differentiate one boy from the other.

Lenore looked alarmed. "My God! This is a crisis. How will we ever keep from mixing them up?"

Her husband, pie-eyed from the cheap champagne he'd consumed in celebration of his patent and the miraculous birth of his twin sons, shrugged his broad shoulders. "Beats me," he answered, using his favorite American colloquialism. "Does it really matter if we get them mixed up? I mean, what's the difference? They'll wind up the same either way."

"Don't be ridiculous!" Lenore scowled at her husband. Her face looked pale and tired and pudgy from her nine-month ordeal. She felt quite certain she never wanted to give birth again. "Of course it matters. We can't just mix them up. Like colored socks. My God, Will, these are our sons! Our flesh and blood. They're people, for crying out loud, not gerbils!"

William, not truly convinced it mattered, shrugged again. But because he could not stand his bride being upset with him for even one second, he swiftly devised a plan. He took a black felt-tipped marker from his shirt pocket and made an X on the sole of John's right foot. At least he believed the sole he marked belonged to John.

"Okay," he told his wife, "for now we mark John with X. Later, after their brains and their bodies start to develop, we find other ways to tell the boys apart."

PART TWO
JUNE 7, 1999

MONDAY MORNING ROUNDUP

Early morning now on the East Coast. Before dawn. A whole slew of ghosts wander around John Hancock's bedroom at the posh town house up on Beacon Hill. It could be a party. A Boston Tea Party. William and Lenore Hancock, their heads cradled in their arms, float about the room in a kind of cosmic stupor. They still, even after all these years, have no idea what happened out there on the San Diego Freeway.

And their lawyer, Frank Hagstrom, he's here, hanging from the ceiling, a noose around his neck. He keeps making threats, telling Hancock he'd better cut him loose right this second. The longer Frank's neck gets, the higher his voice goes. He sounds more and more like a screeching hyena.

And Zelda, she's here. Zelda Cosgrove, literary mentor to the Hancock boys. Older sister of the soon-to-be-announced Mad Dicky Cosgrove. Zelda, God rest her soul, died back in '86. Murdered. In cold blood. Hancock was once a suspect. Briefly.

So the room's a little crowded, but Hancock doesn't mind. Crowds don't bother him at all. Still, it's time to get up and get moving. He throws back the sheets and climbs out of bed. His brother, he knows, is about to call. He can feel it. It's an identical-twins kind of thing. John pulls on sweatpants and climbs the stairs to their third-floor office.

Brother Will sits in a phone booth at the international terminal of Heathrow Airport outside London. He has just finished checking in for his flight to Miami. Thomas Young will be flying Business Class today, seat 9B.

Will picks up the phone and begins to dial.

John crosses to his desk and opens the bottom right-hand drawer. There's a phone in the drawer, an old baby-blue Princess model. No cordless or cellular features. No call forwarding or call waiting or caller ID. Not even a redial button. Just a plain old basic telephone. Or so it would appear.

John picks up the receiver, punches in a long sequence of numbers, then sets the receiver back on the cradle. This sequence of numbers is an access code that makes the phone operable. Without the access code the phone looks and acts like an old unit shoved into the back of a drawer.

The second John puts the receiver back on the cradle, the phone rings. John is not surprised. He picks up the receiver and asks, "Jefferson?"

"Adams?"

"Are we secure?"

"I think so. What's up?"

"I beeped you yesterday. I was hoping you'd call last night."

"I did," lies Will. "You must've gone to bed or had the phone turned off."

"I waited till after midnight."

"I called about one."

"Yeah," says John, not wanting the conversation to go in this direction. "Okay."

"So what's going on?"

John does not waste time. "The cops were here yesterday."

"The cops?" Will sounds surprised. "What did they want?"

"They said they had a report that you were missing."

"That *who* was missing? You or me?"

"You."

"Little unlikely for a dead man to go missing, wouldn't you say?"

"I would, yeah," agrees John. "But they claimed they had a missing person report filed on Mr. Will Hancock."

"That's pretty strange. Who would have filed a report like that?"

"Clara."

"Clara?"

"That's what the cops said. Will Hancock reported missing by Ms. Clara Dare Hancock."

Will hesitates again, then, "I don't get it."

"Neither do I, believe me. That's why I'm calling."

"So what else did the cops say?"

"Not much. I told them you were dead. Long dead. Almost twenty years dead. They looked pretty confused."

"I'll bet they did. Have you talked to Clara?"

"I called her in London. She was with that jackass Byrnes."

"Byrnes, huh?"

"They were having dinner together."

"He's harmless."

"You think so?"

"Absolutely," says Will. "He's like Clara's English sheepdog. Her pet when she's abroad. No need to worry about him. Now tell me what she said."

John thinks his brother is a little blasé about Byrnes. Not Will's typical reaction with anyone or anything regarding their wife. Usually he's full of spit and venom. Very controlling and possessive. But for now John does not push it. He's happy to stick to the original subject. "She didn't say much," he replies. "If she's the one who filed the report, she wasn't fessing up to it."

"Did you ask her?"

"Not straight out, no, but I gave her every opportunity to say something."

"So what do you think? You think she's toying with us?"

"Who knows? We both know it's always been a possibility."

"Maybe," muses Will, "it wasn't Clara who filed the report."

"The thought crossed my mind."

"It could be one of our readers," says Will. "Someone who's read the novels. Read all the articles about John Hancock. And now this reader's put it all together and figured out the twin brother didn't really drown down in Belize. Remember, bro, the body, my body, was never found."

John cringes at the sound of his brother calling him *bro*. "Actually," he says, "I've put together a list. I guess you'd call it a list of suspects. People who might've called the police."

"List of suspects? Jesus, John, you're beginning to sound a little paranoid. Who's on this list?"

"I've got Clara on top. And I've got Byrnes right underneath her."

"Byrnes?" asks Will. "Why Byrnes?"

"Because he's a son of a bitch and he has the hots for Clara."

"Come on, John, Byrnes is a weakling and a coward. Besides, there's no way he could know that your long-assumed-dead brother could possibly be alive."

"In days gone by," says John, "you've sounded pretty irate about old Rodney Byrnes. Hot enough to rip his throat out. You've kind of changed your tune. Now you seem to be saying he's not worth worrying about."

Will clears his throat. He sees no need to mention his little visit to Byrnes's flat or the voodoo zombie powder. "He's a bum, bro. Definitely not worth worrying about. Now who else is on this suspect list of yours?"

John's curious about Will's change of heart regarding Byrnes, but decides to keep his curiosity to himself. At least for now. "Well," he says, "I asked myself this question: Who knows, for sure, that the twins live?"

"That's a pretty short list."

"Exactly. It's basically you, me, and our old Belize buddy Rafe."

"Rafe. Jesus! There's a blast from the past. My recollection of Rastaman Rafe was a man not bright enough to keep his teeth clean, much less file a missing person report."

"I don't know," says John, "if he's bright enough or not, but he's on my list."

"I'd call Rafe a pretty long shot. But okay, no need to cross him off. Anyone else?"

"Not as far as people we know who definitely know you are still alive."

Will pauses briefly, then says, "There's Zelda Cosgrove's brother."

"Mad Dicky?"

"Yeah."

"I thought about him," says John. "But he doesn't know you're alive. He might think you are, but he doesn't know for sure. Besides, he's still in the nuthouse."

"Dicky might still be in the nuthouse, but that wouldn't prevent him from picking up the phone and calling the cops. Last I heard, even certified loonies can use the telephone."

"Okay," agrees John. "I'll put him on the list, even though I think he's a waste of time. Anyone else?"

"What about Leland?"

"Leland? You must be kidding?"

"Hey, you can laugh, but Fisher has been wondering for years if I might still be alive. I've always thought maybe Zelda put the idea in his head before she got whacked."

John does not want to think about Zelda Cosgrove getting whacked, or about Will possibly having done the whacking, so he quickly moves the conversation along. "So you're saying our good buddy Leland maybe called the cops just to see what kind of dust he might kick up?"

"It's possible," says Will, thinking of their publisher's lustful bride.

"No way," says John. "But if you want Fisher on the list, I'll put him on the list."

"I don't care if you put him on the list or not," Will responds. "I really don't see the point of your list anyway. You told those cops I was dead. They went away. That's probably the end of it."

"Somehow I don't think so."

"If it's not, there's not much we can do. Other than wait for our suspect to make his next move."

"Or *her* next move."

"Whatever."

John thinks about it. "Okay, I guess you're right."

"Can I go now?"

"Where are you?"

"Exuma," lies Will.

"Bonefishing?"

"Not as long as we're on the phone." Will has already decided not to tell John about his trip to Scotland, followed by his brief stopover here in London. He just needed to take care of some business. No reason for John to hear all the particulars.

"Call me tomorrow," says John. "Same time."

"If not tomorrow, Wednesday."

"Try and make it tomorrow. In the meantime, I'll see what else I can find out about this missing person business."

"Let's not panic, bro," says Will. "I'm sure whatever happens, we can handle it."

John Hancock goes back to bed after getting off the phone with his brother. Their conversation did not do much to relieve his anxiety about all this missing person business. If anything, he's even more uptight. Not only was Will apathetic about the whole situation regarding the police, but his lackadaisical attitude concerning Rodney Byrnes did not jive with his typically jealous and suspicious nature.

But John does not have time right now to ponder all the possibilities. John junior and little Willy come racing into the room and hurl themselves on the bed for their morning snuggle. Just about every morning the boys slip between the sheets, slide around like a couple of burrowing prairie dogs, then finally come to rest, one on Dad's right side, one on Dad's left side.

About all they say this morning is, "Golden retriever! Golden retriever!"

Dad is saved by Nicky who shows up in the doorway and tells the boys the time has come to get ready for school. The nanny only has to tell them once. Nicky is a tougher taskmaster than her sweet and demure demeanor would lead one to believe.

The telephone rings just seconds after the boys troop out of the bedroom. Knowing Sylvia is no doubt busy with breakfast, John scoops up the receiver, hoping it might be Clara. She'd called last night to talk to the boys, but maybe she just felt the desire to call again this morning. It would not be unusual.

"Hello?"

"Hancock?"

"Yeah?"

"It's Fisher."

"Lee! How the hell are you?" John glances at the clock: 7:56. "Jesus, Lee, it's not even eight o'clock. Everything okay? This is about the time you usually go to bed."

Despite the fact that he might soon have to start hating John Hancock, Leland Fisher smiles at the author's infectious good humor. "Up by eight," he replies, holding up his end of their oft-repeated cliché, "you're workin'."

"So you've always told me, Lee."

"I've been thinking about changing it to nine."

"Good idea. Make it ten. What the hell? Who says eight's written in stone?"

"Noon sounds good to me."

John laughs. He likes Leland. And not just because the guy's his publisher and editor and primary source of income. "Lee, the last time I saw you, you were three sheets to the wind."

"Saturday night?"

"Believe so."

"I got into the Jägermeister."

"I guess you did. How did you feel yesterday when you got up?"

Leland cannot believe he's having a normal Hancock conversation. Joking and kidding around. His expectations had been quite different. "Like death warmed over," he answers. "So I took the edge off with a couple Bloody Marys."

"Nice."

"It worked."

"Hey, I'm not on the lecture tour here, Lee, but you better watch your liver."

"Screw my liver. I'll get a new one." Leland, still out at his house in Woods Hole, paces back and forth across the living room, cordless phone pressed to his ear. Everyone else in the house is still asleep: Hillary, Jaguar, Lois, the babies. Well, maybe not quite babies anymore, but still Leland's sweet little girls. Hillary arrived home last night around seven, said she'd been out in Chatham at some save-the-beaches fund-raiser. A relatively quiet evening followed. No arguments or accusations. No intimacy or carnal activity either. Leland kept wanting to ask his wife about Hancock, but he didn't have the guts.

Finally, after a pretty much sleepless night, he found the guts to call Hancock. But now that he has Hancock on the phone, and Hancock, as usual, is making light of everything, Leland has no idea what to say. Maybe ask something like, "So, Hancock, how's the ride in the back of my Bentley? Smooth enough for your horny ass?"

But Leland has never been able to ask the tough questions, so he settles on a more subtle approach. "Say, John, who was that good-looker you were with Saturday night?"

"The brunette? Pretty sweet, huh?"

"Quite something. And young."

"Not as young as you might think, Lee. But young enough."

"So who is she?" Leland asks.

"She be Linda."

"Clara know about Linda?"

"Leland! Are you suggesting I'd screw around behind Mrs. Hancock's back?"

Several venomous retorts pop into the publisher's brain, but he settles for a rather watery and impotent reply. "We all stray from the barn from time to time."

"Yes, we do, Lee. But not this bull. I've got the finest and most beautiful heifer in the pasture. Be an idiot to even snort at another cow."

"So who's Linda?" persists Leland, thinking Hancock is a very smooth-tongued liar.

"Linda is Clara's best buddy. Has been since before we got married. I'm surprised you haven't met her before."

"So she was your date for Saturday night?"

"Something like that. See, Clara went to London to peddle some Picassos or some Pissarros to some fat-cat Arab with too many petro dollars. That left me solo to The Boston Press's centenary shindig. So Clara, always thinking of her guy, set me up with Linda."

"Clara must be a very secure woman."

"And smart enough to send me off with her pal, rather than leave the entire evening to chance."

"So your relationship with Clara is solid?"

"Absolutely," answers Hancock. "Like a rock." And then, "Pretty personal stuff for so early in the A.M., Lee. But as long as we're on the subject, how's life with Hillary?"

"Great," Leland wants to say, "until the two of you started screwing in the back seat of my Bentley." Instead, he settles for mimicry. "Oh, like a rock."

John, lying in bed, thoughts once again spinning, suddenly decides Will might be right: Maybe Lee Fisher is a contender for the suspect list. The guy is acting awfully weird. This early morning call, for instance. During the nearly twenty years they have been acquainted, John has never known Leland to call before noon. And this is the first time he has ever asked him any intimate questions about his relationship with Clara. Strange. Very strange. The whole last twenty-four hours has been strange.

"So, Lee, you in the city?"

"No, I'm out on the cape. But I'm heading back later this morning."

"Gotta get to the office, hey, Lee?"

Leland chooses to ignore Hancock's sarcasm. His heart's already pounding away; any harder and cardiac arrest will surely bring him to his knees. He wants to just unload his burden, ask Hancock if he's having an affair with Hillary, find out if his fourth marriage is really in jeopardy, if another divorce looms on the murky horizon.

"What about lunch?" he asks abruptly.

"Lunch?"

"Yeah?"

"When?" John asks. "Today?"

"Why not?"

Now John *knows* Leland has something on his mind. Not only does his editor rarely call before noon, and never on Monday, but calling and making a lunch date for the same day? Never happens. Something is definitely up. The question is: Does it have anything to do with those cops showing up at his door?

"No reason," John answers. "Lunch today's good with me."

The main reason Leland wants to do lunch is because it buys him some time, allows him to put off asking the tough questions.

"Okay," he says. "Two o'clock?"

"Two o'clock's fine."

"I'll make reservations."

"You sure you want to do this today, Lee? Monday's usually your day for R and R."

"No, today's perfect. Meet me at the office around one-thirty." Leland hangs up without bothering to say good-bye.

John hears the click in his ear. He sighs, shakes his head, and hangs up the phone. FISHER, LELAND, he thinks, will definitely have to go on the suspect list.

A couple seconds later the boys come screaming back into the bedroom. "Golden retriever!" they shout.

"Golden retriever!" They climb all over Dad. Almost time to leave for school. Hugs and kisses before they go.

Like John Hancock, Al-the-Gumshoe Brown was up before the sun. He sits in his minivan on Louisburg Square across the street from the Hancock town house. It's a very nice minivan, late-model domestic, top-of-the-line all the way. Al paid over thirty grand for her. Then another ten grand to set her up for surveillance. Al does a lot of surveillance. It's probably the biggest part of his job, next to trying to collect payment for services rendered. Some days Al spends as much as twenty hours in his minivan waiting for someone to do something that someone else wants to know about.

Al is well suited to all this waiting. He used to do photography for the *National Enquirer,* traveled the world in search of the rich and famous. The goal was to catch Madonna in the buff or Lady Di necking with the royal gardener or Liz Taylor bingeing on a bucket of the Colonel's extra crispy. Very lofty work. Filled with social significance and personal satisfaction. Pulitzer Prize for photojournalism kind of stuff.

But then Al met the woman of his dreams while in Boston hunting up one of the Kennedy clan. This woman fell in love with Al, but told him in a very pleasant and not at all possessive way that she did not really want to marry a guy who spent ten months a year on the road taking photos of public personalities doing private things.

So Al quit and married and settled in the suburbs of Beantown. His new bride had a good job with excellent benefits with one of the high-tech computer companies. Al took a couple months off to figure out what he wanted to do with the next phase of his life. He came into the gumshoe business by accident when a neighbor dropped by to borrow some whiskey sour mix. The neighbor wound up staying for an hour and a couple of highballs. During the visit he spotted Al's large collection of photography gear, including some very powerful telephoto lenses. After the second highball the neighbor asked Al if he wanted to make some money by doing some spying. Seems the neighbor suspected his spouse of some rather unsavory sexual shenanigans. Al thought it over, and the next day, after negotiating his fee, he went into the private eye biz. He did his surveillance on that first job right from the living room windows of his house. And sure enough, his neighbor's wife was doing the mailman. And the UPS man. And the Federal Express man. A regular nymphomaniac with a proclivity for delivery guys. Al got the goods with his Nikon. Showed them to the neighbor. The neighbor paid Al three hundred and fifty bucks, then beat the hell out of his wife. Al felt bad about that, but figured the guy would have found out eventually anyway. More importantly, Al had enjoyed the work. So he applied for a license to make himself legit, and the rest, as they say, is history.

Now Al sits and watches Hancock's front door. His five-hundred-millimeter lens rests on the passenger seat. His client called late last night and told him he wanted more proof of infidelity. Positive proof. Meaning indisputable photos of the client's wife and this John Hancock fellow partaking of a sexual interlude.

To amuse himself while on stakeout, Al-the-Gumshoe Brown enjoys listening to books on tape. This morning he's listening to John Hancock's *The Settlement,* read by the author. Al, not a very literary fellow, finds it an entertaining tale. In thirty-two words or less, it's the story of a woman who wants a divorce from an abusive and controlling husband. Too bad he's not the divorcing type. He'll kill her before he'll let her go.

So engrossed is Al in the slippery and twisted plot that he does not immediately see the front door of the town house swing open. Fortunately, the rapid movements of two springy youngsters bounding through the doorway and down the brick steps catches Al's eye. He spots Hancock standing on the front stoop, waving and shouting, "Have a good day, guys! See you this afternoon!"

Al switches off the tape player and scoops up his Nikon. Viewfinder pressed to his eye, he pumps off several shots of

John junior, Willy, and Nicky the nanny as they go through the wrought iron gate and head north, away from the square.

No need really, Al knows, to take these shots of the kids, but he takes them anyway. It's proof he's been on the job when his client starts whining about the bill. So far Mr. Leland Fisher has not been a problem, but then, they rarely are while the investigation is ongoing. It's later, once they have what they want, that Al's bills suddenly start looking a little swollen. Oh, yeah, Al's been stiffed plenty of times. That's why he always keeps the negatives.

He sets down the Nikon. Satisfied Hancock is inside the town house, Al gobbles a glazed doughnut, downs some lukewarm coffee, switches on the tape player, and settles in to hear who's going to win this fictional cat-and-mouse game: the terrible husband or the terrified wife. Al's listened to enough suspense stories to know it will undoubtedly be the wife. Unlike in real life, in novels, especially best-seller types, the good guy (or woman) always gets the bad guy and walks off with the loot and the blue ribbon for upstanding moral vigor. Just once he'd like to see the bad guys get the victory.

RAFE

Rafe's doing some surveillance work of his own this morning. Only he's not hiding in some fancy minivan; he's hiding behind a eucalyptus tree, maybe the tallest tree on Caye Caulker. Rafe loves the smell of eucalyptus, all at once powerful and pungent and sweet. It is his favorite smell in the world.

Right now Rafe's waiting for Matilda, the Canadian transplant who runs the ear-piercing, seashell-swapping, travel-to-the-edges-of-the-earth shop on Main Street. Rafe knows Matilda opens and closes like the whims of the wind, sometimes at nine, sometimes at noon, sometimes not at all. Sometimes Matilda disappears for days at a time. Usually she heads for the mainland, say some, to visit the Mayan ruins. But this is not accurate. Matilda has meetings on the mainland. Secret meetings. At undisclosed locations.

When on Caye Caulker Matilda never wears shoes. She likes to tell people she always had to wear shoes in Canada, cold country, usually hand-me-downs from an older sister, shoes that never fit right and inevitably made her feet hurt.

Only trouble is, Matilda's an only child. And she did

not grow up in Canada. She grew up in Michigan, a little town on the Upper Peninsula near the south shore of Lake Superior. Attended the University of Michigan at Ann Arbor. Same as Gerry Ford. Did graduate work in International Studies at Duke University down in North Carolina. Now works for DEA. Field agent. Undercover.

Rafe doesn't know any of this. He just knows his pockets are bulging with cash and if he doesn't buy himself an airline ticket to the States ASAP, he'll surely start blowing the dough on more frivolous pursuits.

So, like Al, Rafe amuses himself while waiting by indulging in a bit of Hancock fiction. He, too, has a copy of *The Settlement*. Only his copy is a hardcover one. Rafe's read the first ten pages like six times, but he's just not getting it. Sure, there's some thin, gorgeous piece in silk pajamas being knocked around by her husband. That part Rafe gets. But while the broad's taking the beating, she's doing all this thinking. Like to herself between blows. It's all this thinking Rafe can't quite keep straight in his head. Plus it's making him think about his own wife, who he smacked once during an argument, right in the jaw. But she's a tough little chicken. Smacked him right back. Gave him a black eye.

Rafe cusses and closes the book and throws it on the ground. Damn book's making him think about all kinds of crap he doesn't want to think about. He definitely doesn't want to think about his wife. Maybe lying naked with some other guy. He can't think about that shit right now. Make him crazy. Make him do something stupid.

Rafe checks again for Matilda, then he checks his pockets for the three hundredth time this morning. It's still there: the wad. Folded in two and held together by a rubber band: Two grand. Actually fifty bucks less after last night's bender: beer and rum and reefer. The ruin of many a good island man. Still, nineteen hundred and a half left. In hundreds and fifties. American greenbacks. That's how the two teenage gringos paid him for the boat. Cold hard cash. The one gringo must've had ten grand on him. He ripped fourteen hundreds and twelve fifties off his roll like a man paying for a shot of tequila and a lobster tail. Said he and his buddy wanted to do some fishing. Rafe just smiled and pocketed the cash. Man says he wants to fish, not a problem. But Rafe knew better. Plenty of good fishing charters out of Caye Caulker. With captains who know the waters. No, these two fresh-faced gringos had something else in mind. Lot of dope smuggling through Caye Caulker in the last few years. A very profitable business, Rafe knows. But it can also very easily land you in jail over in Belize City. Which is not a good place for a couple of fresh-faced gringos.

But Rafe doesn't give a damn about them. He has their dough and soon he'll have his ticket to the States. And after a nice little visit with his old friend John Hancock, he'll have his ticket to paradise.

JOHN & RODNEY

Hancock's not getting anywhere with his suspect list, and he's definitely not getting any writing done. Will may have told him not to sweat it, but he's sweating it nevertheless. First those cops showing up out of the blue, then Clara playing it coy, then Will acting so blasé, and then Lee Fisher, Jesus, calling him at the crack of dawn. On a Monday.

So he dials up the local precinct, tells the girl who answers it's not an emergency, and promptly gets put on hold. Seven minutes pass before some gruff and testy desk sergeant comes on the line.

"Hello," John says politely, "my name's Hancock. John Hancock."

Immediately the desk sergeant, a tough Irishman with eighteen years on the job, and who has heard every wisecrack in the book, says, "Yeah, and I'm Ben Franklin. Now what can I do for you?"

John ponders a witty, wise-guy retort, but shrugs it aside. He learned years ago the absurdity of being anything but perfectly polite to officers of the law. They have a control complex. So John calmly explains about the two officers who came around to see him Sunday morning, then he says, "I was hoping to talk to them again. Get some more information on this missing person report."

The desk sergeant asks, "Names?" He's still not convinced this Hancock guy isn't some crank.

"The one guy was named Raymond."

"Last name Raymond?"

"Yes. And the other one was Collins. Or maybe Connor. Something like that."

The desk sergeant takes less than a second to answer. "Not from this precinct."

"Neither of them?"

"That's right. I've got no Raymond, no Collins, no Connor. Not in uniform and not upstairs with detectives. I do have an Officer O'Connor."

"Maybe that's him."

"Maybe. If one of your visitors wore a bra."

John manages a chuckle, then asks, "So how can I find them?"

"Call headquarters. Personnel. They should be able to help you out."

"What about the missing person report?"

"Can't help you with that, friend. We don't handle missing persons here. That's divisional."

John gets a few telephone numbers from the desk sergeant before the cop hangs up on him. One by one Hancock calls the numbers. Nothing but dead ends. He can't find anyone in the Boston Police Department to confirm a missing person report on a Mr. Will Hancock. Nor is there any record of a report of any kind being filed by a Ms. Clara D. Hancock. And even more disturbing: There is not a single policeman on the entire force with the surname Raymond. There is a cop named Connor, but he's a rookie foot soldier down on the south side.

John makes a couple more calls. He finds out on-duty Boston police detectives do not drive their own vehicles. And they definitely do not drive bloodred Ford Mustangs. John curses himself for not getting the license plate number of that car.

He paces around his office, aggravated and uptight.

Usually, if he can't find a solution in a couple minutes, he leaves it for his brother. Does it all the time when they're working on a novel. John likes the freedom and creativity of the first draft. Leaves all the details and drudgery and editorial nit-picking for Will.

He thinks about calling the Adventure Travel Enterprises cell phone, but decides the beeper might be the better choice. Still not a full-blown emergency.

But before John can pick up the receiver and dial the 800 number, the telephone rings. And the mess gets messier.

"Hello?"

"Hancock?"

"Speaking."

"You bastard! You sick fucking bastard!"

"Who is this?"

"Who the hell do you think it is? I should have you arrested! I should have you killed! Murdered! Exterminated!"

John, reeling from the verbal attack, finally thinks he recognizes the screeching voice. "Byrnes?"

"That's right, asshole! Rodney Byrnes! I have no idea what you had that freak blow in my face, but it just about killed me. My stomach's all knotted up. I have the worst bloody migraine. And my mouth feels as though I've had small rodents running around inside of it."

"Sounds to me, Byrnes, like you've got the grippe. I recommend three aspirin, two large glasses of water, and straight to bed."

"Fuck you, Hancock! Do you hear me? Fuck——you!"

"I hear you, Byrnes. But really, old sport, I haven't a clue what you're blowing off about. I had nothing to do with any freak blowing something in your face."

"Liar! Stinking, rotten asshole of a liar! You'll pay for this, Hancock! Do you hear me? You'll pay!" And Byrnes slams the phone down with a mighty crash.

YOUTH

Despite the fact that William and Lenore could not tell their infant sons apart, subtle differences began to emerge between John and Will at a very early age. For instance, John, slightly more coordinated, walked a couple days earlier than Will, but Will, always more cerebral, uttered his first complete sentence a week or so before John.

But by the time the boys headed off to kindergarten, they had already become superbly skilled at impersonating one another. The only one who could tell them apart with any accuracy was their mother. And even Lenore occasionally had problems.

Young John and Will made a game of keeping the outside world confused as to their true identities. They practiced one way of walking, one way of talking, one way of laughing, one way of answering the phone, one way of eating their breakfast cereal, one way of tying their shoelaces. In later years they would hone their mannerisms to perfection, but even by the age of six they had become accomplished mimics. In the blink of an eye, John could be Will and Will could be John.

Precisely why they performed this illusion is tough to

say. Probably they did it to entertain themselves. Childhood games and all that tomfoolery.

As the family moved relentlessly up the economic ladder, the twins grew more and more indistinguishable. William Hancock's umbrella was a success. His factory in Queens could not produce them fast enough. They sold by the hundreds of thousands. The Hancock Umbrella Company now had a small cadre of salesmen scouring the countryside in an effort to place a Hancock umbrella in the hands of every American who might one day encounter rain, sleet, or snow. William worked tirelessly on his product; he also had plans, big plans, to expand into hats, gloves, and galoshes.

"America," William told his sons, "is by far the greatest consumer nation the world has ever known."

By the time John and Will reached the fifth grade, they had been educated at schools in New Rochelle, Chappaqua, and Greenwich, Connecticut. Everywhere they went, they excelled. They both tested in the ninety-seventh percentile on the IOWA Test of Basic Skills. Will actually scored in the ninety-ninth percentile.

On tests, the boys had a strange propensity to miss the same questions. In fact, so acute was this inclination, that teachers often made them take tests over to find out if they'd been cheating. The teachers always gave these new tests under intense surveillance. But it didn't matter, the results were always the same; if Will missed problem number six, John missed it also.

They possessed athletic gifts as well as intellectual gifts. Generally they could run faster, jump higher, and throw farther than their classmates. They could do more push-ups and pull-ups and sit-ups. Teachers, coaches, and principals spoke glowingly of their many talents.

Rarely, William and Lenore learned, did identical twins excel to such an extent. In most cases identical twins displayed little more than average intelligence. And if they did, it was usually only one of them, with the other one lagging far behind.

Yes, the praise flowed like water over Niagara. It came during parent-teacher conferences, telephone calls, and notes at the bottom of quarterly report cards.

But, inevitably, all this praise came with a caution: "John and Will are outstanding students, Mrs. Hancock. They are two of the brightest students I've seen in all my years as a teacher. But, they are quite a handful. Mischievous. They love to play games and stir up trouble. I wouldn't call them malicious, just restless. Very restless."

Or this: "I want you to know, Mr. Hancock, that it is a pleasure to coach your sons. Both have reached a level of skill far beyond their years. But they are difficult to control. They like to do things their way or no way."

Or this: "A couple of fine, strapping young boys you have there, Mr. and Mrs. Hancock. Fine boys. Fast learners. Very capable. Sharp as tacks. Especially John. At least I believe it's John. It could be Will. But that's the problem, you see. It's impossible to tell them apart."

All William and Lenore could do was nod. They knew well the difficulties. They also knew it did little or no good to lecture their boys or give them a spanking or really punish them in any way. John and Will were nice boys with good manners and excellent dispositions. Rarely were they rude or belligerent. But they were, after all, twins, identical twins. They moved to the rhythm of a drummer no one else could even hear. They were like one person; one person with two heads and two bodies and the incredible power to be in two places at the same time. And ultimately, they had loyalty only to one another.

In the sixth grade, in Greenwich, the principal, a towering, no-nonsense guy named Mr. Lowell, took the bold step of separating the boys, of putting them in different classes. John and Will complained bitterly to their mother about this move. Lenore listened, but did nothing. Actually, she told them, it might be for the best.

The boys did not agree. But there was nothing they could do; they were just boys, after all, twelve-year-olds. For a week or more they moped around, shoulders slumped, spirits low. This was really the first time in their lives they had been separated.

John snapped out of it first.

"This is good," he told his brother up in their bedroom. "Yeah, this is perfect. Think about it."

"I don't need to think about it," said Will. "I think it stinks."

"No, listen, we've been looking at this the wrong way. We have to see it as part of the game."

"What game?"

"The 'Us Versus Them' game."

Will, uncertain, asked, "Us versus them?"

John flashed Will his most prankish smile. "Tomorrow I'll go be you in Mrs. Hirsch's class, and you'll go be me in Mrs. Wyatt's class."

"Huh?"

"We'll trade places."

"You think," Will, dubious, asked, "it's okay if we do that?"

"Is it okay? Of course it's okay. Anything we want to do, little brother, is okay. We just have to get away with it. Anything we can get away with is okay."

"Don't call me little brother. You're only, like, three minutes older than me and I'm just as tall as you."

"You're right, you're just as tall. We're exactly the same height. Now let's see if we can convince people we're exactly the same person. Let's see how good we really are."

"How good we are at what?"

"At being each other."

Will, his doubts obvious from the furrow in his young brow, slowly began to fold under his brother's power. "You really think it's okay?"

"Absolutely," John assured him.

Will took a deep breath and said, "Okay, but I need to know a few things first."

"Like what?"

"Like where do you sit in class? Do you raise your hand or just blurt out the answers? Who do you sit next to? What homework do you have? Stuff like that."

"Oh, right," said John. "Good thinking."

Right from the beginning John was the idea man, the inspirational spark. Will was better suited to filling in the blanks, taking care of details, making sure they covered their backs. It would be the same when they started writing novels. And even more so after that, when they started living the life of one person.

They stayed awake deep into the night making plans. They drew up diagrams of their respective classrooms. They quizzed one another on who sat where. They gave the low-down on their teachers. They did each other's homework, slept in each other's bed.

"Hey," said John, as their heads finally hit their pillows around four A.M., "it's all for the cause."

"Right," agreed Will, "the cause," even though Will was not sure what his brother meant by *the cause*.

When Lenore woke them at seven-fifteen, they had only been asleep for a few hours. But no matter. These two were pumped up, raring to go. They gobbled down their toast and juice and shredded wheat, kissed their mother good-bye, and sprinted to the bus stop.

For the entire week John played Will and Will played John. Then, the following week, they went back to playing themselves. Back and forth they went for the entire school year. One week on, one week off. No one ever suspected. Variations in their temperaments and abilities occasionally surfaced, but not enough that anyone noticed. John was naturally more boisterous and extroverted, always ready to speak up when the teacher wanted an answer. Will was slightly more reserved. Both his questions and his answers tended to have a little more depth than his brother's. But because the boys changed roles with such regularity, no one really took note of these trifling differences.

Teachers, used to erratic behavior from adolescent males, chalked up these minor fluctuations to good days and bad days, lack of sleep, changes of diet, mood swings.

And if a teacher did occasionally suspect that Will might really be John or John might be Will, they simply pushed their doubts aside; they had twenty-two other kids to worry about. Why worry about the Hancock boys? They were excellent students. Quarter after quarter they both earned perfect report cards. Sure, they liked to stir up the pot, cause a ruckus now and then, but everyone agreed: These were not bad boys; they simply had high spirits and excessive amounts of energy. . . .

JOHN & DOCTOR DOPE

At the moment, John Hancock, now a forty-year-old man with a career and a wife and kids, cannot stop pacing back and forth across the office he shares with his brother. They have never actually been in the office at the same time, that would be far too risky, but the space and its contents nevertheless belong equally to both of them. If Will were here now, however, he would not be pacing. He would be sitting at his desk, quietly, letting his mind, not his body, do the work. When writing a book, John furiously scribbles scene after scene, rarely pausing to consider unity or focus. That's Will's job. He takes John's scenes and patiently turns them into something plausible and coherent. Although, of late, Will has not been doing much writing or editing. John has several times asked his brother about this, but Will merely says it's a phase and will no doubt shortly pass.

Right this second, John is not writing much either. He's far too wound up to write.

He makes his way back to his desk, back to his pad of paper. He turns to his suspect list, runs down the short list of names:

HANCOCK, CLARA
BYRNES, RODNEY
RAFE,?
COSGROVE, DICKY
FISHER, LELAND

For a couple minutes he contemplates who else might belong on the list. A few names pop into his head, but no one worth writing down.

Then his eyes fixate on COSGROVE, DICKY. He begins to conjure up the face from memory and imagination. More than a dozen years ago now. A tall, scrawny kid in his early twenties at the time. Some old acne scars on his hollow cheeks. A good ten years younger than sister Zelda. Very bright. Super-high IQ. MENSA range. But weird eyes. Scary eyes. Occasionally violent. Usually against himself. Smack-his-head-against-the-wall type of stuff. Nasty temper tantrums. Self-mutilation. The shrinks finally diagnosed him manic-depressive. They threw schizophrenia in as an afterthought.

Hancock recalls various medications keeping the guy reasonably stable: Lithium, Valium, Thorazine. But then sister Zelda got whacked and Dicky floundered. Totally dependent on his sister for both financial and emotional support, her violent death threw Dicky straight off the board into the deep end. Then he got it in his craw that Hancock had done the deed. For weeks he blew through Cambridge telling anyone who would listen that John Hancock had murdered his sister. He persisted with his accusations even after Hancock proved that he had not even been in the state of Massachusetts on the day Zelda was slain in her Cambridge apartment. Hancock had an airtight alibi. And absolutely no motive.

Still, Dicky did not relent. He insisted Hancock had killed his sister. And if not John Hancock, then his brother, Will Hancock. All interested parties told Dicky that scenario was impossible. John Hancock had been at a writer's conference in Boulder, Colorado. And Will Hancock was dead. Dead men do not commit murder.

Dicky would not listen. He continued to hurl his charges.

But soon thereafter Mad Dicky proved himself absolutely, certifiably insane: He attacked John Hancock outside of the Hasty Pudding Theater just off Harvard Square. Attacked him and tried to plunge a sterling silver letter opener, decorated with the head of a lion, into Hancock's heart.

Only the timely appearance of Mac Oosterhaus, Harvard Crimson's left tackle, saved Hancock from a lethal encounter. Mac, two hundred and sixty-eight pounds of raw power, scooped up scrawny Dicky, ripped that letter opener from his hand, and tossed him out into Holyoke Street like a sack of old onions.

For his homicidal act, the authorities committed Mad Dicky to the loony bin out in Great Barrington and threw away the key.

Too bad, for Hancock anyway, somebody found that key and decided to let Dicky out.

A year or so ago, a new regime came to power at the psych hospital, a regime with an extremely liberal bent on the use of powerful new agents to alter the behavior of maniacs and psychotics. Eventually they took a look at patient #637—Cosgrove, Richard E. For years, they learned, Mr. Cosgrove had been wandering the halls doing the Haldol Shuffle. More dead than alive, Dicky could barely remember his name. He had next to no idea what was happening from one minute to the next.

This new crop of drug docs found Dicky's catatonic state totally unacceptable. They took him off the Haldol and put him on a strict diet of Librium and Prozac. For ten or twelve weeks they messed with his dosages. Until, lo and behold, a new man began to emerge. A calm man. A happy man. A smiling man. A man ready to put his volatile past behind him and boldly reenter society.

John Hancock does not have the Director of Operations of this new regime out at Great Barrington on the horn for more than five minutes before he has heard all about Cosgrove, Richard E.'s remarkable, indeed magical return to reality.

"So what are you telling me?" Hancock demands, after the babbling brook of a shrink finally shuts up. "That Dicky Cosgrove is *loose*?"

"Quite correct you are, sir. Mr. Cosgrove, after careful and exhaustive study, was released on fifteen April of this year. Our entire staff unanimously agreed that twelve years and nine months of incarceration was long enough."

Almost thirteen years, thinks Hancock. Jesus.

"Tell me, doc, do you have any idea why that sick fuck was in your coop for all those years? I'll tell you why. Because he tried to filet me with a letter opener."

"*Sick fuck* is not a particularly positive way to describe a man suffering from mental illness, sir. I understand your feelings of trepidation, but perhaps—"

"Feelings of trepidation! He's a loony and I wanna know why the hell you let him out? Especially without telling me. The S.O.B. could be stalking me right now, and I—"

"Sir, we are not obligated to inform you or anyone of Mr. Cosgrove's release. Mr. Cosgrove is not a threat to you or to anyone else. Trust me, I have been in this business for twenty-six years. I know when a patient has been successfully rehabilitated."

"Successfully rehabilitated! What a fricking crock. Tell me this, Doc, what do I do when Mr. Successfully Rehabilitated comes after me? Or worse, when he comes after my family? You have kids, Doc?"

"No sir, I do not."

"Yeah, well, I do. Two of them. And they're *little* kids. About the same amount of sense as month-old puppies. They still trust the world. So what do they do when this loony comes up to them all slicked up on this newfangled dope you're feeding him and starts messing with them? What if he—"

"Highly unlikely, sir. *Highly* unlikely. Mr. Cosgrove has over and over again expressed his deep sorrow for the difficulties he caused you during his time of intense grief following the loss of his sister."

"You know he thinks I killed Zelda?"

"That's what he *used* to think, Mr. Hancock. He no longer thinks that."

"Is that what he told you?"

"Yes, he did."

"And you believe him?"

"Yes, I do."

"Then you're as nuts as he is."

"I can tell you are upset, sir, so I will not take offense. I will only tell you that I believe you can forget about Mr. Cosgrove causing you any trouble. I feel one hundred percent confident that your path and Mr. Cosgrove's path will never cross, unless by some strange coincidence."

"Strange coincidence, huh?" Hancock is getting sick and tired of coincidences. First the cops. Then Clara. Then Will. Then Leland. Now this shrink telling him Mad Dicky Cosgrove is out on the street. Probably right out on Louisburg Square. Bearing weapons of destruction.

"Relax, Mr. Hancock," he hears the dope doctor tell him. "You're in far more danger driving your car across town than you are with Mr. Cosgrove once again a free man."

"Yeah, okay, Doc, I'll relax. Just as soon as you tell me where Dicky C. is hanging his hat these days."

"I'm afraid I have no idea, sir. Mr. Cosgrove is an unshackled citizen of the United States of America. He is under no obligation to report to me. Or anyone else. He is free to come and go as he pleases."

"That's swell, pal," replies Hancock. "Really super. Right at this moment I am proud to call myself an American. And I'll tell you this: if Dicky Cosgrove comes up out of the sewer and messes with me or my family, you can absolutely count on me coming out there and messing with you."

"Is that a threat, sir?"

Hancock slams the phone down without answering.

The psychiatrist sighs. A man of complex psychological

bearing, he has a couple of diametrically opposed thoughts as this particular conversation concludes. On the one hand, he thinks the volatile Mr. Hancock would benefit greatly from some interactive drug therapy. A couple mils of Prozac with his morning java would decrease his aggressive tendencies. On the other hand, it might be more fun if Cosgrove, Richard E. looked up the foul-mouthed slob and maybe rearranged a few of his teeth.

DICKY

So where is Dicky C.? And what are this free man's intentions?

Question one does not pose a problem. A man's whereabouts, as long as he does not have an identical twin, is typically easy enough to figure out.

But question two falls into a far more slippery category. Penetrating a man's intentions is a very tricky business. Especially when you factor in how rarely a man truly knows his own intentions. Much less anyone else's. A man's intentions change with the wind. They change every time he combs his hair, every time he gets behind the wheel of his car, every time he sees a good-looking woman, every time he pushes on his sunglasses and thinks maybe he's the coolest guy on the planet.

Dicky C.'s intentions? That's a toughie.

But just look around if you want to find Mr. Cosgrove. The man is not trying to hide. Right now he's sitting in the main reading room of the Boston Public Library down on Copley Square. Dicky has been sitting there pretty much every second the library has been open over the past three weeks. Which is precisely the amount of time Dicky has been in Boston. His reading material, which he hides in the evening back in the bowels of the stacks, consists of the entire John Hancock oeuvre. Dicky has read and reread and reread again the novels and short stories of John Hancock. He knows, however—in fact, he feels absolutely certain—that the novels and stories were penned not by John Hancock, but by the team of Hancock & Hancock, John and Will. His certainty lies in the fact that sister Zelda shared a great secret with him a few months before her death.

"I'm going to tell you something, Dicky," she told him. "But it has to remain our little secret. It can't go any further than this room." (That being the living room of her small apartment just beyond Harvard Yard on Berkeley Street. The room where she was murdered.)

"No problem, Zelda," said Dicky, nodding his head vigorously. "No further than this room."

"It's about John and Will Hancock."

"What about them?"

"I think they're both still alive."

Just three months after this announcement, Zelda was dead. And now, thirteen years later, Dicky wants revenge. Forget what the guy told Doctor Dope out at the bin in Great Barrington. That was all a massive lie. Dicky told Doctor Dope and Doctor Dope's team of psycho elves whatever he had to tell them to stop doing the Haldol Shuffle and escape the confines of that dreary psych ward. Once they took him off the Thorazine and the Haldol and his brain started functioning again, he assessed the situation and began to weave his tale of sorrow and regret and redemption. He convinced Doctor Dope that he was, in fact, a good boy who had temporarily lost his way. And with some patience and understanding and, of course, the proper chemical agents, he could once again become a solid and even productive citizen.

Too bad Dicky tossed his bottles of Librium and Prozac out the window of the bus while riding on the turnpike from Stockbridge to Boston.

Which is why right now, sitting in the reading room of the Boston Public Library, the man has both the look and the feel of a full-blown kook. One look at him, and you know the guy's not quite right. The reading room's crowded, but Dicky has a big table all to himself. No way anyone's sitting near this dude. He's sweating and he smells and he has those weird, faraway eyes that remind people that the world is often an unsafe and inhospitable place. Watch your step.

Even the library staff, used to a daily parade of seamy and homeless characters shuffling through their corridors, has been whispering about "the stinky, crazy-looking one down in the reading room." They would like to ban him from the premises, but there are laws against tossing smelly, scowling nut cases out of public places. Thank the ACLU for those pillars of legislation. As long as he doesn't mutter too loudly or kick the other patrons or relieve himself in the corner, the staff has no choice but to leave Dicky alone. This country has a Bill of Rights, after all. A man can stink if he wants to.

Dicky is not even aware of his odor. Or of the hostile demeanor oozing from his pores. No, the man is totally preoccupied with his mission. He has no time to pull on a fresh T-shirt.

And really, the man should be given some credit. Anyone keeping track of the number of hours he has spent at that table over the past few weeks knows this one is a hard and diligent worker. And in America hard and diligent work is applauded. And often rewarded. True, murder as the end result of all that hard and diligent effort might not be held in the highest esteem, but no one has figured out yet that Dicky has homicide on his mind. Even Dicky himself has not quite figured that out.

BABE

Babe Overton stares out the window of that speeding Greyhound while she pops peanut M&M's into her mouth. M&M's, however, are not a typical component of Babe's diet.

A couple hours ago, when the bus stopped in tiny Thoreau, New Mexico, Babe left her seat to stretch her legs. For a hundred miles or more she had been dreaming of a tall and frosty glass of freshly squeezed orange juice, paired with a warm bran muffin. But when she entered the murky Deli-Mart next to the dusty gas station that doubles as the Thoreau bus depot, she faced disappointment. A rather violent spring thunderstorm had rocked Thoreau a couple days back, leaving the small interstate outpost with a blown generator and not a lick of electrical power. Cold juice and warm dough were out of the question. Babe had to settle for lukewarm lemon-lime-orangeade and two bags of ever-so-slightly-melted M&M peanuts.

Now, back on the road, the wheels of that big Greyhound spinning eastward beneath her feet, Babe wonders if it will be raining in Beantown. She has never been to Beantown, has no idea why they call Boston Beantown, possesses no real knowledge of the city whatsoever, only that she expects to encounter quite a lot of rain and probably fog. More than likely Babe's impression of the Cradle of Liberty comes from a movie she saw several years ago with Paul Newman, wherein he played a drunken, ambulance-chasing, down-on-his-luck attorney who, of course, in the end saves the day, gets the girl, and preserves justice and the American way. Babe remembers it raining a lot during that flick. Or maybe Paul just thought it was cool to wear a scruffy raincoat with the collar turned up.

Anyway, Babe thinks it would be wise to buy an umbrella, and maybe a rain jacket, before she reaches Boston. Babe has not owned a rain jacket or an umbrella in years. It doesn't rain in the City of Angels.

Thinking about L.A. makes Babe think about Mary Ann, her roommate. She should have called Mary Ann, told her not to worry, she would be back in a week or so. Babe knows Mary Ann worries about her sometimes. And Babe worries about Mary Ann. She thinks Mary Ann goes out with the wrong kind of guys. Guys who use her and discard her. Guys who want whores, not lovers. Guys who want mothers, not wives. She tries to tell Mary Ann that, but Mary Ann just laughs and lights up another cigarette.

Still, Babe should call. She also needs to get some decent food. And the umbrella, don't forget the umbrella. And the rain jacket.

Babe makes a mental note to take care of all these little things. Then she closes her eyes, leans her head against the window, and dozes.

Moments later, either from a dream or from her own conscious thoughts, Babe suddenly conjures up this little girl named Mary Ann who gets caught in the rain and climbs aboard the bus. She sits in the empty seat beside Babe. It winds up being Babe's long-lost little girl, the child she never had with Frank Hagstrom. Babe dries the little girl's hair with a towel and dresses her in a brand new sundress, just like the one Babe is wearing.

The little fantasy quickly fades, but not before a thin stream of tears runs out of Babe's eye and down across her cheek.

LOUISBURG SQUARE

No rain in Beantown today. Blue skies, green grass, trees and flowers blooming up a storm. Too bad John-the-Psychological-Suspense-Writer-Hancock, normally a keen observer of the natural order, sees little of this splendid urban landscape. He's too preoccupied looking for that fire-engine-red Ford Mustang. A little ripple of anxiety spirals up and down his spine. He doesn't spot the Mustang, so he takes a long and dubious look at each and every vehicle parked on Louisburg Square. Many of the vehicles look familiar. He sees them parked out there everyday. The blue Mercedes sedan. The black Miata with the tan top. The Jeep Cherokee Limited. But many of the cars he has never seen before. Like that old Audi 100. Or that Lincoln Continental. He feels sure those cops are probably sitting in one of those cars. The question is: Is Mad Dicky Cosgrove sitting in there with them? Or is he maybe sitting in one of the other ones? Watching and waiting? How many different people, John now wonders, are after him?

He barely notices the Town and Country minivan sitting across the street just a few doors down. Probably half a dozen minivans dot the Square this Monday afternoon, each more nondescript than the last. Hancock has no reason to give the vans a second glance. In his mind the silly-looking boxes on wheels are driven by harried mothers toting kids and groceries and a wide array of grimy athletic gear. No way are guys who want to hassle and possibly hurt him driving minivans.

Al-the-Gumshoe Brown sits in his minivan and dips a doughnut into his cup of joe. Al is no fool. He knows the perception people have of minivans. That was the main reason he bought one, rather than going for a full-size. Full-size vans, at least in the eyes of the law and the mainstream, carry *banditos* and construction workers and drug addicts. Absolutely no good for surveillance work. Much too conspicuous.

Al rests a moment from his doughnut-dipping and takes a look over at the Hancock town house. Right away he spots Hancock up in the third-floor window. Al assumes the author is taking a little break from the word grind to catch a quick glimpse of spring. See, Al doesn't know a thing about those two detectives visiting Hancock yesterday. He doesn't know about the missing person report. Or about Clara. Or Will. Or Rafe. Or Babe. Or Dicky. Al doesn't know about any of it. He just thinks John Hancock is this guy having an affair with his client's wife. Very run-of-the-mill private-eye stuff. Al deals with this infidelity nonsense every day. Probably ninety percent of his business consists of spying for husbands and wives who think their mates have slipped out of the coop for a little unscheduled nooky.

John spots a suspicious-looking man out on the sidewalk. The man is tall and gangly, and just a little too interested in Hancock's town house. The guy actually stops, puts his hand on the gate, and stares at the front door. John pulls back, hides behind the lace curtains. After a moment he steals another glance. Sure enough, the gangly intruder lingers, eyes still fixed on the front door.

Christ, John wonders, squinting for a better look, could it be him? Could it be Mad Dicky?

Heart pounding, John maneuvers for a closer look. Definitely the right height and the right scrawny build, but the

face . . . hard to tell from here . . . could be him . . .
maybe not. It's been so long. Thirteen years, for chrissakes.

Suddenly the gangly man pulls a map out of his back
pocket and studies it for most of a minute. Both John
Hancock and Al-the-Gumshoe Brown watch the man
closely.

What the hell, Hancock wonders, is the guy looking at?

The tall, gangly fellow begins to nod. Then he folds up
his map, puts it back in his pocket, and unceremoniously
walks away.

And that's when John finally gets it. He sighs and clocks
himself on the side of the head. "Dammit," he says to no
one but the walls, "just some tourist. Some out-of-towner.
Probably some wanna-be writer looking for the Louisa
May Alcott house on the other end of the Square."

CLARA

As she departs the Savoy, Clara Dare Hancock has at her side Ms. Joanne Smith, her London gallery manager. She expected to have Sir Rodney Byrnes here with her also, but he sounded miffed when she called him earlier to see if he was coming along. When he said, "No, I think not," in a snitty little voice, Clara responded with *"C'est la vie,"* and hung up.

Rodney didn't say a word about last night's intruder. He didn't have the guts.

Also in tow is a handsome young gay couple whose names have slipped Clara's mind, though she knows one of them works part-time at her gallery. The duo look cool and chic, with gold and silver loops decorating their ears and noses and lips. Which is precisely why Clara has invited them along. She likes the energy that youth gives her entourage.

Clara loves these scenes—the chaos and confusion, the pile of luggage rolling across the Savoy lobby, bellhops and concierge practically groveling at her feet, the dancing eyes of the other guests, especially the men. She can feel them glancing at her, wondering who she is and where they have seen her. In the cinema, perhaps? On the television? In the glossy magazines?

Clara, a lofty little smile on her smooth and pretty face, slowly crosses the exquisite marble lobby. Head high, her eyes stare off into the distance. She gently pushes a few strands of short blond locks out of her eyes. But even this apparently benign motion happens with practiced perfection.

Clara's theory is this: If you're going to bother walking across a room, you may as well enjoy it.

And then, moments later, on those long, lean legs, Clara is swept through the revolving doors and into the idling stretch limo parked at the curb.

It has not always been this way for Ms. Clara Dare Hancock. No silver spoons in this one's mouth when she burst upon the scene. On the contrary, Clara grew up poor, practically impoverished. Plenty of hard times in this girl's past.

CLARA'S MOM & DAD

In the winter of 1963, a troupe of actors arrived in Boston to do Shakespeare at some of the local college campuses. One night after a performance, several of the actors went out for a bit of libation at a neighborhood bar near Northeastern University. One of the players was a good-looking, sweet-talking young fellow named Rudy (Rudolph) Mooch. Mooch was his real name, but some years earlier, after deciding he wanted to act, he changed his name to Turk Daniels. He figured this macho, ruddy-sounding title would serve him better once he got to Hollywood. (Which, by the way, eventually he did. And where he appeared in over twenty feature films, mostly as a cowboy or a gangster in westerns and shoot-'em-ups.)

Anyway, Turk was really Rudy, but that night at Murphy's Pub on Huntingdon, he told the pretty girl in the corner booth his name was Bertram Rose, a slight derivation from the name of the wily character he had played in that evening's performance of *All's Well That Ends Well*: Bertram, Count of Rousillon.

The pretty girl's name was Patricia Breen McGuire, but everyone called her Patsy. Patsy was a tall, fine-looking, rough-talking Irish lass who lived with her father in a row house on Fullerton just a long fly ball from Fenway Park, home of the Boston Red Sox. Shea McGuire worked as a maintenance crew chief at Boston University. Recently he'd found employment for his daughter, mopping hallways and dusting classrooms. Patsy, of course, didn't like the work, bitched about it all the time, but she did like the money. Mostly she drank up her paycheck cruising from college bar to college bar several nights a week, with a group of friends she'd had since grade school.

So that cold winter night Patsy let Bertram "Call me Bert" alias Turk alias Rudy buy her a drink. No beer or wine for this girl. She liked whiskey. Irish whiskey. Bushmill's, thank you very much. Neat. In a small glass. Just the way her father liked it. And his father. And his father's father.

Bert told her some jokes, made her laugh, bought her another drink, sat close in that narrow booth, their thighs and shoulders touching. Then Bert made an excellent move by telling Patsy she was "really interesting" and did she know any place where they could get a cup of coffee and talk some more? Sure, said Patsy.

They wound up at an all-night diner over on The Fenway where Bert alias Turk alias Rudy proved himself quite a talker. Oh yes, he spun a mighty tall tale that night. More tale than Patsy could handle. And Patsy, though only nineteen, had heard plenty. Nice-looking girls always do.

It took Bert three days (nights, actually) to coax Patsy up to his room at the Lenox Hotel on Boylston. Kind of a run-down, fleabag joint whose glory days had long passed, the Lenox nevertheless impressed young Patsy McGuire. After all, she'd never spent a single night in a hotel before. When Bert ordered strawberries and champagne from room service, she damn near swooned. Of course, she *didn't* swoon. Not Patsy. Patsy saw herself as far too tough and savvy to swoon. But she was definitely impressed. So impressed that halfway through that bottle of champagne she took her shirt off. Not long after that, however, she passed out.

So it took a few more visits, but eventually Bert alias

Turk alias Rudy got all of Patsy's clothes off. She was terribly close to sober when he accomplished this magical feat. Thin and sinewy, like her daughter would later be, Patsy had been naked with boys before. But those had just been boys. Bertram, as she liked to call him, was a man.

Patsy and Bertram had sex that night. Pretty good sex, actually, despite Patsy's Irish Catholic uncertainties. In fact, they had sex every night for the next fourteen nights, the exact same number of nights Bertram had left to play Beantown. Then, on the morning after the fourteenth night, Bert alias Turk alias Rudy packed up and slipped out of the Lenox without bothering to say a word to Patsy. He felt kind of bad about it, but not that bad, and besides, the troupe had a gig down in the Big Apple. Rudy had a hard-and-fast rule about his professional life taking precedence over his personal life. And if people, typically of the female variety, occasionally got hurt, well, them's the breaks.

Patsy cursed and yelled and kicked the wall when the pimply-faced kid behind the front desk informed her that the actors had all checked out that morning. Bad enough Bert left—but leaving without even saying good-bye made him, in Patsy's Irish eyes, a shit-faced, low-life coward.

Well, all that unprotected sex had some other consequences. In the late spring, after Rudy had been gone for a good three months, Patsy's skinny belly began to bulge. There could be no doubt about it: Bertram had blown Beantown, but he had left a little of himself behind.

Shea McGuire threw his daughter out of the house when she told him she was pregnant. And just to show the "little slut" that God punishes sinners, Shey used his clout with the union to have Patsy fired from her job. Not very nice things for a father to do, but let it be said that Shea McGuire lived another sixteen years, and in that time the man never really experienced another day of peace. He suffered big-time for his selfish and sanctimonious attitudes.

And so where did Patsy turn? Not to her mother, who had died of leukemia when Patsy was just eleven. Nor to her aunts or uncles or grandparents, who were either dead, dying, living in the Old Country, or feeling very much the same self-righteous way her pappy felt.

No, Patsy had only herself to rely on. But she was an independent and resilient girl, definitely up to the task. She found a cheap boardinghouse across the Charles River in Cambridge. She found a job cleaning classrooms at Radcliffe. And she found a young female obstetrician willing to help her with her pregnancy for not too much money.

Tiny Jane McGuire, named after her late grandmother on her mother's side, entered the world on a very interesting day: November 22, 1963. Mother Patsy arrived at Mass General, her contractions coming with incessant frequency, just as word began to ripple through the hospital that the President had been shot.

An hour or so later, Walter Cronkite solemnly announced to the nation that President John Fitzgerald Kennedy was dead. He made this announcement at precisely the same moment Jane McGuire, who would, seventeen years later, change her name to Clara Dare, slipped into a world that had abruptly changed forevermore.

JOHN & HILLARY

Very few people know the true story of Clara's lineage. She prefers instead the wholly fabricated ancestral line she produced out of thin air after she changed her surname to Dare. Clara has spent most of the last two decades trying to bury her past.

Hancock knows most of the story, though not quite all of it. A fact here and a tidbit there Clara intends to take with her to the grave. But Hancock knows enough of Clara's secrets to respect her all the more. Coming from such humble beginnings, raised without a father, never having a chance to go to college—these hurdles, he knows, were difficult enough to overcome. But then to achieve so much success, plus have such a firm grasp of what really matters in life—good health, a fine family, a sense of adventure—these are the qualities that make John love his wife with total and undying devotion.

The fact that years ago he deceived her so completely and so willingly brings him daily pain. And the additional fact that he continues to deceive her only makes the pain worse. It is a problem for which there does not seem to be a solution. It remains the single greatest cross he has to bear.

But right now, John has a more immediate problem on his hands. He stands in front of the intercom in his office. "You're absolutely sure she said her name was Fisher?"

"Yes, sir," answers Nicky. "Hillary Fisher."

"And she's at the front door?"

"Yes, sir. And she's most determined to see you."

John has no idea why Hillary Fisher would want to see him. Certainly he knows Hillary, but not all that well. A cocktail party acquaintance. Hancock likes her well enough, though he's always found her bossy and hyperactive. He never really expected Leland's fourth try to be his last.

"You'd better show her into the living room," he tells Nicky. "I'll be right down."

John snaps off the intercom. He can't just leave Hillary down there. That would be rude. But he will have to get rid of her soon. He has to leave shortly to have lunch with her husband.

While across the street, Al-the-Gumshoe Brown tries to calm his pounding heart while tripping the shutter of his Nikon at breakneck speed. Sitting there behind the wheel of his minivan just a few minutes ago, listening to Hancock narrate *The Settlement,* the Gumshoe very nearly nodded off. Not because he didn't like the story, but because he'd been sitting there with virtually no action for over six hours. The man was bored. But a good thing he didn't nod off, because all of a sudden that big blue Bentley turned off Pinckney and double-parked right in front of Hancock's town house. Al almost could not believe his bleary eyes. Especially when the client's wife stepped out from behind the wheel, tugged on her rather short suede skirt, and then, little snippet of a nose pointed at the sky, strode in the direction of Hancock's front door.

Al, in his excitement, spilled his coffee. "Shit!" But then, like a house cat stalking an unsuspecting cardinal, he snatched up his Nikon, equipped with the big-barrel five-hundred-millimeter lens, and started firing. Boom! Boom!

Boom! Three shots before his mark reached the gate. Three more before she reached the front door. Two more while Nicky opened the door. Half a dozen more while the two women chatted, not very amiably.

And now the rest of the roll, while the client's bride stands there, stern and with arms crossed, presumably waiting for Hancock.

But when the door reopens, it's not Hancock. It's the nanny again. She ushers Mrs. Fisher into the house. The Gumshoe gets a shot of her strutting across the threshold. The door closes. Heart firing on all cylinders, Al reloads. Oh, yeah, a whole lot of waiting in this line of work, but when the action starts, it's fast and furious.

Hillary Fisher taps her expensive Punchini black pump on the hardwood floor of the Hancocks' living room. An only child, she has believed since birth that the mighty sun rises and sets at her feet. Misery to the men who have unwisely entered her whirling dervish of a world. And many men there have been. Hillary has long moved with reckless abandon through the Kingdom of Sexuality. She has always, since just a teen, enjoyed her sex. Especially fast sex. The faster the better.

As a youth, Hillary trained rigorously as a gymnast. She proved particularly skilled at the uneven bars and the floor exercise. And now, at thirty-three, she retains many of her best moves. She is short (five feet two inches), slight (ninety-three pounds), springy, and supple. Perfect for sex in the back seat of a Bentley.

Tap, tap, tapping away with her handmade Italian pump, she thinks about having a cigarette. She wants a cigarette. She needs a cigarette. No, she doesn't. Yes, she does. No, she doesn't. Does. Doesn't. Of course she does. But dammit, she's not going to have one. No way. She quit six months ago. But a couple times a week, she binges. Smokes like a chimney. A dozen Winstons in ten minutes. Then she won't have one for a week.

Leland is her second husband. And probably not her

last. She drove the first one, a housing contractor out in Lexington, absolutely insane. She'll no doubt do the same to Leland. He's well on his way already. Of course, he never should have married her in the first place. He married her because at the time, almost six years ago, he was forty-four and she was just twenty-seven. God, all that youth and vigor sure looked good. And a sexual appetite like he had never encountered before.

Right now John Hancock comes down the front stairs, not with his usual bounce, crosses the front foyer, and enters the living room. A formal room filled with tiger maple antiques from the mid-eighteenth century, the family does not really use the space all that much except when entertaining.

"Hillary!" he says in a loud and friendly voice, mostly for the benefit of Sylvia and Nicky who no doubt linger beyond the kitchen door, "how nice to see you. How have you been? And how is Leland?"

Hillary scowls at him, but is, thank God, sharp enough to play along with this bit of hokum. She has domestic help of her own. And she knows how they can chatter.

"I'm just fine," she tells him, sneering. "And Leland is quite well also, thank you."

John, wondering why she seems so perturbed, smiles. "And to what do I owe the pleasure of this unexpected visit?"

Another sneer, then, "Oh, I was in the neighborhood and thought I'd say hello."

"Yes, well, that's very nice."

They make small talk. It's a bit of a strain. Sylvia, without being asked, brings coffee. She lingers, glares, for just a moment, at this *other* woman, finally departs.

John pours the coffee. And while he does, Hillary crosses the room and not very subtly closes the double doors leading to the foyer. She doesn't actually slam them closed, but anyone on the first or second floor would certainly get the idea.

John steadies himself and holds up a cup. "Cream and sugar?"

Hillary glares at him. "I must have called you ten times in the last hour. That damn maid of yours wouldn't put me through."

Ah, John thinks, so that's why Sylvia looked ready to kill. Sylvia is extremely possessive.

"I'm sorry about that, Hillary. It's my fault. Both the housekeeper and the nanny are under strict orders not to disturb me when I'm working. Writing's a delicate matter, you know. One needs one's privacy."

Hillary cannot possibly care less. "I told her it was important."

"They all tell Sylvia that," he wants to say, but diplomatically doesn't. Hancock has no idea why Mrs. Fisher is so worked up, but he assumes if he waits long enough, she will tell him.

"I'm sure it's very important," he replies, his voice subdued and sincere. "Why don't we sit down and you can tell me what's on your mind?"

"I don't feel like sitting down."

John nods. "Okay, we'll stand."

"It's Leland."

"What about Leland?"

"I think he knows. Or at least suspects."

"Suspects what?"

Hillary scowls. "He's acting weird. He won't talk to me. Won't touch me. Usually he has his fat little hands all over me. Gropes so much I feel like a goddamn piece of fruit."

How swell to know these things, thinks Hancock, but says, "Maybe he's upset about something."

Hillary's voice goes up another octave. "Goddamn right he's upset about something. That's what I'm trying to tell you. He knows."

"He knows what?"

"Oh, Christ, Hancock, don't be such an ass. He knows you're fucking me."

John just about spews a mouthful of coffee through his lips. And then, in a moment of pure clarity, two very obvi-

ous realities come clear: Will must be having sex with Hillary, and Leland must have found out. Jesus! What the hell
is Will doing messing around with this twit, the goddamn
wife of their publisher? What the hell's he thinking?

"Dammit, Hancock, did you hear me?"

John manages to nod. He struggles to pull himself together. "I did . . . yes . . . I heard you. I was just taking
a second to think it through."

"We don't have a second!"

John thinks he will surely have to break one of Will's
legs. Or worse. He cannot believe Will has done such a
stupid and selfish thing. And so close to home.

"Now hang on," he says to Hillary. "What do you actually think Leland knows?"

Hillary shrugs impatiently. "I don't know exactly what
he knows. But he knows something. And both last night
and this morning your name popped out of his mouth for
no good reason."

"*My* name?"

"That's right. *Your* name."

"That's not good."

"No, it's not."

John sighs. "So what are we going to do?"

Hillary crosses the room and steps right up to Hancock.
She grabs his private parts and gives them a squeeze.
"What about a quickie? Help cut the tension."

John steps back. "I don't think so, Hillary. Not the right
time. Or place."

And a good thing, too, because anyone looking out the
living room windows will see some guy stepping out of a
minivan toting a Nikon with a very long telephoto lens.

Sure enough, the Gumshoe's on the move, cautiously,
but hoping he might be able to squeeze off a few interior
shots.

"Chickenshit," taunts Hillary.

"Come on, Hillary," says Hancock, trying to keep her
calm, trying to keep the situation under control, "I just
don't think we should do anything foolish."

"You're being boring, Hancock."

"I'm being realistic. The wise move would be to cool it . . . at least for a while. Give Leland a chance to settle down."

Hillary offers a long and noisy sigh. "Okay, we'll cool it for a while. If that's what you want. But first you have to fuck me real nice, right here on this comfy old couch."

"Hillary, be serious. My kids will be home from school soon. For chrissakes, I sit on that sofa with my wife."

"Well, aren't we awfully fussy all of a sudden. You didn't have much concern for my domestic space when you violated me in the back seat of the Bentley."

"*Violated* you?" Hancock's just winging it now. "That's an interesting choice of words. Maybe we better settle down and work on being reasonable."

"That's ridiculous, John. We both know I am not a reasonable woman."

John takes a deep breath. He knows it's critical to handle this delicately. The slightest slip, and all kinds of new and even more formidable problems could arise. He is definitely going to castrate Will. The second he gets his hands on him.

"I think," he tells her, "we should meet later."

"When later?"

"This afternoon."

"It's already afternoon."

"I know, but I have a lunch date with Leland at two."

"For what?"

"Business, dear. He is my editor and publisher, after all."

"Whoop-de-do. So when should we meet? And where?"

"Say five o'clock. Downtown. Out in front of the Public Garden."

"I'll pick you up at the intersection of Commonwealth and Arlington. Right in front of that big statue of George Washington."

John thinks he just about has her out of the house. "Five o'clock at the statue."

Hillary steps up and squeezes his balls again. "Don't be

late, Johnny Boy. And don't forget to bring these with you."

John forces a smile as Hillary turns, struts across the living room floor, and pulls open both doors with a dramatic flourish. "And, oh," she adds as she steps into the foyer, "give Leland a big kiss for me."

Al-the-Gumshoe Brown, trying hard to look like just another out-of-town visitor, sees his client's bride glide through the front door of Hancock's town house. Away from the cover of his minivan, he cannot simply lift his camera to his eye and start snapping photos. He has to play it cool. He's no longer some sleazy paparazzo and Hillary Fisher some famous femme fatale. Still, the guy has been taking pictures of people for a long time. He manages to pop off a couple shots as she steps back into that double-parked Bentley and accelerates away along that old cobblestone-and-asphalt street.

John Hancock, standing in front of one of the floor-to-ceiling windows in his living room, also watches the Bentley pull away. His eyes wander along the Square. That's when he spots the guy across the street. The guy with the camera. "Jesus!" he wonders aloud, "who the hell is that?"

The guy takes a picture of the fast-moving Bentley. But then, a moment later, he nonchalantly turns away, as though that fancy British sedan is of no real interest to him whatsoever. Hancock watches with narrowed eyes as the guy crosses the Square, stops in front of the stone statue of Christopher Columbus, studies the ancient mariner, then finds the right angle and takes the sailor's picture.

John sighs. Just another tourist. Beacon Hill crawls with them this time of year. Sometimes he thinks he might just move the family out to the suburbs. Maybe out to the country. To the old stone farmhouse outside Stockbridge.

He thinks about Will. This time his brother has gone too far. Way beyond the limit. Romantic flings when off on Adventure Travel Enterprises business are bad enough, but this stunt is too much. Absolutely unacceptable.

John turns away from the window. The penetrating stare of Sylvia standing at the end of the foyer gives Hancock pause, but he does not think stopping will give him much pleasure, so he pretends not to see her and continues on to his third-floor retreat.

Life, he thinks, is getting complicated.

RAFE & MATILDA

Rafe could not agree more. Like right now, sitting across
the desk from Matilda, the travel agent-seashell seller-ear
piercer.

"Going to the States, hey? Business or pleasure? How
long will you be staying? Need a car? Hotel reservations?
Be staying with friends?" Blah blah blah blah blah.

"Mind your own business, Tilly," Rafe feels like saying,
but, of course, doesn't. He keeps smiling and telling lies,
mostly about his half-brother up in New Jersey who's dying of some rare blood disease and Rafe has to get up there
pronto to give blood or the guy will croak. He knows
everyone on Caye Caulker will have heard about this fictional half-brother by dusk, but he has to tell the white
broad something. Rafe cannot believe how Matilda can
live down here in the tropics and stay so fricking white.
Pure white. Like a goddamn hotel room sheet. Like goddamn virgin snow. Not that Rafe's ever seen snow, except
in pictures, but he can dream.

"Okay," she says, studying her computer screen, "I
can't get you to New York until Thursday. And the only
seats left on that flight are, like, way expensive. But if you
wait till next week we can get you a discount fare."

"No way. I can't wait that long. The guy'll be dead."

"I hear you," says Matilda, who does not believe for one second this tale of family blood disease, "so what about this? I get you on a flight to Houston tomorrow. Then a connection up to Chicago. Wednesday morning you fly into New York. And you do all this for less than half what you'd pay for a direct."

"How much?"

"Six fifty."

Rafe likes the sound of that number. It leaves a nice wad in his pocket. "And I'm out of here tomorrow?"

Matilda nods. "Late morning."

Rafe thinks about it for eight or ten seconds. "Book it."

Matilda right away starts tapping the computer keyboard. "And how will you be paying?"

"Cash."

Matilda sneaks a peek at Rafe. She knows all about Rafe. She knows he's a slacker. But then, the island's populated pretty much with slackers. Especially the males. They're like lions in the wild: just come out to feed and fornicate. This one's really no worse than the rest.

"Tell me, Rafe, I know you have a lot on your mind, what with your half-brother ill and all, but would you be interested in making some money?"

"Making some money? How do you mean?"

"It wouldn't be a big deal. Really just a matter of an extra bag."

"An extra bag?"

"And a pretty small bag at that."

Jesus, thinks Rafe, I can't be hearing this right. Matilda, running dope? Who would have thunk it? He leans forward. "Exactly how big a bag we talking here, honey?"

Matilda shrugs. "You could probably carry it in your pocket. And if you don't want to carry it, you could swallow it before you go through Customs."

"Or do a rectal insert."

Matilda smiles. "Whatever you fancy."

"And what's in it for me?"

"Five thousand."

"Not much. Considering the risk."

"Hey, if you want to take a big bag with a big risk, I could probably get you twenty-five."

"Twenty-five grand?"

"Easy."

"You mean a big bag, like the size of a carry-on?"

"Exactly."

Rafe thinks it over. For fifteen seconds. "Maybe I'll try a little bag first time around. Where's it go?"

"You said your final destination is New York?"

Rafe tries to remember what he told her. "New Jersey, actually."

"Right. New Jersey. Well, the bag goes nearby."

"Where's it go?"

"New York City."

"Where in New York?"

"A nice little retreat called the Ambassador Hotel."

"The Ambassador Hotel?"

"That's right, Rafe, the Ambassador. But don't worry, I'll give you all the details."

Rafe can already feel his gut churning as he thinks about smuggling dope across the border. Not a very bright idea. But Jesus, he sure could use the dough. Especially if this thing with Hancock fails to take hold. He takes a look at Matilda. And thinks if even this mousy little bare-foot white babe is in the illegal drug trade, the world is pretty well screwed. Royally.

Will Hancock, traveling as Thomas Young, chats up the pretty flight attendant on that Miami-bound flight. "Listen," he says above the whine of those jet engines, "I'm flying out to the Bahamas this afternoon. Little island called Exuma. Hotel Peace and Plenty. Lovely spot on the water. You have a layover, you could join me for a day or two."

The pretty flight attendant smiles. She has had plenty of offers like this before. "That would be nice," she says. "Can I bring along my husband and son?"

Will smiles back and shrugs. "How old's your son?"

"Seven."

"I have two," says Will. "Five and six."

"Well, then," says the flight attendant, "I'm not sure you should be inviting strange women off on exotic vacations."

"You're right," agrees Will. "But my wife and I spend so much time apart that I get, you know, lonely."

The flight attendant, whose name is Pam, and who is often lonely when away from her family, squeezes Will's arm. "I know, honey. Sometimes life's nothing but a great big bitch."

Will nods. He's a thirty-nine-year-old man who has traveled solo all over the world, spent hundreds of nights in strange hotels, but often he's as lonely as an eight-year-old on his first night at sleep-away camp.

Pam slips by him into the aisle. "Time to go back to work." She squeezes his arm again. "Listen, thanks for the invitation. You seem like a sweet guy. Call your wife. Tell her you miss her."

Will would like to do that, but, of course, he can't. It's not his turn. So instead he returns to his seat, pushes it back, and closes his eyes.

Will Hancock is, essentially, a solitary man. But like many solitary men, he does not really enjoy being alone. He likes people nearby, just a few people, people he knows, people he feels safe with, people he trusts. Out here on the road, covering his duties for Adventure Travel Enterprises, he fights a tough battle between indifference and depression, between physical freedom and emotional bondage. All over the world he wanders. And has wandered for many years. With virtually nothing to worry about. No responsibilities to impede his progress. No one demanding to know where he is or what he's doing. No one to call. No one to check in with. Six times a year, every other month, for weeks at a time, Will is free to come and go as he pleases. Nothing and no one stand in his way. Plenty of cash and platinum cards in his billfold. Business travel or better every step of the way. Fishing, hiking, skiing—whatever his heart desires.

And yet, the man is often miserable. He would prefer to be at home, back in Boston, making love to his wife, raising his boys, writing his books, rowing his scull on the Charles. But no, not this month. This month it's once again his turn to do the vanishing act. No calls, no letters, not even a postcard from some distant port. No easy long-distance banter with Clara. No quick chats with the boys to say good night, sleep tight, don't let the bed bugs bite. No communication at all until the end of the month. Until another segment of his life sentence is served. Until he can once again assume the role of John Hancock.

But Will does not feel like going over it all again. He has been over it and under it and around every side of it more times than he cares to remember. So he just sits here high above the Atlantic, isolated and alone, and allows his thoughts to wander into the past. A past that is very quickly beginning to intrude upon the present. . . .

BOARDING SCHOOL

The summer of '72. The family room of the big colonial on Maple Street in Greenwich, Connecticut. Mom and Dad (Lenore and William) came into the room, switched off the television, and asked Will and John how they'd feel about going off to boarding school in the fall.

John right away liked the idea, thought it would be a great adventure. Will was not quite so enthusiastic. He did not really want to leave home. He did not want to leave his mother.

But John's eagerness, as always, carried the day.

Lenore had conceived the idea of boarding school after concluding that her husband had an obsession with moving (five different addresses in less than seven years). Probably William's restlessness stemmed from his ragged youth, running first from the Nazis and then later from those dirty and paranoid commies. Lenore decided all this moving from house to house and from town to town was not healthy for her two young sons. They needed more continuity in their lives. And so, despite the fact that she would miss them dreadfully, Lenore enrolled the twins in a top-notch boarding school up in the Connecticut hills, just an hour or so from home.

Will, when he could manage a few minutes alone with his mother, pleaded with her to let him stay home. He did not want to go. Lenore comforted her slightly younger, but far more needy and insecure son by assuring him she would visit every weekend. She told him it would be fun and challenging and extremely educational. Then, once she had him convinced, Lenore told Will to always be his own man, to make his own decisions. She knew John tended to dominate their relationship, control the flow of emotions and activities. John led and Will followed.

And so Will, despite his reluctance, went off to boarding school. He really had no choice. He had to go. If he hadn't gone, if he had stayed home, alone, John would have ostracized him. And nothing, not even missing his mother, could possibly have been worse than that.

The small, picturesque campus with its towering oak trees and ancient, ivy-covered buildings offered plenty of beauty and security. Will and John had their own room on the second floor of one of the ivy-covered dormitories. The ivy grew right through the windows, right through cracks in the stone walls.

Will felt at home in that room almost right away. Lenore had made sure to bring along all his favorite things. He had his favorite books on the shelves, his favorite posters on the walls, his favorite blankets and pillows on the bed.

And, of course, he had his brother. All the time. Every day.

That winter William Hancock flew out to Los Angeles to sell his umbrellas. Very few people in L.A. even owned an umbrella, but this fact did not deter William for a second. He had bigger fish in mind. Even though he spent most of his waking hours trying to build his fortune, William had never for a moment lost his love of American movies. So when he heard that Warner Brothers was considering a remake of *Singing In the Rain* with Warren Beatty reprising the Gene Kelly role, William packed his bag and several of his top-of-the-line umbrellas and headed west. For a week or more he tried to get through the door at Warner Brothers. He wanted to offer them free use of Hancock umbrellas in the shooting of *Still Singing in the Rain.*

William Hancock was a first-class salesman, but even his best efforts proved futile. No matter. A man born and raised in Berlin, one of the dreariest places on earth, William fell in love with sunny California and the California life-style, especially all that warm and wonderful weather. Back home in Connecticut, winter lingered with a cold, wet vengeance. But here in L.A.: bright sunshine day after day, not a cloud in the sky.

He called his wife. "Pack your bags, Lenny. We're relocating."

"Relocating? To where?"

"To California."

"California! What about the boys?"

"The boys? Hell, they're fine. They're in school. Leave them be. They can come out west for holidays and summer vacations."

Back at boarding school, the Hancock boys continued to plow ahead with both academic and athletic success. Their primary competition both in the classroom and on the playing field came from one another.

At times, this competition was far more intense than anyone knew. To all eyes, John and Will presented a strong and united front. As teammates, their skills meshed perfectly. No question that when they faced a common adversary, the Hancock boys pulled together with a concentrated ferocity.

But what about when they faced each other? Head to head? What happened then? A sibling rivalry definitely existed, though they worked hard to keep it suppressed. They instinctively seemed to understand that their survival depended upon cooperation.

Their youth had passed with only a handful of physical confrontations. But during Thanksgiving break of their sophomore year, they engaged in a classic confrontation, a full-blown battle, a war of wills that brought to the surface years of deep-seated fraternal feelings and bitter resentments.

Their classmates had gone home for the holiday. John and Will were supposed to fly to California, but at the last minute their father had to go to Mexico on business. Lenore accompanied him. So against his better judgment, Headmaster Masters gave the boys permission to stay in their dorm room. Calm prevailed for the first couple of days. They studied, walked into town for meals and movies, and played hours of one-on-one basketball over at the gym.

These games inevitably became heated. Plenty of pushing and shoving. John definitely had a slight edge with his quickness and his shooting prowess. But Will made up for any deficiencies with his almost desperate desire to win. He had the power to will the ball into the basket and the stamina to play until his opponent dropped.

On this particular Saturday morning, John got off to a fast start. Hitting jumpers from beyond the foul line, then driving the lane when Will tried to play him close, John won the first two games with minimal trouble.

They played for almost three hours. Nonstop. They never sat down, never leaned against the wall, never even put their hands on their knees. A whole slew of seething passions began to slowly bubble to the surface.

They played ten games. John won six of them. Will eked out victories in the other four, never winning one by more than three hoops. Still, Will demanded an opportunity to bring things even.

John stood at the top of the key, hands on hips, breathing hard. "That means at least two more games. Then another one if you're lucky enough to win those two."

"Yeah, so?"

"So I've had it. I'm whipped. If this is a war of attrition, brother, I guess you win."

"Faggot."

"Don't call me a faggot."

"I'll call a faggot a faggot, you faggot."

The boys might have rumbled right there in the paint if old Ernie the janitor hadn't come limping through with his mop and bucket. They didn't want to upset Ernie; he was the guy who let them into the gym. So they grabbed their gear and headed for their room.

Tempers very much on edge, the big trouble came later that night. As with most sibling battles, this one erupted not over the conflict at hand, but rather over a host of irritations that had been building for God knows how long. A single careless word could have set it off. A wrong foot forward. A sneeze. A cough. A sideways glance.

They probably should have known better, but after dinner they broke out the backgammon board. More competition. And because backgammon uses dice, luck plays a vital role and victory is often arbitrary. But play enough games, and the better player usually prevails. In this case that would be Will. His brain made the small calculations quicker and with just a hair more precision than his brother's brain. He played the game with ruthless abandon and incredible speed. He often made his move before his dice came to rest.

John had no choice but to play a bit slower. But if he took an extra second to puzzle over his move, Will jumped all over him, told him to hurry up, to quit wasting time.

They played half a dozen games. Will won all but two of them. Losing did not excite John anymore than it did Will. John wanted to win at all cost. Would he cheat to win? His brother thought so.

In the middle of the seventh game the telephone rang out in the hallway. Will went to answer it, thinking it might be their mother. But it was just a wrong number. "Some guy," Will told John as he came back into the room, "looking for Tony's Bar and Grill."

"Never heard of it."

"Me, neither." Will picked up his dice and gave them a shake while he studied the board. His eyes narrowed. "Hey. Wait a second. What's this?"

"What's what?"

"You didn't have that many pieces in your home zone."

"The hell I didn't."

"The hell you did."

"What are you saying," asked John, "that I cheated?"

"I'm saying you moved some of your pieces while I was out of the room."

"So you're saying I cheated?"

"Call it what you want. You definitely moved some of your pieces to give yourself an advantage."

"You're paranoid."

"Don't call me paranoid."

"No? What are you going to do? Throw one of your dice at me?"

That simple question did it. That blew Will's fuse. He threw one of his fists at his brother. It landed on John's jaw. John retaliated by kicking the backgammon board out of the way and advancing with all possible speed. He thrust his head into his brother's chest and drove Will back against the wall. Will needed only a moment to recover. He swung a leg, then an arm at his brother. Both made solid contact. A second later, four arms and four legs flailed wildly about the room.

It took fifteen minutes for the rage and fury to abate. Not too bad, really. Months, probably years, of suppressed hostility, and it all blew away in a few ticks of the clock. That quarter of an hour, however, took its toll. Will sprained his wrist when a left hook went awry and slammed into the wall. John banged his knee up when it smashed into the steel bed frame rather than his brother's rib cage. But all told, the room fared much worse than the Hancocks. Lamps lay shattered upon the floor. Desks had serious injuries, as did bureaus and beds and night tables. Closet doors suddenly bore holes the size of a teenage boy's fist. Cracked mirrors hung crooked on the walls.

It took the boys several hours to come fully to their senses. They went their separate ways the moment the battle ended (John on a tour of the dark streets, Will to the TV room where he sat staring at the blank screen). But by midnight they had met again on the battlefield, this time under a flag of truce.

Throughout the night and well into Sunday morning the boys toiled to repair the damage. They knew that that afternoon, students and faculty would begin the post-holiday return. No way did they want anyone to know what had happened up in Room 226 of Buckley Hall. It was not the physical damage to the room: It was the damage to their image that most concerned them, the nasty blemish the damage would have upon their reputations. They were known as cool guys, wise guys, smart guys, competitive guys. No one saw them as bad guys or violent guys. And no one, as far as they were concerned, ever would. The Hancock brothers were a unit; a single, focused unit. The outside world would never see anything but peace and harmony between them.

And so, John and Will diligently cleaned their room of all splintered wood and broken glass. Chairs and lamps were discarded in the trash bins out behind the gymnasium.

By noon on Sunday the room looked better than it had before. No one ever knew what had happened. No one ever even suspected.

JOHN & LELAND

Will Hancock stirs when he hears the announcement for the final approach into Miami. He shifts his weight and rubs his neck. Will remembers well that battle up in room 226 of Buckley Hall. The battle and the ensuing cover-up. And he knows, even though he has done a masterful job of denying it for more than two decades, that much of his life has been a lie and a cover-up. The whole concept of the Hancock boys has been a facade, a magic trick, smoke and mirrors.

John Hancock hasn't thought about that battle up in room 226 for years. But then, John's never been real big on dredging up the past. Too much going on in the present. Especially these days. Stuff coming at him from all angles. Stuff about Will. Stuff about Hillary Fisher. And Rodney Byrnes. And Dicky Cosgrove.

But John can't stop and think about all that stuff right now. It's almost one thirty. Time to go meet Leland. Try and put out that fire.

On his way out the door John tells Sylvia to tell Nicky

to have the kids here at the house around four-thirty. "I want to take them to the park."

"And the puppy," Sylvia reminds him. "You promise to take them to see the new puppy."

"Right, the puppy."

"Just you do not forget. It very important with children not to forget."

"Don't worry, Sylvia. I won't forget."

John goes out onto Louisburg Square, stops, takes a look around. He doesn't spot Al-the-Gumshoe Brown sitting in his minivan, because not only does Al have tinted windows, but he's slumping pretty low in his seat, no more than the top of his head showing over the steering wheel.

John goes to the end of the Square and turns left on Mount Vernon Street. Al-the-Gumshoe Brown does not follow. Al already knows where Hancock is headed. He's been instructed by his client to take a two-hour lunch break and renew the surveillance again around three-thirty outside Ristorante Toscano down on Charles.

Hancock turns right on Walnut and cuts over to Beacon. He pauses for a moment to look out across Boston Common, then he starts up the hill in the direction of the State House. Just past Joy Street he reaches the offices of The Boston Press. This two-hundred-year-old Charles Bulfinch-designed brick town house has housed The Boston Press since its establishment in 1899 by Leland's great-grandfather, Isaac Fisher.

John enters the lobby. Plenty of carved cherry woodwork and Italian marble here, but it's the books that grab the eyes. Thousands of books. Tens of thousands. One copy of every book The Boston Press has published in its one-hundred-year history rests upon these bookshelves. Hancock's books are here. All seven of them.

John sticks his head into the receptionist's office, where ancient Mrs. Tellison, who some say occupied that post when Isaac ran the place, sits reading a mystery and waiting for the phone to ring. "Hello, Mrs. Tellison!"

The tiny gray-haired woman looks over her half-glasses and squints. "Yes?"

202 *Thomas William Simpson*

John knows she's half deaf and half blind, but he also knows Leland is too much the softie to ever ask her to retire. "It's Hancock!"

She takes this in, processes it, finally says, "Oh yes, young John. How are you?"

"Fine, Mrs. Tellison! Leland in?"

"Leland? Of course, Leland. The son. Let me call upstairs."

"That's okay, Mrs. Tellison! I'll just go on up."

Mrs. Tellison picks up the phone, but young John is already halfway up that first flight of wide marble steps. He knows the way to Leland's office. After all, he's been coming here for almost twenty years now. Leland bought and published John and Will's first novel, *Boarding School Blues,* way back during their postgraduate days at Harvard.

Leland's office is the same office his father, his grandfather, and his great-grandfather occupied before him. These other Fishers, however, actually ran the company. They were hands-on publishers involved in every aspect of the book business, from acquisition through distribution. When Leland's time came, things began to change. Leland did not have much interest in the book business, or, for that matter, even working for a living. Leland, born with the proverbial silver spoon in his mouth, did not really need to worry about having a vocation. His family had money. And connections. These connections gained him admittance to Harvard University, where he graduated dead last in his class.

After this memorable academic career Leland spent several years playing at the Bohemian lifestyle. He lived down in Greenwich Village for a while, got married, had a couple kids, got divorced. Then another wife. Another kid. Another divorce. Then he came back to Boston and his father put him to work. He spent a couple years toting around the titles Associate Editor and Assistant to the Publisher. He didn't really do much editing or assisting. But he did gain a reputation as quite a party boy at all of Boston's hottest night spots.

Then, in 1983, Bernard Fisher broke into a heavy sweat, stood up from his huge mahogany desk, collapsed, had a few convulsions, and died.

Leland, thirty-four at the time and still ripe with bad habits, had to step up to the plate. But the last thing he wanted to do was run a publishing house. So practically his first move after coming to power was to put The Boston Press up for sale. Within days the offers came rolling in from the megapublishers in New York, London, and Germany. The Boston Press possessed that magical combination of profitability and respectability. It had a golden reputation and an impressive backlist. Leland took his time and eventually got what he wanted: umpteen millions, limited autonomy in acquiring new material, and continued occupation of the family's third-floor office for the rest of his working life. Guilt, he recognized even then, would drive him to an early grave if he didn't make a stab at keeping the family name in the book business.

Now here comes Hancock, through the door without knocking, big and broad, smiling from ear to ear. "Lee! How the hell are you?" Across the thick carpet in a couple of loping strides and all over Leland like some kind of good-natured grizzly. He grabs Leland's fat little hand, squeezes his neck, massages his scalp, does just about everything but kiss him on the lips.

The bastard saves that, thinks Leland, for Hillary.

Some pleasant, if somewhat forced, chitchat follows.

"How's sales?" asks Hancock.

"On *The Settlement*?"

"Yeah."

"Slowing," answers Leland, "but still pretty good. We could jump-start it again if you'd be willing to do a tour. TV, radio, the whole shtick."

The Hancock boys don't do book tours. Too much exposure. With two of them out there roaming the planet, they don't need a whole lot of strangers recognizing them. It hurts sales, but they have more important things to protect. At least this is what they tell one another when the issue is discussed. Individually, however, they would both like to do more to promote their work.

"I don't think so, Lee."

"I knew you'd say that, but figured I'd ask."

"No harm in asking."

Leland shrugs. "How's the new one coming?" Leland might be pretty riled up about Hancock having sex with his wife, but business is still business.

"Slowing," John mimics, "but still pretty good. We could jump-start it if you want to fork over some more dough, maybe—"

"Your humor titillates," interrupts Leland, then turns and heads for the refreshment center along the wall of his vast office, dominated by that mahogany desk and a whole arsenal of plush leather chairs and sofas. "Something to drink? Beer? Scotch?"

"A little early, Lee. Maybe a Coke. I thought we were going out for lunch."

"We are. But I called late and couldn't get a reservation till three."

"Where?"

"Toscano."

"Jesus, Leland, is that the only place you eat?"

Leland frowns. He does not like being kidded. "I eat lots of places."

John crosses to the big desk. "Let's order in and eat here. With the weather turning nice there's too many tourists out there anyway. Hell, an hour ago I had some guy taking pictures of my house."

Leland's eyes narrow. He wonders if it was Al-the-Gumshoe Brown. "Pictures?"

John nods. "Like he's standing in front of the damn White House or something . . . So what do you say we eat here?"

"Eat here?"

"Yeah. We'll order from Rebecca's down on Charles. They have excellent soups and seafood. You'll love it."

Leland tries to think of some reason why they should go out to eat, but too late. Hancock already has the phone in hand. He knows the number by heart. He and Clara order in from Rebecca's whenever Sylvia's off for the night.

Leland reaches into the beverage center and pours himself a healthy splash of Wild Turkey on the rocks. He's decided to cut back on the booze, but right now he hopes a drink or two will give him the gumption to say here today the things that need to be said. A while ago he had a call from the Gumshoe. Al told him all about Hillary showing up at Hancock's house. She didn't stay long, but goddammit, she went over there like it was perfectly goddamn acceptable.

"Jesus, Leland," says Hancock, hanging up the phone after placing their order, "whiskey at two in the afternoon? We ain't twenty years old anymore, friend."

"Bugger off. What's yours?"

"I don't know. I guess a beer if you have a cold one."

Leland pulls an ice-cold bottle of Samuel Adams out of the small fridge. "Mug?"

"No, thanks."

Leland hands over the beer, then returns to the beverage center for another splash.

John crosses to the picture window that dominates the front of Leland's office. Beacon Street and most of Boston Common spread out before his eyes. "Hell of a nice view you have here, Lee."

"Yeah, it's not too tough to take." Leland points out to the west. "In the winter, with the leaves gone, you can see clear down to the Public Garden."

"Really?"

Leland nods. "You know that statue of George Washington?"

John sneaks a peek at Leland out of the corner of his eye. "Yeah."

"You can see it once the leaves drop. Hell, I remember one afternoon a few years ago I was sitting here getting plastered, and I swear to God, old George gave his steed a kick and off they trotted. Straight down Commonwealth to battle the redcoats. Blew me away."

John laughs, but he's not really seeing the humor. What

he's seeing is himself and Hillary making plans to rendez-vous later this afternoon at George's statue. Is this, he wonders, Leland's not so subtle way of telling him he knows all about their little five-o'clock tryst? Does Leland have the phones tapped? The house bugged?

"George," he says, because he has no idea what else to say, "was one hell of a general. Despite what the revisionists scribble."

Leland drains his glass. "I read somewhere that he was one of the richest guys in the country when he ran off to fight in the war."

John can't believe they're playing this game, chatting about old George. No doubt about it: Leland definitely knows what's going on. John would like nothing better than to bring Will in here and coldcock the stupid son of a bitch right in front of Leland. But he knows he can't do that, so he sips his brew and plays along. "Hey, back in those days, people had conviction."

"Horseshit," snaps Leland. "The way I see it, Washington must've figured he could make even more dough if he cut the king out of the loop."

"You're not suggesting George and his continental cronies had anything but the most selfless and altruistic motives, are you, Lee?"

Leland's already on his way back to the bar. "I'm suggesting Man is essentially a self-absorbed sleazeball, primarily interested in his own survival and good times."

So, thinks Hancock, here we go.

Leland pours himself another generous dose of medicine. "Take us, for example," he says, turning back to Hancock. "We use each other to get what we want. If I didn't have what you want and you didn't have what I want, shit, we wouldn't be standing here now having this conversation. We wouldn't have anything to do with each other."

"Sure we would, Lee. We're buddies. Have been for almost two decades. If you wanted to quit publishing me, I'd understand. I might not be happy about it, but I'd get over it and we'd still be pals."

Leland drinks off almost half his glass of sour mash. "That's crap."

"Lee, we've had a lot of good times together. I don't know how you feel, but I count you as one of my closest buddies."

"Buddies don't fuck each other's wives."

John does not even flinch. He's seen that one coming ever since Hillary grabbed his private parts earlier in the afternoon. He puts on his best puzzled expression and asks, "What did you say?"

"You heard me."

"Yeah, but I'm confused. Are you telling me you're having sex with Clara?"

"Don't fuck with me, John. I know you're screwing Hillary."

"Oh, so I'm screwing Hillary, but you're *not* screwing Clara?"

Leland has certainly thought what an enormous pleasure it would be to bed Mrs. Hancock, but at the moment he refuses to be distracted. "I've seen you together." This, of course, is not quite true. Leland has only seen the photographs.

"You've seen *who* together? You've seen me with Hillary? And when was that, Lee?"

"It doesn't matter."

"You're accusing me of sleeping with your wife, but when I ask you when, you say it doesn't matter?"

"Just admit it."

"I won't admit what's not true."

"You're a fucking liar."

"Whoa, Lee, you really got a snake up your ass about this." John knows he has to take a chance, and right now is as good a time as any. "You know, I warned Hillary about you."

Leland scowls at Hancock. "What do you mean you warned *her* about *me*?"

"Warned her that you were a jealous and possessive little cretin, and if she and I started rendezvousing on the sly you'd find out and there'd be hell to pay."

"Well, you're goddamn right: There's going to be plenty of hell to pay."

John's plan may not play, but it's the only plan he's got. "Yeah? And aren't you going to feel like a horse's ass when you find out what our secret rendezvousing is all about."

"I know what it's about. It's about you not being able to keep your damn dick in your pants."

"Leland, with an imagination like yours, you should be the one writing the books. Hillary and I are not having sex. We're not even thinking about having sex. No offense, man, but I really don't have much interest in having sex with your wife. I mean, she's good-looking and all, but . . . well, hell, I don't know. I don't really think we should go there. Know what I mean?"

Leland finishes his third glass of Wild Turkey and takes a long, hard, incredulous look at Hancock. He might not be distracted, but he's thoroughly confused. "So what are you telling me? That you're not having sex with my wife?"

"Afraid not, friend. I haven't had sex with any woman other than my beautiful bride since the day we wed."

"Then what the hell have you and Hillary been doing sneaking around together?"

"Okay, Lee, I can see I'll have to tell you. Your wife will be plenty ticked off at me, but I'll tell you anyway. I'll tell you because you're obviously freaking out over all this bullshit. So I'll tell you—"

"Shut the fuck up and *tell me!*"

"Okay, okay. Take it easy."

"You take it easy!"

"Any idea what's coming up, Lee? This summer? In, like, four or five weeks? Right around the Fourth of July?"

Leland continues to scowl, but with a bit less bite. His mouth stays closed. He doesn't say a word.

"You do," continues John, "don't you?"

Leland won't answer, but the scowl melts away. He decides not to pour himself another drink.

"That's right. July the eighth. Leland Fisher smacks head-on into five-zero. Half a century. The big five-oh. Fifty years old. Only happens once in a lifetime, Lee. Hillary and I thought we might throw you a little party. We both know how you love parties. But if you'd rather freak out and think I'm having an affair with your wife, well, go right the hell ahead. Don't let me stand in your way. Have a couple more drinks, too. Turn yourself into a ranting, raving, paranoid drunk. What the hell do I care? It's nothing but middle-of-the-afternoon entertainment to me."

John winds down, and as he does he wonders how many times he's covered up for brother Will. Too many times. Too goddamn many times. And now he's sick of it. Sick and tired. Putting not only their personal and professional relationship with Leland on the line, but their marriage, for chrissakes. Their *marriage*. And their family. Easily the most important thing in John's life. His wife and his boys. Clara would be absolutely livid if she found out about such a grotesque act of infidelity. One way or another, John knows he must deal with his brother.

The telephone on Leland's desk buzzes. Head down, lips tight together, he pads across the carpet and picks up the receiver. "Yes, Mrs. Tellison?"

"There's a boy here from Rebecca's."

"Rebecca's?" Leland has forgotten all about lunch.

"Rebecca's Restaurant," says Mrs. Tellison.

"Oh, right," says Leland. "Send him up."

Leland hangs up the phone, hesitates, then turns to Hancock. "Food's here."

John rubs his hands together. "That's the best news I've heard today. I'm ravenous."

LONDON & PARIS

Suddenly, Sir Rodney, too, is ravenous. He feels like he could eat a horse. Just an hour or so ago he felt like he might not ever be able to eat again. Whatever that maniac blew into his mouth and nose last night did terrible things to Rodney's stomach. And to just about every other inch of his body.

Hancock denied knowing anything about it, but Sir Rodney does not believe that for a second. The lunatic with that black crap spread all over his face kept babbling about Clara. Hancock definitely must have sent him.

The question now is: What is Sir Rodney going to do about it?

He has already decided against calling the police. Nothing was stolen. Nothing in the apartment is amiss. Except, of course, for the mess on the outside of the door. Which Rodney has already cleaned up, for fear the neighbors might think he has some kind of weird sexual fetish. He's afraid if he tells the police, or anyone else, what happened, they might think he's gone around the bend.

Rodney was raised to always, above all else, keep up appearances.

So it is up to him to respond. To retaliate. He has various options. He could hire someone to hurt Hancock. But who would he hire? And how much would it cost? Sir Rodney is quite tight with a pound.

No, Rodney will not be hiring anyone. He will have to take care of this business himself, in his own way. If he can find the guts.

Too bad Sir Rodney, as Will's voodoo acquaintances in Haiti would say, is now one of the Invisibles. His body may live, but his spirit is dead.

Clara is dining at Maxim's, easily the most famous restaurant in Paris. Perhaps the world. Even though years ago the owners stopped worrying about the quality of the fare. People would come, even if they served up puppy chow. The point, after all, was not the food. The point was the place. The atmosphere. To be seen at Maxim's. To be recognized. And whispered about at adjoining tables.

These are certainly the reasons Clara reserved a table for her party that recently swelled to seven: her entourage of four from London, plus the manager of Galerie Dare, Jeanette Boucher, and her hairless husband Roland and their artist son, Gerard, who has been painting for six years but has not yet allowed anyone to view his work. Gerard is a beautiful and delicate boy with sparkling blue eyes and, thinks Clara, a tortured face. Over two hours they have been at Maxim's and Gerard has barely uttered a word.

Clara has consumed practically nothing: A few bites of an asparagus and feta cheese appetizer and two glasses of exquisite champagne.

Maybe she would eat more if Hancock were here. And the boys. She misses them terribly. She wishes Hancock was right now at her side. Laughing and squeezing her thigh under the table. Telling his risqué jokes. Practicing his terrible French.

Clara pushes back her chair and smiles at her guests. "I shall return," she tells them. "Please, order dessert, or more wine, or anything you'd like." She floats away on a pair of stiletto heels. Plenty of heads turn as she makes her way across the dining room.

Clara goes into the ladies room and has a little cry. Not a big event, just a few moist tears. The combination of the tortured look on young Gerard Boucher's face and the too many miles separating her from her family has taken its toll. Clara presents such a study of strength and determination to the world, but inside, she is fragile and even, occasionally, afraid.

An hour later and she's back at the Ritz. A large and lovely room overlooking the Place Vendôme and all of its most affluent artifacts to the material world: grand marble banks, exotic jewelers and perfumeries, designer clothiers, galleries with rare antiques and fine art, including the Galerie Dare just beyond the square (really an octagon) along the Rue de la Paix.

Clara gazes out the window at the evening lights while waiting for someone to pick up the phone. Finally Sylvia answers in the kitchen. The cook chats with Mrs. Hancock for a few moments, but soon enough hands off to the boys, whirling and rambunctious with Mom on the line. Young John, a year older and stronger, manhandles the receiver away from his little brother. Young Willy does not waste time. He races into the family room and snatches up the extension. They both talk at once.

"Mom! You should've been there at school today. It was wild. We had this fire drill. But it wasn't just a pretend drill. It was a real fire. With fire trucks and firemen and everything!"

"Really? Tell me." Clara listens while the boys tell her in detail about the smoke and the sirens and the flames shooting out of the cafeteria. They take turns, and Clara spurs them on with an occasional exclamation of incredulity. The more they talk, the better she feels. Her sadness begins to dissipate.

"But they put the fire out?" she finally asks. "No one got hurt?"

"No casualties," says John.

"But," adds Will, "they told us to bring our lunches to school tomorrow because the cafeteria won't work."

Clara smiles and says, "Sylvia always makes your lunch."

"I know, but if she didn't she would have to, now."

"You've got me there, Willy."

"When are you coming home?" they both want to know.

"Pretty soon. But remember, you're going up to New Hampshire with Auntie Linda for a couple days."

"When's that?"

"Wednesday morning."

"And when is it now?"

"Monday night."

"So when are we going to see you? You've been gone forever."

"I've been gone for two days."

"Well, that's forever."

Tears sparkle in Mom's eyes. "You're right," she says, "it is forever. But I'll be back before you can say, Sally Ann Smithers eats sugary sweet snacks."

"Sally Ann Smithers eats sugary sweet snacks!"

"Sally Ann Smithers eats sugary sweet snacks!"

"Okay, okay. I'm hurrying. I promise. Have you seen the puppy yet? Dad said you were going to see a puppy today."

"We're going later. We're waiting for Dad to get home and take us."

"A golden retriever, right?"

"Golden retriever," the boys say in tandem. "Golden retriever. Golden retriever."

More tears stream down Mom's face. But these, at least, are happier tears.

The kids say they have to go. Sylvia just pulled piping hot chocolate-chip cookies out of the oven.

"I love you," Clara tells them, but they're already gone. She sighs and thinks there's been enough travel. Enough compromises. Enough contradictions. Time now to settle down. Stay home. Enjoy her boys.

But first she has to do this thing in New York. The new gallery. And all the rest of it that can no longer wait.

She wonders if what she plans to do in a few days is the right thing. It seems like the right thing, but maybe not. Maybe it will cause too many complications. Too many added problems.

But no, she assures herself, her sadness is merely making her weak and silly. She has to stay strong and determined.

So, despite the fact it's late, Clara changes into silver-blue tights, blue-and-white high-top cross trainers, and a faded red sweatshirt with NANTUCKET scrawled across the chest. Seconds later and she's out the door and on her way down the hallway at a trot.

She finds the swanky Ritz health club deserted except for the girl who hands her a towel, and a lone, long-haired wolf in the far corner working with the bench press. It is, after all, almost ten o'clock on a Monday evening.

She stretches, rides the bike, climbs the StairMaster, slides back and forth on the cross-country ski simulator. Her heart rate climbs, the perspiration flows. It's no accident Clara has the body of a twenty-year-old.

The lone, long-haired wolf ambles by while she's standing in front of an enormous mirror doing very deep, very slow squats with a couple of eight-pound dumbbells. Clara watches him in the mirror. She thinks he is going to walk right by, not even bother to glance her way, but at the last second his head pivots and his eyes wander. Straight to the back of her legs and then up and over her sweet little behind.

Their eyes meet in the mirror. A smile breaks across his handsome, sweaty face.

Ah, thinks Clara, that's better. Then another look and she realizes, Jesus, it's Brad Fricking Pitt. Absolutely.

She manages to smile back. He nods, does that little

cutesy thing with his mouth that drives the girls crazy, drops his head, and goes out the door.

Clara has no desire to be with Brad Pitt, or any man other than her man. But still, she likes it when men notice her, when she can turn heads and get eyes to roam.

CLARA'S YOUTH

On the day the nation buried JFK, Patsy McGuire took her baby home from Mass General. Home was an old boardinghouse on Decatur Street in Cambridge, about halfway between MIT and Harvard. The residents were mostly graduate students from places like Iran and Ghana and Singapore. A regular melting pot. Quite a place for young Miss Jane McGuire to spend her formative years.

Soon enough Patsy had Arabs and Africans and Asians baby-sitting her little girl while she went to work. And sometimes out on the town. Patsy was, after all, still just a kid herself. Little Janey grew up hearing a dozen different languages and music from around the world. She ate Indian food, French food, Japanese food, Chilean food—all before her fifth birthday. And before she reached seven she had attended classes in Business Administration, Corporate Law, and Molecular Biology. This typically occurred when Patsy failed to arrive home on time and so the young student in charge of Jane would have to bring the youngster to class. Jane sat quietly in those cool, well-lit classrooms, absorbing the vibes, sucking up any and all stimulation the world had to offer.

Those were the sixties. Plenty of paisley and tie-dye and

pot smoking out on the front porch of that boardinghouse on Decatur. And Patsy, still a party girl despite this sudden assault of motherhood, wore the threads and smoked the smoke. She made no effort to shield her daughter from any of it. Maybe some of the sex, but not all of it. For almost nine years, after all, the two shared a bedroom.

Patsy did her best with Janey. She taught her daughter the basics. She taught Janey to dig her dreams and follow her fantasies, but to stay rooted in reality, to see the world clearly and honestly. Have a good time, but remember, the first order of business is survival. And above all else, don't take shit from anybody. Especially men. Use men and enjoy men, but don't believe a word they say. They're bullies and whiners, and virtually every word that spills from a man's mouth is a big, fat, manipulative lie.

When Jane was nine, she and her mother moved into an old Victorian house long ago divided up to make room for the exploding population of students and professors. The McGuires had the whole third floor apartment to themselves. The ceilings ran off at strange angles, but they had their own kitchen and their own bathroom and they each had a bedroom.

Florence Baker lived down on the second floor. Florence was a thirty-one-year-old woman who had already acquired a bachelor's degree in English, a bachelor's degree in philosophy, a master's degree in world religions, and a doctorate in medieval studies. She was a professional student with a small but steady trust fund and an insatiable curiosity for a vast variety of knowledge.

When Patsy and Jane moved in upstairs, Florence was studying nineteenth-century European art as an undergraduate at Boston University. She right away took a shine to the tall and skinny nine-year-old with the shy smile and the blue-green eyes. Watching out for the youngster after she came home from school, Florence told Patsy, would not be a problem. It would be her pleasure.

Florence was small and spare and studious, and extremely intelligent. She immediately took stock of the McGuires' situation. And recognized that she was being presented with an opportunity to give something back. She had been given so much.

Just a few weeks after the McGuires moved in, Florence took Jane over to the Fogg Art Museum on the Harvard campus. Jane had never been to a museum before, except once when she and Mom ducked into the Museum of African-American History over by Boston Common one afternoon during a thunderstorm. Florence took Jane up to the second floor gallery where she encountered, for the first time in her young life, the work of Monet, Renoir, Gauguin, van Gogh, Picasso, Cézanne.

Jane, easily the tallest girl in her class, shifted her weight from one leg to the other while studying those pictures for several minutes. Then she turned to Florence and asked, in a perfectly grave and earnest voice, "Did kids paint these?"

Florence, momentarily shocked, could not immediately respond. She took another look at those famous canvasses. Finally, a smile broke across her usually serious face. "Yes," she answered, "I guess you could say kids did paint these pictures. Adult kids. Grown-up kids still able to see the world with the freshness and innocence of youth."

"I don't know about all that," said Jane, "but I like them. The wild swirling colors make my eyes roll around in my head and the tips of my fingers tingle. Especially that one." And she pointed to Vincent van Gogh's self-portrait, dedicated to Paul Gauguin.

Over the next few years, Florence and Jane visited many museums together. Patsy occasionally tagged along, but standing around staring at paintings never really got her juices flowing. Her interests lay elsewhere. A fun and steady guy, maybe with a few bucks in the bank, was her primary pursuit. But Janey hanging out with Flo, Patsy knew, was a good thing. An excellent thing. She encouraged it. The kid needed every break she could get. Life was not going to be a cakewalk.

Boston's Museum of Fine Arts was Jane's favorite museum. She and Florence passed many afternoons together there, gazing at some of the great masterpieces. And they spent countless hours talking about the paintings and many other things down in the Japanese Garden or out in the Museum Courtyard. Florence listened very carefully when Jane stated her opinion. No one had ever really listened to Janey before. The girl's confidence soared.

The pair traveled far and wide to see the works of the great Impressionist and Post-Impressionist masters. They drove up to Portland and out to Worcester and down to Providence. They even went to New York where they spent three glorious days at the Museum of Modern Art and the grand Metropolitan up on Fifth Avenue.

They stayed in Florence Baker's parents' opulent Fifth Avenue apartment. Young Jane McGuire could not believe her eyes: The views of the city. The gold faucets in the bathroom. The Chinese silk tapestry on the living room wall. The Afghan carpets covering the floors. The embroidered cashmere quilt draped across her bed. The racks filled with French wine. The cupboards filled with exotic foods. The Degas oil in the study. The Picasso sketch in the master bedroom.

This grand tour of Manhattan was Jane's first glimpse of the good life. It was, to a young girl brought up in a boardinghouse with nary a material possession to her name, utterly and completely overwhelming.

But not so overwhelming that Jane did not take it all in, absorb, as always, every last lick of stimulation.

Janey McGuire, now just four years away from changing her name to Clara Dare, returned to Boston wanting more. Lots more. The girl, the young woman, suddenly wanted it all.

The Hancock boys make their way down off Beacon Hill onto the flats. They reach Charles Street. Hancock starts across but John junior and Will call him back. "Hey, Dad, wait! We have to hold hands. Mom says never cross the street without holding hands."

John senior returns to the curb. "Sorry, guys, I was spacing out. Mom is absolutely right." So he takes John junior by his left hand and Will by his right hand and crosses first Charles Street, then Beacon Street. Late afternoon. Five o'clock. Lots of traffic. People getting out of work. Trying to get home.

Amongst the trees and flowering shrubs of the Public Garden, the traffic noise abates. The kids break away to climb on the bronze statues of Mrs. Mallard and her eight ducklings. Dad prods them along to the footbridge over the lagoon where a hundred or more ducks, geese, and swans swim, chatter, and squawk.

The boys, of course, have to stop in the middle of the bridge, hang on the rails, spit in the water, watch the ripples. "Why does that little bit of spit make those great big circles?" they want to know.

"Because," Dad tells them, "you want it to."

They buy this as gospel, and so follow Dad down off the bridge like a couple of obedient apostles.

The giant statue of General Washington on horseback looms ahead. Spotting the statue, the two disciples race off, press against the wrought iron fence protecting the base, and stare up with mouths open at the massive and mighty general on his gallant steed.

John looks around for the Bentley. It's not tough to spot out there on Arlington Street among the Honda Civics and Dodge Neons. Hillary has illegally parked the huge British auto right smack in front of the statue. John can see her behind the wheel, eyes narrowed and roaming. She looks irritated. And why not? It is, after all, almost six minutes after five. Hillary's middle name, Hancock has noticed, could easily be Punctual.

She spots him, rolls down the window, sticks out her hand, gives him a wave.

Hancock pretends to notice her for the first time. He waves back, then turns to his sons. "Hey guys, look. It's Mrs. Fisher. You know, Leland's wife. Let's go over and say hello."

So over they all go, right up to the driver's side of the Bentley. Not a shy bone in either one of these boys. "Wow," says John Jr., "great car."

"Yeah," says Willy. "Can we go for a ride?"

And so they do, all four of them, Hillary figuring it's the only way she'll get Hancock into the car. The kids climb into the back. It's cavernous back there. Hancock slips into the front. Hillary accelerates away from the curb, shoots down Arlington, then zips around the corner and up Boylston.

The scowl on her face and the way she's trying to turn the big Bentley into a Ferrari assure Hancock that this is not exactly what Hillary had in mind when they planned their afternoon rendezvous.

"So," he asks, "where are *your* little ones this afternoon?"

Hillary gives Hancock a ferocious glare, and says, "You did this on purpose."

"Hey, honey, listen, I've got kids. You can see 'em in your rearview mirror. Every afternoon after school we do something together. It's part of the daily ritual. Today we're having a little drive with Mrs. Fisher. Later we're going off to look at puppies."

"How quaint." Hillary glances in the mirror. The Hancock kids kneel on that expansive back seat and look out the rear window. They wave, the way kids do, to the man driving the minivan behind them. That would be Al-the-Gumshoe Brown. Al got a little fouled up when Mr. Fisher and Hancock failed to show at Ristorante Toscano, but half an hour ago he picked up on Hancock again when Hancock left his town house with his sons and walked down to the Public Garden. He pulled over to the side of the road, kept an eye on Hancock through his binoculars, and so was right on top of things when the trio piled into Mrs. Fisher's big blue Bentley.

The Gumshoe does his best to ignore the waving youngsters, but they keep it up for so long and with such determination that he finally waves back. He feels like an idiot, and thinks, Jesus, the things I've done to put a few bucks in my pocket.

While Hillary has to admit, at least to herself, that the Hancock kids are kind of cute, but she's still ticked off at their father for dragging them along. "Maybe you should have mentioned you'd have company when you told me to meet you at five o'clock."

At least, thinks Hancock, she's keeping her voice down. He's confident his sons can't hear. And what little they do hear won't mean much to them anyway. "I didn't know then what I know now."

"And what do you know now?"

"You were right. Leland knows. At lunch he came right out and accused me of having a . . . a, you know, thing with you."

This news kind of takes the venom out of Hillary's voice. "You're kidding?"

Hancock shakes his head. "I wish I was."

"So what did you tell him?"

"I told him he was crazy."

"And what did he say?"

"He said he knew we'd been seeing each other."

"So what did you say?"

"I said, yeah, you and I had been seeing each other some."

"You did not."

"I did, too."

"Christ, Hancock, why did you do that?"

"I told him you and I had been getting together to plan his fiftieth birthday party. I also told him you'd be pissed off at me for letting the cat out of the bag. So play your part if he brings it up."

"Wow," Hillary mutters. "Planning his fiftieth birthday bash. You're quick on your feet, Hancock, I'll give you that. So what did he say?"

"He didn't really say much. But, you know, a guy doesn't want to believe his buddy is putting it to his wife. Give him an out and he'll likely jump on it."

"So you think he believed you?"

Finally, thinks Hancock, the payoff. He shrugs. "I think we better cool it, Hillary, that's what I think. Think about what we've done and then go from there. I mean, you've got a husband and kids . . ." Hancock rolls his eyes back to John junior and little Willy, still waving to that guy in the minivan. "I've got a wife and two fine young boys. We can't be playing these games. There's too much at stake. Too many people who can get hurt."

Hillary's no dope. She sees the logic. She knows Hancock's right. But still, she doesn't like being thrown over. "So what are you saying?"

"I'm saying," John feels like saying, "that the next time I see your lover I'm going to knock loose several of his teeth." But instead he says, "I just think we should both think mighty hard about what we're doing."

"We're just having a little frolic, Hancock. It's not like we're looking to break up our families and run off together to Timbuktu."

"Could you maybe keep your voice down?" Hancock glances back at the boys.

"So are you saying you don't want to do it anymore?"

John has to suppress several biting retorts. "It's not that I don't want to. But I really think we need to be reasonable about this."

But as Hillary pointed out earlier, she is not a reasonable woman. She suddenly pulls over to the curb and slams on the brakes. The kids come tumbling forward.

"Screw you, Hancock! You're nothing but a pussy. Get the fuck out of my car!"

Hancock is already out. He already has the back door open and is checking to make sure John junior and Willy weathered the storm. They're fine. Already up and around and wondering what happened.

"Nothing," their father tells them. "A dog ran out in the street and Mrs. Fisher had to hit the brakes."

The kids climb out of the car. "But didn't," Willy asks, "she use the 'f' word?"

"She did," answers Hancock. "But that was only because the dog running out in the street scared her and she said something she didn't mean."

Both the kids look around for the dog. "Is the dog okay? He didn't get hit or anything, did he?"

"No, the dog's fine," Dad tells them. "Come on, let's go. Mrs. Fisher has other things to do. We'll walk from here." Hancock closes the back door. "Wave good-bye to Mrs. Fisher."

The kids wave.

Hillary hits the gas, and, rubber smoking, makes her departure.

Al-the-Gumshoe Brown, half a block back, stares wide-eyed at this latest scene. He doesn't know what to do next. Where to go or who to follow. He decides maybe he's had enough for one day. A six-pack in front of the tube sounds like a plan.

Hancock looks around, gets his bearings. He sees they're over near Massachusetts Avenue, not far from Symphony Hall. Just fifteen minutes to Gloucester Street, where they are supposed to see those puppies.

"Come on, guys," he says. "Golden retriever time."

"Golden retriever!" the boys chant. "Golden retriever! Golden retriever!"

They start walking. Hancock thinks the scene with Mrs. Fisher could have been worse. Far worse. It actually went fairly well. But he knows it's probably not over. Sexual liaisons rarely end on the first pass.

Will has done this kind of thing before. The last time, John vowed to himself that if Will ever did it again, if he ever put their relationship with Clara in jeopardy, heads would have to roll. No way can he tolerate this kind of threat to their domestic lives.

THE BAHAMAS

The small Bahamas Air plane cruises over the clear blue-green waters bound for Exuma. Out the small oval window, Will can see the shadow of the plane.

Ask Will, and he will tell you he never should have gotten involved with Hillary Fisher. But that's the problem: He knows it was wrong, but he went ahead and did it anyway. For a few minutes of pleasure he jeopardized everything. The same with the stunt he pulled on Rodney Byrnes: He easily could have blown a little too much zombie powder into Rodney's mouth and killed the pompous Englishman. No question about it, Will's moral governor has gone on the blink. Worn out. The man now lives on impulse.

Will stares out the small, scratched, plastic window at the world below, at that wide open expanse of sea. During his many travels for Adventure Travel Enterprises over the past dozen years, Will Hancock has sought out places like the isolated Out Islands of the Bahamas. Places where he can be alone with his fly rod or his hiking boots or his cross-country skis or his kayak. Places where he can hone his skills and focus entirely on the moment. Places where he can empty his mind and calm his aching heart.

Will knows his life is intricately and intimately linked to John's. The ruse they perpetrated down on Caye Caulker in '82 might have divided them physically, but in many ways it bound them even tighter together emotionally. After that, they had no choice but to develop a single persona. A persona, however, much more in harmony with John's natural gait than with Will's.

Sitting on that plane, suspended above the earth, Will suddenly feels the full fury of the past. Two lives, endlessly and inevitably folding in upon one another . . .

MORE OLD BUSINESS

ON THEIR OWN

The western Caribbean. Late December. 1982. Will watched from Rafe's Whaler as John struggled through the surf. John hit the beach running and never looked back.

Rafe, anxious to avoid the Mexican border patrol, turned his Whaler south and opened the throttle. It was the last time John and Will would ever be seen together in public.

Plenty of work to do, though, in the days ahead. Plenty of mind games. Plenty of emotional whirlpools. Plenty of lies to tell. And tell again.

Will sat in the bow thinking about his brother and that damn passport. He could not stop wondering about John's motives for leaving his own passport behind, forcing Will to change identities.

Brother John did exactly what Rafe told him to do: He headed north. For most of the next hour he marched through the soft sand, moving fast, but not too fast, just a good steady pace, not wanting to wear himself out, since he had no idea, despite Rafe's assurances, where he was or how far he might have to travel. With plenty of time to reach Houston, he figured he could walk all the way, if necessary.

The sun soared into the sky. It grew warm. Then hot. John stripped down to his swimsuit. Every half hour or so he took a quick dip in the Caribbean. Floating on his back, imagination spinning, he wondered how long it might take him to swim to the States.

He reached the coastal town of Majahual late in the afternoon. There he hitched a ride to Chetumal on a truck carrying live chickens. The truck pulled into the town square sometime after dark.

John felt a fair amount of trepidation. Here he was in a strange place, with very little money in his pocket and precious little Spanish in his head. And he was alone. His brother, for really the first time in his life, was not at his side. But still, John Hancock felt alive. Intensely energized. His nerves hummed and the adrenaline flowed.

At the Restaurante El Vaticano, he had a cheap but tasty meal of grilled conch and corn tortillas. And for less than two bucks he found a bed with reasonably clean sheets at the youth hostel just north of Obregón.

John Hancock slept like a baby.

Residents of Caye Caulker, sedated by all that warm tropical air, have always loved a good sea disaster. It gives their normally dull and predictable lives a touch of excitement. The Hancock affair proved no exception.

A search party was formed, mere minutes after Will and Rafe reached the town dock and reported the trouble. An hour later, four boats and a dozen divers had reached the site and started for the underwater caves. Another dozen or so folks stayed topside to give support. No one doubted for a second the tale Will Hancock told. Why should they? These were brothers, after all, twins, identical twins. Everyone on the island had seen them together. Foul play did not enter their minds. Will even threw in the bit about how they'd run into that huge hammerhead shark the day before. Several divers nodded upon hearing this news. They, too, had recently seen some big sharks lurking just outside the reef.

The search went on throughout the afternoon and into the evening. The network of caves was vast. The divers combed the area slowly, meticulously. It became clear early on that the twin brother must have wandered off underwater, gotten lost, run out of air, and drowned. No other explanation was really possible. The divers were simply down there looking for the body, hoping to find it and bring it up for proper burial.

Needless to say, they did not find the body. As dusk fell, the rescue team gave up and headed back to town. Will, bereft, thanked them all for trying. Several divers assured him they would try again in the morning.

That night, unlike his brother, Will Hancock did not sleep like a baby. He barely slept at all.

John Hancock, playing the role of the presumed-dead Will Hancock, woke up at dawn not at all certain of his whereabouts. He instinctively took a look around for his brother. Then he remembered their scheme.

He climbed aboard a crowded and smoke-spewing bus bound for Villahermosa and points west. The bus never seemed to go over twenty miles an hour. In Catazajá, just west of the Rio San Pedro, the bus broke down. First the driver claimed it would be fixed in an hour, then in two hours, then not until the following morning.

John found a cheap hotel on the edge of town. The room was dirty and littered with dead cockroaches. Downstairs in the dusty dining room he ate a meal of rice and beans and cornbread. The food was tasteless and soggy. The lukewarm beer did not drive away his thirst.

So his second day of freedom was not such a spectacular success, but John didn't give a damn. His father had taught him to never explain and never complain; just keep pressing forward.

●　　　●　　　●

The whole next day divers searched for the missing Hancock. Will started to feel guilty about them giving up so much of their time.

"Forget it," said Rafe. "They got nothing better to do."

Will sighed. He wondered where his brother was and what he was doing.

Finally, late in the afternoon, the flotilla of small boats gave up the search. Will breathed a sigh of relief. He made a beeline for his room at the guest house, where he stayed in seclusion until the following morning.

In the morning John boarded an old diesel bus heading up the coast for Veracruz. The bus stopped at every cross in the road, but John barely noticed the slow pace. He felt now like he had nothing but time. He sat in the rear with a quart of beer and made friends with anyone who sat near him. He taught two teenage boys to say in slow but perfect English, "I want to live in the United States and become a fat and lazy millionaire."

He shared his beer with a rough-looking older man who told him in a fragmented mix of English and Spanish that Veracruz had the ugliest whores in the world, who were infected with a rare venereal disease that made a man's pecker rot and fall off.

On the third afternoon after his brother's disappearance, Will Hancock had to make a statement to two men who came out to Caye Caulker from Belize City. One of the men was a government bureaucrat, the other one some kind of law enforcement officer. Since Will was now technically John, he had to explain to the two officials, in some detail, the circumstances surrounding his own death. For the first few minutes he felt extremely awkward in such a role, but soon enough his superb story-telling abilities took over. He used his narrative skills to draw a vivid underwater picture for the two somber-faced men in their damp suits. He made sure he mentioned the shark.

The two men listened, nodded, and made a few notes. Sober and formal, neither expressed their condolences before, during, or after Will's statement. After they left, Will wondered aloud if they had believed his story.

"Absolutely they believe you," Rafe assured him. "You told it with emotion and confidence. Besides, those two fools no give a damn. Just bureaucratic bullshit. Forms to fill out. Another gringo drowns in the sea. So what? Who cares? That was good you tell them about the hammerhead. They put that in their report and no one ever wonders why the body was never found."

Will nodded. So that's how it was: People would assume he had been eaten by a shark. What a way to go.

He wanted off the island. He wanted to pack his bag and head for home that very minute. But he had to follow the plan. And the plan called for him to remain on Caye Caulker for another twenty-four hours. Just in case the corpse of his brother turned up. It would look weird if he fled too soon.

So what did Will do with the rest of the day? He pretty much holed up in his room at the Caye Caulker Guest House. Several times he took a look at the green passport lying over on the bureau. The passport with his brother's name inside. Every time Will opened it to take a look, John's face, the face so like his own, smiled back at him. The face did not make Will smile. Had leaving behind his own passport, he wondered, been a simple slip-up, or a premeditated plot?

Will was not sure he would ever have a clear answer.

John took his beer-drinking buddy's advice and stayed away from the whores in Veracruz. In fact, he decided to stay away from Veracruz altogether, and catch the next bus north for Tampico.

This proved propitious, because on that bus John met Felipe Alvarez. Felipe was a feisty little Mexican who claimed he had slipped illegally into the United States fifty-six times in one year without getting caught. Felipe also claimed he had a wife in Cuernavaca and another one across the border in San Antonio. He further claimed he had nine children and an almost-new Chrysler New Yorker that he kept up in San Antonio because it was too damn expensive to get parts for the car in Mexico.

John, himself an occasional teller of tall tales, did not believe or disbelieve Felipe's claims. But he did listen very closely when Felipe described, in some detail, exactly where, when, and how to slip across the Rio Grande without being detected by nasty, overzealous, gun-toting U.S. border guards.

Just before the bus pulled into Guadalupe, John asked Felipe about the possibility of procuring a firearm.

"Not a problem," Felipe told him. "We find you a little something."

"Nothing fancy," said John.

"Oh, no," replied Felipe. "Just something small and simple. Something to help clean up messy situations."

John smiled. "Exactly."

Will followed the plan to a T. Late in the morning on the fourth day following his own death, he packed his bags and paid off Rafe with five hundred in cash. He even gave him a fifty-dollar tip for a job well done.

Rafe smiled and stuffed the money in the pocket of his baggy shorts. "You two brothers have a good time," he said, "doing whatever it is you want to do with one dead and one alive. Stop by Caye Caulker sometime and say hey to Rafe."

"We definitely will," replied Will, while at the same time hoping to never lay eyes on the man again.

Hopes are good, but rarely enough. Rafe, their accomplice, was now part of their lives. Forever.

That evening Will checked into the Bliss Hotel on Water Street in Belize City. He had two shots of tequila before he called Zelda Cosgrove up in Cambridge. Over and over he reminded himself that he was John Hancock now, not Will.

Finally, on about the tenth ring, she picked up. "Yes?"

"Zelda?"

"Yes?" She sounded out of breath.

"It's . . ." Despite his reminders, Will almost said Will. "It's John." He kept his voice low and subdued. After all, he had recently lost his brother.

"John!" Zelda's voice perked right up. "How are you?"

"Okay, I guess. I was just about to hang up. I didn't think you were home."

"We just walked in the door. Dicky and I. Where are you? Back in town?"

"No," answered Will. "I'm still in Belize."

"I suppose you're calling to tell me that you and Will are sick of cold weather and testy Bostonians, so you're relocating to the tropics."

Will, as John, steeled himself. "Nothing so frivolous, I'm afraid."

"No?"

"We've had some trouble."

"What kind of trouble? Money trouble? If you have money troubles, honey, I suggest you call your publisher, Lee Fisher, not me. I'm just your advisor. A lowly professor of literature."

"It's not about money, Zelda. It's about . . ." Will almost said John. He had to be careful. Extremely careful. "It's about . . . Will."

"Don't tell me he's in love with some exotic Mayan princess?"

"No."

"What is it, John? You sound strange . . . not at all yourself."

"He's dead, Zelda. Will is dead." There, he said it.

"What? What do you mean, he's dead?"

Will recounted the story about the hammerhead and the underwater caves, just the way he and John had rehearsed it. "I couldn't find him," he said, his voice cracking, real tears streaming down his face. "He must have gotten lost . . . run out of air."

Zelda listened while standing there in her tiny kitchen.

For a brief moment, she thought John Hancock was playing one of his practical jokes; but no, she could hear the strains of grief in his voice.

"My God, John," she managed say after he had finished his tale. "I don't know what to say. I'm so sorry. This is horrible. Are you all right? What can I do? Would you like me to come down there? I could fly down first thing in the morning."

Will, playing John, assured Zelda he was doing reasonably well. He thanked her for offering to come, but said he intended to fly up to Houston the following afternoon, then on to Boston the day after that.

"I understand," said Zelda. "Let me know when you're coming in and I'll be there to pick you up at Logan."

Will did not want her picking him up, so he said, "I'll call you."

"Definitely do."

"I will."

A brief pause followed before Zelda asked, "What about Will's body?"

"What about it?"

"Will there be a problem getting his body back to the States? For proper burial?"

Will, as John, choked back the tears. "There won't be any burial, Zelda."

"Why not?"

Will did not answer, not right away. He felt his next line demanded a lengthy and dramatic pause. "Because," he said, "we haven't been able to find his body." Will sighed audibly. "We think Will must've been eaten by sharks. Hammerheads."

John crossed the Rio Grande under cover of darkness beneath an almost full moon frequently obscured by high, fast-moving clouds. He had his spare clothes, his wallet, and his brother's passport wrapped in his trusty plastic bag. Only that bag was now inside another bag which was inside another bag.

Another item of some interest occupied space inside those plastic bags. It lay snuggled in the crotch of John's wrinkled khakis: a .38 Saturday night special with two dozen rounds of ammunition, purchased from a friend of Felipe's for one hundred and twenty-five American dollars at a bodega in Guadelupe.

John, as Will, stepped into the Rio Grande on a chilly morning about an hour before dawn. "The best time," Felipe had told him. "The night shift is whipped and the day crew hasn't come on yet."

The crossing went reasonably well at first; the water barely rose above his knees. But about a third of the way across, the Rio Grande, known to those south of the border as the Rio Bravo, began to deepen. It reached over his knees and then up over his waist. Soon John found the water up around his chest, reaching for his neck. Moments later, he could not touch bottom. He started to swim. Clutching his plastic bags, he steered for America. Like his father before him, he was making a clandestine escape.

It did not take him long before he found Texas mud beneath his feet. Thick, slimy mud. He wanted nothing to do with that, so he kept swimming. He stroked until the water was only a few murky inches deep, then he stood and immediately sank into the soft bottom. He slogged up the riverbank in search of dry land. Twice he slipped and fell, covering himself both times from head to toe in the messy ooze.

By the time John Hancock climbed off that embankment, he had mud everywhere, even in his eyes and ears. And dawn was fast approaching. He could see orange light in the eastern sky. If the border patrol spotted him looking like this, they would know in a second he had just entered the United States under suspicious circumstances.

So what did John-as-Will do? He started moving north, away from the Rio Grande, just as fast as his muddy feet would carry him. He crossed some boggy farmland while the sun pushed above the horizon and crept into the blue morning sky. The mud coating his arms and legs and clothes began to dry. Little by little he brushed it off.

The sun was up high and warm by the time he reached blacktop. In the distance, off to his left, he spotted what looked like a small town. He headed that way.

Dreamland, Texas, had signs in English, a Texaco station, a doughnut shop, and not much else. John used the restroom at the Texaco to clean himself up, then he crossed the street and ate half a dozen doughnuts and drank two cups of black coffee. While finishing up his last creme-filled, a fuel truck pulled into the Texaco to top off the station's underground tanks. John paid his bill and strolled over to talk to the driver.

Half an hour later, John was out on the interstate, heading north for Houston in the high passenger seat of an eighteen-wheeler.

Will, as John, was also on his way to Houston. He flew out of Belize in the early afternoon and found himself at the Houston Intercontinental Airport a couple hours later. Palms sweaty, heart racing, he approached the customs officer. He felt nervous, jittery, and guilty as he handed over his brother's passport.

The officer flipped through the pages of the passport. He stopped for a moment to study the photograph. Then he looked up and glanced at Will. Will did his best to act cool and nonchalant, like his brother.

The customs officer dropped his eyes back to the passport. "Anything to declare, Mr. Hancock?"

Will was too busy concentrating on his coolness and nonchalance to hear what the officer said. "Excuse me?"

Instantly, the officer's eyes popped up and zeroed in. "Anything to declare?"

"Oh. No, sir. Nothing at all."

The customs officer kept his eyes fixed on Mr. Hancock for several seconds. A search might be in order. But the line was long, and getting longer. He took an irritable breath, stamped John Hancock's passport, and shouted, "Next!"

Will, safely back on U.S. soil, slipped away into the crowded terminal. He could feel the fear pumping through his bloodstream. But he'd made it, he'd gotten the job done, held up his end of the bargain.

He caught the shuttle bus over to the Airport Marriott and booked a room under his brother's name. He showered and shaved. He watched TV and ordered a hamburger from room service. And he waited. He waited for his brother to come, or at least to call.

While he waited, his thoughts wandered. They wandered all over his personal road map: to his mother and father and their horrible accident, to all the good times they'd had as a family, to all the money his father had made and that prick Frank Hagstrom had stolen, to Hagstrom living up in the Hancocks' beautiful home in the Hollywood Hills, to all the lying and cheating Hagstrom had done to him and his brother over the past six years.

Oh yes, Big Frank Hagstrom was heavily on Will Hancock's mind when a knock hit the door just after ten o'clock that night. Will jumped off the bed, raced across the room, and pulled open the door.

John stood there big as life, bigger even, a wide smile on his face. "Hey, bro. You made it."

The Hancock boys embraced, and then, for the next several hours, they went over virtually every second that had passed since separating off the coast of Mexico. There was much to tell. Those five and a half days had been, by far, the longest separation of their young lives.

Little did they know what lay ahead.

Just before John got to the part about crossing the Rio Grande, he pulled out the .38 special.

"What the hell is that for?" Will wanted to know.

"It's for our friend."

"Who's that?"

"Who do you think?"

"Big Frank?" Will asked quietly.

"Damn right."

"Jesus. We're going to shoot Frank?"

"Unless you have a better idea."

"I guess I hadn't really thought about the method."

"Well, I have. And I think it's best to shoot the son of a

bitch down like an old dog. Just break into the house late one night, steal a few things to make it look like a burglary, then shoot the fucker. Dead as a doornail."

"Sounds kind of brutal."

"It is brutal. No question about that."

"Do you think we have the guts to do it?"

John shrugged. "Excellent question, bro. In theory, it's easy as pie. In reality, I have no idea if I'd actually be able to pull the trigger."

Will nodded. "I know what you mean. I don't think I could do it."

"You're not gonna do it, bro," John assured him. "I'm gonna do it. After all, it was my idea. It's my responsibility. I want you to fly back to Boston, get yourself settled, put our alibi in place, deal with Zelda and Leland and everyone else. I'll pay Hagstrom a visit. I'll take that bastard out."

Will swallowed hard, thinking about his brother shooting Frank Hagstrom. "You're sure?"

John nodded. "Absolutely."

For an hour or more they discussed the situation. They discussed it well into the night. John would do it, but when would he do it? Right away? Or would it be better to wait a while? Put it off for a few weeks or a few months? Wait for the air over Will's *death* to clear?

Finally, well after one o'clock in the morning, exhausted from their travels and their long discourse, the Hancock boys turned off the light and said good night.

For maybe fifteen minutes they lay there in the darkness of that Houston hotel room on opposite sides of the king-size bed. All was silent except for the steady rhythm of their breathing.

Will broke the silence. "John?"

"Yeah?"

"Just one thing I need to ask you?"

"Go ahead."

"I hate to do it, but, well, it's been on my mind."

"Ask away."

"The way you handled that passport business back at the Caye Caulker Guest House?"

John, beginning to nod out, came wide awake now. He had been anticipating his brother's question for days, really since stepping out of Rafe's Whaler. "Yeah?"

"Did you do it on purpose?"

"Do what on purpose?" The question gave John a second to gather himself.

"You know, take mine and leave yours behind?"

John did not immediately answer. He did not want his reply to sound forced or rehearsed.

"Jesus, bro! Of course I didn't do it on purpose. You crazy? You know I'd never do something like that."

"Right," said Will, "I know." His voice sounded reassured. But anyone with the optical power to penetrate the darkness would have seen a face tormented by doubt and fear and suspicion.

ORPHANS

John and Will Hancock first met Frank Hagstrom when they flew out to California after their parents had perished in that freak auto accident on the San Diego Freeway. Frank actually picked the boys up at the airport and drove them to the glass-and-redwood house high up in the Hollywood Hills. That first night he even stayed in the house with them, treated them like his own sons. And in the morning he drove them to the memorial service at Gray's Funeral Home in Westwood. Sat with them while the boys struggled with tears shed in memory of their dear and suddenly departed mother and father.

The rest of the folks sitting quietly in those folding metal chairs were mostly Mexicans who spoke little or no English. They worked in William Hancock's umbrella factory out in Glendale. Only a few of them had green cards. Still, they had come to pay their respects to their boss, and also to maybe find out if the factory would stay open so they could keep their jobs. Sure, they were upset their boss and his wife had been beheaded, but, well, life rolls on. Those Mexicans, scraping by paycheck to paycheck, still had used-car payments to make and beans to put on the table and babies who needed shots against diphtheria and whooping cough.

Little did those Mexicans know, however, that the Hancock umbrella factory was preparing to move south to old Mexico. William Hancock had been planning the move for a year or more, when his Eldorado crashed out on the freeway. It had become far more profitable to make umbrellas down in Mexico and then import them to the rainy cities throughout the U.S. and Canada.

An outfit that made office furniture already had a contract to buy the factory in Glendale. But after William lost his head, Frank Hagstrom killed the contract. He sold the factory to a guy named Stanley from Hermosa Beach who wanted to tear it down and put up California's biggest tittie bar. Stanley paid cash. Frank put a significant amount of that cash straight into his own pocket. Cash that really belonged to Will and John Hancock.

After the memorial service Frank drove the two youngsters out to Santa Monica to the Southern California Crematorium. Seems in their last will and testament, William and Lenore had requested cremation. They found it absurd that perfectly good real estate should be gobbled up by a bunch of dead bodies in wooden boxes.

"When we pass away," they had told their close friend and family attorney, Mr. Frank Hagstrom, "have our boys toss our ashes into the aquamarine Pacific at sunset."

And so, late that afternoon, the boys ventured down to the Santa Monica pier toting two small brass urns. Quite a few people milled around on the pier waiting for the sun to go down. John and Will had a hard time finding some quiet space all to themselves. But finally they did, over behind an old abandoned custard stand.

They opened the urns and prepared to toss the ashes into the surf swirling around the dark pilings holding up the pier. Prayers fell from their lips, more tears from their eyes. The existence of God seemed a dubious thing indeed to anyone watching those two teenage boys trying to deal all by themselves with this traumatic episode in their young lives.

And then, in a demonstration of God's folly, just as the Hancock boys turned those urns over, a breeze kicked up off the Pacific and scattered most of those ashes back into their faces and across the pier. Frantically, the twins fell to their knees and commenced an all-out effort to sweep their parents's ashes into piles and cast them overboard.

The next morning they had an appointment with Mr. Hagstrom at Frank's posh offices on Wilshire Boulevard in Beverly Hills. Frank had an enormous corner office complete with massive teak desk and fancy leather furniture. His law degree from UCLA hung on the wall amidst photographs of local sports heroes and popular politicians. Frank was a big wheel in L.A. The practice of law had been good to Frank Hagstrom. Very good. Frank ran the show at Hagstrom, Hays, Bennett, Barlow & Lunt. He called the shots.

And make no mistake, Frank was a big man, tall and broad. In his late forties at that time, but still pretty fit, not more than eight or ten pounds overweight. He had been an athlete all his life, though recently he had fallen under the spell of golf, a leisure activity providing little or no exercise. The fancy private clubs where Frank drove and pitched and putted insisted the golfers ride the course in carts so as not to slow play. Tough to get the old ticker pumping behind the wheel of a golf cart.

Frank had a wife and three teenage daughters. He had been married for twenty-two years. The Hagstroms were, or so thought the outside world, a happy family. But the outside world rarely knows what's really going on behind closed doors. In this case, daily doses of emotional abuse, and even some occasional physical abuse.

Frank had many rich and famous clients. He also did pro bono work for the poor and downtrodden. He gave generously to a wide variety of charities. Every year he worked as a volunteer on the Rose Bowl parade. Frank was a model citizen.

Too bad he was also a liar, a swindler, and a cheat.

"So," Frank wanted to know after they all took their seats and settled down in his swanky office, "how did it go out in Santa Monica?" His tone rang solemn and sincere.

John and Will just kind of shrugged. They were feeling pretty low. Especially Will. The reality that his parents were actually dead and gone had finally reached the bottom of his gut. The Hancock boys were now orphans. And as orphans, they would have to run an agonizing gauntlet of emotion. Everything they would do, every decision they would make, every direction they would turn, would be shaped and influenced by this tragedy that had happened in a blurry instant out on the San Diego Freeway.

"Not very well," they told Mr. Hagstrom, whom they naturally trusted implicitly.

"No? What happened?"

They told him about the wind kicking up and the ashes blowing all over the place. Will, followed soon thereafter by John, began to cry.

Frank Hagstrom waited patiently for the boys to calm down. One side of his brain wanted to slap them into silence. The other side wanted to press them to his chest, give them solace. He did neither. He passed the time checking his schedule and handing out a few tissues.

"Now, boys," he said, "I know this is a tough time, but I have a few things to go over. I know nothing I can say here today will change what happened to your parents. But I can try to ease your burden."

Frank moved slowly about his office as he spoke. He made plenty of eye contact with both boys as he squeezed their shoulders reassuringly with his massive hands. The only thing that put a damper on Frank's performance was the absolute indistinguishability of William Hancock's offspring. They were identical in every way, right down to the arches in their eyebrows and the length of their fingernails. Frank had no idea which was which. He found the paradox most disconcerting. So what did he do? Like any good attorney worth his wingtips, Frank pushed his doubt aside and focused on the victory.

"First of all," he said, "I want you to know your father

and I were like brothers. He was a fine man: decent and hardworking. One of the most honest men I've ever known. Your father would always go the extra mile to help a friend. Which is exactly what I intend to do for his boys. So any time either of you needs anything, anything at all, just pick up the phone and call me, and it'll be done. I'm here for you guys. Count on it.

"Second, I don't want you worrying about money. I'm going to give you some cash until we get everything straightened out. This may take some time because of the . . . well, because of the suddenness of this whole terrible situation. But believe me, it's better to take a little extra time now and make sure everything gets done in a thorough and proper manner.

"I understand your room, board, and tuition have been paid in full for the rest of the school year. For next year, that should not be a problem either. As for college, well, your father told me you both had your eyes on Harvard. I believe he even said something about early admission due to the excellence of your academic record. Well done.

"I think we can feel confident that this whole mess will be resolved long before any college tuition moneys are due."

"What whole mess?" John wanted to know.

"Well, just the whole complexity of your parents' estate."

John, glum, nodded. So did Will.

"As your parents' attorney, as well as their executor, it is my responsibility to make sure their property is properly dispersed."

"Do you think there will be a problem?" Will asked.

"It must be spelled out in our father's will," added John.

A couple of bright boys, thought Frank. Ever since he'd known William Hancock, he had been hearing about his twin sons and their overachievements in academics and athletics. Frank had not expected this little embezzlement to be a walk in the park.

"Actually, John—You are John, right?"

John and Will glanced at one another. The briefest of smiles, their first in several days, passed between them. "I'm Will, He's John."

"Sorry. It's difficult to tell."

"We know."

Frank caught a note of pride in this announcement. Clearly, these two were a team. There would be no dividing and conquering. Frank would have to tread lightly.

"The truth is," the attorney continued, "your father's last will and testament was in rather a state of flux at the unfortunate time of his . . . at the time of his accident. He—"

"State of flux?"

Frank had no idea why he had used the expression. It certainly was not a legal term. He hated to admit it, but these twins, perfect goddamn mirror images of one another, had *him* in a state of flux.

"Yes, well, his will had been going through some changes. Nothing major, you understand. Nothing involving the bulk of his estate, which, upon his death, was set up to go directly to your mother. But I'm afraid it gets a bit tricky here because your mother never really drew up a last will and testament."

"So what does that mean? What'll happen?"

These kinds of questions always made Frank feel better. He just loved it when he knew the answers and others didn't. Control was one of his favorite things in life.

"Hopefully, nothing will happen. Your father's will clearly states the bulk of his estate should pass to the two of you in the event he outlives your mother. Since there are no other children, I feel confident the court will see its way clear to disperse the assets."

"I don't really want to talk about this anymore," said John. All this talk of death and money and last wills and testaments was beginning to take its toll.

"Me, neither," said Will.

"I understand completely," said Frank Hagstrom. "There'll be time later to cover some of these financial matters. I just wanted to reassure you that everything is under control. The next few months will undoubtedly be tough for both of you, but I think if you go back to school, work hard, prepare for the future, you will get through this tragedy together. And remember," Frank added, "you will always have each other."

The boys liked the sound of that. They stood, shook hands with kindly Mr. Hagstrom, thanked him for his help, and departed.

Outside on the sidewalk, waiting for a taxi to haul them back up to the house in the Hollywood Hills, Will turned to John and said, "Mr. Hagstrom seems like a decent guy."

"Yeah."

"Do you think we can trust him?"

"Dad did."

"That's true."

"I don't think he'd cheat us."

"No way. He was Dad's buddy. Besides, Mom and Dad are gone. No lawyer would cheat two kids whose parents just got decapitated in a car crash."

"I agree. He'll do right by us."

"I think so. It's all written down on paper anyway."

"Exactly. It's pretty tough to change a will."

Not that tough, sonny boys.

So that school year passed. And soon enough another one came. Hagstrom paid their room, board, and tuition, *after* the boys signed a note saying they would pay the money back once the estate was settled. They had no idea why the estate was not yet settled, but they had plenty of other things to think about. Like their applications to Harvard for the following fall. Tops in their class, they had no trouble gaining acceptance.

Then, one day in the spring of '77, just a month before graduation, a letter arrived from the bursar's office at Harvard. The letter contained various information concerning their enrollment the following September. It also contained a bill for their room, board, and tuition: $7,665.00. Each. A grand total of $15,330.

"How are we going to pay for this?"

"I have no idea. We better call Mr. Hagstrom."

They called Frank at his office. After some delay, they were told Mr. Hagstrom was in court and could not be reached. His secretary assured them he would return their call later that same day. He didn't call. They had to call back. Several times. Most of a week passed before they finally got the attorney on the phone.

"John? Or is this Will? Sorry about the delay. I've had an incredibly full plate the last few days. In and out of court more times than I can count. What can I do you for?"

"Well," answered Will, "we were kind of wondering how things were going with our parents' estate. It's been a really long time. Like a year and a half."

"That's not really all that long," replied Frank. "Settling wills takes time and plenty of patience. Too much time and patience, if you ask me. Sometimes I think the courts fail to realize that real people with real problems live behind the mountains of paperwork. But I can assure you, son, I'm doing everything I can."

Will had no reason not to believe him. "I know, but we just received this bill."

"What bill? Not from me." Frank sounded politely defensive.

"No. From Harvard."

"Harvard University?"

"Right. They're looking for their money for next year."

Frank did not immediately respond. His lawyerly brain raced through a few facts, a few different scenarios. "Okay, listen. Send me the bill. I'll take care of it."

"But—"

"But nothing. I told you boys not to worry about anything."

The boys talked it over after Will hung up the phone. John felt confident Hagstrom would pay the bill.

Will wasn't so sure. "What if he doesn't?"

"He said he would."

"But what if he doesn't?"

"Jesus, bro, you have to learn to relax."

Two weeks later, while John was taking a shower, Will, worried about their college tuition, called the bursar's office up in Cambridge. Sure enough, Frank Hagstrom had paid the bill, both bills, on time and in full.

That summer, after graduation, the boys flew out to California. They did not really know where else to go. At least the house up on Edwin Drive in the Hollywood Hills was a place to stay. And there was a car to drive. At least they thought they had a car to drive. But when they went out into the garage, they found nothing but a few garden tools and an oil stain on the floor where the old T-bird used to sit. The 1959 Ford Thunderbird: their father's pride and joy.

The boys stood there, dumbfounded. They could not believe the car was gone.

"Where is it?"

"I don't know. You think somebody stole it?"

"It doesn't look like anyone broke in."

"Maybe we should call the cops."

"Let's call Mr. Hagstrom first. Maybe he knows something."

Frank knew all about the T-bird. Frank had the T-bird parked downstairs in the parking garage under his office. "Oh, yeah, I own that little baby now."

"*You* own it?"

"That's right. I drive it to the office every other day. It takes turns with my sixty-three 'Vette."

"But how did—"

"Hey, let me apologize, I should have told you. It just slipped my mind. Your old man and I had an agreement. If I went first, he got the 'Vette. If he went first, I got the T-bird. It's all down on paper, legal as can be, if you want to see it."

"No," said Will, satisfied but disappointed, "we don't

need to see it. But we're out here for the summer. How are
we supposed to get around?"

"Let me make some calls," the attorney told Will. "I
think I have something you boys might be able to use."

"That son of a bitch," John said when he heard the
news. "Maybe it's time we stopped trusting the bastard."

By the end of the day the boys were tooling around L.A. in
a '68 VW Beetle with AM radio and convertible top. Not
exactly a '59 T-bird, but wheels nevertheless. Frank gave
them money for gas, for groceries, for fun.

John and Will spent most of the summer working out.
They both wanted starting berths on Harvard's freshmen
football team. They went to bed early, lifted weights, rode
their bikes for miles through the Hollywood Hills, and
worked out on the practice fields down at UCLA. John
hoped to play quarterback. Will wanted to play end and
catch John's passes.

In late August, a few days before heading back east,
they received a call from Frank Hagstrom. He wanted to
know if they could come down to his office in the morning.
"I have some news about the estate."

The boys, of course, figured Hagstrom finally had everything settled. They figured they had a tidy sum of money
coming their way. They figured their father must've been
worth at least a couple million dollars. Maybe more. They
really had no idea. But even after legal fees and inheritance
taxes, they would surely wind up with enough cash to get
them through college and maybe even graduate school.
Mom had hoped they would become doctors, Dad engi-
neers or lawyers.

"So, boys," Frank Hagstrom wanted to know, "have a
good summer?"

They nodded from their leather chairs in front of Big
Frank's big teak desk.

Frank looked at them closely. "So tell me something,"
he asked, "how the hell do people tell you two apart?"

The Hancock boys chuckled.

Exactly what Frank wanted them to do. Frank the master manipulator. He'd studied and perfected the art of putting people at ease, getting people to drop their guard.

"Identical twins. You two must pull some pretty fancy stunts."

"Not us," said John.

"We're good boys," said Will.

Frank nodded conspiratorially, then leaned across his desk. "Look, guys, I need to be straight with you. This is no time for me to pull any punches. I hate packing you off to college this way, but, well, it can't be helped. If we're going to move forward, we have to do it now."

"What's the problem?" John wanted to know.

Frank rubbed his eyes, rubbed his chin, rubbed his eyes again. He looked truly concerned.

"What's the problem?" he asked rhetorically. "Now that, son, is an excellent question. And I suppose the answer, in a single word, would be debt. D-E-B-T." Frank spelled out the word as he pushed back his chair. He stirred his large body into motion and began to pace back and forth across his spacious corner office overlooking Beverly Hills and the rolling contours of the Los Angeles Country Club. "Your father and mother, God rest their souls, had too much debt."

"Too much debt!" John snapped. "No way. Our father was the most conservative guy in the country. He never borrowed money. How could he have been in debt?"

Frank shrugged. "Your father was a businessman. And a damn good one. I feel sure, had he lived, he would have worked his way out of this jam and gone on to bigger and better things."

"What jam? What are you talking about?"

"I assume you two knew about the Mexican deal."

The Hancock boys glanced at one another. "Mexican deal?" John muttered. "We don't know anything about any Mexican deal."

Frank sighed and shook his head. He looked sincerely troubled, even though inside he was thoroughly enjoying himself. "Jesus, where to start? . . . Look, your old man was ambitious. He wanted to be rich."

"He was rich."

"Rich is a relative term. In many places across America, your father would have been the richest guy in town. But here, in L.A., he was just another guy with money. Your father didn't want just part of the pie, he wanted the whole damn thing."

"We knew," said Will, "that he was expanding his business."

"Expanding like crazy," replied Hagstrom. "Probably expanding faster than he should have. It takes time, guts, energy, and plenty of luck to make the kind of money your father wanted to make. And unfortunately, your old man was dealing with a string of bad economic luck when his Cadillac plowed into the back of that tractor trailer."

They all took a moment to remember.

Then, "What kind of bad economic luck are we talking about here?" demanded John. "Business was great. At least that's what Dad always told us."

Hagstrom shrugged. "What can I say? I've had a good look at the books. It's there, plain as day: The debt was piling up fast. Your father was moving his entire manufacturing operation down to Mexico. Everything: umbrellas, gloves, hats, boots, scarves, the whole shebang. This move took money, big money. A lot of people, including me, advised him against it. But he believed, in the long haul, it would make him millions. And maybe it would have. But in the short run it meant a hell of a lot more cash flowing out than flowing in. Your father may have been a conservative guy, but he took a gamble and lost. At the time of his death, he had outstanding loans totaling more than two million dollars."

The boys needed a couple minutes for this news to settle. While they mulled it over, Big Frank returned to his desk. He had them down, but he definitely didn't want them out. Not yet. Too early for that. He knew once people felt like they'd hit the bottom of the barrel, like they had nothing to lose, they often became unpredictable.

The time had come for a whiff of good news. "It may not be as bad as it looks," Frank told them. "I've had someone working on this around the clock all summer long. He thinks the assets still might outweigh the liabilities."

The boys started breathing again. "When will we know?"

"I'm afraid it's going to take time."

"How much time?"

"Hard to say. Several months, at least. Not only are we dealing with an extremely complex estate, but also with a foreign government that may or may not be cooperative."

"Mexico?"

"Exactly. A large chunk of the cash your father borrowed was from a government-owned Mexican bank. It was a special loan offered at low interest in an effort to lure U.S. companies south of the border. This will undoubtedly complicate matters. But trust me," Frank added quickly, "I'm on top of it."

"That's good, Mr. Hagstrom," said John, his tone not revealing his growing uncertainty. "But what'll we do till this whole mess gets settled? Neither of us has any money, and we start college in less than a week."

"One way or another, we'll work this out. I'm sending you back east with a couple thousand dollars each. And if you boys need more, I want you to call me. Don't hesitate to call me."

Will did not look well. No color at all in his face. "But you definitely think things will work out? I mean, there'll be something left? For college, and . . ."

"Absolutely." Frank loved that word: absolutely. It never failed to calm his clients.

Will, still trusting, nodded.

"Now, before you go," Frank added, his mind hyperfocused, "I just need the two of you to sign a few papers. Take as long as you like to read them over. There's nothing very exciting, but have a look anyway. Basically you're empowering me to act in your behalf. I've been doing that all along, but I think this should help expedite matters."

The boys definitely wanted to expedite matters. And so, after barely glancing at the lengthy legal documents before them, they signed, in ink, wherever Big Frank's thick index finger pointed.

PART THREE
JUNE 8, 1999

TUESDAY MORNING ROUNDUP

Will Hancock rises early this morning, before dawn, in his room at the Hotel Peace and Plenty on the small Bahamian island of Exuma. Not because he wants to, but because throughout the night Frank Hagstrom kept wandering around in his dreams. In most of these dreams Frank hung dead from the ceiling, but every so often the attorney popped up alive and well and spreading his filthy lies with his velvety-smooth legal tongue. Will has done his best over the years to believe the bastard deserved what he got, but often at night pangs of conscience still make war upon his slumber.

So he rises, and just after first light, Will pays a local fisherman fifty bucks to run him across the bay to Stocking Island, a slender spit of land shaped like a fishhook. They land at a long wooden dock on the island's western shore. Will grabs his fishing gear and sets off along a narrow path made of crushed coral and sand. The path emerges onto a flat and deserted beach. Dead ahead, the sun, huge and orange, rises out of the calm Atlantic. Will looks up and down the long stretch of white sand. He sees no one, not a soul. He knows, at least for the next few hours, it will just be him. And the bonefish.

Which suits Will just fine. He prefers solitude. Unlike his brother, he is not a very gregarious fellow. Often when playing the role of John Hancock, Will has no choice but to take on the demeanor of Mr. Congeniality. This role does not come naturally. Of course, after all these years without a truly grounded identity, Will does not really know what comes naturally. He is a man grappling daily with his emotions and mannerisms. Like at home. He knows his brother never yells at the kids, never cuffs them no matter what they do wrong or how belligerent they become. Will, on the other hand, believes in discipline. He thinks a little corporal punishment is good for the boys. But he has to be careful. He has to play by John's rules. Everything has to be by John's rules.

Will sighs. He doesn't feel like thinking about all this crap. Not right now. Not out on this beautiful stretch of beach with the bonefish biting. Will knows he only has the morning to fish. Originally, he had planned on staying in the Bahamas until Thursday or Friday, but last night, unable to sleep, he decided to return to the States late this afternoon. By tonight he will be back up in Massachusetts, out at the Hancock hideaway in the Berkshires. There are some changes he has been wanting to make, and the time has come to make them.

Brother John begins to stir. But without really too much on his mind other than his boys. In the predawn gloom he makes his way across the bedroom and along the hallway without turning on any lights. After living in the town house for almost seven years, he knows the way even with his eyes closed.

He looks in on John junior and little Willy. Both boys sleep peacefully. John smiles and heads back to bed. He thinks about giving his wife a call. He misses her and wishes she was right now beside him between the sheets.

He checks the clock beside the bed. Just after five. That would make it ten in London. Ten or eleven in Paris. Clara might be up. But probably not. Better to wait. To call later.

That settled, John rolls onto his side, fluffs up his pillow, and searches for a little more slumber.

Clara would not have answered even had Hancock called. She has both her cell phone and her Ritz hotel room phone turned off. She went to bed around one-thirty without the slightest interest in getting up before noon.

After returning from the health club she showered and washed her hair, then lay in bed reading a novel until her eyes grew heavy. Clara reads all of Hancock's novels, but she prefers romance. The light and airy stuff with plenty of passion, where everything works out for the heroine in the end. Hancock's books are dark and spooky. If she reads them late at night she sometimes has trouble sleeping.

Who else stirs at this early morning hour? Rafe? No way. Rafe is sound asleep in his Belize City hotel room. The same cheap, dirty hotel on Cockburn Street where the Hancock boys stayed when they first arrived in Belize way back on Christmas Day in '82.

Rafe came over from Caye Caulker last night so he would be sure to make his plane bound for Houston, gateway to the U.S.A. Bag of coke stowed safely in his duffel, he has a wake-up call coming in at eight o'clock.

And what about Babe? Where's Ms. Overton resting her head at this cool, dark hour? Cross-country Greyhounds make pretty good time in the middle of the night. Every few hours they stop to refuel and take on a new driver, but otherwise they just keep pushing down the highway.

Babe's about fifty miles west of Oklahoma City now. The steady whine of rubber on asphalt and the swaying of that big bus on its soft chassis has made it easy for her to sleep. Only a couple of things are causing Babe any discomfort at all. The first thing is that cold, black, snub-nose pistol buried in the bottom of her handbag. It's pressing against her hip, and every so often she comes half awake to rearrange herself in an effort to make the dull, distant ache go away.

The other thing causing her some discomfort of a mental nature would be that paperback novel resting on the empty seat beside her. She purchased the mass-market psycho thriller at a magazine stand outside of Amarillo, Texas. The cover shows a medieval fighting ax dripping with blood. Above the ax, in bloodred block letters, the title: **REVENGE**. Below the ax, also in bloodred letters, the author: **JOHN HANCOCK**. Though actually, assumed-deceased coauthor Will Hancock dreamed up the title. And a good deal of the plot. Published back in '92, it became their second best-seller.

The novel has been causing Babe some discomfort due to the nature of its narrative. That being the story of a crooked lawyer who screws a woman out of a sizable inheritance after her well-heeled husband dies at the helm of his private jet. The widow winds up freaking out, torturing the attorney with her late husband's collection of medieval weaponry, and ultimately killing him in a most hideous fashion. But Babe hasn't gotten that far yet. She's only up to page forty-seven.

And what about Babe's therapist back in L.A.? Gerdy MacDaniel? Is Gerdy up? Of course she's up. Dealing with a patient. A neurotic, anorexic, female starlet we've all seen many times up on the Big Screen. The once sweet young lass is now bitching and moaning about everything from exploitation of the Dali Lama to the crappy syrup they served at breakfast while on location making her latest period pic, *Ravage,* based rather loosely on Emily Jane Brontë's *Wuthering Heights*. In the film the actress has a nude scene with Heathcliff, but the director demanded a body double due to the protruding ribs and practically concave chest of his female lead. The director feared audiences would think Heathcliff was making love to a corpse.

Gerdy hides a yawn. The starlet bores Gerdy to tears.

Several hours ago, while dozing between patients, Gerdy thought about Babe. Late yesterday afternoon Babe's roommate, Mary Ann, called and asked if Babe had been in recently to see the good doctor. Gerdy quickly realized that Babe had never gone home after their session early Sunday morning. So, just before the anorexic actress arrived, Gerdy called Babe's answering machine and left a message. Asked Babe to please call back.

Gerdy is worried about Babe, worried the poor, distraught woman might do something stupid. People, Gerdy well knows, especially people living and suffering in the past, reach the breaking point all the time.

Leland Fisher and his lovely bride Hillary are sound asleep in their California king in their Back Bay digs, a Super Slumber Machine piping the constant strains of breaking waves into their plush bedchamber. Not so many hours ago Leland and Hillary had sex. The sex did not last very long, but it gave both of them some small amount of solace and satisfaction.

After the sex, Hillary told Leland it would be nice to get away for a few days.

Leland, suspicious, but satiated, asked, "Where do you want to go?"

"Oh, I don't know," answered Hillary. "What about New York? We could get a suite at the Ambassador, see a show, do some shopping."

And get the hell away from Hancock for a while, thought Leland. "New York, sure. I have some things to do at the office tomorrow, but we could take the train down on Wednesday."

Hillary gave her hubby a squeeze. "I'll make the arrangements."

Al-the-Gumshoe Brown lies in bed reading by the dim glow of his Itty Bitty book light. The book is a large, heavy volume containing many of Edward Weston's most famous black-and-white photographs. As a young man, Al had dreams of being another Weston or Ansel Adams or Walker Evans. But one day he found himself following Michael Jackson into the men's room at Kennedy Airport and snapping a photo of Mike while the singer-songwriter relieved himself. Right then and there Al decided to let his dreams of glory die a quiet death.

Beside him, his wife sleeps peacefully. She has rarely had a bad night's sleep in her entire life.

Not too many folks out there who can say that.

Dicky Cosgrove has not gone to bed yet. Sometimes he thinks he may never go to bed again. What good, he asks himself, is sleep? Sleep is for the weak and the infirm.

The less he sleeps, and the further he strays from Doctor Dope's plethora of psycho meds, the crazier Mad Dicky gets. Right now, at five o'clock in the morning, he wanders through Boston's not-exactly-safe-even-in-broad-daylight South End looking for someone, anyone, to sell him a rifle or a revolver or any variety of firearm at all. Anything that will shoot bullets and make holes in the Hancocks.

Last evening, sitting there at his desk in the Boston Public Library, Dicky made his decision: He would shoot the Hancock boys. Shoot them both. Dead.

Only trouble is, he needs a gun. Has to have a gun. Can't do it without a gun. But a gun's not real easy to get. Especially in the Commonwealth of Massachusetts, a state with some of the toughest gun laws in the country. And a good thing, too, because in this case, those laws might just save a few lives. Maybe.

Look at him. Down on East Newton Street. Just cruising along the cracked sidewalk asking every pitiful drunk and homeless derelict he sees if they have any guns they want to sell. Panhandling for weapons. Unreal.

Too bad he smells so bad and acts so weird that even the winos and whackos run for cover when he approaches.

"Goddamn motherfucking son of an old bitch!" Dicky shouts right out on the corner of Newton and Washington.

"I need a gun! I'm an American! I have the right to bear arms!"

But nobody, not even the black dude with the goatee and the gold teeth who runs the show here on Franklin Square, will sell this lunatic a gun. The black dude, known locally as Moses, has immediate access to it all: heroin, coke, speed, Magnums, Colts, AK-47's, hand grenades, even land mines. You name it, Moses can get it. They call him Moses because in this neighborhood, he wrote, and enforces, the Two Commandments: 1) Ain't nuthin' goin' down 'less Moses say it go down; and 2) Moses take a fifty-percent slice of everything, repeat that, everything that go down.

Moses has been watching this "Crazy White Fucker" for half an hour or so through a pair of night-vision goggles. Finally he says to his lieutenant, Stick, "Stick, get that sumbitch outta the 'hood. That Crazy White Fucker gonna be bringin' the heat 'round here wit' all his shit-ass screamin' and carryin' on."

Stick, six feet four inches, maybe a hundred forty pounds when he's packing, nods and goes into action without muttering a word. He always do exactly what Moses tell him to do.

Stick and a couple of other brothers roll up to Dicky in Stick's big Lincoln, load Dicky into the back seat, and smack him around a little. Nothing too rough. Just enough to get his attention, keep him quiet. Then they drive him out to suburban Arlington, where they slow down to ten, maybe fifteen miles per hour and push Dicky out the door.

Dicky, cursing their grandmothers and kicking up a storm, rolls and bounces and finally comes to rest against a stop sign.

DICKY & ZELDA

Dicky Cosgrove had a couple of tough childhood breaks, no question about that. His mother died in a freak accident before Dicky turned three. A wild and free-spirited young woman, Meg Carter-Cosgrove relished reckless pursuits. After giving birth to her second child, she took up skydiving, claiming the excitement of it made her feel more alive than sex. Well, one spectacular spring afternoon she jumped out of an airplane and headed for earth. Halfway down she pulled on the cord to open her parachute, but the chute got tangled and failed to deploy. Meg landed in a Vermont cornfield traveling in excess of one hundred and fifty miles per hour.

Bob Cosgrove, Dicky's dad, took his wife's death hard. She was the love of his life, the fuel that kept his engine running. He turned cold and depressed and distant after her death.

Dicky's upbringing was more or less left up to his big sister Zelda. Barely a teenager at the time, Zelda did the best she could, but for a few years after Mom's death, she couldn't keep old Bob from smacking little Dicky whenever the youngster started crying or whining for his mommy. Bob frequently gave Dicky the back of his hand,

and once in a while his full fist, more times, in fact, than anyone in that family would care to admit or remember. No D.Y.F.S. (Division of Youth and Family Services) around in those days to protect the children, so Dicky took his wallops without the world ever knowing.

Eventually Bob worked through his grief, met a new woman, and got on with his life. But all this happened a little late for little Dicky. The damage had been done.

So a skewed genetic blueprint, some bad chemistry, and a few bad boyhood breaks left Dicky with a big brain but a twisted psyche. He had a superhigh IQ, capable of figuring out highly complex mathematical problems.

Too bad he could never quite get to the root of his emotional difficulties.

Sister Zelda had a few problems of her own. Zelda, by the way, was not her given name. Gretchen, her parents had named her, in loving memory of Grandma Cosgrove. But soon after her mother's precipitous demise, Gretchen read *The Great Gatsby,* and everything else F. Scott scribbled. The teenager soon had herself immersed in a full-blown Fitzgerald fantasy. To the point where she insisted people call her Zelda, the name of F. Scott's pretty blond bride.

When she turned eighteen, Gretchen had her name legally changed to Zelda. And at the time of her death a decade and a half later, Ms. Cosgrove was still totally absorbed with Scott and Zelda Fitzgerald. All through her twenties and into her thirties she wore her bleach-blond hair in one of those Roaring Twenties styles: short, like a boy's. She spoke in an affected manner, smoked her cigarettes through long plastic filters, and never uttered a word unless it qualified as one of the world's ten wittiest remarks.

But despite these eccentricities, Zelda was brilliant, as brilliant as her brother Dicky. Her brilliance swept through the world of language, whereas Dicky excelled with numbers and equations.

Had Zelda possessed a flair for stringing words together

on paper, she might well have gone on to write extraordinary novels. But Zelda was a bit too linear. She was, from
an early age, destined for academia. She had read, at least
twice, virtually every novel of any import that had ever
been published. And she could discuss those novels with
wit and intelligence and insight. To debate, say, the narrative structure of *Beowulf* or the Freudian overtones of *Ma-
dame Bovary* or the psychological impetus of *Lolita* with
Zelda Cosgrove was, at best, nerve-racking, and, at worst,
intellectually debilitating. Zelda could pull plots, characters, settings, major and minor themes, out of her head
from every relevant work of literature from *Canterbury
Tales* to *Catch 22.*

She was just twenty-eight years old when the Hancock
boys made her acquaintance as freshmen at Harvard. At
that time she already had her master's from the University
of Vermont and her Ph.D. from Columbia. Tenure at Crimson U. was her next objective.

HARVARD

The Hancock boys were just seventeen when they arrived at Harvard in the fall of '77. They needed a couple months to get themselves adjusted; the sheer size of the university at first seemed daunting, almost intimidating. Plus it was *Harvard*. The mere utterance of the word spawned images of Thoreau and Emerson, T.S. Eliot and Oliver Wendell Holmes, Teddy Roosevelt, FDR, and JFK. The place was hallowed ground. They walked around Harvard Yard those first weeks with their mouths open and their eyes wide.

Then, right around Halloween, through no effort of their own, word began to spread that the Hancock twins living over in Lionel Hall were direct descendants of that famous Harvard grad and prominent signer of the Declaration of Independence, John Hancock. This rumor brought the boys instant rank and recognition. They became campus celebrities. Suddenly their classmates were looking at them with awe. More than once they heard the whispers, "See those guys? Those are the Hancocks. They're, like, the great-great-great-great-grandkids of John Hancock."

Their efforts to squelch this familial connection proved futile. In fact, it only increased their status as Very Important Harvardites. By denying the connection, the boys showed their modesty and good breeding. And at Harvard, good breeding, i.e., blue-blooded Protestantism, was, despite the denials, a much sought-after designation.

The freshman football coach decided to use them on defense as cornerbacks because of their speed and agility. Too bad the frosh teams at Princeton and Brown and Yale rarely threw the football. Four offensive plays out of five, these other Ivy League schools ran the ball, usually straight up the middle or off tackle. This dull and conservative play-calling precisely mirrored the schools from which they came: Never take chances, hold onto the ball, work the clock, stick to the middle of the field. The Hancock boys, out on the periphery, guarding the corners, saw very little action. By the end of the season they were bored stiff.

Soon thereafter, they discovered drama. The Hancock boys took to acting like birds to flight. They had, after all, been acting all their lives, impersonating one another practically since their days in the womb. Now, suddenly, they had the opportunity to play a wide variety of roles in a wide variety of plays. John and Will performed in several of the classics: as Edgar and Edmund in *King Lear,* as Oliver and Orlando in *As You Like It,* as Jack Worthing and Algernon Moncrieff in *The Importance of Being Earnest.* They traded these roles back and forth, sometimes even between acts. In Act One, John would play Edgar and Will would play Edmund. In Act Two they would trade places, reverse roles. No one ever noticed.

At least they thought no one noticed. But then one evening, after a wild and woolly performance of *Death of a Salesman,* Zelda Cosgrove came backstage to congratulate the boys on a job well done. Zelda taught John and Will that semester in a creative writing course focusing on the short story. From the first day of class she had been intrigued by the pair's sameness, by their perfect symmetry, and by her observation that they seemed utterly inseparable. She had kept a close eye on them ever since.

"The Hancock brothers as the Loman brothers," she drawled, her voice low and husky, an as yet unlit cigarette in its long plastic holder perched between the thumb and index finger of her right hand. "How perfectly quaint." Zelda paused for one of the boys to offer her a light. Too bad neither of them had a match. They did not smoke. But from that day on they both kept a pack of matches tucked away in their wallets.

The boys' infatuation with Zelda had started back at freshmen orientation. Zelda had been on hand to chat up the English department. So as soon as possible the boys took her course in creative writing, not because they had any real interest in creative writing, but because they had a keen interest in Zelda. Her pale and powdery good looks, her powerful feminine mystique, her sexuality, her cocky and confident demeanor—all of these components made their teenage blood boil. And now, here she was, backstage, complimenting them on their performance.

"So," asked John, "you liked the play?"

"Not particularly," answered Zelda. "I find Miller unbearably morose, his primary characters dreary, and his dialogue watery and insipid. Of course, it is the greatest play of the twentieth century."

A chimp could have picked up on her sarcasm.

The boys, barely able to hold in their drool, managed uncertain chuckles.

"But," she added, "I loved the two of you."

"You did?" Like a couple of puppies begging for a pat on the head.

"Oh, yes. Especially the way you took turns with the far juicier role of brother Biff."

The boys exchanged the briefest of glances. "Say what?"

"I found your reversals so . . . Oh, I don't know . . ." Zelda continued to swing her unlit cigarette around in the air, ". . . so, so subtle and amusing. And, of course, so perfectly unselfish."

The Hancock boys did not know what to do, not a notion what to say. Should they say nothing? Should they offer denials? Pretend they had no idea what she was talking about?

Quite a rambunctious brouhaha engulfed the backstage area. Actors and their entourages bustled about, laughing and discussing the performance. The boys, unable to speak, hoped no one had overheard Zelda's remarks.

No one had heard a word, but Zelda had more to say.

"Unselfish," she explained, as though the boys had asked, "because obviously one of you, which one I have no idea, was originally cast to play Biff. But whoever that was made the decision to share the role with his twin brother. Or perhaps it was not a decision at all. Perhaps the two of you share everything. Hmm?"

Zelda waited for a reply, her huge green eyes easily controlling the Hancock boys.

John finally unhinged his jaw. "Ms. Cosgrove," he muttered, "I can assure you, we never—"

Zelda laughed right in his face. "Save it, Hancock. Your secret is safe with me."

"Secret?"

"Oh, I love a good secret," she assured them. "I adore secrets. Secrets make our lives worth living. What fun would it be without a few secrets? And, anyway, I came here tonight looking for some insights. And I certainly found some."

"Insights?"

"Into your writing."

"Our writing?"

"Ever since you handed in your first stories at the beginning of the semester, I've wondered about them. I wondered if they were solo efforts or collaborations. I see now they are most certainly collaborations. It is undoubtedly this duality that makes the narratives so dense and magical and entertaining. Tell me, do the two of you do everything together? Do you play together? Shower together? Shave together? Shit together? Even fuck together? Or do you take turns fucking the same woman? While, of course, leading the poor girl to believe she's fucking only one of the Hancock boys. Women, as you may or may not yet know, love sole proprietorships."

Then, the Hancock boys properly shocked, Zelda

smiled, swirled around, and sashayed off in search of someone to light her smoke.

John and Will, bedazzled and sexually aroused, watched her slip away into the crowd. Quite a lot of time passed before they spoke.

Soon after Zelda's backstage appearance, the Hancock boys decided to ask Ms. Cosgrove if she would be their academic advisor. Both John and Will claimed it had to do with her keen interest in their academic careers, but in truth, both boys were smitten with the stylish, cocky, and ravishing Ms. Zelda.

Their first advisor at Crimson U. was a scratchy old gent named Richard "Hey, call me Rick" Whorlman. Rick had been teaching English lit at Harvard since the days of Milton and Dryden, and try though Rick did to stay cool and current, he was bald and boring and had halitosis bad enough to make even students with heavy head colds recoil in disgust. He also had the nervous habit of asking the boys every time he saw them when they intended to declare a major, what that major might be, and precisely what they intended to do with the rest of their lives.

Specificity, however, was a suit the Hancock boys did not wear well. And never would. They wanted to do a dozen different things, follow a hundred divergent paths. So what did they tell Rick Whorlman, Ph.D.? They told him nothing at all; they ran the other way whenever they spotted him around campus. And, of course, they dumped him as soon as Zelda made herself available.

Zelda did not ask them what they were going to be when they grew up; no, Zelda told them. "There is absolutely no doubt in my mind," she announced, "that the two of you were born to be writers."

"Writers?" asked John.

"Writers," answered Zelda.

"What kind of writers?" asked Will.

"Creative writers," answered Zelda. "Story-tellers."

"Story-tellers? You mean, like, novelists? Like James Joyce? Stephen King?"

Zelda gave them her most engaging smile. "Yes," she said, "exactly. A combination of Joyce and King. I love it."

"But we don't know the first thing about being novelists."

"You know how to write."

"We learned how to do that in first grade. But we have no idea what to write."

"Yes, you do," she assured them. "Just write what you want to write. Write what comes naturally."

"But hell," protested John, "writing's not something you do when you grow up. It's not something you do for a living."

"Mom and Dad wanted us to have careers," added Will. "Professions. Like doctors or lawyers."

Zelda sat behind her metal desk in her cramped office on the first floor of Boylston Hall. Books were shelved and scattered everywhere. Hundreds of books, thousands of books, hardcover books, paperback books, old books and new books. She leaned forward across that desk and gathered in the twins with her penetrating gaze. The fact that they both lusted after her physically made it easy for her to dominate them mentally.

"A profession," she told them, "is basically a vocation with social relevance. I can assure you, the creation of strong literary fiction has all the social relevance any mommy or daddy could possibly want."

"Yes, but—"

"Listen to me," she ordered. "I've read everything: great, good, bad, and revolting. And I can tell you this: Throughout the ages only a handful of writers have achieved greatness: Shakespeare, Cervantes, Dostoyevsky. One writer in a million. One in a billion. This is because creative writing, writing that originates in the soul, migrates to the brain, and oozes out through the fingertips, demands a wide variety of gifts and skills. It is extremely rare for the necessary combination to blend in a single individual. One writer might have the most tantalizing imagination, but no ability to carry off a sustained narrative. Another writer might possess incredible powers to create plot, but no feel whatsoever for the creation of strong, believable characters. Writers fail for many reasons: stupidity, alcohol, poverty, affluence, shitty relationships, no self-discipline, problems with—"

"Okay, but—"

"Quiet!" shouted Zelda. "Don't interrupt me. Ever." She was that kind of gal. "The two of you, writing together, as a team, might possibly possess all the vital ingredients necessary for the creation of extraordinary prose. I have no idea yet which of you brings what to the mix, but at this point, I'm not sure it matters. What matters for the time being is the result: an exquisite blend of focused energy and controlled lunacy. It's all rather like a primitive painting at this stage, but definitely the essential elements are in place."

Zelda seemed to wind down then, but the boys, edgy, decided not to risk another interruption. And sure enough, after a brief pause, Zelda had more to say. "Tell me," she asked, "how do you do it?"

The boys glanced at one another.

"Do what?" asked John.

"Write like magicians?"

Will shrugged. "I don't know. We just do it."

"And why do you do it together?"

"Why?" they asked.

"Yes, why do you collaborate?"

"Oh, that's easy," answered John. "To get the assignments done faster so we can go out and fart around."

"Usually," added Will, "John scribbles out a first draft and then I fix it up."

Zelda knew there was more to it than the boys were willing to reveal. But their cocky answer did not really surprise her. She'd half expected something worse. Like Mozart cackling and chasing his little sister around the harpsichord while composing beautiful symphonies at the tender age of eight.

Right now John's not scribbling much of anything. He
tried early this morning, but gave up as soon as he heard
the kids stir. They had breakfast together and talked about
the golden retriever. Yes, *the* golden retriever. Last evening, the boys picked up and held the five month-old puppies for over an hour. They of course wanted all five, but
Dad said no way. He did, however, finally give in and tell
them they could have *one* of the pups. John knew this
would undoubtedly irritate his brother (Will has never
much liked dogs), but too bad; John loves to make his boys
happy.

After breakfast John walked the boys to school. Along
the way they discussed names.
"Bill."
"Bob."
"Brutus."
"Walter."
"Wolf."
"Wiggles."
Plenty of time to decide.
John waved good-bye at the front door of the school.
He's been pretty much walking ever since. Middle of the

morning now and he has just about completed the Freedom Trail. A tourist route through the historic parts of
Boston, John has walked it many times over the years
when he needs to think through a problem. Today he has
walked past the site of the Boston Massacre, strolled by
Paul Revere's house, stopped briefly in front of the Old
North Church, crossed Boston Harbor on the Charlestown
Bridge, and climbed to the top of the Bunker Hill Monu-
ment up on the summit of Breed's Hill where the rebels
routed the redcoats back in June of 1775.

John likes to see himself as part of history. He has come
to accept as fact the fiction that his ancestor presided over
the Continental Congress and boldly scrawled his signature across the Declaration of Independence. Forget the
Hermann Goering connection; that bit of family trivia has
no place in John's reality. His life is, and always has been,
a fancy and complex arrangement of deceptions and dis-
tortions. And right at this second, his brain working
through all the stimulation of the last couple days, he wonders for just a second if maybe all the deceptions and dis-
tortions have finally caught up with him. If his luck has
maybe run out.

That suspect list keeps circling around in his head. The
names keep flashing in front of his eyes, one after another,
an endless parade of possibilities:

HANCOCK, CLARA
BYRNES, RODNEY
RAFE,?
COSGROVE, DICKY
FISHER, LELAND

Most of the names on the list do not scare him. Certainly Clara's doesn't. Although, John knows he will be
both paralyzed and devastated if his wife has learned the
truth and is now preparing to alter the status quo, perhaps
end their marriage. That might be more than John could
bear.

Byrnes he does not fear. Nor Rafe. Nor Leland. Leland

might be out of his mind with jealousy if he thinks his wife and his best-selling author have been having a fling behind his back. But Leland is a teddy bear. The poor guy would break down and cry before he would do anything violent.

No, the only name on the list that scares John is Dicky Cosgrove. John has no idea what Mad Dicky might do. Call it fear, instinct, intuition, but John can feel Dicky's presence. He knows Dicky is out there. And he's pretty close. And getting closer.

Physically, Dicky's not really all that close. Not yet.

He's taking a little break, visiting the scene of the crime. Like Hancock, Dicky's been doing a lot of walking the last few hours. After getting pushed out of Stick's Lincoln, he walked all the way from Arlington to Cambridge. Other than a few bumps and bruises, he survived his encounter with the asphalt on Medford Street without serious injury.

Right now he's outside the apartment building on Berkeley Street where sister Zelda lived at the time of her slaying. The front door of the three-story brick building is locked. Dicky wants to go upstairs, down to the end of the hallway to 4D, step inside, see if his sister's blood still stains the carpets and the wood floors.

But no one's about to let this guy inside. Not only does he smell and look crazy, but he has blood on his hands and face. His clothes are all torn and tattered. Direct results of irritating Mr. Moses down on Franklin Square.

A Cambridge cop car pulls up to the apartment building. An officer steps out of the cruiser and demands some identification. Dicky hands over his brand-new Massachusetts driver's license, a little something Doctor Dope out in Great Barrington helped him procure as part of his release program.

The cop checks out the driver's license, then checks out Dicky. He gives Dicky a little sniff and asks, "May I ask what you are doing here, Mr. Cosgrove?"

"Waiting for my sister," answers Mad Dicky, sane as

can be. "She lives here. On the fourth floor." He points with his thumb.

"She's not presently at home?"

"No, sir. Not yet. But she should be soon."

"So what happened to you?"

Dicky checks himself over. "Oh, this. I got mugged last night."

"Mugged? Where?"

"Over in Boston. But I'm fine. Really. I don't want to file a report or anything. I only had a few dollars on me."

The radio crackles in the police cruiser. The dispatcher needs officers immediately over on Brattle Street. Domestic incident. Shots fired. Trouble everywhere.

The officer hands the driver's license back to Dicky. "I suggest you get cleaned up, Mr. Cosgrove. A shower and some fresh clothes. You're scaring the neighbors."

"Right," says Dicky, "I'll do that."

The officer climbs back into his cruiser, turns on the siren, and accelerates away from the curb. Little does the cop know that he has just let a potential homicidal maniac walk away scot-free. Nor does he know that the free advice he gave Dicky might well have far-reaching and violent consequences.

For the first time in weeks, Dicky takes note of his disheveled appearance. And his horrendous body odor. He decides immediately to rectify the situation.

FISHING

Will Hancock stands in the warm, waist-deep Bahamian waters off Stocking Island. He casts for bonefish with his nine-weight graphite fly rod. Back and forth the fly line arcs through the air. The fly lands softly in the rippled surf. A small bonefish cruises by, uninterested. Will reels in the line and casts again. Not too many of the silver and sinewy fish biting in this bright, glaring, late morning light, but Will will not be deterred.

Earlier, Will caught one of the spooky bottom feeders: a small two-pounder that gave up without a fight. Will took absolutely no satisfaction in the catch. But he did not give up. He is, if nothing else, dogged in his desire.

Changing rods, changing reels, changing flies—this is what fly-fishing is all about. Patience is needed, and patience Will has, unlimited reserves of patience. He can fish the same stretch of water for hours, placidly tying on one fly after another in an effort to find one the fish will hit. Brother John, on the other hand, if you can even get him to take up a rod, will make a few frenzied casts, then, if unsuccessful, he will move on to the next activity. Getting a fish to bite down on a barbed hook, then jerking that fish around in the water, is not John's idea of a good time. John prefers more adrenaline-pumping pursuits: cycling, white-water kayaking, downhill skiing, mountain climbing. Will goes for the fishing, the hunting, the hiking.

Will reels in his line and remembers for the second time in less than forty-eight hours the day he became John Hancock. Almost twenty years ago now, almost half his life, but rarely does a day go by when he does not think about what happened with those passports down there on Caye Caulker.

Will peers into the clear blue-green water, and there in the shallows, not more than thirty feet from where he stands, he spots a bonefish, its silver scales shimmering under that bright tropical sun. Methodically, Will prepares to cast. The fish moves slowly. It is definitely feeding. Will draws back his rod and throws the fly out directly in the bonefish's path. The fly lands softly. Wham! The bonefish strikes. Then turns and heads out to sea. Will lets him run. No need not to let him run. Will wants to play with him. Not unlike a cat who has cornered a mouse. The cat will let the mouse head for cover, but at the last second will bat the mouse back into the middle of the room. And so Will does the same. He lets that bonefish make a few frenzied runs for freedom, but each time Will reels him back so the chase can begin again. Will takes great joy in this, enormous pleasure.

The battle lasts six, maybe seven minutes. The fish, a strong and able fighter, quickly becomes exhausted. Will brings him ashore to have a look. A healthy six-pound male. Good size for a bonefish. But not really much of a match for a hundred-and-seventy pound man with a rod and a reel and a great big brain.

Carefully, because bonefish have teeth, Will removes the hook from the fish's mouth and tosses the fish back into the sea. Will definitely doesn't want the fish. Bonefish make good fighting but terrible eating.

Satisfied, even satiated, Will takes a break. He sits on the beach. Eats a steak sandwich. Gazes out at the horizon. Beautiful, he thinks. Spectacular. He would like to bring his wife and kids here someday. Someday after all this deception and confusion and loneliness can be swept away.

Will is a calm and patient fisherman. Just as he is a calm and patient man. But his great patience has another side, perhaps a somewhat less virtuous side. Predators, too, have patience. Hawks and owls. Lions and leopards. Spiders and scorpions. They can lay in wait for their prey for hours. For days. Calmly, stealthily, ruthlessly—they wait. And then, in an instant, they strike.

CONNECTIONS

Rafe Paquita stands right at this moment in the lavatory of a Boeing 737 flying at twenty-eight thousand feet. Rafe has a jar of Vaseline in one hand and a plastic bag containing eight ounces of pure cocaine in the other.

That 737 is beginning its final approach into Houston Intercontinental Airport. Rafe knows he has to make that bag of dope disappear before he goes through Customs. Just burying it in the bottom of his ratty duffel bag won't do the trick. So he drops his drawers, takes a couple of deep breaths, lubes himself up, and does what needs doing.

Rafe knows, or he at least believes, that if he wants to get his wife and daughter back, he has to get that dope into the States, deliver it to the Ambassador Hotel in New York City, then get himself up to Boston and have a little chat with Mr. John Hancock.

After that he can relax, take it easy, really enjoy life.

Speaking of the Ambassador Hotel, Mrs. Hillary Fisher is on the phone with the Ambassador at this very moment. She is busy making reservations for Wednesday and Thursday night. When the Fishers travel to New York, they always stay in midtown at the Ambassador. Usually in a suite overlooking Central Park.

Hillary's not really sure why she wants to go to New York. Certainly not to be with Leland. Though he was kind of sweet and lustful last night. But really she just needs to get away from Boston for a few days. Away from Hancock. Think about how she might exact revenge for the way he so crudely cut her off yesterday. And in the meantime, Fifth Avenue will be but a short stroll away. She can shop while she plots.

And Leland can foot the bill. Leland's sitting up in his office over on Beacon Street trying to decide whether or not to call Al-the-Gumshoe Brown and tell him to nip the surveillance of John Hancock in the bud. He has himself pretty well convinced that his paranoia concerning his wife's infidelity was for naught. He decides to give Al a call, get the latest dope, and then, depending on the report, lay the Gumshoe off.

The Gumshoe is outside Hancock's Beacon Hill town house waiting for Hancock to make his first appearance of the day. Al got a late start this morning and missed Hancock leaving around eight o'clock with John junior and young Willy. So he's been sitting here in his minivan all morning sucking coffee, thinking Hancock's inside maybe working on his next psycho-thriller.

But all of a sudden here comes Hancock. Crossing the cobblestones of Louisburg Square. He passes through his wrought-iron gate and goes up the steps to the front door. John forgot his keys, so he gives the solid brass knocker a couple of firm whacks.

"Dammit," mutters Al, reaching for his Nikon, "where has he been?"

Al's cell phone rings. "Jesus. Perfectly quiet all morning long and now all hell's breaking loose." He picks up the phone and turns it on. "Hello."

"It's Fisher."

"Yes, sir?"

"Just wondering what's going on."

"I'm at the Hancock house, sir. We have some activity. I'll call you back."

"I'm at the office."

"Right." Al goes back to the Nikon. He manages to pop off a shot or two before Hancock slides through the front door.

"Hey, Nick," John says to the nanny, "Anything exciting happen in my absence?"

Poor Nicky shakes her head. Earlier, when Mr. Hancock left to walk the boys to school, he said he'd be back in a few minutes. And now, here he is, four hours later. But after eight months on the job, Nicky has finally gotten used to this kind of behavior. She likes Mr. Hancock, and enjoys working for him. He's funny and fair and he gives her plenty of time off. But he's definitely weird. And eccentric. And forgetful. He forgets appointments. He forgets to return telephone calls. He forgets where he left his keys and his jacket. He sometimes even forgets what happened earlier in the day. Nicky has noticed that his wife and kids barely seem to notice these spells of memory loss. She figures maybe it has to do with him being a writer. Maybe writers are just weird and eccentric and absentminded by nature.

Or maybe, Nicky, there are simply two Mr. Hancocks. And maybe one does not always know exactly where the other one left the keys.

"So, Nick," asks Hancock, "anybody call?"

"Mrs. Hancock called. A few minutes ago. She would like you to call back. She's at the Ritz in Paris." Nicky pulls a piece of paper out of her pocket. "Here's the number."

Hancock takes it and starts upstairs. "Thanks, Nick. I'll dial her up directly."

Al punches in the numbers for Leland's direct line. Leland snatches up the phone. "Yeah?"

"It's Brown."

"What's up? You said there was some activity."

"Yes, sir. Hancock showed up just as you called."

"Showed up? Where was he?"

"I don't know."

"What do you mean, you don't know? Christ, man, I'm paying you to know."

"I got here at ten minutes of seven," lies Al. "Except for the two kids leaving for school at eight, there's been absolutely no activity."

"So you're telling me Hancock has been gone since before seven, but you have no idea where?"

"That's correct, sir." Al figures he has to lie; if he gets fired now he'll have a tough time getting the unpaid portion of his bill. "Unless he left later and went out the back."

Leland sighs a mighty sigh. Tells himself he'd better keep this moron on the job. "Don't let him out of your sight again, dammit," he growls and slams down the phone.

Al sighs, too. And has another doughnut.

Another call dialed. Another connection made.

"Hello?"

"Hey, it's me."

"Hey, you."

"I hear you called."

"I did."

"You must miss me."

"I do," Clara tells him in her most seductive voice.

"So when are you coming home? I feel the need to nestle."

"That sounds nice."

"So when are you coming?"

"A day or two. But first I have to go to New York."

"The new gallery?" John asks.

"Yes," says Clara. "I think we've finally worked out the details."

John knows all about the new gallery. He has been hearing about the new gallery for a year or more. Clara's fourth gallery. This one down in the Big Apple. Right smack in the heart of midtown. Within spitting distance of Tiffany's. But a very complex deal. Clara needed several partners because of the tremendous expense operating in Manhattan. Now it looks like maybe, finally, it's a done deal.

"So tomorrow you fly to New York. Are you staying at the Ambassador?"

"Of course."

"What about our little rendezvous? Still up for that?"

"Absolutely."

"With or without the guys?" asks John.

"The guys," answers Clara, "are going off tomorrow morning with Linda."

"Going off where with Linda who?"

"Linda who? Linda Carson. My best friend Linda. The same Linda you took to Leland's bash Saturday night. The same Linda who introduced us all those years ago."

"No need to be facetious, dear. Just wasn't sure there for a second who you meant. So where is Linda going with our offspring?"

"I swear, Hancock, you have the memory of an inchworm. They're going to New Hampshire."

"New Hampshire?"

"To Linda's cabin in the White Mountains. I've already told you all this."

"I'm sure you have. Remind me."

"They're just going for a day or two. To open up the cabin for the summer. Get the place aired out. Do a little hiking. This is not new news."

Hancock tries to remember. He can't, but knows he occasionally forgets a thing or two. It's also possible Clara told Will and Will forgot to tell him before they switched places last week. It's a small problem the brothers have been juggling for years.

"I'm sure it's not," says John. And then, "So they're missing school?"

"Just for a couple days. And believe me, Linda will keep them far more stimulated than their teachers do."

"Do the boys know about all this?"

"Of course they do. I asked them if they wanted to go. They love it up there. Don't you remember what a great time we all had last summer?"

Actually, Hancock doesn't remember. He was climbing in the Alps. Will had domestic duty that week. "Oh, sure," he says, "I remember."

"They'll be fine," Clara assures him. "Linda loves them. She's the closest thing they have to a real aunt."

"I'm not complaining. I enjoy it when my entire family abandons me. Leaves me here all alone."

"Poor boy."

Hancock sighs and asks, "When is Linda picking them up?"

"Sometime in the morning. So don't send them off to school."

"Got it."

"And after they go, you hop on the shuttle and meet me in New York."

"Sounds like a perfect plan."

"You can be there at the press conference."

"What press conference?"

"On Thursday. To announce the opening of the new gallery."

"Free publicity."

"Exactly."

John and Clara cover a few more details, then hang up. Clara feels confident the pieces of her puzzle are starting to fit together nicely. She has always been a superb planner and schemer. Like her assault on the public and private lives of Charles and Anita Dare. That was a work of art, a virtual masterpiece of research, planning, and execution.

CHARLES, ANITA, & CLARA DARE

The day after Clara Dare, then known as Jane McGuire, graduated from Cambridge High School in June of 1981, Jane's mother, Patsy, and Patsy's new boyfriend, Guy, presented the young grad with a check for five thousand dollars. It was mostly Guy's money, money he'd made playing semipro hockey in Boston and Montreal. Now Guy wanted to move to Mexico, and he wanted Patsy to go with him. And Patsy wanted to go, except she was torn about leaving behind her little girl. Who wasn't so little anymore. Jane had sprouted up to nearly six feet, all long and leggy and lean.

"You're almost eighteen now," Patsy told her daughter. "Time to make your own way in the world."

"These five g's," added Guy, who, at the age of thirty-eight, had a full set of false teeth, "will make it easier on ya. When my old man t'rew me outta the house when I was, like, seventeen, I had nuthin' but the clothes on my back and a pair of old skates."

Not entirely true, but it made good copy.

So Patsy and Guy went to Cabo San Lucas out on the Baja, and Janey rented a small two-room flat near the Museum of Fine Arts. Her friend and fine arts mentor, Florence Baker, had long ago departed Boston to study American Indian culture in Albuquerque, New Mexico, but Jane still visited the museum at least once a week.

Jane found a job waiting tables, but spent most of her time wandering around the city fantasizing about fame and fortune and how to get her share of both. She especially loved Newbury Street, Boston's version of New York's Fifth Avenue or L.A.'s Rodeo Drive. In fact, it was along Newbury Street one lovely afternoon in the spring of '82 that Jane, gazing in the windows of the fashionable boutiques and fine art galleries, suddenly had a moment of pure inspiration.

Right then and there she began to hatch her plot.

It was no easy task. It demanded hard work and long hours. But she was used to hard work and long hours. Back in high school, before she began to blossom into a tall and graceful beauty, the boys called her Plain Jane. Plain Janes learn how to work hard.

A full six months passed before she finally felt ready to make a move. By that time she had completely reinvented herself. Her age had suddenly jumped from eighteen to twenty-one. Her résumé included a year at the Sorbonne and working experience at galleries in London and Miami Beach. She had a new wardrobe, not a very large one, but two or three outfits in the absolutely latest fashions for young women in the art world. She had a new hairstyle, short and chic, also the latest fashion. She had the right purse and the right shoes and the right earrings. She had The Look, copied from *Vogue* and researched at Boston's finest boutiques. And she also had a new name. It was her legal name now, said so right on her driver's license: Clara Dare.

Why Clara Dare? Because Charles and Anita Dare owned one of the most exclusive art galleries on Newbury Street. Jane, now Clara, knew all about the Dares. She had made it her business to find out every detail. Charles was seventy-one, Anita sixty-nine. They had been married for forty-six years. Had been in the art business forty-five years. They had galleries in Boston, London, and Paris.

They had loads of money. And lots of valuable paintings. And best of all, from Jane's point of view, they had no children. And no grandchildren. Their only child, David, had died of a heroin overdose back in 1969. All these years later, but they still had not fully recovered from David's death.

Jane had her facts down cold when she stepped through the door of the Dare Gallery on the corner of Newbury and Exeter on a warm autumn afternoon. She knew, for instance, that Charles would be alone in the gallery. It was a Monday, and on Monday afternoons Anita always left the gallery and strolled over to a very exclusive salon on Marlborough Street to have her hair done and her nails polished.

Jane, now Clara, had herself looking good. Really good. Very fine. One look out of the corner of his seventy-one-year-old eyes, and old Charles Dare might just as well have turned over his assets to this tall young beauty in the skimpy black leather skirt before she ever even opened her pretty mouth.

She smiled and closed the door. "I'm so glad you're open," she said, cool and refined.

"Oh, yes," Charles replied, "we're open. We're practically always open. If not to the public, then by appointment."

Jane, now Clara, nodded. "I saw the name on the window and just wanted to say hello." She moved easily across the airy, well-lit space in her black high heels. Paintings, mostly oil paintings, some by very famous painters, dominated the walls, but nothing at all stood between Charles Dare and Clara. Nothing save fifty-some years and a bunch of lies that were about to come pouring out of Jane McGuire like the Nile overflowing its banks.

Halfway across the room, Clara stopped. And took in the Degas hanging on the wall to her left. "My God, look at that! 'The Meet.' That came relatively early in his career, didn't it? Early to mid sixties. It's just magnificent. You could already see where he was headed. I assumed that painting was in a museum."

Charles, impressed, replied, "No, we acquired it last year from a private collection in Luxembourg. But you're quite right about the date. 1864 to be precise."

Clara nodded. She knew the precise date, but being too precise would have been bad form. Oh, yes, she knew all about the painting. She had done her research on many of the paintings hanging in the Dare Gallery. A month or so earlier, she had slipped into the gallery wearing jeans, dark glasses, and a baseball cap.

"So," Charles asked, "you know Degas?"

"I love his brush work. I really don't think anyone has ever handled a brush better."

Absolutely stunning, thought Charles, and an art lover to boot.

And a Dare, Charles was about to find out. At least on paper.

Clara held out her hand. "My name's Clara," she said, for the first time in her life. "Clara Dare." The name sounded good rolling off her tongue.

"Dare?" replied Charles. "Really?"

"Yes. I saw the name of your gallery and had to stop in and say hello. It is not a common name. One does not hear it often."

Clara did a lot more that afternoon than just say hello. She wound up staying for an hour. Almost two hours. Charles offered her a cup of tea. They talked about art. They talked about Clara. She had her story all ready to go. Born in New York. Raised in New York and Florida and Geneva. Her father had been in stocks and bonds. Her mother had been the art collector and aficionado. Very knowledgeable. Especially about the Impressionists. She loved Frédéric Bazille's work best of all, but then, before he ever reached his prime, he was shot in the chest and killed by that Prussian sniper. A dreadful loss to the art world. As for her father, well, he had made some unwise investments, gone broke, and taken his own life with a saber. Her mother had eventually remarried and now lived a quiet life on the Isle of Wight.

Charles Dare, a full-fledged Boston Brahmin, believed

every word this lovely young lady told him. Being a gentleman of education and integrity who always spoke the
truth, Charles believed virtually everything everyone told
him. And he was moved, truly moved, when Clara told
him, a tear in her eye, about her father's premature demise.

"You poor dear. That must have been an extremely difficult time for you."

"It was," she assured him. "It was the worst thing that
has ever happened to me."

And then Charles, much to his own surprise, told Clara
about the death of his son, David. Which, of course, Clara
already knew about. Though she did not let on.

Charles, normally tight-lipped and emotionally Spartan,
shed a few tears of his own. Clara grasped and squeezed
his hand. And their bond was sealed.

Before Clara left that afternoon she told Charles she would
very much like to meet his wife. Charles thought that
sounded like an excellent idea. In fact, in an explosion of
emotion that even Clara could not have hoped for, Charles
invited Clara for dinner. He did this in his typically selfless
way, believing Anita would enjoy having a young person in
the house again.

The house would be the town house on Louisburg
Square up on Beacon Hill. The Dares had lived there for
decades. And so, a few days later, Jane, as Clara, walked
through the front door of that house for the first time. She
presented herself to Anita Dare quite differently than she
had presented herself to Charles. The short skirt and high
heels were gone, replaced with a conservative gray dress
and cordovan loafers.

The two women responded positively to one another
immediately, if for somewhat different reasons. Clara
quickly became the granddaughter Anita never had.

The Dares offered Clara a job at the gallery without her
ever having to ask. Solid, tightfisted Yankees, they did not
pay her much money, but Clara would have worked for
free. What she wanted, what she had been dreaming about

for months, was her foot in the door of the Dare Gallery. And now, suddenly, she had her whole body inside.

Whatever they needed done, Clara did. She mailed letters, went for coffee, packed and unpacked boxes, served cocktails at openings, hung paintings. Clara had never wanted or expected a free ride, just a shot, an opportunity.

As the months, and then the years, swept by, the Dares, growing older and contemplating retirement, gave Clara more and more responsibility. Just as she had hoped, they began to treat her as a member of the family. She came to the house for dinner several times a week. Charles and Anita spoke candidly in her presence about both professional and personal matters. They invited her to join them for holidays and other important events, like birthdays and anniversaries. They sent her to Europe to check on the status of the galleries in London and Paris. They trusted her judgment regarding the sale and purchase of paintings. And they also introduced her to all the right people in Boston society. They procured invitations for her to all the best social functions.

Yes, Clara was in. She was golden. And never for a second did she feel guilty or even remotely uneasy about the deception she had wrought upon these two elderly and generous purveyors of her good fortune. They had helped her go from rags to riches. In return, she had given them her youth and her love. A perfectly equitable exchange.

AMERICA

Rafe's plan to go from rags to riches has turned a bit hairy. If he could find a men's room he would go in there and move his bowels and flush that coke straight down the toilet. But he wants the dough, the rest of the cash he'll get when he hands the goods over to his contact at the Ambassador Hotel in New York. But man, oh man, what if he gets caught in the act? What if they snag him right here at the Houston Intercontinental Airport? They'll throw his butt in jail and flush the key down the hole.

The crowd keeps moving, pushing him closer and closer to where the stern and somber customs agents ply their trade. Rafe feels his bowels groan. He looks around for a men's room, doesn't see one, thinks about asking, decides that would not be a good idea at all. Bad idea, Rafe. Very bad. Stay calm. Stay cool. Easy to say, but tough to do with sweat pouring off your forehead and eight ounces of coke stowed away.

He's in line now, moving forward, moving fast, too fast. Maybe he should make a run for it. But where would he go? How far could he get? He's right behind an old lady with her grandson. Maybe her great-grandson. How the hell does he know? Goddammit, what the hell does he care? Come on, God, give me a break. Help me out here.

See me through this shit and I'll follow you to the ends of the earth. Promise. Cross my heart. Hope to die.

Oh Jesus, here we go.

The customs officer looks Rafe over and says, "Passport, sir?"

Rafe, doing his best not to shake or sweat, hands over his Belize passport. No problem with that. His papers are in order. The United States doesn't mind if Rafe comes to visit; they just don't want him sneaking cocaine into the country and selling it to innocent young schoolchildren.

"Is this a business trip, Mr. Paquita?"

"No, sir. I'm coming to visit my brother. He lives in New Jersey and is very sick."

The customs officer neither believes nor disbelieves Mr. Rafe Paquita's story. "I see. And where in New Jersey will you be staying, sir?"

"Jersey City, sir. One four six eight three Lafayette Street. Apartment two-E." Rafe's not a total idiot; he consulted an atlas before concocting his story.

"Two-E?"

"Yes, sir."

"Are you carrying any agricultural products, Mr. Paquita?"

"No, sir."

"Any firearms?"

"No, sir."

"Any contraband of any kind?"

"No, sir."

"Any illegal drugs?"

"No, sir."

"Marijuana? Heroin? Cocaine?"

The tiniest pause, then, "No, sir. I am not, sir."

"How long will you be in the United States, Mr. Paquita?"

"A week or two, sir, depending on my brother's health."

"I thought you said your mother was ill."

"No, sir. My brother. Leukemia."

The customs officer calls over his assistant. The assistant goes through Rafe's duffel bag. Nothing in there but a change of clothes, some shaving gear, a toothbrush, a John Hancock novel, and a small stuffed alligator he picked up down at the airport in Belize. "For my niece," he tells the customs officers.

The assistant takes out a pocket knife and cuts open the seam of the stuffed alligator. Nothing in there but old shredded newspaper. Very cheap stuffed animals they make down in Belize.

Rafe sweats while holding his sphincter muscle very tight so as not to defecate that cocaine right into his breeches.

"Follow me, Mr. Paquita."

Rafe follows, but he already sees the end of this story: Jail. Prison. Twenty years of incarceration. Hard labor. And for what? Five measly grand? "It's up my butt!" he feels like confessing, shouting at the top of his lungs. "It's up my butt!"

But, incredibly, they don't look up his butt. They look everywhere else, but not up his butt. They let him go, send him on his way.

Later, waiting for his flight to Chicago, Rafe replays the scene in the examining room over and over. The two customs guys making him strip, going through his pockets, ripping the soles off his shoes, sticking a light down his throat and in his ears. But then the one doing the probing suddenly got called away. And never came back.

That would have been the DEA putting in a call to Customs. *Let Paquita walk. We've got our eyes on him.*

Several minutes later Rafe was told to put on his clothes. Which he did. Lickity split. A minute or so later he was out the door and through the gates.

A big red, white, and blue banner read: WELCOME TO THE U.S.A., RAFE PAQUITA! WELCOME TO THE HOME OF THE BRAVE AND THE LAND OF THE FREE!

Well, maybe not, but it sure felt that way.

DICKY

No big blue banner greets Dicky Cosgrove as he trudges up the front steps of his boardinghouse in Cambridge. No, not the same boardinghouse Patsy McGuire and her little girl Jane lived in thirty years ago, but one exactly like it, just down the street.

The rumors are true: It's a small world.

Up the steps and through the door goes Dicky. He's up on the second floor. A lovely little studio apartment. Psychopath Central. Ratty old sheetless mattress on the floor. A couple lamps without shades, also on the floor. A small black-and-white TV (do they still make black and whites?) perched atop a cardboard box, an untwisted hanger serving as antennae. Clothes and shoes strewn into corners, everything dirty and smelling of B.O. Some hard-core porn rags hanging around the mattress, many of the pages mutilated and stuck together.

Off to the side, the filthy little kitchenette. Nothing in there but some cans of Dinty Moore Beef Stew. Dicky usually doesn't even bother to heat the stuff up. Just cracks the lid and wolfs it down.

And across the way, the bathroom. Best just stay out of there. The toilet hasn't worked in over a week.

Might as well be a sign on the front door of 2B: BE-WARE! PSYCHO DWELLS WITHIN.

A psycho with an agenda. Or is that redundant?

Dicky's in high gear now. Straight to the shower, green and sour with mold. He needs fumigating, but settles for plenty of hot water and most of a big fat bar of Zest. Dicky scrubs himself Zestfully clean. He even pares the wax out of his ears and digs the crusty crud from between his toes and fingernails. His hair gets washed three times. Dicky stays in there until the water runs tepid.

The whiskers come off next. He scratches away with a dull Bic disposable until his chin and cheeks run as smooth as a baby's bottom. Next he breaks out the toothbrush and a flattened tube of Crest. He pushes out some paste and brushes his filmy yellow teeth three times.

Dicky dresses in the cleanest clothes he can find. No, not very clean, pretty smelly and gross actually, but they'll pass muster till he buys new. Then a couple twisted glances in the cracked mirror over the bathroom sink, and out goes Dicky to take on the world.

He's already walked about fifty miles in the past twenty-four hours, but he sets off walking again. Up Pearl Street to Massachusetts Avenue and down into the heart of Cambridge to the Harvard Square Business District. He knows the District will provide him with all the goodies he needs.

At the Gap on Brattle Street he buys two pairs of dark blue chinos, three blue T-shirts, and a couple of blue oxford button-downs. Blue makes Dicky feel safe. And for some reason powerful. He walks out of the Gap wearing new chinos, new T-shirt, new oxford button-down. The old gear he left in the dressing room. The rest of the new gear rests in a plastic Gap bag under his arm.

Next stop: Le Foot Sportif over on Auburn. Dicky tries on several pairs of snazzy sneakers. Sneakers with a purpose. Sneakers with an attitude. Tennis sneakers. Basketball sneakers. Running sneakers. Walking sneakers. Dicky's eyes roll around in his head at the abundance of different styles and colors.

Too bad the young salesgirl, her hair dyed green and a

gold hoop earring pierced through her lower lip, has no idea she's selling sneakers to a psychopath.

Dicky finally settles on a pair of flashy blue-and-white Nikes specially made for soft-court tennis. Nike's ad tag, scrawled across the box, says it all: JUST DO IT!

Exactly what Dicky intends to do.

He also buys a couple pairs of fresh socks. Blue ones. Wearing one pair of the new socks and his brand-new sneaks, Dicky slips through the door of Le Foot Sportif feeling extraordinarily light on his feet.

Next stop: the Globe Bookstore on Church Street. Dicky immediately spots the floor-mounted display. It's this big colorful cardboard cutout contraption with a damn near life-size reproduction of John Hancock smiling out at the book-buying public. And next to this giant monstrosity of a poster: fifty copies of the new Hancock thriller, *The Settlement.* Dicky wants to spit on the big photo, lay a louie right on Hancock's eye, but that would attract attention, something he definitely does not want to do. So he picks up a copy of the book, then slides toward the back of the store where they shelve the paperbacks.

In Mysteries & Suspense, Dicky locates the Hancock section. Being a local author and a Harvard grad, Hancock gets a big play in all the Cambridge bookstores. The Globe does a brisk business in the early Hancock titles. Dicky picks up one of each, six paperbacks in all, including *The Killer,* a story in which Dicky feels the Hancock brothers decimated his character. Just one more reason why he intends to end their lousy, stinking, conniving, murderous lives.

The young man at the cash register smiles pleasantly at Dicky when he sees the stack of Hancock books. "You must be a big fan."

Dicky returns the smile, nice as can be. "I'm hoping to get them autographed."

Wasn't that crazy SOB who shot Lennon outside the Dakota out buying Beatles albums just before he put a couple slugs in John's chest? What was that loony's name? So hard to remember all these little details.

Anyway, next stop for Dicky: Shades, down on Dunster. Dicky needs shades. Not to block out the sun, but to hide his eyes. He doesn't want people watching his eyes, trying to figure out what he might do next.

He tries on a dozen different pairs. Finally settles on some traditional Wayfarers with a tortoiseshell frame. He pays, pushes the shades up onto his nose, and struts out of the store, back out onto the street. Check him out. Dicky could easily pass now for a Harvard prof who likes contemporary jazz and plays a pretty mean game of singles over at the Baren Tennis Center across the Charles. The guy looks downright dapper in his Gap duds. And he doesn't smell at all.

His next stop, however, carries with it the pungent aroma of weirdness: Colonial Cutlery over on Holyoke, just a few short steps from where big Mac Oosterhaus, Harvard Crimson's left tackle, took that sterling silver letter opener away from Dicky all those years ago, then picked Dicky up and tossed him out into the street.

Colonial Cutlery sells letter openers, but they also sell lots of other very sharp and lethal instruments. Dicky, you see, has decided, after his run-in with Moses and Stick, that it's just too darn tough to get a gun in this city. Hell, he doesn't really even want to use a gun anymore. Too easy. And far too impersonal. Good for random assassinations and acts of international terrorism, but utterly inappropriate for revenge killings. Revenge killings demand close proximity. The victim should be able to smell your breath, see the hate in your eyes. Lots of common, everyday items found around the house can be used to carry out the damage: an iron skillet, a shovel, a pickax, even a curtain rod or a brick. But Dicky has decided knives best suit his needs and his personality. Serving the upscale cutlery buyer, Colonial Cutlery carries the finest European brands: Henckels, Sabatier, Wüsthof-Trident. Dicky stares at the vast array of cutting paraphernalia.

"May I help you, sir?" asks the salesclerk, a chubby woman who would be about the same age as Dicky's mother, had Dicky's mother's parachute opened all those years ago over that Vermont cornfield.

"Oh," says Dicky, "I'm just browsing. My wife's along the street here somewhere buying God knows what. I'm just staying out of trouble."

The chubby woman smiles. She's selling knives to help put her son through med school. When she's not selling knives she crochets and gossips on the telephone. "Always a good idea to stay out of trouble. Let me know if you'd like to see something."

Dicky says he sure will, then watches as she waddles down the counter to service another customer. His eyes soon enough return to the glistening blades inside the glass showcase. He checks out the small stuff first: the paring knives, the peeling knives, the fluting knives. Then the medium stuff: the utility knives, the steak knives, the fillet knives. And finally the big stuff: the ham slicers, the salmon slicers, the cleavers. His mouth begins to water. A thin stream of drool runs down his chin and drops onto the top of the glass showcase. Wiping it up with the cuff of his new blue oxford, Dicky thinks about filleting the Hancock boys, boning them, slicing and dicing them, hacking off fingers and toes and hands and feet with one of those cleavers.

But then, down at the end of the showcase, he spots something special. And he knows instantly, instinctively, that this is what he wants. This is what he needs.

And so he calls Chubby over and asks her if he can have a look.

"Of course, sir." She unlocks the case and slides open the door. "Not too many people use these anymore, but those that do claim this particular model has absolutely the sharpest and finest blade in the world." She picks up the instrument and hands it to Mad Dicky.

He right away enjoys the way it feels resting in his palm. The size. The weight. The smooth, carved-bone handle. And the folding blade: a thing of exquisite beauty.

"It's an authentic Solingen, sir. Made in Germany. Handcrafted from the finest materials."

"Yes," says Dicky, dreamily, "I'm sure it is." He swings open the blade and runs his thumb across the edge. Not along the edge, but across it. Running his thumb along the edge would instantly open up a deep and bloody gash.

"Careful, sir, it's extremely sharp. Far sharper than even the best mass-produced blades you buy at the drug store."

"Yes," Dicky mutters again. "No doubt." And then, pulling himself together, putting on his best display yet today of passive, middle-class manners, he adds, "You know, ma'am, I've always wanted to try shaving with a straight-edge razor. I think I'll take it."

Chubby smiles again. She loves to make a sale.

Back out on the street, his new blade inside its protective cloth, Dicky feels the joy of a satisfied consumer. Shopping does indeed have its rewards.

DOUBLE TROUBLE

Thomas Young shows his passport to the customs officer at Miami International Airport. The officer checks the photograph inside the passport. Then he glances at Mr. Thomas Young. A perfect likeness. "Anything to declare, Mr. Young?"

Will Hancock shakes his head. "No, sir."

The customs officer stamps Mr. Young's passport and waves him through.

Will strolls through the terminal. He wonders if Mr. Thomas Young has just made his last trip abroad. Before retrieving his baggage, he finds a relatively quiet area with a pay phone. He dials the town house up on Beacon Hill.

Sylvia answers. "Hancock residence."

"Yes, hello," says Will, disguising his voice, "Leland Fisher here. Is Mr. Hancock available?"

"A minute please, Mr. Fisher. I'm sure he is."

Sylvia buzzes Hancock on the intercom. "Mr. Fisher on the line, sir."

John, back in pacing mode, picks up the phone. He hopes Leland doesn't have any new evidence to unleash on him. "Hey, Lee."

Will waits for Sylvia to hang up, then says, "You've got connection problems."

The line goes dead. But John gets the message. He unlocks the bottom drawer of the desk, pulls out the blue Princess telephone, plugs in the access code, and turns on the ringer. Ten seconds later, it rings.

"Jefferson?"

"Adams?"

"Are we secure?"

"I think so."

"What's up?"

"We need to talk," says Will.

"You're goddamn right we do," says John. "Where are you?"

"Fort Ticonderoga," lies Will. Their code name for the old stone farmhouse in the Berkshires outside of Stockbridge.

Will's present location surprises John. "I didn't know you were coming back so soon."

"Yeah, well," says Will, "I got to thinking about that missing person report and decided we should talk it over. Put our heads together and figure this thing out."

"Excellent idea," says John, furious, but working to keep his anger in check. "But first you better tell me what the fuck is going on."

"What do you mean?"

John feels pretty sure he should keep his mouth shut, but now that he has Will on the line he can't bring himself to do so. "Maybe we could start with Hillary Fisher."

"Hillary Fisher? What about her?"

"What do you mean, *what about her?* You're screwing her, for chrissakes."

Will laughs. "Technically, bro, *you're* the one screwing her."

"And what the hell does that mean?"

"It means dear Hillary thinks she's doing you, not me. If you get my drift."

"Oh, I get your drift," says John. "And it's pretty damn sick."

Will laughs again. "Just kidding, bro."

"Yeah, sure, just kidding. Very funny, *bro*. Well I got rid of her. Cleaned up *your* mess. Again. Now do all concerned a favor and stay away from her."

"Or what?"

John backs down. "Christ, Will, what possessed you to screw her in the first place? She's awful."

"Like I said," replies Will, enjoying the exchange, "it was you doing the screwing, not me. I'm dead. Remember?"

John's had enough. He decides to change the subject. "You lied to me."

"About what?"

"About being in the Bahamas."

"Bullshit I lied. I was out on Exuma until late this morning."

"I don't know about this morning, but the other night you were in London."

No chuckle from Will this time. "No way."

"Don't bullshit me, Will."

"I'm not bullshitting you."

"I think you are, and I think you should remember we're in this thing together."

"Absolutely right. Peas in a pod. Have been for almost forty years."

"Exactly. So this is no time to start lying to each other."

"Hey, listen," says Will, "I don't know about you, but I'm all the way on the up-and-up. True blue. Ready to do anything to keep the good ship Hancock afloat."

John thinks he hears an edge of lunacy in Will's voice. He takes a deep breath. "Okay. So tell me what you did to Byrnes."

Will has already anticipated this. "I suggested it might be wise for him to reconsider his feelings for Clara."

"From what he told me it sounds like you almost killed him."

"You talked to him?"

"He called."

"Then I guess I didn't kill him. But I could have. Easily."

John can feel his brother beginning to spin out of control. Hillary. Byrnes. What next? "So you're out at the farmhouse?"

"Sure am."

"And you think I should come out there?"

"I do, yeah. Like I said before, we need to discuss this missing person business."

"You're right," says John. "We do."

"So let's do it."

"Tonight?"

"I was thinking you'd drive out tomorrow," suggests Will. "After the kids go to school."

"They're not going to school tomorrow."

"Why not?"

"They're going up to New Hampshire with Linda Carson. You forgot to tell me."

"This is the first I've heard about it."

"Clara didn't tell you?"

"Nope."

"You sure?"

"Absolutely."

John mulls this over. "Maybe she told me and I forgot."

"So why are they going to New Hampshire?"

"Just to go, I guess." John hadn't really thought about why they were going.

"What about Clara?"

"What about her?"

"Is she going with them?"

John hesitates. Decides not to mention his and Clara's rendezvous at the Ambassador in New York. "I don't know."

"What do you mean, you don't know?"

"Christ, Will, let's just decide what we're going to do."

"You're going to come out here tomorrow so we can talk about me suddenly being a missing person instead of a dead person."

"Right. Tomorrow. Late morning." John figures that

way he can deal with Will for a few hours, then drive down
to New York and meet Clara.

"Late morning?"

"Right."

"I'll see you then," says Will. "Drive safely. And remember, if you get killed in a car wreck, I'm up shit
creek." And he hangs up.

John holds the receiver at arm's length. For several seconds he just stares at it. His thoughts swirl out of control.
So much confusion. Then an idea occurs to him. He gets a
dial tone and punches in *69. But instead of the last number to call the house, Hancock gets this prerecorded message: *"We're sorry. The last number to call your line is not
known. Please hang up now."*

"Shit!" John shouts, as he slams down the receiver.

A second later he snatches it up again. He dials the
farmhouse out in Stockbridge. The phone rings and rings.
Will does not answer. After the fifth ring, he hears his own
voice on the message machine: *"You've reached Adventure
Travel Enter—"*

Again, John slams down the receiver. "Where the hell is
he?" he asks the empty office. "And what the hell is he up
to?"

Less than a minute later the house phone rings again. Sylvia answers down in the kitchen. She has the phone in her
left hand and a large Oriental cleaver in her right. She has
been using the cleaver to chop vegetables for this evening's
stir-fry. Polish by both birth and temperament, Sylvia can
nevertheless create culinary delights from around the
world.

After listening to the person on the other end of the line,
Sylvia again crosses to the intercom. She buzzes the third
floor. "I am sorry for bother you, Mr. Hancock, but a lady
on the phone making herself most insistent about talking
to you."

John doesn't care about the intrusion. He's not working
right now anyway. He's just sitting at his desk, brooding

about his brother, about his wife, about his boys. While he broods, he doodles on a piece of paper. Over and over, in neat block letters, he writes: SWEET WEDNESDAY NIGHT, THE AMBASSADOR HOTEL, NEW YORK, N.Y. . . . SWEET WEDNESDAY NIGHT, THE AMBASSADOR HOTEL, NEW YORK, N.Y. . . .

"Most insistent, you say? Who is it, Sylvia? Not Mrs. Fisher, I hope."

"No, sir. Not that lady. This lady is I think Daniel. Gerd Daniel."

"Gerd Daniel? Who the hell is that?"

"I do not know, sir. She calls from California. Should I say you are not here?"

"No, Sylvia, better let me check it out."

Hancock picks up the phone. "John Hancock here."

"Yes, hello, is this John Hancock? The author?"

"Who's calling, please?"

"Yes, I'm sorry. My name is Doctor MacDaniel. I am a psychiatrist in Los Angeles, California. I have a patient by the name of Babe Overton."

"Yes? So?"

"I don't mean to sound forward, sir, but before I say anything else I would like to make sure I am speaking to the correct Mr. John Hancock. It would be most embarrassing to make a mistake."

Yes, Gerdy, indeed it would. But have no fear, you have the right John Hancock on the line. As the two of them soon enough figure out after they establish a connection between Babe and John and Frank Hagstrom.

"Jesus," says John, "I remember Babe. Beautiful girl. I couldn't believe she wanted to hang around with that old fart Frank. What a waste."

"I don't want to alarm you, Mr. Hancock, but Babe is not well. She has not been well for quite some time."

"Sorry to hear that, but what's it got to do with me?"

"Well, I have reason to believe she has concluded that you, and/or your brother, were responsible for Mr. Hagstrom's death."

"Say what?" But Hancock does not have to ask the question. He heard what Gerdy said loud and clear.

"She has herself convinced," continues Gerdy, "that you killed her lover, Frank Hagstrom, in retaliation for something he did to you. Or maybe to your parents. I'm not exactly sure of the details."

Christ, thinks Hancock, another loony on my tail. Maybe Babe Overton called in that missing person report. The cops said it was a woman. Of course, there's a damn good chance the cops weren't even cops.

"And so let me get this straight. You think Babe's after me?"

"I might not go that far."

"How far might you go?"

"I think it's possible she might pay you a visit."

"Is that what she told you? That she was coming to visit me?"

"Not exactly in those words, no. But I've been in this line of work a long time, Mr. Hancock. I can tell when someone has reached the breaking point."

"So you think Babe has snapped? You think she's violent?"

Gerdy hesitates, sighs, then answers. "Babe Overton is capable of violent thoughts, but I do not think she is capable of violent actions."

"Then why the call?"

"I believe in being cautious."

"So you think I should be careful."

Another sigh from Gerdy. "Babe does not return my calls. Her roommate has not heard from her since Saturday night. I guess I believe the possibility exists that she is either in Boston or on her way."

"You guess?"

"I'm not normally an alarmist, Mr. Hancock, and in this case I hope I'm totally off the mark, but the last time I saw Babe she was extremely distraught. She also knew where you lived."

"Well, isn't that good news."

"I thought you should know."

"Of course you did."

"I'm only trying to help."

"Of course you are." Hancock sighs and rubs his eyes. He and Gerdy talk over the situation for a few more minutes. Gerdy assures him she will call the moment she hears from Babe. Until then, they both agree it might be best for Hancock to exercise a certain amount of caution and vigilance.

Poor Babe. People talking about her this way. A woman who once had such a full and happy life, such deep pools of potential and enthusiasm.

Look at her. Sitting there on that noisy, over-air-conditioned bus. Not a friend in the world. Face drawn. Eyes sad. Mouth gloomy.

Gerdy thinks Babe has murder on her mind. And now Hancock probably thinks so, too. She does have a gun. But the chances of Babe actually using that gun, despite the thoughts she's had, are roughly equal to the chances of an asteroid slamming into planet Earth sometime before the end of the millennium. A possibility, yes, but highly remote.

Babe is just a sad and broken woman. Look around. You'll see them everywhere. In the malls. On the roads. At the airports. And the bus stations. Some hide it better than others. Babe does not hide it very well. She has those sad, faraway eyes.

If only she'd found a lover. Someone kind and decent. Someone to take her to the movies and out to dinner and for an evening stroll down Sunset Boulevard. Someone to give her flowers and candy and make love to her in the morning and again before bed. Someone to marry her and give her babies and mow the grass on Sunday after church.

Poor Babe. Nothing quite so sad in life as a tired and lonely middle-aged woman on a Greyhound bus forty miles west of St. Louis, Missouri.

And now here's John Hancock, right there on the proverbial edge of freaking out, adding OVERTON, BABE to his list of suspects.

FRANK & BABE

After their sophomore year at Harvard, John and Will traveled west to California to check on the status of their parents' estate. Right from the start the trip did not go well. Trouble started as soon as they arrived at their parents' lovely home up in the Hollywood Hills. Their front door key refused to turn the lock.

A minute or so after ringing the bell and banging the brass knocker, the door opened to reveal a young woman wearing nothing but a sheer black negligee and a thin gold anklet. She had a body like an hourglass, shoulder-length blond hair, and a beautiful face. The kind of smooth and pleasant face you see on TV advertising toothpaste. She looked fresh and innocent, with about as many years experience on Earth as John and Will Hancock.

"Hey, babe," came a familiar voice from somewhere deep inside the house, "did I hear someone at the door?"

"You sure did, pumpkin. And he's cute," added the pretty blonde, her eyes smiling at the twin brothers. "Both of them."

"What did you say?"

"I said we have company."

The boys and the young lady stood there at the front

door staring at each other for thirty or forty seconds. Will wanted to ask her why the hell she was in their house, but her beauty and that black negligee had his tongue tied.

And then, wearing red silk boxers and a V-neck T-shirt, Big Frank Hagstrom came strutting into the entrance foyer. But one glimpse of those Hancock boys and he quit strutting in a hurry. He came to a dead stop. His eyes grew wide. He had the look of a big buck suddenly caught in the glare of oncoming headlights.

But years of lying and weaseling out of tight spots had taught the attorney how to avoid disaster. "Hey, boys," he said with all the nonchalance of a right cross to the bridge of the nose, "how's things?"

The Hancock boys glared.

Frank crossed to his young pet, thinking she might be able to take the edge off. "So you boys meet Ms. Overton yet? John, Will, this is Babe Overton. Babe, these two fine-looking young men are the Hancock brothers. John and Will. Don't ask me which one is which. I don't have a clue."

Babe smiled. She had no idea what was going on. Innocent as a newborn lamb.

The Hancock boys smiled back, but continued to glare at Hagstrom.

And then John Hancock, not at all happy with the lay of the land, brushed past the pretty blonde, gave Frank a little shove, and strode into the vast living room with its high ceiling and glass facade overlooking the great smog-filled city of Los Angeles. Brother Will followed close behind.

The living room was cluttered with cardboard moving boxes and furniture covered with moving blankets. The Hancock boys, hands on hips, waited for an explanation.

Frank, no shrinking violet, and well trained in aggressive warfare, went directly on the offensive. "Sorry you had to find out this way, boys. I had a letter in the—"

"Find out what?" John demanded.

"About the house," said Frank. "I had a letter in the works. All ready to go. In the legal business you hurry up and wait, and then, all at once, things happen."

"What things are we talking about here, Frank?" It was the first time John had ever called Frank Frank.

Well, Frank babbled on as only an attorney who bills by the second can babble, but it all boiled down to this rather obvious piece of business: Hagstrom now owned the house on Edwin Drive up in the Hollywood Hills. He owned the locks, the views, and the crystal chandeliers. He owned it all.

He had moved in just a couple days earlier. With his '59 T-bird, his law books, and his luscious young bimbo Babe. And boy, oh boy, did Babe look luscious back in those days. Nothing at all like the sad and tired lady on that Greyhound bus.

All of the furniture and most of the cardboard boxes belonged to her. A few of the boxes belonged to Frank, but not too many. Frank had pretty much jettisoned everything, including his wife and his kids and his Outstanding Citizen of the Year Award. He made the dump soon after meeting Babe. One session in the sack with the twenty-something Ms. Overton, and this whiny, middle-aged voice in the back of Frank's head kept shouting, "Younger is better, Frank! Go for the gold! Younger is better, Frank! Go for the gold!"

Frank, hovering right around fifty, went for the gold, all right.

As for the house, well, it was all perfectly legal; legal but unbelievably sleazy. For nearly four years, ever since William and Lenore had lost their heads, the mortgage on the house had gone unpaid. Frank, of course, knew this, but chose to do nothing about it. Nothing, that is, but crouch and wait, like a panther stalking its unwitting prey. And sure enough, just before the bank moved in for its final foreclosure, Frank stepped up to the plate with his secret money market account. He bought the property for pennies on the dollar.

"The house was going, one way or another," Frank explained, thick arms folded across his T-shirt. "I just saw an opportunity and grabbed it."

"An opportunity, huh!" shouted John, his face awash

with rage after listening to the lawyer justify his actions. John was the far more volatile of the two brothers back in those days, far more likely to lose his temper. He quickly closed in on Hagstrom. "Well, maybe I see an *opportunity* to beat your stinking brains out."

An old law professor had once told Frank, "Never under any circumstances back off. Back off, even one step, and you're through. You're a loser." So Frank stood his ground. "Calm down, son. I doubt beating my brains out would do you much good."

"It wouldn't do you much good either, *pumpkin*."

Will grabbed his brother by the arm. "Take it easy, John. Hitting the son of a bitch won't solve anything." Good old Will. Always calm. Always rational.

John yanked his arm away. He shoved his face right up into Hagstrom's face. "Now I see what you've been up to all these years. Slowly but surely sucking us dry. Dragging our father's good name through the muck. Telling us he was broke and in debt. You lying son of a bitch. You're going to pay for this. Do you hear me, *pumpkin*? You're going to pay. You're standing there now, but believe me, you're as good as dead." John turned to his brother. "Look at him, Will. He appears to be alive, but he's not. He's a dead man."

Will said nothing. Will rarely lost his cool. Even in the tensest situations. But, of course, that all changed. Later.

Frank felt himself swallow, then he puffed out his chest and asked, "Is that a threat?"

"Fuck you."

"Fuck me?"

"That's right, pal: fuck you. And you can also consider yourself fired. As of this moment, you're no longer our lawyer. You've screwed us around long enough."

Frank recovered nicely. A bold smirk actually spread across his face. "But son, I never was your lawyer. I was your father's lawyer."

"Which made you our lawyer after he died."

"Sorry," replied Frank, "not true. I'm the executor of your parents' estate. It's right there in your old man's last will and testament. And, as executor, I am doing everything in my power to bring your father's wishes to fruition."

"Bullshit!"

Frank shrugged. "I'm sorry you feel that way, son."

John did his best to burn holes in Frank's flesh, but attorneys have thick skin; they do not burn easily. "Let's roll," he said to his brother. "I can't stand the stink in here."

But Will was not quite ready to go. He turned to Hagstrom. As calmly as possible, doing everything in his power to steady his pounding heart and his angry thoughts, he asked, "What about all the stuff that was here? The furniture and the clothes and the paintings?"

"It's all in storage," Frank assured him. "Safe and sound. Why don't you call the office tomorrow. Talk to my secretary. She'll give you the details."

"We want the details now!" demanded John.

"I don't think so," said Hagstrom. "Tomorrow would be better."

"Fuck tomorrow!"

Hagstrom took a step back. The time had come to decrease the chances of physical conflict. "Relax, Mr. Hancock. And watch your mouth in the company of a lady."

Babe stood off to the side watching the unfolding drama as though it was nothing but a bit on her favorite daytime soap. Never in her wildest dreams would she have thought that this particular scene was the beginning of the end of her charmed life.

"Lady, my ass!" shouted John. "That's no goddamn lady."

Will put his hand on his brother's shoulder. "Come on, John, let's get out of here before something ugly happens."

John nodded, but didn't move.

And then Hagstrom, the coward, instead of defending Babe's honor, had the gall to say, "I want you boys to know how bad I feel about all this."

John mumbled an obscenity or two, then thumped the

attorney on the chest with the tip of his index finger. "Like I said before, *pumpkin*: Consider yourself a dead man."

"Listen," replied Frank, now cool as a cucumber, "I understand how you feel, son. I really do. This hasn't been easy for you, or for any of us who cared about your mom and dad. But I think I should tell you: I'm a little strapped for cash right now, what with the divorce and buying this place and all. I think if you want to stay in school you better apply for some student loans, maybe get yourselves some part-time jobs. I'd sure hate to see those Harvard educations go down the tubes because of this mess."

MAXWELL EDISON

The Hancock boys did not retreat east with their tails between their legs. Before returning to Cambridge, they hired
a new attorney. They found his name in the Los Angeles
Area yellow pages. There were literally thousands of lawyers listed under this heading. More lawyers than doctors.
More lawyers than movie producers. Which one to pick?
Which one could they trust? John and Will had no idea.
They could only guess, and hope. Their eyes combed the
ads and the long list of names. After nearly an hour of
studying the lists, they both suddenly stopped dead at the
same name: Edison, Maxwell, Attorney-at-Law. 32119
Wilshire Blvd. Santa Monica. 555–9989.

They dialed up Max immediately.

The boys were heavily into The Beatles at that time.
They owned every Beatles album and had listened to every
album hundreds of times. Their favorite album was *Abbey
Road*. And one of their favorite tunes on *Abbey Road* was
"Maxwell's Silver Hammer," starring that psychotic bad
boy, Maxwell Edison.

Can you think of a better way to eenie-meenie-miney-
moe pick an attorney?

Max agreed to see the Hancock boys later that same

afternoon. The offices of Maxwell Edison on Wilshire Boulevard did not look quite as spiffy as the posh space occupied by Hagstrom, Hays, Bennett, Barlow & Lunt over in
Beverly Hills. Max was a lone wolf. He shared a secretary
with three other lone wolves. His office overlooked an auto
body shop. But John and Will noticed none of this. They
knew from the name that Max was their man. He was
young, hip, well-dressed, and very, very eager. And so
what if the law degree hanging in the shadows at the back
of his dingy, dusty office had been granted by the Podunk
School of Law back in East Podunk, Illinois?

Max listened intently while the boys spilled their tale of
woe. He nodded and took notes. And when the boys finished, Max assured them he'd do everything in his power
to clear their father's good name and settle the family estate.

John and Will thanked him, solemn expressions on their
twin faces. Then they flew east believing Maxwell Edison
would solve all of their legal and financial problems.

It would be remiss to bluntly accuse Maxwell Edison of
being yet another crooked lawyer. The man had reasonably decent scruples. But, like all of us, Max had bills to
pay and desires to fulfill. So, when Big Frank Hagstrom
offered him a generous stipend simply for keeping his
mouth shut, Max had to think seriously about zipping his
lip.

But that came later. In the beginning, Max really
wanted to help the Hancock boys. He wanted to help them
for three reasons: to collect a handsome fee after the estate
was settled, to take on the powerful L.A. attorney, Frank
Hagstrom, and, lastly, to serve the needs of his clients to
the best of his abilities.

For several weeks, months even, Maxwell Edison
looked into the matter. He put together a thick file filled
with dozens of fascinating facts. Facts about William and
Lenore Hancock. Facts about the Hancock Umbrella Company. Facts about Frank Hagstrom. And finally, feeling he
had sufficient ammunition, he made an appointment to see

Mr. Hagstrom at Frank's Beverly Hills office. He had to wait a week.

At the appointed hour, Max strolled into Hagstrom's enormous office wearing his best suit. He felt like he had finally made it to the big show. This was his moment to shine.

"Have a seat," said Frank. Frank was already behind his massive desk, looking tall and powerful and very lawyerly. He did not bother to get up.

Max sat in a small wooden chair which had had the legs cut down several inches. It was a special chair Frank brought out for special occasions. Occasions like this when he wanted to totally dominate his adversary.

"What can I do for you today, Mr. . . ." Frank checked his notes. "Mr. Edison? Any relation to Thomas Alva?" Hagstrom threw Max his most charming smile.

Max, suddenly feeling small and intimidated, actually answered. "We like to think there is a distant connection."

"That's swell," replied Frank. And then, "So I understand you're representing John and Will Hancock now. Doing a little mercenary work, are you, Max?"

Max was not entirely naive. He could see what was happening here. So he took a deep breath and told Hagstrom the boys had hired him to find out why it was taking so long to settle William and Lenore Hancock's estate. Frank listened carefully as Max droned on about the '59 T-bird and the house up in the Hollywood Hills and the fortune William Hancock had made in umbrellas.

Frank listened, and didn't say a word. He let this slick young whippersnapper talk himself mute.

Finally, after Max had run out of fuel, Frank shuffled a few papers around on his desk, cleared his throat, and asked, "Tell me, Max—Do you mind if I call you Max?—have you done much estate work?"

"I've handled a number of wills."

"Wills. Excellent. Ever been an executor?"

Max had to shake his head. "No."

"Well, tell me this, Max: Do you have the slightest idea what kind of complexities are involved in trying to settle a private, multimillion-dollar estate when the principals bow out," and Frank Hagstrom snapped his fingers together, "just like that?" The snap echoed through the vast office.

Max tried not to fidget in that tiny chair, but he could not help craning his neck to ease the muscle tension. He was beginning to feel like maybe he had overstepped his bounds, waded in where perhaps the water ran too deep. "I know it takes time."

"Damn right it takes time."

"Yes, but, well, the fact remains that the Hancocks lost their parents in that terrible auto accident almost four years ago."

"And you think four years is a long time?"

"Well, I think—"

"I've seen estates take twenty years to settle. Five years is not uncommon."

Max tugged on his tie. It suddenly felt warm in there, like maybe the air conditioning had gone on the blink. "Look, Frank, Mr. Hagstrom, I'm not trying to—"

Frank held up his hand. Max fell silent.

"Let's not waste each other's time here, son. I've got things to do, and maybe so do you. You'll never be able to touch me on this thing. Not in a million years. Not that there's anything to touch. But knowing the financial situation facing those twins, I would have to say you signed on to help them on a contingency basis. They don't have two dimes to rub together for an attorney. So I suggest you and I do a little business."

"Business?"

"That's right. It's very simple. I'll go through it once, and only once. Here's how it works: I throw some civil cases your way. Nothing too complex. You bill me at any rate you think fair. I'll expect to pay through the nose for your expert legal services. In return, all you have to do is give those two Harvard boys some reassurance. Tell them all is well here in the Golden State."

Max had sweat under his arms and on his brow. (Frank had, in fact, cranked the thermostat up to eighty.) "I don't know," Max mumbled. "It doesn't sound ethical to me."

Frank did not waste a second. He struck hard. He was a
master of knowing exactly when to strike. "Don't give me
that ethical crap, Edison! You think it's ethical for you to
waltz in here on your high fucking horse and start accusing
me, Frank Hagstrom, pillar of the Los Angeles legal community, of manipulating a client's estate? I patiently gave
you an opportunity to speak, sir. But now you're out of
line. Way out of line!"

Maxwell Edison, by this time, was little more than a
calamity of nervous, sweaty tics. "No . . . I . . . Let me
apologize . . . I just wanted—"

"I don't give a damn what you wanted, boy. I've heard
enough. Now I have work to do. Real work. I strongly
suggest you take the deal, Edison. It's by far your best way
out of this mess."

Right about then is when Maxwell Edison, hefty payments to make on his used 911 Targa, decided it might be
best to zip his lip.

THE HANCOCK HIDEAWAY

Young Willy and John junior have a hankering for a bed-time story, so Dad interrupts his forays into the past, gets the kids into bed, and tells them a wild tale about knights and dragons and damsels in distress. Not much plot or continuity (those are not John's strong suits), but plenty of blood and gore and kisses for the good guys.

As the story winds down and the boys begin to drift off, John's thoughts return to that little ferret of a lawyer, Maxwell Edison. Every three months for almost two years Max called them up and assured them his investigation into Frank Hagstrom was turning up nothing unusual, certainly nothing illegal.

Little did John suspect that Max was on the dole.

Will, however, suspected. And several times he suggested to John that they fire Max and hire someone new. But John thought Max was doing a fine job. Plus he was doing it for free.

Oh yes, Will remembers. He remembers everything. Every last detail. Like the passport switch down on Caye Caulker. And the way John kept insisting he would get rid of Hagstrom, but never did. And the way John claimed he was only interested in sharing Clara for a year or two.

After that he would move out and move on to greener pastures. So how many years ago was that now? Seven years? Eight years? No question about it: too goddamn many years.

Will exits the Massachusetts Turnpike in his big silver BMW 750il (brother John has one exactly like it) and heads southwest along Route 102. Will retrieved his BMW from long-term parking at Logan International Airport just a couple hours ago.

He drives slowly through the small town of Stockbridge. For nearly a decade now Stockbridge has been the boys' home away from home. When not back in Boston or off gallivanting around for Adventure Travel Enterprises, they hang their hats here in this peaceful little New England village with its Norman Rockwell museum and old-fashioned general store. Will passes the Red Lion Inn on his left and St. Paul's Episcopal Church on his right. He makes no stops. He drives straight through town and out into the country.

A couple miles north of Stockbridge he turns right onto Church Street. Half a mile or so later he makes another right onto Old Meeting House Road. A narrow, dirt and gravel lane, Old Meeting House climbs sharply into the hills. At the top of the third rise Will swings the big BMW into a stone drive protected on both sides by a tall forsythia hedge. The high, bushy hedge easily keeps out any prying eyes. The Hancock boys definitely do not want any prying eyes.

The driveway winds for thirty or forty yards through a stand of mature sugar maples. At the end of the drive stands the Hancock Hideaway, where one brother hides from the world while the other brother performs the role of John Hancock: author, father, husband, and all-around good citizen. Up here, in this old stone farmhouse, tucked away in the rolling Berkshires of western Massachusetts, a million miles from Boston, John and Will play out their dual lives.

They bought the house and the eleven private acres for a

song some years back when their third novel, *The Killer,*
hit the best-seller list. An uninhabitable mess at the time of
the closing, they have slowly whipped it into shape. Mostly
with their own hands and their own sweat. They now have
an almost fully restored two-hundred-and-fifty-year-old
stone-and-mortar farmhouse where they can write and relax and plan their Adventure Travel Enterprises trips. No
one else in the world even knows they have this place. It's
their little secret.

The outside of the house is ivy-covered, with a blue slate
roof. Around the house there are perennial gardens, many
of the beds beginning to come to life after the long New
England winter.

Dusk settles slowly on this late spring evening. Almost
nine o'clock now, but Will can still see the old wooden
barn where they keep their lawn and garden equipment
and their fine German automobiles during inclement
weather. For several years Will has had plans to make his
own private studio in the barn, but thus far he has not
gotten beyond the planning stage. And if things go as he
hopes in the next twenty-four to forty-eight hours, there
will be no need for a private studio.

Between the house and the barn stands the property's
third and final structure: a low, squat, stone building with
a steeply pitched slate roof. On the front of the building a
set of stone steps leads directly underground. A concrete
ramp on the back side leads down to a large wooden door.
Before refrigeration, the bunkerlike building was used by
farmers to store ice and roots and potatoes and anything
else they wanted to preserve.

Will has recently spent quite a lot of time down in this
old root cellar. He thinks he might have found another,
more contemporary use for the underground space.

Right now he climbs out of his BMW, takes a leisurely
look around, and starts up the brick path to the house.
Someday he hopes to bring Clara and the kids here. The
boys, he knows, will love it. Plenty of room to run wild.

He enters the farmhouse through the front door, a wide

but rather low opening that forces both brothers to duck a bit when coming and going. All the doorways in the house are low, a testament, no doubt, to the fact that Americans were a shorter lot, back before the War for Independence.

The farmhouse is small, not more than twelve hundred square feet, but during renovation the Hancock boys tore down walls and opened up the tiny, colonial rooms. The downstairs is one large space now with areas for cooking, dining, reading, and writing. In the middle of the room sits a large, cast-iron wood stove. Upstairs is a large sleeping loft and a thoroughly modern bathroom complete with Jacuzzi.

In the corner that receives the most morning light, the boys have set up their office. A large wooden desk sits against a wide bay window. Several tables surround the desk. On these tables sit various pieces of electronic equipment: computer, printer, scanner, fax, modem, telephone answering machine, even a shortwave radio. This is corporate HQ for Adventure Travel Enterprises. Travel books, guide books, and brochures from all over the world are piled high everywhere.

The digital read-out on the telephone answering machine indicates there are twenty-one messages. Will decides to deal with them later. Or maybe he won't bother dealing with them at all. Ever. Could be time to put Adventure Travel Enterprises to rest. Will is sick and tired of traveling. Will feels like staying home.

Still, he figures he'd better listen to the messages. There might be one from John.

But first he needs a drink. He crosses to the bar and pours himself a stiff one.

Drink secured, he returns to the desk and hits the play button.

"Yes, hello, my name's Lee Brush. I'm interested in receiving your newsletter. My phone number is 973–555–7819. My address is . . ."

"This is Pete Christopher. I'd like to subscribe to your newsletter. My phone number is 908 . . ."

"Yeah, this is Steve French. I'm interested in making a trip to . . ."

On and on they drone, one after another. Will pours himself another Scotch and listens to the voices without really hearing a word they say.

CHICAGO

Rafe doesn't really hear much either. Just a steady hum of white noise. He's high as a kite wandering around Chicago O'Hare International Airport. On the flight up from Houston he needed almost half an hour in the lavatory to extract that plastic bag of cocaine from his rectum. And once he finally did, he decided to have a little sniff to help calm his frayed and twitchy nerves.

Well, as anyone who ever snorted coke knows, one line very often leads to another line which leads to another line. And so the coke goes. By the time Rafe reached Chicago he'd pulled half a dozen long, thick lines up his nostrils.

Now he's feeling good. Got a smile working from ear to ear. The world flowing by in slow motion. No worries, mon. He feels like hearing some music, like maybe doing some dancing. Head bopping, hips rolling, feet sliding, Rafe heads for the exit in search of a taxi to take him into the Windy City.

He has an early flight to the Big Apple, but to hell with six-thirty in the A.M. He'll get a later flight. Or take a train. Or a bus. See a little of the USA. No worries, no hurries. Hancock, he feels sure, ain't going anywhere. And the drug dude he has to meet at The Chase inside the Ambassador

Hotel, that's not till Thursday around noon. Plenty of time to make that gig. Loads of time.

Rafe spins through the revolving doors. Out into a warm Chicago night. He glides along, practically on a bed of air. Oh, yeah, so fine. Money to spend. Coke to blow.

He pulls open the back door of a yellow cab. "Downtown, sire," he says to the driver, an amiable Indian fellow who grew up in Bombay. "Someplace with reggae and dancing and lots of black chicks."

"Oh, yes, dancing," says the driver, checking out Rafe in the rearview mirror. "I show you dancing."

Frank used to take Babe dancing. In fact, he was going to take her dancing the night he died. They had a date. For ten o'clock. Too bad Frank never showed up.

Babe had a gig that day. At a studio out in Burbank. For Prell. Or maybe Head & Shoulders. One of the hair products. There weren't so many back in those days.

The shoot ran late. The producers brought in dinner. Babe called Frank. They agreed to meet at the Roxbury for a drink and a couple trips around the dance floor.

"Bye, baby."

"Bye, sweets. See you soon."

Their last words.

Babe waited at the Roxbury down on Sunset Boulevard till about eleven-fifteen. A couple times she called the house up in the Hollywood Hills. Frank didn't answer. Frank couldn't answer. Frank was tied up.

Babe finally got home around midnight. Where she found Frank, dangling from the living room ceiling.

She sees him again now. She sees him in the darkness outside the window of that Greyhound bus. She sees him hanging there in the living room. Stretched and ghost-pale and dead. And then she sees the Hancock brothers. Both of them. John and Will. Standing there, making threats. Threatening to hurt Frank. Threatening to kill him.

"You're a dead man, pumpkin. Do you hear me? You're a dead man."

Oh, yes, Babe hears it all. And sees it all. Tears roll out of her sad eyes and down her cheeks. Babe feels for the handgun in the bottom of her purse. She looks out the window again and spots a sign along the side of the interstate highway: CHICAGO 250 MILES.

JEFFERSON & ADAMS

John kisses the boys good night. They are both already sound asleep. He retreats quietly, turns off the light, and closes the door. But he does not close it all the way. He knows the boys like it left partway open so they can see out into the hallway in the middle of the night.

John climbs the stairs to the third floor. He picks up the phone and dials the number out in Stockbridge. He waits for the message, his message, to finish, then he says, "Yo, Jefferson, if you're there, pick up. I have something to report."

Will, another scotch on the rocks in hand, hesitates, but answers. "Adams?"

"That's right."

"You're still coming tomorrow, aren't you?"

"I'll be there. But we had another little piece of business a while ago I thought I'd pass along to you."

"What?"

"I had a call from some shrink out in L.A." John tells Will about the conversation with Gerdy MacDaniel.

"Jesus," says Will, "I remember Babe Overton. Beautiful girl. We both had the hots for her."

"Yeah, well," says John, "this Doctor MacDaniel

doesn't think Babe's the violent type, but she still thinks it would be wise for us to be on guard."

"So is she dangerous or what?"

"I don't know. But maybe she's behind that missing person report."

"You think so?" asks Will, a pretty good buzz going after several ounces of scotch.

"Who the hell knows," says John. "I have no idea what to think anymore."

"Why don't you just get your butt out here and we'll figure out what to do about everything. The whole mess."

"You sound," says John, "like you've been drinking."

"Just a nip or two."

John decides not to push it. It's just that he knows Will has been boozing a lot at home lately, and that is not a good thing. "Like I said earlier, I'll be there late morning."

They say good-bye and hang up.

John sighs. And thinks again about the booze. He knows his brother used to drink very little. But lately, Will's been drinking like a fish.

Will finishes his scotch. He wonders how Babe Overton is looking these days. But wondering about Babe gets him thinking about Frank, which is not something he wants to think about, so he crosses to the bar and refills his glass.

Then he returns to the desk and switches the answering machine back on. That long list of messages continues to unwind. Most of the messages have been painfully dull.

He is now up to number fourteen. Number fifteen. Sixteen. Will barely hears a word the callers say. Nothing but distant voices. He's sitting here at the desk, eyes half closed, hoping the scotch will just send him off to sleep. Off to never-never land.

Seventeen. Eighteen. Nineteen.

But then, coming from far away, from the vast and alien interior of that telephone answering machine, he hears a familiar voice. A very familiar voice. A voice that causes Will Hancock to suddenly become perfectly sober.

"Yes, hello, I received your name and number from a friend of mine. I'm interested in taking my family on a nice

*summer vacation in July or August. My husband and my
two young sons. Scandinavia sounds fun, but really I'm
looking for suggestions. And also a guide. You know,
someone to set up the trip, kind of take us by the hand so
we can just relax and have some fun.*

*"You come very highly recommended, so I hope you
can get in touch with me as soon as possible. My name is
Clara Dare Hancock. You can reach me in Boston at 617–
555–9917. Unfortunately, you will not be able to reach me
there until Friday or Saturday. It would be much better if
you called me in New York at the Ambassador Hotel anytime after, say, two o'clock on Wednesday afternoon. That
way we can start planning something right away. I just
hate putting things off. Don't you?*

*"So again, that's Clara Dare Hancock. I believe the
number at the Ambassador is 212–994–4000. Or better
yet, if you're in New York, just stop by the hotel and see
me. In fact, that's definitely what you should do. The Ambassador is located on Fifth Avenue at Sixty-third Street,
near the southeast corner of Central Park. Ciao."*

Will, out of his chair, breathing short and frantic,
throws up all over the wide pine floor boards.

Will's well known for puking when the going gets
tough.

SOME MORE OLD BUSINESS

COMMENCEMENT

The Hancock boys graduated from Harvard University on a beautiful and hopeful spring afternoon in early June of 1981. Harvard Yard looked glorious on that June afternoon: the sun shining bright, the flowers in bloom, birds chirping away, the crimson robes of the graduates flowing in the gentle spring breeze. The audience was filled to overflowing with smiling parents and grandparents, brothers and sisters, aunts and uncles. You could see the joy and the pride, like halos, hovering over the heads of these proud family members. It was Harvard, after all, about to celebrate something like its three hundred and fortieth commencement.

But the Hancock boys had no one out there among the masses; no one other than their mentor Zelda Cosgrove and a handful of other professors who had enlightened and encouraged them along their academic way. They had recently turned twenty-one, but they felt more than ever like orphans.

All of this might have been a slight overdramatization. The boys certainly had a place to go: just a stone's throw from Harvard Yard, over on Prescott Street. The upstairs of that old converted row house with its peeling clapboards and sagging porch might not have been the finest digs in the world, but it was cheap and convenient, and for the first time in their lives John and Will each had a bedroom of their own.

After much debate about what to do next with their lives, the boys had decided to stay on at Harvard and pursue a master's degree in creative writing. This course of action had originally been proposed by Professor Cosgrove, who very much wanted to keep the Hancock boys within her immediate sphere of influence. Zelda feared if they spread their wings now, she would never get them back to the nest.

John had balked at the idea of hanging around Cambridge after graduation. He figured four years in that environment was enough for any man. He wanted out. He wanted to clear his head, see some new places.

"Hell," he told his brother, "I don't care if we wind up being writers or doctors or bicycle mechanics, the time has come for us to get out and see the world."

"I agree," said Will, even though he had mixed feelings about leaving the security of the Cambridge community, "but we have one small problem."

"And what's that?"

"Money."

"Money?"

"We don't have any. In fact, we're in debt. Something in the neighborhood of twenty-five thousand dollars, because of our student loans."

"Thanks to that son of a bitch Hagstrom. If that bastard hadn't ripped us off we'd be on easy street now. We'd be off to Europe for the summer."

"You think?" asked Will.

"Damn right, I do. But don't worry, bro. We'll get to Europe, and every other corner of the planet. Just you wait and see." The concept of Adventure Travel Enterprises had already taken root in John's furtive and restless imagination.

•   •   •

That summer the boys only made it as far as Baxter State Park in Maine, for a week of hiking and camping. And they managed that trip only after working menial jobs for the university all through June, July, and most of August. They painted dorm rooms, cleaned gutters, cut grass, and pruned hedges.

Even after classes resumed in the fall, they had to keep working to pay their bills. They had rent to pay, food and books to buy, clothes to put on their backs.

And all the time, almost every day, they had Professor Zelda Cosgrove breathing down their necks, telling them the time had come to start a novel, to make their first big push toward a literary career.

"Exactly when are we supposed to write this stupid novel?" was inevitably John's response.

"That's up to you," Zelda always replied. "Ayn Rand wrote *The Fountainhead* in the middle of the night while raising children and holding down a full-time job."

"Ayn Fricking Rand."

"Fine," countered Zelda, "waste your talent. Go play basketball. Go out drinking and carousing and looking for women. I don't give a damn. Just don't hand me those two-bit excuses about not having the time. You have the time if you want to make the time."

John typically stormed out during Zelda's tirades. He did not enjoy criticism.

Will, however, almost always hung around. One day he asked her, "So let's say we start a novel. What's it about? What's the first line?"

Will had been trying, for months, to get a story started. He had not told anyone, but he'd been working at it every spare minute. Unfortunately, his imagination was not as fertile as John's. Will had a problem creating something out of nothing. John could fill blank page after blank page without pausing to take a breath. But Will feared the blank page. His skills came into play once the early draft, the inspirational spark, had been whipped up by his brother.

As for Zelda, she had been thinking about the Hancocks' first novel for a long time. "It's about a couple of teenage boys at boarding school," she now told Will. "Twins, actually, who lose their parents and have to face the world all by themselves."

Will took all this in, then went back to work. But he couldn't do it. Page after page after page fell flat. He tore the pages to pieces and threw them in the trash.

But John, too, was working on a first draft. And he was doing so on the sly, without his brother or Zelda or anyone else knowing about it. Zelda's challenge had taken root. John wanted to prove he could do it.

He started in late one autumn night when he couldn't sleep. It began as a short story for one of his classes and just kept growing, chapter after chapter. Most of a month passed before he actually admitted to himself that the seventy-five pages he had written constituted the opening move of a real novel. Each night as he worked, some-times—à la Ms. Rand—into the wee hours of the morning, he kept himself revved up with the idea that this was his way out. By writing and selling a novel, he could pay off his debts and get out of Cambridge, slip away, whenever he felt like it, to Caracas or Katmandu. That's what John Hancock wanted to do: hit the road, see the world, live out of a suitcase.

But no question about it: his plot had started to drift, his characters had lost their focus. He needed Will's input. And soon.

The boys had Thanksgiving dinner at Zelda's apartment on Berkeley Street. After the meal, John produced two cop-ies of his typed manuscript, which by then had swelled to over a hundred pages. He handed one copy to his brother and one copy to Zelda.

Both of them looked mildly shocked.

"Read it when you have time," he told them, "and let me know what you think."

Zelda smiled, stood up, and headed for the bedroom. Just before closing the door she said, "Don't go anywhere till I get back."

Zelda stayed in her room for well over an hour. Will didn't feel like reading the manuscript in the presence of his brother, so they turned on the tube and watched the Detroit Lions defeat the Philadelphia Eagles.

A couple times they heard Zelda laugh out loud.

When Zelda returned, she kept it brief. "It's good. A little rough around the edges, but you've written some very funny scenes." She looked John dead in the eye. "I want you to keep pushing forward until you finish the first draft. Don't worry about details. We'll work those out." Then she turned to Will. "You need to read these pages through at least two or three times. Get a grip on the story, on what your brother is trying to do. Then go to page one and start working your magic." Zelda, all wound up, paced around the small room. "If I can keep you two focused and we can come up with an ending, I think we could definitely stir up some interest."

John, looking like a happy mutt, smiled and wagged his tail.

Will, ticked off his brother had kept the existence of the manuscript a secret for all these weeks, did not look quite so pleased. Nevertheless, he went home that night and went straight to work, exactly as the good Professor ordered.

John and Will worked on the novel all through the winter and into the spring. Zelda monitored their progress with a zealot's intensity. They held weekly meetings to discuss the narrative and to solve any problems that had arisen. John frequently missed these meetings. He claimed writing was a far better use of his time. Though usually he was out drinking and playing pool, while Will and Zelda pored over the manuscript.

His absence at these meetings did not really matter. John had provided the spark. It was Will who had to keep the engine running smoothly, who changed the oil and followed the maintenance schedule. With Zelda's wickedly sharp eye, Will kept the story firing on all cylinders.

On the Ides of March, 1982, satisfied with the first half of the manuscript, Zelda dropped by to see Mr. Leland Fisher. Leland had not yet assumed control of the family publishing business, The Boston Press, but he did occupy a small office in that lovely old brownstone on Beacon Street, just off Boston Common.

Leland pretty much came and went as he pleased, believing, more than anything, in the importance of getting drunk and stoned at least once a day. But officially, Leland was an editor at The Boston Press with the power to purchase and publish books. In fact, his father, in an act of flagrant nepotism, encouraged him to do so.

Zelda knew all this. Zelda knew everything. And everyone. She had known Leland Fisher and Leland's father for years. More importantly, she knew Leland would like the Hancocks' novel. She knew he would love the title: *Boarding School Blues*. Leland had been a boarding school brat. So she tossed the manuscript on his desk, leaned over so he could view her voluptuous chest, and told him to take a look.

"At those?" Leland asked, pointing at Zelda's breasts.

"No, Leland," she replied, tapping the top of the manuscript, "at this."

"And what is this, dear? Not another dreary novel from one of your morose and far-too-serious colleagues across the Charles."

"Actually, I think you'll find this rather humorous, perhaps even touching."

Leland recoiled in mock horror. "I hate touching."

"No, you don't. You just like to pretend you do."

Leland stared longingly at Zelda. "If I read it will you sleep with me?"

"Not a chance."

"Not even if I offer you a million dollars to publish it?"

"Not even then."

Leland sulked, but read the manuscript anyway. He read it five times over the next few days. He first read it drunk, then sober, then stoned, then drunk, then once more sober. Each time he laughed and laughed and laughed.

"Jesus," he told Zelda, "this thing is hilarious."

"You liked it?"

"Liked it? I loved it. This guy can write. Who is he?"

"Not he," Zelda told him. "Them. Two of them, actually. Brothers. Twin brothers. Identical twins. The Hancocks. No relation to John Hancock, though they'll try to tell you otherwise. They lie about everything. A very fucked-up pair. Lost their parents when they were kids. Psychologically they're a mess."

"But they can write."

"Oh, yes, they certainly can do that. And get this."

"What?"

"They're only twenty-one years old. Twenty-two in a couple months."

"Yikes," said Leland, and he bent down to the beverage center in the bottom right-hand drawer of his desk. "I better have a cocktail."

"So," asked Zelda, "you want to buy it? Do you want to publish it?"

Leland mixed himself a bourbon and water. "So what's the deal, Zelda? Are you their agent? Their mentor? What's in it for you?"

"Nothing's in it for me, Leland. Nothing at all. Except, of course, the sheer joy of seeing exceptional prose brought to the reading public."

Leland sipped his drink. "You know, Zelda, it's a pain in the ass dealing with such an honest and selfless soul. Takes all the fun out of it."

"Sorry, baby, I'll try to be a bitch."

Leland laughed and took another sip. "So when do I see the rest of it?"

"It shouldn't be long," answered Zelda. "Sometime over the summer."

"They write fast, do they?"

"Oh yes, very fast. As long as you can get them to sit down."

"So you're their mother as well?"

"Something like that. Now what about some money, Leland?"

Leland decided it might be best not to draw up a contract just yet. Better to see the finished product and then make an offer. But he did give the boys five thousand dollars of his own money to help them finish their novel. The only stipulation on the dough was that he got first crack at the completed manuscript.

John and Will continued to work on the book all through the spring and into the summer. They even used some of the money Leland Fisher had given them to rent a place on Martha's Vineyard for a couple weeks in late July. It was there, at a moss-covered cottage outside Chilmark, that they put the finishing touches on the manuscript.

John thought it would set them free.

Will thought it was just a beginning.

John wanted to quit the master's program and go out on the road.

Will wanted to stay in school.

Zelda, of course, sided with Will. After reading the completed manuscript, she asked John, "What's the hurry? I feel confident Leland will buy this, but not for a lot of money. It's a first novel. You have to be patient."

Leland bought the novel for fifteen grand; not a bad sum for a first novel.

But John had expected more, a lot more.

Will was perfectly satisfied. He thought they should start in right away on their next book.

John had other ideas. He had spent a lot of time and energy on *Boarding School Blues*. Now he wanted to get back to playing hoops and drinking beer and running after the girls.

Will tried to get the second book started on his own, but, as usual, with no success. He needed his brother to provide that first burst of inspiration. The blank page gave Will a headache and heartburn.

They started the second year of their master's program

with a promise from Leland Fisher to publish *Boarding School Blues* the following fall. Leland had actually wanted to publish the novel that spring, but Zelda had sat on his lap, pressed her breasts against his chest, and asked him to please put it off for a few months. She knew John was chaffing at the bit, and she did not want him or his brother running out on her anytime soon. Professor Cosgrove wanted her share of the credit when the praise and kudos started to flow. And flow it would, if Zelda had her way. She had already started the publicity wheels turning.

Boarding School Blues was not a long novel. It ran just over seventy-five thousand words. It had only one locale: Canterbury Prep. Canterbury Prep was a small, private boarding school in the foothills of western Connecticut. The school had wide, open lawns and big shade trees and ivy-covered buildings built back in the days of old. In the private school catalogs, Canterbury Prep liked to call itself, "a school for blue bloods and stuffed shirts." All were welcome at Canterbury Prep, as long as you were "white, wealthy, and reasonably Protestant."

"We educate snobs," the headmaster liked to tell the parents of prospective students.

Canterbury Prep, at least on the surface, looked like a pretty dull and conservative spot where the young lords and ladies of the well-heeled were prepared academically and athletically for the likes of Harvard, Radcliffe, Smith, Princeton, and Yale. Everyone at Canterbury Prep had exquisite manners. An impolite word was rarely uttered. The school motto, TRUTH, HONESTY, RESPECT, adorned the gold seal over the entrance to the main hall. But, of course, all was not as it seemed. Scratch the surface and all this truth, honesty, and respect business began to bleed thick blue blood.

Zelda, tireless promoter, hailed *Boarding School Blues* as, "a contemporary masterpiece in the tradition of *A Catcher In The Rye, A Separate Peace* and *This Side of Paradise.*"

This might have been a slight exaggeration, but the boys did produce a pretty vivid and biting tale. Along the way they managed to throw money, manners, and morality on the table and bludgeon them to death with their youthful wit and irreverent attitudes.

But all they could do now was wait. Wait for Leland to publish the novel. Wait for the reviews. Wait to see if anyone bought it. Wait to see if anyone liked it. Wait and wait and wait.

A LETTER & A PHONE CALL

While they waited, the letter, the check, and the bill for services rendered arrived in the mail. It was just a few weeks before Christmas, 1982.

Dear John and Will:

I sincerely hope this letter finds you both well. I know it has been quite a while since we last communicated. Let me apologize profusely for this long lapse.

As you probably have assumed from the unreasonably long delays, your parents' estate has proved extremely difficult to settle. The firm has spent enormous amounts of time and money trying to unravel all of your father's business dealings. The investments he made in Mexico were especially beguiling. But I am pleased to inform you the matter has finally been resolved.

For a long time I thought the bottom line would look a lot worse than it actually turned out in the end. Until just last month, I feared I would not be able to send either of you a nickel. But here, enclosed, is a check for $17,753.13. Not a king's ransom, I know, but certainly better than nothing at all. And, of course, you will be *extremely glad to learn that all of your parents' creditors have been paid in full.*

With one small exception. I do this with enormous regret, but I feel I must nevertheless enclose a bill for legal services provided by Hagstrom, Hays, Bennett, Barlow & Lunt. I want you to know, however, that I certainly do not expect you to pay this fee until the day comes when both of you are financially on your feet. This sum, $46,850.68, represents only a fraction of what this firm has invested to make this settlement. Last year alone, I spent almost two months in Mexico working on your behalf. But I feel a paternal responsibility, so I do not care to burden either of you with any additional debt.

Please feel free to contact me at any time if I can be of service to either one of you in the future. Merry Christmas, and may the Lord be with you in this joyous season.

Very sincerely yours,
Frank Hagstrom, Esq.

"Do you believe this son of a bitch!" John shouted, waving the letter in the air.

"The nerve!"

"Two months in Mexico!"

"On our money!"

"I'll kill him!"

"I'll help you."

"Dad would want us to kill him."

"We should tear his fucking head off!"

For the next few days the boys walked around Cambridge seething, wanting in the worst way to do violent things to Frank Hagstrom's body. They had no idea how much money Hagstrom had stolen from them, but their imaginations had no trouble conjuring up some pretty serious numbers.

Seventeen grand! They could not believe they had

wound up, after waiting all these years, with a measly seventeen grand. They had once expected millions.

Then, a couple of weeks later, on the first day of winter, always a cold and gloomy affair in Boston, John Hancock, unable to deal with the depressing prospect of spending the entire Christmas-New Year's holiday in their crappy little apartment freezing their butts off, stopped at a travel agent over on Bow Street and bought two tickets to Belize, departing early on Christmas morning. He had been wanting to visit Belize for years, and now, dammit, the time had come.

Will put up only a mild objection. Not only did he need a vacation, but he knew his brother would not be deterred.

On Christmas Eve they had drinks with Zelda and Leland. They toasted the success of *Boarding School Blues* and all future projects. Then, around ten o'clock, John said they had to go home and pack. Zelda kissed them goodbye and asked them, maternally, to please call so she would know they were all right.

The telephone was ringing when the boys walked into their apartment. Will picked up the receiver. "Hello?"

"Mr. Hancock?"

"Yes?"

"Is this John or Will?" The voice sounded slow and slurred.

"Who wants to know?"

"Edison . . . Maxwell Edison . . . Do you remember me?"

"Sure," answered Will, "I remember you." Will covered the mouthpiece and whispered to his brother. "It's that lawyer we hired out in L.A. a couple years ago to check up on Hagstrom. Maxwell Edison."

"What the hell does he want? Don't tell me he wants to steal some of our money, too? That bastard never did shit for us. Just assured us all was well, then pretty much told us to get lost."

"I tried to tell you that a year and a half ago."

"Don't lecture me," snarled John. Then, "Find out what he wants."

"I think he's drunk."

"Let me get on the other line." John went straight into his bedroom and picked up the extension.

"I wanted to call you up," Maxwell Edison slurred, "and . . . and . . . and wish you and your brother a very happy Christmas. And tell you that . . . that all the stuff I told you before . . . last year . . . about Frank . . . Frank Hagstrom being on the up-and-up . . . about all being swell in the Golden State . . . well, that was . . . that was lies. Big fat filthy lies!"

"Lies?" asked Will.

"Lies," answered Max. "I'd say two million . . . Maybe even three mil—"

"Two million what, Max?" John wanted to know.

"Dollars!" Maxwell Edison shouted. "Two million dollars!"

Oh yes, Max had definitely drank a tootful. His blood-alcohol level had soared off the charts. All that booze had brought on a pretty good case of guilt. Sitting all alone in his apartment on Christmas Eve, Max had suddenly encountered an almost desperate desire to unburden his pitiful self. Soon thereafter, he had dialed up the Hancock boys.

"Stolen! I tell you . . . Swindled! . . . Embezzled! . . . And no one will ever know. Never ever! A sly and very sneaky . . . fucking fox . . . that Frank Hagstrom! He never took a step . . . not one tiny step . . . without brushing clean the footprint he'd left behind!"

The Hancock boys tried to ask questions. They made every effort to solicit more information, to extract more details, to find out exactly how much money Frank Hagstrom had stolen from them. They worked Max over for a good twenty minutes.

Too bad Max had befriended a fifth of Jimmy Beam. The sour mash had turned Max's brain and Max's tongue to mush. Max could only babble. Max soon became incoherent. Then Max dropped the phone onto the floor. The boys could still hear Max whining and slurring in the background, but it sounded more like the noise of a rabid animal than a member of the California state bar.

They hung up and finished packing. Three million dollars and their father's good name dancing in their heads.

A few days later Will was dead. Drowned off the coast of Caye Caulker. Food for the fishes.

At least that's what John Hancock, who was really Will Hancock, told the public.

CLARA MEETS THE HANCOCKS

The Boston Athenaeum. Late June of 1991. Eight and a half years after that call from Maxwell Edison. Almost eight and a half years after Will Hancock's "death." Eight years after the publication of *Boarding School Blues*. A sultry summer night. A dinner for the library's trustees. The organizers invited John Hancock because he was a local author with a new book in the bookstores.

He was standing there in the elegant Bow Room of the Athenaeum signing copies of *The Killer* and sipping a not very dry martini when into the room flowed this tall and beautiful blonde with just about the longest legs John had ever seen. On her face she wore that slightly annoyed expression that John had seen on a lot of good-looking women's faces. He figured it probably had something to do with guys staring at them and coming onto them all the time.

Which was pretty much exactly what John Hancock unsuccessfully did for the rest of the evening.

But a couple weeks later, through the help of mutual friend Linda Carson, John called Ms. Dare and asked her out for dinner. She hedged, but finally agreed to go.

John thought long and hard about where to take her,

finally settling on the Library Grill on the corner of Beacon and Brimmer. It proved an excellent choice. The food was tasty, the ambiance pleasant and subdued, and the view of the Public Garden exceptional on that breezy July evening.

Best of all, John made Clara laugh. Not always an easy thing to do. John had to tell her three or four jokes before finally hitting on one that Clara found amusing.

After dinner they took a stroll through the Public Garden. They did not hold hands. Nor did they share a kiss when John walked her to the door of her apartment building on Commonwealth Avenue. But Clara, much to her own surprise, said, "There's a Van Gogh exhibit opening at the Museum of Fine Arts next week. The night before the show opens to the public, the museum is having a black-tie fund-raiser. Would you like to go?"

Of course John wanted to go. He was already head over heels in love. He would have followed Clara just about anywhere. Even to a museum to stare at paintings; easily one of his least favorite things to do.

"That would be great," he told her. "I love Van Gogh." Not really. John knew Van Gogh's work. It amazed him the guy had become so famous.

As fate would have it, John was scheduled to leave the morning of the fund-raiser on an Adventure Travel trip to Alaska. The day before departing, John told Will about Clara Dare and the gig at the museum. He hesitated asking his brother to fill in, but finally decided Will would make an excellent impression, with his knowledge of art and artists.

Reluctantly, Will agreed to go to the fund-raiser with his brother's latest flame. Will did not really like big parties or crowds of any kind. Nor did he enjoy dating his brother's girlfriends. He and John had very different taste in women. John wanted long legs and good looks. Will wanted a little more depth.

•   •   •

Nevertheless, Will Hancock fell in love with Clara Dare the moment he laid eyes on her. One look and he wanted to marry her, spend the rest of his life with her.

Clara wore a clingy, pearl-colored gown. It wrapped around her long, lean body like a close-fitting glove. She took his arm as they walked through the grand entrance of the Museum of Fine Arts. Will felt like he was at the Academy Awards. The men were all in black tie. The women wore designer gowns and lots of jewelry. Usually Will stayed clear of this kind of event, but suddenly, with the gorgeous Clara Dare on his arm, he felt ready to take on the world.

Will was, of course, playing the role of brother John. A role he had been playing in public by that time for nearly a decade. But he only played the role up to a point. He had his own distinct personality, and he refused to bury that personality entirely. So it was a fact of life to all who knew John Hancock that he was a difficult person to know well, a complex man, prone to many different attitudes and many different moods from light gaiety to somber contemplation. He could give you a big hello one day and walk right by you on the street the next. Some people labeled him a snob, but most simply found him eccentric. No one knew, of course, that there were two of him.

So that night at the Museum of Fine Arts, Will, as John, did not tell any jokes, but he did make a fine and lasting impression on Ms. Dare. Will had paid attention during the Art Appreciation class he had taken as an undergraduate. He was able to speak about Van Gogh's work with intelligence and insight. The fact that, like his brother, he found Van Gogh way overrated never spilled from his mouth. Will could see that the lovely Ms. Dare simply adored the crazy Dutch artist. No way was Will going to take the opposite point of view. He had long ago become a very accomplished liar.

As he and Clara made their way through the exhibit, they stopped in front of nearly every canvas to admire and comment on the work. Clara was thoroughly impressed with her date's knowledge and grasp of the Post-

Impressionist movement. Will was equally impressed with his date. Not only was she physically overwhelming, but she easily held up her end of their intellectual foray into late-nineteenth-century painting.

Most of the women John dated and then handed over for Will to try out were mental midgets, barely able to grasp the narrative chicanery of even the most elementary Hollywood movie. But Clara, Will could see at once, had it all: beauty, brains, and breeding. No way would Will have believed that Clara Dare had grown up Plain Jane Mc-Guire in a crummy boardinghouse over in the seedy section of Cambridge.

Of course, just as unlikely was the fact that the extremely intelligent and sensitive John Hancock was really Will Hancock playing John Hancock, and Clara now had two extremely smitten suitors pursuing her as one.

Quite a romance was beginning to stir.

Later that same evening, not only did Will, as John, hold Ms. Dare's hand, but they shared a long and rather sumptuous kiss on her front stoop. And that came *before* she invited him upstairs for a nightcap.

Nothing happened up in her apartment that night, except for a few more kisses and some full-body hugs in the standing position. But an agreement to go out again, and soon, was reached before Will, as John, took his leave.

John made love to Clara first. But only after they had been dating for almost two months. Clara did not commit herself physically very easily. Which made it all the sweeter once she finally did.

John played it soft and slow, not his usual mode. Usually he had far more interest in his own needs and physical wants than he did in the young lady lying at his side. He would say and do the things that needed saying and doing, but beyond that his own desires came first.

But not so when he lay with Clara. Chalk it up to love. No question about it, for the first time in his adult life, John was in love. Love changes a man. And when a man is in love with a woman, he makes love to that woman very differently than he does to a woman with whom he simply wants to have a sexual interlude. Her needs and desires come first. Only if she finds satisfaction does he find satisfaction. And so it was with John and Clara.

And again later with Will, as John, and Clara.

Both couples shook the earth.

"She's perfect," Will said to John.

"Damn close," John said to Will.

"She's smart."

"And gorgeous."

"And fun."

"And sexy."

"She could be the one, John."

"You're right," agreed John. "I think she could."

"I want her."

"So do I."

Will sighed. "So what are we going to do?"

John shrugged. "Really only one solution, bro."

Will thought about it and frowned. "No, we can't."

"Yes, we can."

"Christ, John, it's sick. The whole idea of it is sick."

"Together we can make her happy. And make ourselves happy, too. The best of all possible worlds."

"It's wrong."

"Screw wrong, bro. Who's to say what's right and wrong? I say this is right for us. All three of us."

Will looked pretty dubious. He had done some bad things in his life. Some terrible things. But this, potentially, could be the worst thing of all. He shook his head.

"Look, she might say no and then you won't have to worry about it."

"But what if she says yes?"

"If she says yes we'll plow ahead."

"But," said Will, not much above a whisper, "I'm not sure I want to share her. I want her all for me."

"But she's not just yours, bro. She's ours."

"I know, but—"

"Listen, Will, you know me, I'll probably only stick at it for a year or two anyway, then you can go full-time."

Will studied his brother with narrowed eyes. He had not forgotten, not for one second, the whole passport fiasco. Nor had he forgotten about Hagstrom; Will blamed his brother for that, also. "You swear to God, John? After a year or two you'll bow out?"

"Hey, you know my history, bro. I get bored easy."

"But what if you don't?"

"Christ, Will, can't you just go with the flow for a change? Have some fun?"

Will frowned, but after talking it over for a few more days, they decided to go ahead and ask her.

John, in an act of appeasement, told Will he could do the proposing.

They were back at the Library Grill, back at that same table overlooking the Public Garden. Only this time, Will, as John, was sitting where John had been sitting less than nine months before.

But John was in the restaurant also. He sat at the bar wearing the exact same clothes as Will, right down to the same color underwear and the same color socks. But he also had on a pair of wire-rim eyeglasses and a fake beard. He sipped a Dewar's on the rocks, same as Will, while he followed the action out of the corner of his eye.

Will waited until they had ordered dessert. Well, until he had ordered dessert. Clara never had dessert, though she always liked a bite or two of his. Chocolate mousse tonight, Clara's favorite.

Heart pounding, palms clammy, Will reached into his jacket pocket and felt for the engagement ring, a nice gold band mounted with a fat diamond that had set the Hancock boys back a few grand.

"Clara?"

"Yes, John?"

"I've been . . . Well, I've been thinking . . ."

"About what?"

Will had this all planned out. He knew exactly what he wanted to say. But suddenly some crazy cat had hold of his tongue. It wasn't cold feet, but rather terror of rejection.

A minute or two passed. Eventually Clara apologized, stood, and headed off to the ladies' room.

Will waited until she was out of sight, then he beelined for the bar.

"What happened?" asked John. "What did she say?"

"She didn't say anything. I didn't ask her. I couldn't do it. You have to do it."

John did not waste a second. He stepped off his bar stool, motioned for Will to follow, then steered for the men's room. Once inside he pulled off the fake beard and the eyeglasses. "Put these on," he told Will, "and give me the ring."

Will, perspiration beading up on his forehead, handed over the ring and accepted the disguise. "You'll do it?"

John smiled. "Have no fear, bro."

John fussed with his hair and his face in the mirror for a minute or so, then, ring in his jacket pocket, he headed for the table under the window. Clara, notorious for long stints in the powder room, had not yet returned. John snacked on his brother's mousse. He glanced over at the bar. There sat Will, wearing beard and eyeglasses, sipping his Dewar's and water.

John stood and held Clara's chair upon her return. "I was beginning to think you'd gone home."

She reached across the table and gave his cheek a squeeze. A puzzled expression raced across her face, but she quickly recovered and replied, "Funny boy."

He smiled at her with his best boyish smile and asked, "So, I was wondering . . ."

"Yes?"

"Want to marry me?"

Clara, clearly thrown by the question, did a double take and asked, "What?"

John pulled out the ring, held it up between his thumb and his index finger, and said, "Listen, you know I'm crazy about you. Madly in love with you. And you tell me I make your toes curl. You might not ever find another guy who can do that. So what do you say? How 'bout we get hitched?"

Clara, rarely at a loss for words, gaped across the table at Hancock. Several seconds passed before she asked, "Married?"

"That's right, baby. Married. Like in wedded bliss."

"Jesus . . ."

John reached out and took her hand. "Why don't we see how she fits?"

Clara took a deep breath, then held out her hand. Hancock slipped the diamond ring onto her finger. It fit perfectly; snug, but not too tight.

Will, watching from the sidelines, was ecstatic to see the ring slide onto Clara's finger. But he was also extremely annoyed and irritated that he was not the one doing the sliding. . . .

PART FOUR

JUNE 9, 1999

As another morning dawns, Clara, John, and Will Hancock find themselves remembering those early days of their infatuation.

Even Clara was up bright and early this morning. She awoke at seven-thirty, Paris time. Out of the Ritz and into the limousine by nine. Then to the Air France terminal at Charles-de-Gaulle by ten. On board the Concorde by eleven. In the air by eleven-thirty.

Now, somewhere over the Atlantic, traveling at the speed of sound, Clara pushes back her seat and rests her head against a thin cotton pillow. She squirms around a bit in her seat trying to get comfortable. A rather small, hard seat. Even up here in first class. The price one pays, Clara reminds herself, for speed.

Her thoughts have wandered into the past, but for now she has had enough of days gone by. So she closes her eyes and breathes slowly and steadily. It would be nice to have a little nap before reaching New York. It will no doubt be a long day. And tomorrow, too, will be a long one. Oh, yes, plenty to do tomorrow. But Clara feels confident about her plan. She has thought long and hard about her plan. And now the time has come to put it into motion. To wait any longer would be foolish, and even selfish.

John Hancock's been awake most of the night. Tossing and turning, thinking things over, trying to sort things out. He keeps telling himself to get up, get moving, head for Stockbridge now. But it's tough getting out of bed when it's still dark outside, when the house is so quiet, when it's so warm and cozy under the sheets.

He thinks about his first nights with Clara. Unbelievable nights. The best nights of his life. He wishes she were here now. He'd lie here with her all morning and into the afternoon, if he could get her to stay still that long. But Clara never stays still for long. Always going. Always on the move. Even when making love she keeps moving. Always changing position. Top. Bottom. On her side. On her knees. On top again. Like having sex with a tornado. But ask John and he'll tell you there's no one in the world he'd rather make love to than Clara. She excites and stimulates him today as much as she did the first time they ever made love, almost eight years ago.

Brother Will cannot sleep either. He paces back and forth across the first floor of that old stone farmhouse north of Stockbridge. He, too, finds himself thinking about those first days and weeks and months with Clara.

But he is thinking about plenty of other things as well. It is now close to dawn. Will has been up all night. Hasn't even bothered trying to go to bed. Hours ago he knew lying down would be futile. So he's had plenty of time to think it all over. He's been back and forth across the major avenues of his life three or four times.

Last night, after throwing up, Will pulled himself together long enough to listen once again to that message from Clara. He listened to it a third time. And a fourth time. And a fifth time. He listened to every subtle nuance of her voice, every inflection, every intonation. He tried to figure out what she knew and what she did not know. All from that sixty-second message. Was it possible she knew nothing? That calling Adventure Travel Enterprises was simply a coincidence?

Will does not think so. Not for one second. Will thinks Clara knows. Everything.

For openers, the entire message sounded contrived. Not at all like anything Will could imagine Clara saying. That bit about ". . . *a nice summer vacation in July or August. My husband and two young sons.*" No way. That didn't sound like Clara. Same with the part where she said, "*. . . take us by the hand so we can just relax and have fun.*" Clara never lets anyone take her by the hand. Stubborn and independent through and through. But maybe worst of all was that mess near the end where she said, "*Or better yet, if you're in New York, just stop by the hotel and see me.*" Right. Like she'd just make that invitation to a complete stranger on a message machine. And then signing off, "*Ciao.*" Will could not ever recall his wife using that expression before in his life.

No, she knows. She definitely knows. Somehow she's figured it out. Figured out the whole damn convoluted mess. After all these years, his and John's massive deception is finally out in the open.

But how? Will keeps asking himself. How did she find out? And when? And who told her? Did John tell her? And if he did tell her, why did he tell her? What the hell is going on? Are they in on this together? Against him?

Will, his paranoia running rampant, sees shadows everywhere.

Just a few short hours ago Will believed he had everything under control. He had his brother on the run and a plan to take control of his life. But now . . .

He tries to relax, takes a few deep breaths. Some decisions will have to be made, some actions taken. And soon, very soon. He knows he will need to have his wits about him in the hours and days ahead.

•   •   •

So just barely dawn, but already we find John, Will, and Clara wide awake and extremely active. But what about their friends and foes? What are they up to at this early hour?

Leland's sound asleep in his Back Bay digs. And there's wife Hillary, right beside him, also asleep. They had sex again last night. Hillary didn't have an orgasm, but she faked a little one so Leland would stop trying so hard. She lay there afterward and pretty much decided to somehow let Hancock's wife, that snobby bitch Clara Dare, know that her husband was a philandering bastard. Exactly how she would pass along this lovely bit of news was as yet undetermined, but Hillary felt sure she could figure something out before their return from New York.

She and Leland will be leaving for the Big Apple in a few hours. The alarm is set for eight-fifteen. They have a ten o'clock train to catch from South Station. Leland takes the train whenever possible. He hates to fly. Since childhood he's had recurring nightmares wherein he perishes in a fiery plane crash.

Babe, of course, refuses to fly. She will not fly under any circumstances. That's why she's right now dozing in the lounge of the Greyhound Bus Station on West Harrison Street in Chicago, Illinois.

The bus from St. Louis got in before dawn. Babe could have stayed aboard and continued on for New York and Boston. But she found out an express bus for the Big Apple would be leaving at nine o'clock, so she decided to wait. Until then she dozes on a plastic chair, her head resting on her shoulder, her leather handbag on her lap, her suitcase under her feet.

This grim life is about to change. But not the way Babe thinks it will. Oh no, things are about to happen to Babe that she would not be able to imagine in even her wildest fantasies.

•   •   •

Not far from the Greyhound Bus Station, Rafe sleeps the sleep of the dead. The cocaine dead. Rafe had himself quite a night last night. His first and only night in Chicago, and he did it all. Sex, drugs, and rock 'n roll. Well, that wasn't actually rock 'n roll he heard last night at the Cotton Club. More of an R&B beat. Funky rhythm and blues, and here came Rafe, all the way from Caye Caulker, out of that yellow cab and through the front door. Floating all the way. Bebopping to the pulsing bass lines and twangy electric guitar licks.

Rafe had no trouble making friends. After all, the man had a nice smile, an easy manner, a Caribbean cool. And oh, yes, a rather large bag of blow. Which, as the night wore on, grew somewhat smaller. His new friends kept leading Rafe into the rest rooms, both the men's and ladies', where Rafe was invited to make peace offerings. Something like Lewis and Clark as they made their way west. Only instead of trinkets and tobacco, Rafe cut thick lines of cocaine on the white porcelain sinks. Sniff, sniff went the natives.

Wanda finally came to his rescue. Wanda June. A sweet young milk-chocolate-colored babe who grabbed Rafe's crotch and whispered in his ear, "Come on, honey, let's trip this joint."

Which they did. Out the front door they went and, remarkably, straight into a waiting cab. Driven, coincidentally, by Rafe's old Indian friend from Bombay. "Regency International," ordered Wanda, while she stroked Rafe between the thighs.

Rafe moaned and wondered what had taken him so long to come to America.

The Regency International stood old and decrepit a couple miles up South Michigan. It used to be quite a famous hotel in its heyday. Democrats held a couple of their national conventions there in the first half of the century. Now the place attracts a slightly seedier crowd.

Rafe paid for the room out of his wad of cash. And up they went, in a creaky old elevator and down a long hallway with peeling wallpaper and threadbare carpet. Rafe didn't even notice. He had more carnal pleasures on his mind.

Wanda did not disappoint. She had Rafe naked and frolicking on that saggy queen-size mattress just seconds after they entered room 636. The sheets were somewhat damp, probably due to the fact that the room had not been fully serviced after the last happy couple had checked out just a few short hours earlier.

Wanda needed to work pretty hard on Rafe. The guy had snorted a lot of coke and consumed a lot of tequila.

"What's a matter, baby," she cooed in his ear, "don't you love Wanda?"

Rafe grunted and groaned and finally came. Soon thereafter he passed out. "Jesus," Wanda muttered, slipping out of the clammy bed, "I should have listened to my mother and stayed in school."

She rifled through Rafe's pockets, swiftly locating his wad of cash. It both looked and felt substantial. She dressed and slipped the wad into her panties. Rafe stirred. Time to scoot, throught Wanda, and out the door of room 636 she went.

Rafe's old Indian friend from Bombay was waiting for her outside of the Regency International behind the wheel of his yellow cab. "Did you get the money?" he asked.

Wanda handed over the wad. "Feels like a nice take."

Rafe's old Indian friend turned on the overhead light and counted the money. Two thousand seven hundred and sixty-two dollars. Rafe's old friend smiled. "Very, very good, Wanda. Now what about the cocaine?"

Wanda smacked herself in the head. "Christ, I forgot the coke. He started waking up and I just hauled ass out of there."

Rafe's good buddy from Bombay turned and slapped Wanda sharply across the face. "Stupid dumb bitch."

Stupid dumb Rafe would be more like it. Rolled on his very first night in the States. And by a couple of amateurs. Wait till he wakes up from his coke stupor and realizes what happened. Won't he feel like a jackass?

He sold his boat for two grand. Matilda gave him

twenty-five hundred as a down payment for hauling the coke. He blew almost fifteen hundred of that on plane tickets and various other travel expenses. Then he lets Wanda June steal another twenty-seven hundred right out of his damn pockets. Which means he's suddenly down to about three hundred bucks. Three hundred exactly, actually. At least he was smart enough to stuff three one-hundred-dollar bills into the toe of his left shoe before leaving his shack, back on Caye Caulker.

Way to go, Rafe.

But he has even bigger problems than a shortage of cash. He has only half a bag of cocaine left. Which probably will not make his contact at the Ambassador Hotel real happy.

But for now, Rafe sleeps, oblivious to the churning of the world beyond the sour walls of room 636 of the Regency International, Chicago, Illinois.

Also asleep at this early morning hour, believe it or not, is Dicky Cosgrove. He crawled onto his filthy mattress on the floor last night after returning from his shopping spree. Feeling a bit fatigued, he thought he might just close his eyes and catch a few winks. Pull himself together. But Dicky was way beyond fatigued. The guy was exhausted, mentally and physically drained; no more gas in the tank.

But he can still dream. And dream he does, vividly and in living color. Dicky also dreams in reality. Or at least as close to reality as his twisted brain ventures.

This morning he's dreaming about sister Zelda's death; his version of her death anyway. It begins with that conversation between the two of them wherein Zelda tells Dicky that she believes both of the Hancock twins are still alive. Then things bounce ahead a couple months and there's one of the Hancock twins, tough to tell which one, knocking on Zelda's apartment door over on Berkeley Street. Zelda answers, smiles at Hancock, invites him inside. Of course she invites him inside. They're friends. They sit at the kitchen table, share a pot of tea, talk about the new book.

The new book would be Hancock's third book, the one he has recently started writing. It will be totally different from the first two. More of a psychological thriller with plenty of plot, lots of suspense. Mayhem, sex, and violence. Hancock has had enough of the literary stuff. Too hard to write, and then no one reads it except for a few pompous and disgruntled reviewers who inevitably trash the work.

Zelda, however, is not real happy with the decision. She wants Hancock writing literature, not pop crap for mass consumption. They argue. Hancock insists the decision has been made. Zelda says no, it hasn't. Hancock says yes, it has. Zelda says she knows a secret or two and that she will reveal those secrets if Hancock insists on writing pulp. What kind of secrets? Hancock demands.

"Secrets about you and your brother," Zelda tells him. "I know you're both alive. I can see it in your writing. Neither of you has the skills to write so well on your own. Alone, each of you is nothing."

Hancock gets mad, calls Zelda insane. He slams the door on his way out.

Dicky stirs, thrashes, rolls over, goes back to his dream.

It's a few days later. Hancock returns to Zelda's apartment. But which Hancock? That's anyone's guess.

Again he knocks on the door. Again Zelda lets him in. This time Hancock has on gloves. Leather driving gloves. Though he does not even own a car. He also has a length of steel pipe with him. Heavy gauge. He whacks Zelda over the head and the blow knocks her unconscious. Down she goes with a fractured skull.

Dicky thrashes some more. He lashes out, tries to save his sister. But too late. Too late.

And then, mission complete, Zelda's blood everywhere, Hancock departs.

At least this is the way Dicky dreams it. And has dreamed it a thousand times or more over the years. In his dream he sees Hancock leaving his sister's apartment and strolling down the hallway, as calm and contented as a well-fed tabby cat.

The sight of his sister lying there in a pool of blood brings Dicky wide awake. In a flash he's off that filthy mattress, fire in his eyes. He glances at the clock on the kitchen stove. Nearly twenty after seven. In the morning. Wednesday morning.

"Fuck!" Dicky shouts. He wanted to exact his revenge last night. In the dark, quiet hours before dawn. Now he wrings his hands while reformulating his plan.

A moment later, he's on the move. He showers and shaves, brushes his teeth, gets himself looking good. Then back into his new blue chinos, new blue T-shirt, new blue oxford, new socks and sneakers. And finally, he slips his new straight-edge razor into the pocket of his chinos. Well hidden but easily accessible.

A quick look in the mirror and he's ready to go. He heads for the door, taking the Gap bag filled with his new duds and his bag of Hancock novels with him.

Al-the-Gumshoe Brown blew it yesterday morning; no way is he going to blow it again today. He pulled up in his minivan around six-thirty. Now it's almost seven-thirty. No activity at the moment over at the Hancock house. He's seen a few lights pop on, but no one has come or gone yet. Around eight-fifteen, he figures, the kids will leave for school. Probably nothing much will happen till then. And probably not a whole lot after that either. At least he hopes not. Al has a date to meet his wife down at Starbucks on Charles Street. They decided last night it would be nice to get together for half an hour or so over a cup of coffee and a Danish.

Al figures he'll head down there about nine, be back by nine-thirty, quarter of ten at the latest. He feels confident he won't miss a beat.

John Hancock, showered and shaved and dressed in a nice pair of khakis and a cream-colored cotton sweater, comes into the kitchen. Sylvia busies herself making coffee and biscuits. The kids love warm buttermilk biscuits.

"Morning, Sylvia."

"Good morning, Mr. Hancock."

"Coffee ready?"

"Two more minutes." Sylvia makes the coffee exactly the same way every morning: She grinds the six scoops of Colombian beans and dumps them into the French coffee maker. Into the glass beaker she pours precisely forty-eight ounces of boiling water. She allows the water to mix with the coffee grinds for six minutes. Not one second more or one second less. After six minutes she pushes down the plunger, separating the grinds from the water, and presto: fresh perfect coffee.

John waits for the okay, then pours himself a cup. While he adds a bit of sugar he says, "I'll be gone most of the day, Sylvia. In fact, I won't be back till tomorrow. So if you want, take the day off."

Sylvia is not one to mince words. She takes the biscuits out of the oven and asks Mr. Hancock, "You're not going with that Mrs. Fisher woman? She is not nice woman. And not nice also for Mrs. Hancock for you to be with her."

John just about chokes on his perfect cup of Colombian. "Relax, Sylvia," he manages to tell her, "Mrs. Fisher is just the wife of my editor. You're so suspicious. It must be from growing up in a Communist country."

"No," says Sylvia, "not from Communists. It is from early learning that men lie and cheat. You may not know, but I was pretty girl when I was young. Men lie and cheat to me all the time to get what they want from my body. Men can no be trusted. Not in Poland or in America or anywhere."

John drains his cup and sets it on the counter. "Well, I don't know about that, Sylvia. All I know is that you are the only woman for me." He puts his arms around her and gives her a squeeze. "You and, of course, Mrs. Hancock." But at the same moment John finds himself wondering if his brother can be trusted.

Sylvia smiles and melts just a bit. But she quickly recovers. "You make game of everything. Whole life a big game. A big joke. But you should know better. Your wife is fine woman. She is good wife, good mother, and good, too, at making money. Not many women good at all that. You should love and respect her more."

"Now, Sylvia, you know I love and respect Mrs. Hancock more than anyone in the world. And as for other women, there hasn't been another woman in my life since the day I laid eyes on Clara."

Before Sylvia can respond, John junior and young Willy come hurtling down the stairs and into the kitchen. "I smell biscuits!" they both shout. "Buttermilk biscuits!" They both wolf down a couple of biscuits lathered with butter, then ask, "When's Linda coming? Is she here yet? Is it time to go to New Hampshire?"

"Not yet," Dad tells them, "but pretty soon." Then Dad launches into a short lecture on the importance of being polite and safe while away from home. "We don't want either of you getting hurt. So think before you act."

•   •   •

Linda is running a little late. She's right now crossing the Longfellow Bridge from Cambridge in her Volvo wagon. She thinks about the things she needs to do before leaving the city and heading north for New Hampshire: Pick up the boys, gas up the car, get some bagels and fruit for the ride.

Better pick up John and Willy last. They'll be sitting in the car long enough.

Who else is using the Longfellow Bridge this morning to cross the Charles from Cambridge to Boston? None other than Mr. Richard Cosgrove. No wheels for Dicky, so he hoofs it. Linda zips right by him in her Volvo. She doesn't even give him a glance. Of course, she doesn't know Dicky Cosgrove from the Sultan of Brunei.

The Longfellow Bridge, named, of course, for the poet Henry Wadsworth, has not always been known by that name. You only get stuff named for you after you die.

Dicky pauses a few seconds in midspan to contemplate the cluster of fine homes on the high ground dead ahead. Hancock, he knows, lives among those homes. "Though not for long," Dicky says aloud, his words caught and scattered by the warm breeze.

Dicky reaches Cambridge Street. His eyes wander while his stomach churns. Yes, Dicky has developed a case of nerves. But he's also ravenous. He needs food. There, across the street, a diner, a greasy spoon. He crosses without bothering to look either way. Horns blare, brakes squeal. Dicky shoves his neck down into the collar of his blue oxford and hurries across the street. He goes into the diner and takes a seat at the counter.

The gum-chewing waitress comes over with a pot. "Coffee?"

Dicky shakes his head. "I want four eggs, fried and runny, four pieces of white toast, home fries, and a chocolate shake."

The waitress smacks her gum and turns toward the kitchen. She mutters, "A fine morning to you, too, friend."

But Dicky doesn't hear. Dicky's in a zone.

Al Brown's in a zone, too. The Gumshoe is hyperfocused on the front door of the Hancock town house. It's way past time for the Hancock kids to have left for school, but still no sign of them. He thinks maybe they're sick. Or maybe it's some kind of holiday and he just forgot.

He glances at his watch: 8:51. He has to leave to meet his wife pretty soon. Like any minute.

A car pulls up in front of the town house. One of those boxy Swedish station wagons. A woman steps out. Al doesn't recognize her, but she's a good-looker, with long reddish-brown hair. He picks up his camera and pops off a couple shots.

The woman gets halfway up the brick walk when the door opens and the two Hancock kids come running out. They practically jump into her arms. Al's seen photographs of Clara Dare Hancock and this is definitely not her. The wife, he knows, has short blond hair.

Hancock comes through the front door next. He carries a couple of small backpacks. He kisses the woman on the cheek. Al captures the moment on film. Hancock and the woman chat. The kids circle like Indians.

The cook and the nanny join them. More hugs and kisses for Dad. Long hugs and extra kisses. Then they bound down the brick walk, through the wrought iron gate, and into the back of the station wagon.

Hancock gives the woman another kiss on the cheek, and then she, too, climbs back into the car. The engine starts and off the trio goes.

To where and for what, Al hasn't a clue. And right now, he doesn't really care. He just wants to get out of here, spend a little time with his wife.

So, the second Hancock and the cook and the nanny go back into the town house, Al fires up the minivan and heads down the hill for Starbucks.

•   •   •

Back in the town house, Hancock doesn't waste much time either. He tells Sylvia and Nicky he will call later, that he plans on going down to New York to rendezvous with Mrs. Hancock. Then he grabs the keys to his BMW off the hook beside the back door. But he stops and reconsiders. It's a beautiful spring day. He'll want to drive with the windows down. He likes driving with the windows down, the air screaming through the cabin, the radio turned up loud. But something's wrong with the windows in the BMW. Half the time he presses the buttons the windows won't go down. And when they do go down he can't get them back up.

So he hangs the keys back on the hook and grabs the keys to Clara's car. She bought a Mercedes ML320 SUV a few months ago. Hancock really hasn't had a chance to drive it much. Just a few times to pick up the boys.

Now he goes out the back door and across the driveway to the detached garage in the back. He pulls open the door and climbs into the ML320. He backs out, closes the garage door, and is soon underway: across Louisburg Square and down the hill along Pinckney.

Halfway down the hill, at the corner of Pinckney and West Cedar, Hancock slows to let a pedestrian cross the street. Good brakes, he thinks, nice and strong.

That pedestrian would be Richard Cosgrove, moving quickly up the hill in the direction of the Hancock town house after his pit stop for fried eggs and choco shake. He doesn't even see the Mercedes-Benz coming down Pinckney. No, Dicky's still in a zone, a killing zone.

Hancock goes to the end of Pinckney and turns left on Charles. He drives right by Starbucks, where Al-the-Gumshoe Brown sits at a table in the front window with his lovely and very well dressed wife.

COFFEE

"I like those new Benzes," Al says to his bride while sipping his Guatemalan Hazelnut Latte. "Maybe I'll trade in my minivan on one of those."

"I don't like them," says his wife. "They made the emblem on the front grille too large. It screams at you whenever you drive by: 'Look what I've got!' "

And Al knows his wife is right and that he will never buy one. He reaches for a piece of her chocolate croissant. She smiles and slaps his hand.

While Hancock, happy behind the wheel of his sporty SUV, stops just long enough to get a black coffee to go. Then he gets a ticket at the Mass Pike toll plaza, and accelerates out onto the turnpike in anticipation of his rendezvous with Will. He tries not to think too much about it. He just hopes Will has not totally flipped his switches.

Clara sips her coffee at forty thousand feet. She likes it black with one packet of Equal. Too bad Air France does not have Equal. They have the bitter, nasty stuff in the pink packet. But Clara knows this from experience. That's why she always carries several packets of Equal in her purse.

Clara believes in being prepared.

Leland and Hillary have coffee at the coffee shop at Boston's South Street Station. Neither of them says much. They're not big talkers this early in the morning.

The lady in the Jones New York business suit sitting in the next booth is reading a copy of John Hancock's *The Settlement*. Both Leland and Hillary spot this little detail, but neither mentions it.

Babe gets her morning cup of coffee out of a vending machine at the Greyhound Bus Station in Chicago. She pops in four quarters, pushes the button for coffee with non-dairy creamer and sugar, and watches as a styrofoam cup drops out of the chute, then fills with a steamy, watery blend barely recognizable as coffee.

Babe drinks it anyway. Then she heads for the New York express.

Rafe orders a large coffee, black, four sugars, from a woman old enough to be his grandmother at a Dunkin' Donuts on West Harrison Street, just a block and a half from the Chicago Greyhound Bus Station.

It's almost quarter of nine, Central Daylight Time. In the hour or so that Rafe has been awake, he's figured out exactly what went down last night. He knows that kinky bitch Wanda stole his wad, but thank the Lord, she didn't snag the bag o' coke. Or the three one-hundred-dollar bills stuffed into the toe of his shoe.

Of course, at least half the bag of coke has been snorted, and Rafe's smart enough to know that'll be trouble once he makes his connection in the Big Apple. But he'll figure something out. There's always a tale to tell. And he has until tomorrow at noon to get it all straight in his head.

To celebrate his eventual arrival in Hancock's home-town, Rafe gets two Boston Creme doughnuts to go, then he departs Dunkin' Donuts and heads up Harrison for the bus station. He called ahead from the hotel, found out there was an express leaving for New York at nine o'clock.

RAZOR'S EDGE

Midmorning in Beantown. And here comes Dicky C., looking like a young, urban professional taking Wednesday off from work to do a little shopping, maybe get a few things done around the house. He turns off Pinckney onto Louisburg Square. Opens and walks through the Hancocks' wrought-iron front gate like he has done so a hundred times before. A thousand times.

Which, of course, he has. In his daydreams.

He climbs the steps to the door and rings the bell. Not even a moment's doubt or hesitation enters his mind. A young woman answers the door. She only cracks it a few inches, the length of the steel chain bolted to both the door and the doorjamb. This is a big city, after all. Lots of crime. Plenty of nuts. Can't be too careful.

"Yes? May I help you?"

English, thinks Dicky. Must be the little nympho who takes care of the kiddies.

He smiles. "Good morning, miss. My name's Dave. Dave Wilson. I'm a bookseller here in the Boston area. I was looking for Mr. John Hancock."

Normally, Nicky would just tell Mr. Wilson that Mr. Hancock wasn't home, but the Hancocks no longer want her to say that. There's been some crime in the neighborhood recently, breaking and entering, right in broad daylight. So now, especially when the kids are home and the parents are out, Nicky has been instructed to say, "Mr. Hancock is not available right now."

"Not even for a minute or two?" asks Mr. Wilson. "I have these copies of Mr. Hancock's very fine novels that I would like him to sign." Dicky shows the young English girl the bag of books. "I have a client who is a collector and she has been begging me to get Mr. Hancock's signature."

Nicky has no fear of this well-groomed and pleasant-enough-looking man standing at the door. No fear at all. "Maybe you could leave the books with me and I could ask Mr. Hancock to sign them later. I'm sure he'll do it. Then you can come back and pick them up this afternoon or tomorrow."

Dicky nods, but allows a look of disappointment to wash across his face. "You don't think he could do it now?" Dicky feels some sweat gathering under his arms. What he really wants to do is lower his shoulder and ram the door.

And look, here comes Al-the-Gumshoe Brown, turning off Charles and starting up Pinckney, coffee break with his wife at an end.

"Probably better just to leave them," says Nicky. "Mr. Hancock does not like to be disturbed."

Dicky smiles. "Busy writing, is he?"

"Something like that."

"All right then, I'll just leave them." Dicky can see there is not enough room to shove the bag of books through the small opening in the door. This young English twit will have to disconnect the chain.

"Hang on a second," Nicky tells him. She closes the door.

Al Brown turns off Pinckney onto the far side of Louisburg Square. The Gumshoe drives slowly around the Square, eyes searching for a parking spot.

Nicky frees the steel chain and again opens the door.

But she does not open it very far. Just far enough so that
Mr. Wilson out on the stoop can hand her the bag of
books.

Which Dicky does, eyes still smiling. "This is very nice
of you, miss. Thank you very much."

Al sees a spot not far from the Hancock town house. He
drives by, then puts the minivan in reverse and executes a
very nice parallel parking job.

While Al parks, Dicky swings into action.

The instant Nicky takes the bag of books, Dicky grabs
her wrist. She tries to shake free, but too late. Dicky has
her now. He pushes the door open with his foot and
quickly steps inside.

The door closes, and locks, just seconds before Al shuts
down the minivan, picks up his Nikon, and fixes his eyes
on the Hancock town house. Gone less than an hour, but
the Gumshoe has missed it all.

Dicky goes to work. He cups his hand around Nicky's
mouth and drags her into the living room. She kicks and
scratches and tries to scream, but all in vain. Dicky grabs
Nicky by the hair and slams the back of her head against
the wooden floor. She goes out like a light. Dicky drags her
behind the sofa, out of view.

"Nicky!" Sylvia calls from the kitchen.

Dicky freezes.

"Nicky! Was that a knock on door?" Sylvia is in the
hallway now, coming toward the foyer.

Dicky slips across the living room and hides behind the
door. He pulls the straight-edge razor from his pocket and
opens the blade.

Sylvia steps into the living room. "Nicky?"

Dicky slams the door shut, grabs and twists Sylvia's
arm, presses the gleaming blade against her throat. "I suggest, sister, that you not make a sound."

Sylvia has been terrorized before. Back in Poland. "Let
go of me. Who are you? What do you want?"

Dicky twists her arm tighter. "I don't want to hurt you.
Just tell me where Hancock is."

"Mr. Hancock not home."

"Bullshit. Where is he? In the kitchen? Upstairs?" He twists her arm even tighter, tight enough to very nearly break the bones. "Where?"

Sylvia grimaces. "I tell you he leave. Just half an hour ago. Not even. Ten minutes."

"You lie."

As a young child Sylvia saw people tortured and beaten to death. She does not know who this man is or what he wants, but she can feel his brutality and smell his insanity.

"I do not lie," she tells him. "I tell you Mr. Hancock gone for day."

Dicky does not believe her, but nevertheless asks, "Where did he go?"

"He does not say. He never say. He just go."

Behind the sofa Nicky groans.

Sylvia tries to break free.

Dicky, his fury so long bottled up, slides the incredibly sharp blade of that straight-edge razor from left to right across poor Sylvia's neck. The blade slices easily through Sylvia's jugular.

Not much more than a whimper spills from her mouth. Blood spurts everywhere. It spurts halfway across the room as the primary artery from the heart tries to push blood to the brain.

Dicky, revolted by the blood, releases his grip.

Life swiftly slipping away, Sylvia turns to face her killer. This simple movement causes several spurts of blood to cover Dicky's new blue oxford, as well as his face and hands. He shoves her backward. Sylvia crumples to the fine Persian carpet, the blood pulsing out of her gaping wound every time her dying heart beats.

Nicky groans again.

Dicky crosses to her. Nicky's eyes are open wide. Dicky cannot bear to look at her eyes. He bends down and without a moment's hesitation swipes the bloody blade across Nicky's lovely throat. Poor girl. Not even old enough yet to have known the love of a man.

Dicky wipes the blood off his razor blade onto Nicky's

white silk blouse. Then he stands and slips out of the living room, closing the door as he exits.

For several seconds he stands in the front foyer and listens. Two human beings abruptly dead, but the house does not make a sound. Two brutal, senseless murders, but the world's clocks just keep ticking.

Dicky sweeps through the downstairs, straight-edge at the ready. He checks the dining room, the family room, the kitchen. No sign of Hancock.

Up the carpeted stairs he goes, two at a time. One by one he searches the rooms, even the closets and under the beds. Hancock, he thinks, could be hiding anywhere.

In the master bedroom he finds the bed unmade. And on the bureau, pictures of Hancock and Clara and the kids.

The door to the third floor is closed, but not locked. Up goes Dicky, stepping lightly, not wanting those stairs to creak. But even up in the office he finds no sign of Hancock.

The phone rings. It rings a second time. And a third time. On the fourth ring the answering machine picks up. The message has recently been recorded by John junior and young Willy. *"Hi, none of us are home right now. Please tell us who you are and what your number is and we will call you back."*

And then the caller, Clara Dare Hancock, calling from Kennedy Airport. *"Hey, where is everyone? So early and everyone's already up and gone. I just wanted to say hi to the boys before they left with Linda. And John, I wanted to tell you I've arrived and will soon be on route to the hotel. Maybe you're already on your way. I hope so. And if not, hurry along. We'll have dinner. And then, whatever. Love you all. Bye."*

The phone goes dead. Dicky has not moved a muscle since the phone rang. He stands perfectly still for several more seconds. Then he makes a move in the direction of Hancock's desk. He wants to replay the message. But in the middle of the desk he finds a pad of paper. On the top sheet he finds Hancock's handiwork from last night: SWEET WEDNESDAY NIGHT, THE AMBASSADOR

HOTEL, NEW YORK, N.Y. . . . SWEET WEDNES-
DAY NIGHT, THE AMBASSADOR HOTEL, NEW
YORK, N.Y.

Dicky has heard of the Ambassador Hotel. A swanky
spot near Central Park in midtown Manhattan.

Back down the stairs he goes. He does not give a single
thought to the two dead bodies lying in the living room.
And why should he? In his sick and twisted perception of
the world, people die for no good reason all the time. His
mother. His sister. What did they do to deserve death at an
early age? Ask Dicky and he will tell you not a single
goddamn thing.

So, a couple people got in Dicky's way and now they're
dead. Tough luck. Too bad.

Now Dicky has places to go. Things to do. More people
to kill. But first he has to get to New York. To the Ambassador Hotel in New York City. Tonight. Today. Right
away.

But how to get there? Plane? Train? Bus? Car?

Dicky goes into the kitchen and out the back door. He
crosses the driveway to the detached garage and peers in
the dusty window. There's a car in there all right, a big
silver job, some kind of luxury import. He pulls open the
heavy garage door and crosses to the car. Too bad the
BMW is locked.

It doesn't take Dicky long to find the keys. They're right
there hanging on that hook in the kitchen. Dicky grabs
them, locates his bag of books and his bag of clothes, and
prepares to go.

But first he rips off his bloody oxford without bothering
with the buttons. The tee shirt comes off next. Then the
pants. Almost naked, he washes up at the kitchen sink.
Practically takes a bath in an effort to remove all that
blood and gore. He dries himself with half a roll of paper
towels. Then, leaving his mess in a heap on the kitchen
floor, he pulls on fresh duds and heads for the garage.

He backs out of the driveway onto Louisburg Square,
traveling at a rather excessive rate of speed. Then he slams

the transmission into drive and burns rubber as he peels
out onto Pinckney.

Al-the-Gumshoe Brown watches this hasty exit with no
small amount of wonder. Where, he wonders, is Hancock
going in such a hurry in his big German sedan?

So, knowing Mr. Fisher would want him to, Al powers
up the minivan and follows the BMW at a discreet distance.

The Gumshoe doesn't know it yet, but he won't be
home for supper.

CLARA & LINDA

The day after John Hancock proposed to Clara Dare, Clara invited her friend Linda Carson over for a late breakfast.

"He asked me to marry him."

"What? Who did?"

"Hancock."

"You're kidding?"

"No, I'm not."

"When?"

"Last night."

"Jesus."

Clara and Linda sat out on the terrace of Clara's apartment overlooking the Charles River. It was a lovely morning, warm and sunny. Birds chirped. Clouds drifted by. And the girls, having recently sworn off coffee, sipped tea. Some kind of weird herbal tea with ginseng and ginger root.

"So what," Linda asked Clara, "did you tell him?"

"I told him yes."

Linda could not believe her ears. "You've only been seeing him for, like, six months."

"Almost nine months, actually."

"Still, not very long."

"Long enough to know he's the one."

"Maybe, but—"

"You don't approve?"

Linda, still stunned by this sudden news, needed a moment to respond. "Approve? Of course I approve. It's just so weird. It seems like only last week I was trying to get you to just go out on a date with the guy. And now you're getting married."

Clara was all smiles. "Pretty wild, huh?"

"Really wild. Especially coming from a woman who has been insisting for years that she would never settle for just one guy. That one guy would never be able to satisfy all her needs."

Clara, still smiling, sipped her tea. A nice rich cup of Colombian would taste so much better.

"Who," she asked innocently enough, "says I'm settling for one guy?"

Linda studied her friend with narrowed eyes. "Well, dearie, if you're getting married . . ."

Another sip of the awful tea and Clara asked, "Want to hear a little secret?"

"A secret? Sure."

"It's a juicy one."

"How juicy?"

"About as juicy as it gets."

"I can take it."

Clara offered up her wickedest smile. "Twins."

"Twins?"

"That's right."

"That's what?"

"There are two of them."

"Two of who?"

"Two of them."

Linda was thoroughly confused. "Who's them?"

"John Hancock. There's two of him."

"Clara, what the hell are you talking about?"

So Clara had to explain. In some detail. It took a while. In fact, the two girls made coffee and drank the whole pot.

But really, it all came down to this: Within a month of meeting John Hancock, Ms. Clara Dare had started to wonder. Her curiosity soon enough led her to hire a private investigator. No, not Al-the-Gumshoe Brown. This gumshoe, whose name was Pete, followed John Hancock night and day for over a fortnight. Eventually he followed Hancock all the way out to the old stone farmhouse in Stockbridge. Where he managed to get a roll of superlong-range photos of the Hancock boys standing side by side out in the front yard. Photos which, all these years later, Clara still has in her possession. Has at this very moment, by the way, in her Ferragamo handbag.

Now Clara was, as one can easily imagine, upon first seeing those photographs, both alarmed and incredibly angry. And who wouldn't be? After all, the nerve of these two scoundrels. Using her in such a despicable manner. Taking turns with her, for God's sake. Having sex with her. It was terrible. Unconscionable. Punishable by death.

For several days she refused to see John Hancock or even take his calls. *Their* calls. And make no mistake, they called every day. Several times a day. They were in love with her, after all. Both of them. Only Clara never let on, not for one second, that she knew there were two of them.

Clara wanted to kill them. Short of death, she wanted them arrested. But arrested for what? For impersonating one another? Okay, so she would not have them arrested. She would have them injured. Beaten. Maimed. Bruised and bloodied.

But strangely enough, some time passed—a few days, a week, almost two weeks—and Clara began to miss him. Miss *them*. For the first time in her life she had that lost and lonely feeling that only lovers experience when separated from their mate.

And so what did the strong and stoic Clara Dare do? She called John Hancock on the phone and asked him if he wanted to come over.

Of course he wanted to come over. In less than an hour he knocked on her door, though that day it was Will as John who went over to Clara's apartment, not John. John was on his way to Chile to do some rock climbing in the Andes.

Will as John or John himself, it made no difference to Clara. She longed for and loved them both. Her anger was gone. Swept away on the wings of passion and emotional intrigue. Two for the price of one. How tantalizing.

Clara loved the whole bizarre notion of it. Especially now that she was back in control. *Their* little secret now *her* little secret.

Linda Carson, driving her Volvo wagon at a nice, safe sixty miles per hour, crosses the Massachusetts border into the Live Free or Die state of New Hampshire. Young Willy and John junior sit in back. All wear their safety belts. E.B. White's *Charlotte's Web* echoes through the speakers. John junior fidgets. Willy sits calmly, hands folded across his lap. The boys smile, a couple of happy guys. Brothers all the way. Though really only half brothers. Same mom. Different dads. Though, genetically speaking, their fathers are pretty much exactly the same.

Linda keeps a close eye on them. Always has. She found out years ago she could not have children. That was a difficult cross to bear, but at least now she has the Hancock boys. She loves them like her own.

Linda is a little worried, however, about Clara's plan. Worried because she fears it might bring emotional distress to the boys. And at their young and innocent ages, she would hate to see them emotionally damaged. But Clara, Linda well knows, is a strong-willed woman. Once Clara decides to proceed in a particular manner, she rarely changes course.

Her insane scheme to marry the Hancock brothers remains for Linda the supreme example of Clara's willingness to make a plan and stick with it to the bitter end.

After listening to her best friend that morning almost eight years ago, Linda asked a few simple questions: "So you're serious? You're really going to marry him? Marry them? Both of them?"

"That's right," Clara answered. "That's exactly what I'm going to do."

"And you're not going to tell them?"

"Tell them what? That I know there are two of them? That I know they've been deceiving me? That I know they're trying to pull the wool over this pretty girl's eyes?"

"Yes. All of those things."

Clara shook her head. "No, of course I'm not going to tell them."

"But Clara," said Linda, "that's crazy. Certifiably insane. You can't live that way."

"It's not crazy at all. And why can't I live that way? Telling them I know would be ridiculous. It would ruin everything. Take away all the fun. All the adventure. It's much better for me to know and for them to not know I know."

Linda, just south of Manchester on Interstate 93, shakes her head as she recalls the conversation. She has to admit, somehow Clara has made it all work. She's kept her rather strange and undoubtedly illegal marriage together, given birth to two beautiful boys, created a wonderful home for her family, and made buckets of money along the way.

But now, in the midst of all that success and good fortune, Clara is, as always, looking for more.

Linda sighs. She knows, despite her worries and her reservations, that she will help and support her best friend any way she can.

FRANK HAGSTROM HANGS

It's more than fifteen years ago now that Hancock stood outside that glass-and-redwood house high in the Hollywood Hills, watching Hagstrom climb up and down off the coffee table. Finally he drew the conclusion that Big Frank did not have the guts to hang himself. So Hancock decided to slip into his parents' old house and pay the stinking, thieving, lying lawyer a visit. Give the son of a bitch a helping hand.

But first Hancock had to get into the house. No problem. He crept back into the shadows in search of an open door. All were locked. So he unzipped his backpack and took out the ice pick and the ball peen hammer. The door leading into the kitchen looked easy enough to jimmy, so Hancock quietly hammered and pried until the lock gave way and the door sprang open. Then he returned to the front window to check on Hagstrom. The attorney, dressed to the hilt, as always, in his custom suit and polished black wing tips, continued to dither with death.

Soon enough, Big Frank made another approach on his makeshift gallows. The second he began his ascent, Hancock sprinted around to the kitchen door, pushed it open, and slipped silently into the house. The door did not make a sound. Nor did Hancock's footsteps across the tiled floor. Beautiful tiles his mother had picked out to match the light cherry cabinets and the rose-colored marble countertops.

At the door into the living room he drew the .38 Saturday night special his brother had procured down in Mexico from Felipe Alvarez. He stopped, took a couple of deep breaths. There, less than ten feet away, stood Hagstrom, balanced precariously on top of that dining room chair on top of the glass coffee table. The attorney had that noose around his neck. And he had the most pitiful expression on his lying, cheating face. Too wrapped up in his own miseries, Hagstrom neither saw nor heard Will Hancock.

Will stood there and wondered what he should do. He had two choices: move forward or retreat. Retreat, he knew, was the simple way out. For over a year now, ever since he had supposedly drowned down on Caye Caulker, he and John had been taking turns stalking Hagstrom. But neither of them had yet found the guts to knock the attorney off. Now, suddenly, Will had an excellent opportunity to do the job. All he had to do was walk in there and kick that chair out from under Hagstrom's feet.

But if he did, if he killed Hagstrom, that would pretty much seal his fate. He would never be able to resurrect his own life again. Right now, fifteen months after faking his own death, Will knew he could still come back and announce to anyone who cared to listen that his death had been highly exaggerated. The stunt might even provide some publicity for their nicely reviewed but slow-selling literary debut, *Boarding School Blues*.

On the other hand, murdering Hagstrom would lock in the status quo. Will would forevermore be taking turns playing the role of John Hancock.

What to do? Will stood there wondering. Is this son of a bitch worth the trouble?

In the end, Will walked into that living room for many reasons. He walked in there because of his dead mother and his dead father. Maybe Hagstrom hadn't killed them, but he had certainly dragged their names and reputations through the muck. He walked in there because of the money. Because of the three million bucks Hagstrom had stolen from him and his brother. He walked in there because fate seemed to be pulling him in that direction. But the main reason he walked into the living room was brother John. Will wanted to prove to John that he could take care of this mess, that he had the courage to carry out the execution. All along John had been insisting that he would be the one to kill Hagstrom, but Will no longer believed John had the guts.

So he pointed the .38 special at the lawyer and said, "Hello, Frank."

Big Frank, unnerved by being caught in a rather compromised position, nearly lost his balance and toppled off the chair. Had he done so he would have hung himself right then and there. But he managed to hang on.

"What the fuck are you doing in my house?" Big Frank tried to sound tough.

"This is my house, Frank. My family's home. You stole it."

"Bullshit. Get the hell out. I'm not in the mood for visitors."

"I can see that, Frank. Having a bad day?"

"Screw you, Hancock." Hagstrom reached up to remove the noose from around his neck.

Will took a step closer, shoved the .38 right up into the attorney's groin. "Drop your hands, Frank, or I'll blow off your testicles."

Hagstrom dropped his hands. He was so pale he already looked dead. "What the hell do you want?"

"I want you, Frank."

"You and everyone else in this crummy town. So, what are you going to do, Hancock? Shoot me?"

"Thinking about it."

"You don't have the balls to shoot me."

"Maybe I don't have to shoot you, Frank. Maybe all I have to do is give you a little shove." To demonstrate, Will took his left hand and pressed against Big Frank's belly.

The attorney struggled to keep his balance.

Will actually smiled. Despite his reservations, he was enjoying himself. He liked being in control of another human being's fate. Life and death. It made him feel potent.

"What's this all about, Hancock? The dough, right? You're pissed off about the dough?"

"Do you have a camera, Frank? I want to take some pictures."

"Pictures? Of what?"

"Of you. In that humiliating position."

"Fuck you, Hancock."

"You already said that, Frank. Now where's the camera?"

"In the bedroom. On the bureau."

Will backed up to the bedroom door, never for a second taking his eye or that gun off the attorney. Once he reached the doorway, he took a quick look inside. There it was, on the bureau, right beside Frank's billfold and solid gold cufflinks, a 35-mm Minolta. He grabbed it and returned to the living room. Hagstrom had not moved a muscle. Will checked the film. The camera was loaded, with several frames still left to shoot.

"Okay, Frank," said Will, "I just want a few photos of you standing up there with that noose around your neck. Then, if you want, I'll let you get down. But the photos are the price you have to pay for me sparing your life."

"Go to hell."

"Be nice, Frank. You're going to do this for me." Will sounded confident. And he looked and felt pretty confident, too. Maybe he really could do this. Maybe he could take Hagstrom out. Maybe murder wasn't such a big deal after all. John, Will knew, had tried to do it, but John had failed. John didn't have the guts. John was all mouth. It was up to Will now. Will was the man.

But first he had to get the photos. To prove to John he had been here.

"Okay," said Frank, "take your goddamn pictures. But make it quick."

"Don't sweat it, Frank. Just take it easy. Draw that

noose up snug. I want these photographs to look authentic."

"Thirty seconds," countered the attorney. "I'll give you thirty seconds to take three pictures. But first I want you to back off. Give me some room. Ten feet at least."

Will obligingly backed off, halfway across the vast living room.

Frank took a deep breath and drew the noose against his Adam's apple. The sensation made his skin crawl.

"You ready, Frank?"

"Take your damn pictures."

Will brought the camera up to his eye. "Okay, Frank—smile."

"Screw you!"

Will popped the shutter.

"That's one," announced Frank.

Will moved around the room in search of another angle. Reason and reality had by this time leaked out of his conscience.

"Come on, goddammit! Take the picture."

"Easy, Frank. You can't rush the artist."

"Just do it."

Will snapped another shot.

"That's two. One more is all you get."

"Okay," said Will, "but let's make this last one a good one." Will kept moving around the room, circling, moving closer to Hagstrom as he peered through the viewfinder.

Frank did his best to keep an eye on young Hancock, but Will would not stand still.

"Take the damn photograph!"

Will worked himself in behind Hagstrom. He had his adrenaline pumping, his instincts twitching.

"Where the hell are you, Hancock!"

"Right here at your side, Frank." Will grabbed the back of the chair and gave it a little shake. He was over the edge now, well on his way down Insanity Row.

"What the fuck!" Hagstrom's voice had found a new pitch.

Will laughed and shook the chair again. "Having fun yet, Frankie?"

"Damn you, Hancock!" Hagstrom, in a panic, started to lose his balance. His knees buckled. The noose tightened.

This is when things could have gone either way. Will could have saved Frank from falling. Maybe saved his own life, his own sanity anyway, in the process. Or he could have simply watched in the hope that Frank might fall.

Will, in by far the boldest and sickest move of his young life, decided to take charge. Be assertive.

He ripped that chair right out from under Big Frank's feet. Frank screamed and came rushing through the air. Then, rather abruptly, just six or eight inches above the top of that glass coffee table, Big Frank suddenly stopped falling. A quick bounce, then he just hung there with his legs kicking and flailing, his toes struggling to grow longer in an all-out effort to reach terra firma. That six or eight inches might just as well have been a mile.

Frank next tried to reach up with his arms and grab the rope with his hands in another mighty effort to take some of the strain off his lengthening neck. But Will, in his purest and most murderous moment yet, hopped up onto the coffee table and held Frank's arms behind his back.

"Easy, Frank," he told the lawyer, his voice calm and comforting. "Time to stop struggling. It's all over now."

Frank tried to respond, but nothing would come out.

"This is no big thing, Frank. You're simply getting what you deserve."

Unable to breathe, life draining away, Frank soon ran out of steam. His arms, and then his legs, went limp.

Will hung on, just in case, for another minute or two. Then, finally, he climbed down off the coffee table. He looked up, and there hung Frank Hagstrom's body, slowly swaying back and forth across the middle of the living room.

Will felt something rumbling deep down in the pit of his

stomach. Before he could make a move for the bathroom or the kitchen sink, he found himself doubled over and retching all over the luxurious, deep-pile carpet.

Not the last time Will would puke when the going got tough.

CORNERED

Will would puke again in Zelda Cosgrove's apartment a couple years later, in June of 1986. He never could stand the sight of blood. And then again, just last night, upon hearing his wife's voice on the Adventure Travel Enterprises answering machine.

Will once again replays that message from Clara. He replays it several times. The message from hell, he has labeled it. The message that has come out of the blue and looks as though it might well change everything.

Right at this moment, Will is not real certain what to do or how to proceed. The four walls of that stone farmhouse in Stockbridge suddenly feel like a cell. He feels cornered, like a caged animal. His thoughts swirl, nothing but a cloud of confusion.

John, he knows, will be here soon, looking for answers.

He paces for ten minutes, then picks up the phone. He dials the 800 number Clara left on the message.

After several rings a woman answers. "Good morning, Ambassador Hotel. How may I help you?"

"Yes, Clara Dare Hancock, please."

"Room number?"

"I don't know."

The operator punches some information into her computer terminal. "I'm sorry, sir, Ms. Hancock has not checked in yet."

"But she does have a reservation?"

"Yes, sir. She has a suite reserved for tonight and tomorrow night."

"I see. Any idea when she is scheduled to arrive?"

"Sometime this afternoon, sir. I would be happy to leave her a message if you would like her to return your call."

"Not necessary," says Will Hancock, and he hangs up.

One last time he replays the message from Clara. But this time he barely hears her foreboding words. He has his mind focused now on other matters.

When the message finishes, Will hits the erase button. No need for anyone else to stumble upon Clara's message. Especially John. Not that John will have much chance.

BABE & RAFE

On that Greyhound bus, a couple hundred miles or so east of Chicago, Rafe does his best to deal with the forced confinement. He would not have made a good submarine man. He likes fresh air, wide open spaces.

So what does Rafe do? He gets up out of his seat near the rear of the bus and strolls forward. He exchanges a few morning pleasantries with the driver, Fred, a happy-go-lucky guy from Dayton, Ohio who used to drive a tour bus for a heavy metal rock band named Blister. Drove the band all over the country, Fred tells Rafe, while members of Blister hung out in the back shooting heroin and screwing scrawny, black-eyed white girls who didn't look old enough to have their periods.

Rafe, having heard enough, turns and heads back to his seat. About halfway back on his left he spots a good-looking blonde sitting by herself. He can see she's pretty well engrossed in some paperback book. Doesn't even look up when Rafe passes. Which Rafe thinks is too bad because he'd like to give that blonde his best smile, maybe take that empty seat beside her, talk her up for an hour or two. It sure would help kill the time on the long haul to New York City.

Rafe's most of the way back to his seat when something clicks in his brain: that paperback book! Rafe backs up, all the way back to where the blonde sits reading. And sure enough, it's a John Hancock novel: *Revenge.*

Rafe cruises back to his seat and fetches *his* John Hancock novel, *The Settlement.*

He returns to the middle of the bus. "Hey," he says, his best smile in place, "sorry to bother you, but, well, I was just wondering if you were a fan?" By way of explanation Rafe holds up his copy of *The Settlement.*

Babe, lost in her own world, needs several seconds to make the connection. Except to ask directions to the ladies' room or to order food, Babe has not really spoken to anyone since leaving Doctor Gerdy's office *three* days ago.

"A fan?" Babe looks up at the smiling black man. "Oh, a fan. I see. No, it's mostly something to pass the time." She quickly lowers her eyes.

A shy one, thinks Rafe, who has been making moves on vacationing white chicks for twenty-five years. "I was just wondering," he says, his brain searching for an angle, "because, well, I'm an old friend of his."

At this announcement, Babe's ears perk up. Normally Babe does not strike up conversations with strangers, especially male strangers, but she might just have to make an exception for an old friend of John Hancock's.

"Are you an author, too?" she asks.

"Actually, no," answers Rafe. "I'm an, uh . . . I own a hotel. Down in Belize."

"Belize? That's Central America."

"Central America. Right. My place is actually out in the Caribbean."

"The Caribbean?"

Rafe nods. "On a small island called Caye Caulker."

"Your own tropical island hotel. Sounds wonderful."

"It's just a modest place. But it's very beautiful. A little piece of paradise on earth."

"I imagine."

"The Hancocks have been my guests. Several times."

Babe's ears really perk up now. "The *Hancocks*? You mean the author and his wife?"

"Actually," says Rafe, in a moment of almost divine innocence, "the author and his brother."

"His brother?" Babe does a mediocre job of hiding her incredulity.

"Yeah, well, that was years ago."

Babe practically slaps herself in the face to regain her composure. For just one second she wonders if this black man is real.

Rafe is as real as they come. And now that he has the conversation going, no way is he going to let up. He slips into the empty seat and says, "Let's put it this way: John Hancock used to have a brother. A twin brother. Will Hancock. But he died. Down on Caye Caulker. Skin diving. I was there when it happened."

My God, thinks Babe, so the story of Will Hancock's death is true. All of this time I thought his death was a lie. I thought he was alive. Alive and well and killing Frank. And now, out of the blue, this man shows up to tell me otherwise.

Rafe, totally unaware of the blonde's interest in the Hancock boys, makes his next move. "I have business in New York," he tells her. "Hotel business. At the Ambassador on Central Park." He figures that has to sound impressive. "Then," he adds, "I'm on my way up to Boston. To see, believe it or not, John Hancock." Rafe taps the hardcover book. "Figured I better read his latest before I get there."

Babe, still reeling from this blast of reality, asks, "John Hancock? Really? You're going to see him?"

"Yup." And then, in that casual island cool, he adds, "You could come along if you'd like."

Babe is certainly not in the habit of accepting invitations from black male strangers. Still, a face-to-face meeting with John Hancock . . . "Well, actually, I'm on my way to Boston, also."

"Then come with me when I go to see Hancock. I'll only

be in New York for a few hours. Then straight up to Boston. You really should meet them. They're great guys."

Babe's brain spins in circles. Maybe, she thinks, I misunderstood him. This is all happening so fast. "Great *guys*? I thought you just said one of them was dead?"

Rafe leans over close. He's a master of contrived intimacy. "Be interested in a little secret?"

"A secret?"

Rafe smiles. "Yeah. A secret."

"About John Hancock?"

Rafe nods.

Babe says, in a low and conspiratorial voice, "I love a good secret."

Rafe, his face now just inches from this good-looking blonde's face, asks, "And how good are you at keeping a secret?"

Babe actually smiles. "Very good."

And so Rafe, thinking if he plays his cards right he might just be able to get something going with this white chick, begins to tell, for the first time in his life, his big secret. All the way across Indiana and most of Ohio, Rafe spins his tale of a staged death off the coast of Caye Caulker in the western Caribbean. Of a dead Hancock who is not really dead at all. The more Rafe fantasizes about bedding this blonde, the more details about the Hancocks pour forth.

Babe, of course, cannot believe what she is hearing. She comes to think this man, this Rafe, must surely have been sent by God to deliver this message. The message, just as she has long suspected, that the Hancock boys live.

A MIGHTY BLOW

John Hancock parks the ML320 in front of the old stone farmhouse. He steps out of the vehicle and starts up the brick walk.

The door opens. Will steps out onto the porch. He stands there in jeans and a sandy-colored cotton pullover. Exactly the same combination worn by John. Neither brother seems surprised by this identical fashion statement.

They shake hands. And then, reluctantly, embrace.

"Kids okay?" asks Will.

John nods. "They left with Linda a couple hours ago."

"For New Hampshire?"

"Right."

Will begins to say something, but stops. He sighs.

His sigh does not provide John with any comfort at all. Several seconds pass. Half a minute.

"So," says John.

"So," says Will.

Another silence.

"Why don't we go inside," suggests John.

"I'd rather stay out here," says Will. Then, after a moment, adds, "It's a beautiful day."

"Yeah," says John. "Beautiful."

Will steps off the porch onto the brick walk.

John looks around at the fresh spring grass and the flowers in bloom. "Place looks great."

"Always does this time of year," says Will.

Okay, John tells himself, time to get on with it. "I've been thinking about those cops," he says. "And I don't think they were cops at all."

Will bends down and pulls a dandelion out by its roots. "No?"

"I think they were just impersonating cops."

"Why would they do that?"

John shrugs. "I don't know. You have any ideas?"

"Not really," Will says.

"Okay," says John. He tells himself to relax. "But I did drive all the way out here so we could discuss the situation, so let's at least give it a try."

"We'll discuss everything," Will tells him. "Just take it easy. Don't be in such a hurry."

"I'm not in a hurry. I have all day."

"Good, then come with me. I want to show you the wisteria growing up the side of the barn. It's about to bloom."

Will turns and starts across the lawn.

John hesitates, but follows. He doesn't give a damn about the wisteria.

Neither does Will. Out in the middle of the lawn, Will stops.

John stops beside him. He remembers how, back in the old days, they used to talk for hours. Talk about everything: everything under the sun. But it hasn't been that way for a long time. Now they just have quick, five-minute exchanges about Clara and the boys, maybe about the latest book they're writing or their new contract with Lee Fisher.

John suddenly thinks the whole thing is pretty sad, pretty pathetic really. Damn near tragic.

And then, right on cue, Will, who has decided to proceed with his plans despite Clara's message, says, "You're right, bro, they weren't cops."

"Huh? How do you know?"

"Because I sent them."

"What do you mean *you sent them*? Why?"

"Those fake cops were harbingers, John. Harbingers of change."

Stay calm, John tells himself. Stay cool. This is not totally unexpected. He feels sure he can talk Will through whatever craziness is going on in his brother's head. "What kind of changes are we talking about?"

"Well, bro," says Will, "I have to tell you, I've about had it."

"Had what?"

"It! The whole thing. The whole situation."

"I know sometimes it's tough on you. All the time on the road."

"And all the time at home being *you*. I'm sick of it. I've had enough."

"Okay. I hear you. So what do you think we should do about it?"

"The way I see it, you've fucked me over pretty good through the years. Fucked me over several times. The first time, of course, was down on Caye Caulker when you stole my passport. The second time was leaving it to me to take out Hagstrom because you were too much of a pussy. And the third time, and maybe the worst time of all, was lying to me about how long you would hang around with Clara."

If there's one thing John's learned over the years, it's not to respond too quickly when the heat is up. He's never heard Will get it all out in the open so cleanly and clearly before. Over the years everything has always been suppressed, beneath the surface, alluded to but never actually broached. John feels certain this is not a good sign.

And he's right; it's not. Will's scheme has been hatching in his head for months, years even. The execution of that plan has now arrived. It has suddenly grown a little tricky, what with Clara possibly aware of the truth. But Will figures he will just have to cross each bridge as it comes.

"Look, Will," says John, "I can see you're angry and

you're hurting. But we need to talk this out. That passport thing—I told you then and I'll tell you again now, that was nothing but a misunderstanding."

"Bullshit."

"And don't be trying to blame me for Hagstrom. You killed him in cold blood."

"Because you wanted me to."

"No, I didn't, Will. I didn't want either of us to kill him. Not really. I never thought we'd do it. I was pissed and it was just kind of cool, thinking we might do it. Tough guys, you know?"

"Fuck you, John. You were just too much of a coward to kill him yourself."

"Whatever you say, Will. You want to blame me for Hagstrom, I can't stop you. But what about Zelda? Why did you go and kill her? She was our friend, for chrissakes."

"I didn't kill her."

"You killed her. Same as you killed Hagstrom. I tried to believe you didn't kill her. For a long time I had myself pretty well convinced. But I knew, down in my gut, that you killed her after she threatened to tell the world that we were both alive."

"I did it," Will confesses, "to protect us. To protect you."

"Bullshit, Will. You did it to protect yourself. Because you'd killed Hagstrom and were afraid if Zelda blew the whistle you'd get caught."

"No!"

"Yes."

"Goddamn you, John! You still should have left Clara to me. You promised you would."

"You're right, Will, I did. And I'm sorry. But promises cannot always be kept. I love Clara. And I love those boys. No way could I have left them in your hands. You're sick in the head, Will. Look what you did to Rodney Byrnes a few days ago. And this insane affair with Hillary Fisher. Christ, Will, you're self-destructing. You're going to destroy everything."

Will has heard enough. "I've made a few decisions," he tells his brother. "Decisions about the future."

John takes a deep breath. "Such as?"

"Such as this."

And with that utterance Will, standing just a foot or so away from his brother out there in the middle of the lawn, puts his right knee into motion. He drives that knee hard into John's groin.

John does not see the knee coming. But he sure enough feels that knee the instant it makes contact with his flesh. His testicles fly up into his stomach. The air whistles out of his lungs. A feeble cry sputters out of his mouth as he doubles over, both in agony and to protect himself from further blows.

But the next blow does not come from below. It comes from above. Will clenches his hands together and slams them down across the back of his brother's head.

Down goes John. Flat out onto the grass.

Nothing sudden or subtle about Will's attack. He came out of the farmhouse knowing exactly what he had to do. What he wanted to do.

Now he turns John over and blows a small pile of voodoo zombie powder into his brother's mouth and nostrils. Not too much powder. About half as much as he blew at Sir Rodney a few days ago. But enough to render John more or less inanimate for the next few hours. A little voodoo zombie powder goes a long way.

Satisfied John will not be blabbing at him or putting up any resistance or trying to escape, Will goes out to the barn and fetches the large wheelbarrow the brothers use to haul dirt and rocks around the property. Feeling no guilt at all about the attack he has leveled against his brother, Will pushes the wheelbarrow up to John's limp body and begins loading him into the bucket.

Will carefully wheels the barrow down the concrete ramp of the old root cellar and through the large open doorway. He came down here an hour ago and unlocked the door, made sure everything was in order for his brother's stay. A small act of premeditation.

No longer much evidence of the way this root cellar used to look, when farmers stored their roots and vegetables and hard cider for those long New England winters. No more cold stone walls or dirt floor. No more darkness or chill in the air. Will has made some changes. Maybe not as many changes as he would have liked, but time grew short, so his improvements will simply have to do. A concrete slab has been poured over the dirt floor. An inexpensive grade of industrial carpet covers the concrete. Drywall blocks out the old stones. There is electricity, though no plumbing or heating. Will wanted to install these conveniences, but execution of his plan came a little sooner than anticipated.

The almost finished space measures about twenty by twenty. It is basically one large room, with a kitchen section divided off by a Formica countertop perched upon a pair of sawhorses. The kitchen has a small refrigerator, a toaster, and a hot plate.

The rest of the space is mostly empty except for a sofa that folds out into a bed, a couple of wooden chairs, and a wooden table. An Apple computer, similar to the ones in the farmhouse and up in their Beacon Hill office, sits on top of the table.

Not exactly a luxury suite at the Ambassador, but, for now anyway, this is the best Will can do for his brother. After all, the game has changed. Will is quite sure things will never be the same again. John is his prisoner now, and will remain so until Will can get a handle on what to do next. Until he can figure out just how much Clara knows.

Will unloads John onto the floor in the middle of the room. Then he drags his brother up onto the sofa and puts a soft pillow under his head in an effort to make him more comfortable.

John moans and groans. He has started to recover from the blow to the back of the head. The voodoo zombie powder, however, still holds him in his grip.

"It's okay," Will tells him. "You took a nasty fall. Just rest easy."

John, his brain filled with cobwebs, makes no effort to

respond. Not that he could even if he wanted to; the zombie powder has temporarily robbed him of speech and virtually all control over his muscles. Plus his whole body hurts. His memory is foggy. He remembers being in the ML320. Driving west on the Mass Pike. Passing through Stockbridge. Turning down the driveway. Stepping out of the car. Seeing Will at the front door. Embracing. Talking it over. Accusations and repercussions. And then falling. He thinks he recalls falling. But he can't be sure. . . .

In the distance, far away, he hears his brother's voice. "Just rest easy. You'll feel better in a couple hours."

John thinks he should respond, but he cannot bring himself to speak. He feels paralyzed. And in pain. He feels like it would be wonderful to rest, to sleep. And within just a few seconds, he does exactly that.

Will checks on him. John's breathing and his pulse are slow, but adequate. In a few hours, he'll be fine. Relatively speaking.

Will checks the door leading to the stairway. It is a new door, thick and very solid. It is locked from the outside, triple locked, actually. A key lock and a couple of heavy-duty dead bolts. A stick of dynamite would be needed to get that baby open.

Will turns and crosses to the large, thick, wooden door leading to the concrete ramp. He exits, closes the door, turns the lock, then throws into place those two brand-new solid steel dead bolts.

GAS

Linda Carson pulls off Interstate 93 near Plymouth, New Hampshire. The Volvo needs gas. The boys need to use the restroom.

Linda decides to call John Hancock, let him know his boys are well. She dials up the Hancock town house down in Boston. No one answers. No one can answer. Everyone is gone. Or dead.

The answering machine beeps. *"John, hi, it's Linda. I know it's only been a few hours, but I just wanted to check in, let you know we're doing fine. We should reach the cabin in about an hour. No telephone there, but you can call my cell phone if you want to chat with the boys. Talk to you later. Bye."*

Young Willy and John junior return from their trip to the restroom. They've raided the vending machines along the way. In their hands they carry Cokes and Hershey bars and small bags of Famous Amos chocolate chip cookies. Linda, not a big junk food advocate, is not real happy with their purchases. But when they hand her a bag of cookies, she melts and says nothing. Except thank you.

Linda loves these boys. Loves them like her own.

They climb back into the Volvo and head north for the White Mountains.

Al needs gas. He's annoyed with himself for not filling up yesterday on his way home from work. Now he's west of New London, Connecticut and damn near running on fumes. For almost three hours he's been following that big BMW. Hancock barely even stops at stop signs. Just slows and rolls on through. He drives like a maniac. Weaving in and out of lanes. Driving eighty-five, then fifty, then seventy. Totally erratic and sometimes reckless. Al has had a hell of a time trying to maintain visual contact.

Several times the Gumshoe has called Leland Fisher to keep his client apprised of the situation. He knows Mr. Fisher is on his way to New York City, but thus far Al has only been able to leave voice mail.

But now, suddenly, near Lyme, Connecticut, things begin to happen. The big BMW exits. Al follows. The BMW pulls into a Mobil station. Al pulls into an Exxon across the street. "Fill 'er up," he tells the attendant. "Fill 'er to the brim."

The attendant, an angry and despondent teenager with long red hair and a grimy Grateful Dead T-shirt, who recently dropped out of high school, shakes his head at Al's request and turns his attention to the pump. The teener hates everyone over the age of twenty.

The Gumshoe doesn't care. He's a happy man listening to the sound of high test rushing into his tank.

Across the street, Mad Dicky cannot get the window of the BMW to go down. This irritates him thoroughly. He curses, opens the door an inch or two, and grumbles to the attendant, "Fill it!"

The attendant, a retired schoolteacher who last year realized his life savings and pension could not begin to make ends meet, manages a smile and says, "Yes, sir. Will that be cash or credit?"

Dicky scowls. "Cash." And he slams the door.

The attendant is used to this kind of belligerent, adolescent behavior. He taught seventh and eighth grade science and math for thirty-two years.

Al watches through the window of his minivan. But a combination of too much distance and a midafternoon glare on the windows make it impossible for the Gumshoe to tell that the driver's seat of that BMW is not occupied by John Hancock.

His cell phone rings. "Brown here."

"It's Fisher," Leland says softly into his own cellular phone. "What's up?"

"Mr. Fisher, thanks for calling back."

"I'm on the train," says Leland. "Just outside New York. My wife went to the can, but she'll be back any second. I've only got a minute."

Al quickly brings Leland up to speed on his pursuit of John Hancock through Boston and then south along Interstate 95.

"Christ," grumbles Leland, "I wonder if the SOB is headed for Manhattan."

"Could be, sir," says Al. "I'd estimate we're about three hours out of the city right now."

Leland sighs. Poor Leland. Last night he told himself he would not have a single drink during this little getaway to the Big Apple, but right about now he sure could use a Scotch sour or a Bloody Mary.

He tells Al, "Okay, just keep tailing him. And be sure to keep me informed. I'll be at the Ambassador Hotel at Fifth Avenue and Sixty-third Street. Maybe my wife told Hancock we were going to the Ambassador and the SOB decided to drive down and pay her a visit."

"Maybe."

"Here she comes. Gotta go."

The line goes dead.

Al hangs up and looks out the window. The big BMW pulls out of the Mobil and starts up the ramp for I-95 South.

The Gumshoe pays the surly teener and follows. If nothing else, he figures this little escapade will make a great story to tell his wife.

*   *   *

The Greyhound cruiser heads into the Angola, Indiana, bus depot not far from the Indiana-Ohio border. Time for fresh fuel and a new driver. Babe and Rafe barely notice the bus has stopped. They are deep in conversation now, sharing secrets, telling lies. Several times Rafe has made Babe laugh. Once or twice she actually even giggled. Something she has not done in years. Had started to believe she might never do again.

Rafe's off the whole Hancock story now. He'll go back to it if he needs to. But right now Babe is getting a kick out of hearing about all the strange and eccentric characters living down on Caye Caulker. Rafe has told her about Matilda, and Jackie of Jackie's Bar & Grill, plus several others, some of whom exist and some of whom Rafe has just conjured up out of his imagination.

Rafe likes to see Babe smile. He can see she hasn't smiled nearly enough in a long time. She's older than he first thought, a little worn and wrinkled around the edges, but she's still a good-looking woman, and he's having a fine time sitting beside her, talking her up. Sure beats sitting alone thinking about what might happen when he hands over that depleted bag of coke.

Babe, now that she has someone to talk to, is also enjoying the trip. She's really like most of the rest of us: often isolated, but rarely happy about it. She's had nary a bad or negative thought since Rafe sat down beside her.

And, of course, most incredible of all: he knows the Hancocks. John and Will.

If all goes well, Babe sees herself sitting in the Hancock home in Boston as early as tomorrow evening. She'll waltz right in on Rafe's arm, shake Hancock's hand, have a seat in his living room. And at some point in the conversation, she will nonchalantly ask, "So, John, remember me? I'm Babe Overton. Frank Hagstrom's fiancée. Is your brother Will around? I'd like to have a little chat with the two of you."

.   •   •

Will Hancock is not thinking about Babe Overton. He's thinking about Dicky Cosgrove. He's thinking about Dicky because directly across the street from the Amoco station where he's refueling his BMW, there's a sign for the Great Barrington Psychiatric Center.

"Yes, sir?" asks the attendant, who also happens to be the owner-operator. "What can I get for you today?"

"Fill it with premium," says Will. "And would you please check the oil?"

"Sure."

"Thanks."

Lenore taught her boys to always say please and thank you.

Will stares at the sign for the psychiatric center. He shakes his head. All these years, and Mad Dicky was just down the road.

From the old farmhouse outside of Stockbridge to the entrance gates of the Great Barrington Psychiatric Center, it cannot be more than ten or twelve miles. Maybe fifteen or twenty minutes. Neither of the Hancock boys, however, ever stopped by to pay Dicky a visit.

Understandable, considering the circumstances.

Will nevertheless thinks about Dicky as that Amoco Ultimate sloshes into the tank of his 750il. He soon enough starts thinking about Zelda. He loved Zelda. The first real love of his life. He just about died after she died. After she was murdered. Of course, her murder was inevitable. She knew too much and made way too many demands. But Will does not want to think about that. So he thinks about his plan. His new plan. Nothing but a hasty variation of his old plan.

All of Will's thoughts are muddled and confused. And tainted with a past gone sour and a future filled with uncertainty. His plan was to take John out of the picture, plain and simple. Become the one and only John Hancock. Full time. But now there's a glitch to that scenario. Will does not like glitches.

He sighs and rubs his eyes. Then he pays for the gas, pulls out of the Amoco, and heads southwest on Route 23. He will soon reach the Taconic State Parkway and steer south for New York. If he drives like the wind, he figures he can reach the Ambassador Hotel in less than two hours.

EARLY ARRIVALS

Clara's limo pulls up to the Sixty-third Street entrance of the Ambassador Hotel. The doorman, all decked out in his gray uniform with gold trim, opens the limousine door. Clara steps out, rested and looking radiant.

It would be impossible to call any one of New York's many grand hotels the absolute finest, but the Ambassador certainly finds itself near the top. The simple yet elegant lobby welcomes Clara as she comes through the revolving doors. An enormous vase of cut flowers dominates the large round table in the center of the vast space. Clara registers, then is led to her suite on the fourteenth floor by the bell captain, a man with impeccable manners and sparkling white teeth. Hands clasped behind his back, he assures Clara that if she needs anything, anything at all, she need only ask.

He shows her around the suite: the sitting room with its large television and fully stocked bar. The bedroom with its king-size bed covered with a lovely lace spread. And the lavish bath complete with Jacuzzi and bidet.

The bellhop brings her luggage, places everything discreetly out of the way. Very professional. Very polite. Clara gives the captain and the bellhop generous tips.

Then down to business. She spends an hour or so on the telephone organizing and conferring and confirming appointments.

She calls the concierge to make sure she has a room reserved for tomorrow's press conference at noon.

She calls her publicist to make sure the proper media people have been contacted about the press conference.

Then, only partially satisfied, she calls three or four acquaintances who write about the arts. Clara believes in the adage that if you want something done right, do it yourself.

While Clara makes her calls, Leland and Hillary Fisher pull up to the Fifth Avenue entrance in a New York yellow cab.

Leland does not really like the Ambassador. He prefers the Regency over on Park, but if they stayed at the Regency and everything did not go perfectly, Hillary would bitch and moan and complain. There would not be a moment's peace. And no way does Leland need that.

Right now he's just hoping for a couple of restful days. But this business with Hancock driving south on I-95 has Leland's blood pressure on the rise. And the Ambassador, he has to admit, has an excellent bar. The Chase is a large and airy lounge with walls covered with famous fox hunting prints. Horses and foxes decorate the ashtrays and the matchboxes and the beverage coasters. Leland has always liked The Chase. He intends to pay a visit to the bar just as soon as Hillary heads south for Tiffany's and Bergdorf's.

But first he has to deal with a bit of a ruckus concerning their room. Exactly the kind of thing that keeps Leland from insisting they stay at the Regency.

It seems Hillary requested a suite with a view of Central Park. But she only called to make the reservation yesterday. The hotel is quite full. They have either suites without a view or rooms with a view.

Hillary hears this and immediately starts screeching at

the desk clerk, then at the floor manager. Finally, with Leland practically disappearing into his suitcase, his lovely bride settles for a room with a view, up on the fourteenth floor. Room 1466.

On the opposite end of the hall from the Hancock suite.

BURIED

John feels a little woozy. A lot woozy. Like he used to feel back in the old days after a night of too much booze and too much grass. But those days are over. John's a family man now. And a damn good one. Except for the fact that he shares the domestic duties with his psychotic brother.

Haitian voodoo zombie powder does a number on short-term memory, so John has been having some trouble piecing together precisely what happened after he stepped out of the ML320. He's pretty sure he had some kind of encounter with Will, but the substance of that encounter has vanished.

The back of his head hurts. His neck hurts. His testicles hurt. John begins to think Will must have kneed him in the groin and then clobbered him over the head. Either that or he got run over by a truck.

He stands. Dizziness swiftly forces him to sit back down. After a few seconds he tries standing again. He looks around, works to get his bearings. His surroundings do not look familiar.

His nose itches. He scratches it. His finger comes away covered with a dirty white residue. John, confused, examines the residue closely. Then it dawns on him. The voodoo powder! Will knocked him out with the voodoo zombie powder. Jesus!

John takes some deep breaths, does some deep knee bends, walks, unsteadily, around the room. Now he knows why Rodney Byrnes was so ticked off when he called the other day.

The dizziness returning, he sits again on the sofa. He looks around the room. It still does not look familiar. But it's plenty Spartan. Just the sofa, a couple chairs, a table, some kind of a small kitchen on the far side of the room.

But where, he wonders, am I?

Another look around and John realizes the room does not have any windows. Not a single one. The only illumination comes from a couple of bare bulbs hanging off the ceiling. Basically, it's pretty dim in the room. Dim and dank. And damp. Almost wet. Like it might be underground.

John pushes himself out of the sofa and crosses to the smaller door on the near side of the room. It's locked. He flips the locking mechanism on the knob, but the door does not open. He pulls on it, shakes it, even gives it a kick, but all he does is hurt his foot. The door does not move.

Blood rushes to his head. For a second or two John fears he will pass out. But he grabs the doorknob, steadies himself, waits for the dizziness to pass. Then he turns and slowly crosses to the larger door on the far side of the room.

As he approaches the door, it hits him. It's the door to the old root cellar, out by the barn! The bunker, he and Will have called it ever since they bought the old farm back in the eighties.

Panic immediately charges through John's body. He moves forward, grabs the handle of the door, and gives it a vicious pull. But nothing happens. The door does not budge. It's locked. Dead-bolted, he quickly realizes, from the outside.

Instantly the entire scene comes clear. Will must have knocked him out cold on the lawn, then dragged him here to the old root cellar. Buried him in the bunker. Buried him alive.

Dizzy, John sits. He cannot believe how stupid and careless he was to waltz right into Will's trap. All the signs of Will's growing insanity were plain enough to see. John knows he should have been far more aggressive in responding to the situation. But hindsight is an utterly useless art. All he can do now is try to extricate himself.

He rises. Crosses to the nearest door. Fiddles with the lock. Bangs with his fists and kicks with his feet. The door does not give an inch.

Exhausted, he collapses on the floor. What, he wonders, does Will have in mind? What's his plan? Does he plan on keeping him locked up down here forever? Or does he have something else in store? Maybe murder? John knows full well Will has murdered before. At least twice.

Escape. He must escape. But how? There's no way out.

John rises and slowly makes his way to the table. He sits in the chair and flips on the Macintosh computer. A very nice unit. Similar to the one in the farmhouse.

The computer boots up. Several icons appear on the screen. A large one right in the middle quickly captures John's attention. It's a Word document, entitled: MEMO FROM W. TO J.

John double-clicks the mouse and the document begins to open. While it opens John sighs and rubs his eyes. He cannot believe he has put himself in this vulnerable and compromised position. What, he wonders, is he going to do? What about Clara? What about the boys?

He reads:

Dear John,

If you're reading this I'll assume you're feeling reasonably well. And that by this time you've tried the doors and figured a few things out. I've always been the craftier one, but you're certainly no dummy.

I'm sorry about all this. Really I am. But what's an

unhappy brother to do? Stand idly by while you plot against me?

I had to lock you down here because I can't simply get rid of you. You are my brother, after all. My twin brother. Fratricide is out of the question. At least for the time being.

There is, of course, the writing to consider. We still, even after all these years, need each other for that.

So, for now anyway, you'll just have to stay down here and make do the best you can. I didn't get a chance to finish the place (the lack of plumbing is of particular concern), but in the days and weeks ahead we'll get you a TV and some exercise equipment, make the place a little more homey.

Try not to be upset about this, John. Just look at it as the next phase of our lives. I might have more fun and more freedom than you in this new phase, but maybe that will help even things out.

Don't sweat the solitude. I'll be around to see you real soon. I promise.

Love,
Will

John reads the note over a second time. What scares him the most is its matter-of-fact attitude. As though this particular scenario is all perfectly sane and normal. Will has clearly gone stark raving mad, but he's acting like he's just gone down to the corner store to buy the newspaper and a cup of coffee.

John, sweating profusely, can feel his heart pounding against the walls of his chest. He can feel the terror spiraling along his spine.

BIG MAC ATTACK

Al-the-Gumshoe Brown has also started to sweat. It's all that coffee. Al's been seriously contemplating for the past twenty or thirty miles just peeing in his pants. If he had a fresh pair to change into, he'd do it right here and now.

Dead ahead, he sees it—Nirvana! The right side blinker of John Hancock's BMW flashing on and off.

Yes, Dicky, too, needs to use the can. He also has a yearning for a Big Mac or two. Been fourteen years since he's been through the golden arches.

But really neither the can nor the Big Mac is the primary reason Dicky has decided to exit a few miles east of New Haven. No, the real reason is that minivan he keeps seeing in his rearview mirror. He saw it back in Boston. He saw it up in Rhode Island. He saw it when he stopped to refuel. And he's seeing it now.

So Dicky exits. And sure enough, the minivan exits. Dicky pulls into McDonald's. The van does, too. Dicky heads for the rear of the parking lot and parks the BMW.

Forgetting and ignoring all proper surveillance techniques, Al parks, shuts down the engine, and literally sprints across the parking lot and into the restaurant. In the back right corner, he spots a sign for the men's room.

He goes for it with all possible haste. In his enthusiasm he begins pulling down his zipper. He very nearly exposes himself to a group of young Americans bouncing around Ronald McDonald Land. But he slips safely through the door and steps right up to the urinal. Nothing in his entire life has ever felt so wonderful as the joy and satisfaction he feels once the stream starts flowing.

Al needs way over a minute to fully purge his bladder. Almost two minutes. It just goes on and on and on. A combination of pleasure and relief causes him to moan with delight.

A kid with ketchup and mustard on his face stares at Al like he must be some kind of freak. The kids today know a freak when they see one. They see them all the time on TV. Freaks blowing up airplanes. And bombing buildings. And shooting kids in schoolyards.

But this kid has it wrong. Al's not the freak. The freak's out in the restaurant. Right now Dicky's paying for his three Big Macs, two large orders of golden fries, and two chocolate shakes. Dicky loves his choco shakes.

Dicky pays, then stands off to the side to wait for the guy from the minivan to come out of the head.

The Gumshoe comes out soon enough. He takes a look around the restaurant. He's looking, of course, for John Hancock. Not spotting him, he goes outside. He sees the big BMW parked in the lot, not too far from his minivan. No sign of Hancock inside the car, so Al goes back to order his lunch. As long as the BMW is out there, Al knows Hancock cannot be far away.

Al's wife does not approve of McDonald's. "Fat, sodium, and profit," she always says when Al suggests pulling in for a burger. So Al does his fast-food bingeing on the sly. Like today. He, like Mad Dicky, goes for the Big Mac. A pair of them.

Dicky watches all this from a booth along the side of the restaurant. He eats and watches the mildly overweight, balding guy from the minivan. A few minutes ago the guy looked right at Dicky, but then looked away. Took no interest in Dicky whatsoever. But he's awfully interested in

Hancock's car. He's been tailing the BMW for hours. So what, Dicky wonders, is going on? Does he think he's following Hancock? Definitely a possibility. But who is he? And what the hell does he want?

Dicky takes a break from his burger and goes into the head to relieve himself.

Al pays for his lunch and grabs some napkins. All the while he keeps looking around for Hancock. No sign of the author anywhere. Dammit. Al decides to go back to the minivan, eat his burgers, and just wait for Hancock to return.

Dicky comes out of the head just in time to see the minivan guy walk out of the restaurant. He watches him climb into his Town and Country and close the door. But the guy doesn't drive away. He sits there. And eats.

Dicky moves to another booth where he can keep an eye on the minivan. He sucks down one of his shakes and opens up his second Big Mac.

Al eats and watches.

Half an hour passes. Then another half an hour. Al keeps wondering what could have happened to Hancock. Weird. Very weird.

Dicky, anxious to get to New York and kill Hancock, orders a third chocolate shake and tells himself to stay calm.

Leland Fisher sits at a booth in The Chase. He sips his Chivas and stares at the pictures of humans on horses pursuing foxes. Now there, thinks Leland, is one stupid leisure activity.

Leland's been sitting here now for an hour or so, ever since Hillary went off to shop. Leland hates shopping. But he does love bars. He's on his third Chivas double.

The cocktail waitress, in her skimpy black dress, strolls over and smiles at Leland. "Another Chivas, sir?"

Leland smiles back. Infidelity is so easy. Especially the mental variety. Leland has always thought the statistics about husbands and wives being unfaithful to one another were highly exaggerated. He thinks most of the cheating goes on upstairs. In the brain. All that desire and lust stirred up by the imagination. Like right now. His brain has no problem inviting this waitress up to his room, carrying her over the threshold, ravaging her on that king-size bed. They could be in and out of the sack before Hillary ever walked through the front door of Saks Fifth Avenue.

But thinking, fantasizing, Leland knows, is a hell of a lot different than doing. And that's all he thinks most husbands and wives ever do: fantasize.

Except his wife. She does more than just fantasize. Her and that son of a bitch John Hancock.

And right then, out of the corner of his eye, Leland spots his old friend. There, out in the corridor. Walking past the entrance to The Chase. Leland needs a couple seconds to register the specter.

Then he stands and crosses the bar. He goes out into the corridor. "John!" he calls.

But too late. Hancock steps into an elevator and the doors slide closed.

Hastily, Leland returns to his booth. He snatches up his cell phone. He dials up Al-the-Gumshoe Brown. The waitress brings his fourth Chivas. Leland thanks her and, all carnal thoughts history, takes a sip.

Al picks up his cell phone. "Hello."

"Fisher here."

"Yes, sir?"

"Where are you?"

"New Haven, sir."

"Connecticut?"

"Yes, sir."

"Then why the hell is Hancock here at the hotel? I thought you were tailing him."

"I am tailing him, sir. Have been for hours. We're right now at a McDonald's just off I-ninety-five."

"Can you see him?"

"Well, no," admits Al, "but I can see his BMW. I'm parked near it and I'm waiting for him to return."

"How long have you been there?"

"I don't know. Maybe an hour."

"You moron!" shouts Leland. "Hancock's not in New Haven. He's here, in New York City. At the Ambassador Hotel. I just saw him with my own eyes."

Al finds that a little hard to believe. But reminds himself that the client is always right. "If you say so, sir. But I really don't see how he could have gotten all the way to New York in so short a time."

Leland sighs. Maybe it wasn't Hancock who stepped into that elevator. Though it sure looked like him. "Okay," he tells Al, "then go find him. And make a positive goddamn identification. As soon as you do, call me back. And I mean soon." Leland snaps off the cell phone and takes another hit off his glass of Chivas.

The Gumshoe, flustered, closes up his cell phone. Then he hurries back into McDonald's.

Dicky has not taken his eyes off the minivan for one second. Now he watches as the guy behind the wheel of the van comes back into the restaurant, stands at the front entrance, and surveys the crowd.

Jesus, thinks the Gumshoe, where could he be? Deciding the men's room is a possibility, Al heads in that direction.

Dicky does not hesitate. He stands and departs the moment the fat man walks past his booth. Dicky goes through the door and across the parking lot.

The Gumshoe checks the men's room. No sign of Hancock. Al nevertheless takes the opportunity to once again purge his bladder. No sense getting caught out on the road again.

On his way back to the minivan, he buys another burger. The thought of calling Mr. Fisher and telling him Hancock has somehow slipped away has made Al hungry all over again.

Leland has already forgotten about Al. Leland has just been to the front desk. He just learned that the Hancocks have in fact checked into the hotel. This very day. Their room is registered to Ms. Clara Dare Hancock.

But John, Leland knows, is here also. Hell, Leland saw John with his own eyes.

Like the Fishers, the Hancocks are up on the fourteenth floor. Suite 1424.

Leland's back in his booth now, thinking about a fifth Chivas. His cell phone rings. "Yeah?"

"Mr. Fisher. It's Al Brown."

"Right."

"Sorry, sir, no sign of Hancock. His car's here, but he managed to give me the slip. Maybe in a taxi or something." Al is back behind the wheel of his minivan, cell phone in one hand, burger in the other.

"Like I told you before, moron," snaps Leland, "Hancock is not in New Haven. He's in New York."

"At the Ambassador Hotel?"

"Absolutely goddamn right."

"Jesus."

"Fuck Jesus," says Leland. "You're fired!" And with that announcement he once again hangs up on the Gumshoe.

Al sighs and turns off his phone. "Dammit," he says right out loud, "I'll never get any money out of this deal now."

A fraction of a second later two large meaty hands grab Al's neck and drag him up over the top of the seat and into the rear of his minivan. Al, as shocked as he has ever been in his whole life, struggles, but Mad Dicky is far too strong and much too insane. His fingers dig deeper and deeper into Al's neck, cutting off his windpipe. Pretty soon the Gumshoe can't breathe. Not too long after that he's unconscious. A couple minutes after that the Gumshoe is dead. Stone dead. Dicky's third victim. Today.

Dicky lays Al's body out on the floor behind the front seats. He covers Al with a nice plaid quilt. That would be the Browns' picnic quilt, the one they use when they go out into the country on pleasant summer afternoons.

Then, Dicky steps out of the minivan and crosses the parking lot to the BMW. He removes his personal belongings, including his bag of clothes and his bag of Hancock novels. He locks up the car and returns to the minivan. He climbs in behind the wheel. But he can't find the keys. So he goes over the front seats, digs through the dead man's pockets, and finds not only the keys, but the dead guy's wallet.

A few minutes later, back out on I-95, heading south for New York City and the Ambassador Hotel, Mad Dicky Cosgrove takes a long look through Al-the-Gumshoe Brown's bulging billfold.

WILL & CLARA

Will made it to New York from Stockbridge in record time. But now that he has arrived, he's all of a sudden feeling nervous. Uncertain. Just a couple hours ago the guy locked his own brother in that root cellar. He's not feeling real good or real secure about that maneuver. If something happens to him, John could be trapped down there. Forever. He could starve to death. Die of thirst. Unless, of course, he figures out some way to escape. Will knows his brother is a very resourceful guy. He could be out of there already. On his way here. To the Big Apple.

So, ambivalence surging, thinking maybe he should have just whacked his brother once and for all, buried him out behind the barn, Will knocks softly on the door of Suite 1424.

Inside, Clara has just finished her phone calls. She has bathed and changed into a pair of jeans and a close-fitting black silk turtleneck. The knock on the door does not surprise her.

She smiles. She has been looking forward to this for quite some time.

And so, her thin and lovely hand upon the brass doorknob, she inquires, "Who is it?"

"Your loving husband," comes the answer.

"Which one?" asks Clara, turning the knob and pulling the door open.

All of Will's suspicions and paranoias instantly snap into place the moment he hears this one innocent little question. Still, he manages to look confused while asking, "Sorry, baby, what did you say?"

Clara smiles at him, grabs him by the belt, and pulls him into the room. "I said, what took you so long to get here? I've been waiting for hours."

Will, shaken, musters up a smile of his own. "Heavy traffic."

Clara takes a look at her husband. She has to admit, even after all these years, that it is incredibly difficult to tell the two of them apart when they are just standing there, fully dressed. The casual observer would never in a hundred years guess there were two Hancocks. But then, Clara is no casual observer. She has been at this for quite a long time. On a rather intimate level. She realized she was dating not one John Hancock but two John Hancocks as soon as sex crept into their relationship. The bodies of her two lovers were ever so slightly different. As were their techniques. John is a bit more muscular, especially through the chest, and he has always been more aggressive in bed. He prefers to instigate, control, and dominate the action. Will tends to hang back, let Clara dictate pace and position. A perfect combination for a woman who is easily bored and difficult to satisfy.

But after all this time Clara does not need to get the Hancock boys naked and frolicking to tell them apart. All she has to do is look into their eyes. John's eyes have held their youth. Forty looms on the near horizon, but his eyes still sparkle with vigor and enthusiasm. Will's eyes have lost some of that zest, grown more serious, but also more mature. The years, as well as this massive deception her men have orchestrated, have taken their toll far more on Will than on John. Which is just one of the reasons why Clara has decided to bring the whole charade to an end. She loves both her husbands equally, adores them. They have given her so much happiness and adventure. She has no desire to see either of them suffer.

Of course, she does not know that Will has committed murder. Twice. Or that, if thoroughly diagnosed by a reliable psychiatrist, he would surely be categorized a full-blown psychopath.

Clara leads Will through the sitting room to the bedroom. Will, his insides churning, would definitely like to know what's going on, but he has never been able to resist his wife's sexual advances.

And soon enough they are on the bed, kissing and hugging, squirming out of their jeans and pullovers, pressing their bodies close together. Because the Hancock boys spend only half their time with Clara, they are always extremely desirous and passionate. Never any halfhearted efforts. This afternoon is no exception.

In the middle of the action the phone rings. Neither Will nor Clara makes any effort to answer the call. It's just Leland Fisher anyway, still downstairs in the bar, working on another Chivas, calling to say hello, see if he can find out why the hell Hancock is in New York City.

But the call will have to wait. The Hancocks are preoccupied.

The phone rings again. In the heat of the moment Will and Clara barely even hear it ring. It's Linda Carson this time, calling from her cabin up in the White Mountains. She just wants to let Clara know they have arrived, the boys are fine, they are all about to go out for a hike.

But right now Clara has no desire whatsoever to talk to anyone about anything. She latches onto Will and pushes while the heat rises and her body convulses.

Will hangs on tight, all his suspicions and paranoias temporarily suspended. Before long it is his turn. He does not hold back.

Afterward, they lie side by side, shoulders and hips touching, not saying much, once in a while turning their heads and smiling.

This, Clara knows, is another difference between her two guys. After lovemaking, Will is much quieter and calmer. John tends to get energized and animated. He likes to clown around. Make goofy faces. Talk in foreign accents. Make Clara giggle.

Clara loves it either way. She also loves that old cliché: Variety is the spice of life.

She turns to Will. "I love you. You know that, right?"

"Of course I know."

"It's important you know I love you."

"I agree," says Will, not entirely comfortable with the tone of Clara's voice. "It's very important."

"And it's just as important for you to know that I love both of you."

"*Both* of us?"

Clara ignores Will's mystified expression. "You got my message, right? On the Adventure Travel Enterprises answering machine? You're here to help me set up my summer vacation?"

Will knows he should have anticipated this. He should have known Clara would handle the situation in this perfectly calm and calculating way. Make love and then make the announcement. Just straight to the nitty-gritty. But somehow he has managed to convince himself that Clara did not really know the truth. Before locking John in the root cellar he even talked himself into believing that her call to Adventure Travel was nothing more than a coincidence.

"What," he asks, his voice reasonably calm, "are you talking about?"

"You know exactly what I'm talking about."

"I do?"

"Yes, Will, you do."

Hearing his name uttered after all these years causes some rockets to go off in Will's brain. He is not at all sure he likes hearing his name. He might be Will Hancock, but today he is here as John Hancock. It is John Hancock who locked his brother in the Bunker, not Will Hancock. John who has been contemplating fratricide, not Will. There is no Will. Just two Johns. At least for now.

After a fairly lengthy pause he says, "Will's our son, Clara. I'm John."

Clara swings her feet off the bed, plants them on the carpet, and stands. "You're not really going to play it this way, are you?"

"Play what?" Will does not really know how else to play it. He has lived with this deception for so long. No one, except for his brother, has called him Will for almost twenty years.

"Look," says Clara, pulling on a silk robe, "I know the truth. I've known from the beginning. Since before I married you. Before I married both of you. Quite frankly, it has always amazed me that you and John actually had yourselves convinced that I didn't know there were two of you. I've always found it a bit insulting. Though, in the end, it's just a testament to the enormity of the Hancock brothers' egos. Because the truth is, Will, the two of you are not even that much alike."

"Clara, are you okay? Has something happened you haven't told me about? You know I don't have a brother. Not anymore. You know my brother died off the coast of Belize, back in 1982."

Clara laughs. Then she crosses to the bureau, picks up her brush, and begins to run the bristles through her glossy hair. Sex always leaves it a tangle of knots.

"Really, Will, I'm a little surprised. I would have expected these petty denials from John, but not from you."

"But I am John."

"Yes, and I'm Joan of Arc."

Clara laughs again. "Will, listen to me: it's over. You don't have to pretend you're John anymore. That should be a relief, not cause for more lies. It's okay, I'm not mad. I love you. I love both of you. Nothing's going to change."

"Clara," Will says, patiently, "with the trip to Europe and the new gallery and all your other responsibilities, I know you've been under a lot of pressure. But really, you're scaring me. Why don't you lie down. I'll get you a cool, damp cloth."

Clara's smile vanishes. She's actually starting to get

mildly miffed. This was supposed to be fun, not annoying. "Okay, I can see this is turning into a waste of time. So I'll just tell you what I want. I want you to call your brother and tell him to get his butt down here to the Ambassador. He should have been here by now. But obviously you two have powwowed and cooked up some silly scheme, after concluding that your stupid blond bride Clara finally, after all these years, figured things out."

So, thinks Will, John knows Clara is here. Of course he knows. Clara would have told him. This whole thing is a setup. A goddamn setup. Only I've got John locked in the bunker up in Stockbridge. A little detail neither John nor Clara had anticipated.

"Look, Clara," he says, as calmly as possible, "I really don't know what this is all about. Maybe you're just stressed. Maybe—"

"Actually, my love," interrupts Clara, "I am stress-free. Without stress. And as for what this is all about, well, it's about you and John and me. It's about our boys and our lives. Truth and lies. Books and art and Adventure Travel Enterprises. It's about—"

"Adventure Travel Enterprises?"

"For chrissakes, Will, why don't you listen? I know everything. I've known all along. And I don't care. Like I just said, I don't even want anything to change. Well, maybe a few things. Things that I think will make our lives even better. But we'll talk about it later. When all three of us are together."

"All *three* of us?"

"Will, you're beginning to bore me. In all the years you played John, you never bored me once. But today you're playing yourself and already I'm bored to tears."

"Sorry," pouts Will. "This is just so bizarre. I mean, all this stuff you're saying. I don't know how to respond. I think maybe—"

Clara has heard enough. Her expectations for this scene had been far grander than these stupid and endless denials. "Will," she interrupts, "be quiet. I have better things to do than listen to your jabbering." Clara takes off the silk robe and pulls on her jeans and black turtleneck. "I have a meeting across town with my partners in the new gallery."

"A meeting?"

"That's right. A meeting. I'll be gone an hour or so. That'll give you time to think about what I've said. Start dealing with reality. Get past your denials. Then get John here. We have things to discuss. And I want to do it this evening. Tomorrow morning at the latest."

Clara picks up her purse. She opens it and pulls out a thin stack of four-by-six photos. She tosses them on the bed. "Here," she says. "Maybe these will help jog your memory about that brother you say drowned off the coast of Belize."

They are, of course, the photographs Pete the other gumshoe took of the Hancock boys outside their Stock-bridge hideaway seven or eight years ago.

Clara does not wait for Will to look at them. She heads for the door, pulls it open, and turns. "Don't get all upset over this, Will. It's been a long time coming. Now we just have to deal with it. But like I told you before, I love you. I love you for you. You don't have to be John anymore. Not for one more second."

Their eyes meet. Clara smiles, turns, and slips through the door.

HEADING FOR THE AMBASSADOR

"Good afternoon. Ambassador Hotel reservations. How may I help you?"

"I know it's short notice, but I was hoping you might have something available for tonight."

"Tonight, sir?"

"Yes."

"How many in your party, sir?"

"Just one."

"Let me check." The reservations clerk scans her room chart. She knows the hotel has several vacancies, but she has been trained to make last-minute callers think they might be getting the absolutely last available room. That way the hotel can charge an even more exorbitant rate.

"Yes, sir," she says, "I see we do have one or two single rooms still available."

"Could you book one of those for me? I should be arriving in about an hour."

"Certainly, sir. I'll just need a credit card to hold the room."

"Of course."

"Can I first get your name?"

"Yes. It's Brown, Allen Brown."

"And your credit card number, Mr. Brown?"

Mad Dicky reads the Visa number off the late Al Brown's credit card. He does this while driving the late Al Brown's minivan and talking on the late Al Brown's cell phone.

So yes, Al may be dead, but his legacy lives on.

Several hundred miles to the west, the bond between Ms. Babe Overton and Mr. Rafe Paquita grows. Just a few minutes ago Rafe had his fingertips playfully dancing across Babe's thigh. Now they're just north of Norwalk, Ohio, not far from the birthplace of Thomas Alva Edison.

Hour by hour, even minute by minute, their relationship broadens and deepens with each new lie Rafe tells. His friendship with the Hancock boys, his lavish Caribbean hotel, his leisurely and affluent lifestyle in the tropics—all these little tidbits have made quite an impression on Babe.

Exactly why Rafe is travelling by public motor coach has not yet come up. And if Rafe has any say in the matter, it won't. He's hoping if things work out at The Chase bar inside the Ambassador Hotel tomorrow at noon, maybe he and Babe will book a room, spend a few days in the big city becoming even more intimately acquainted.

Babe, however, will definitely not be shacking up with Rafe. She likes Rafe, but she is not that kind of girl. And besides, she's more anxious now than ever to get up to Boston and have that little chat with the Hancock brothers. She's fully expecting Rafe to give her a personal introduction.

Back in the Big Apple, Hillary Fisher slowly makes her way up Fifth Avenue. She carries several large shopping bags (Tiffany's, Saks, Bergdorf's), but these hefty sacks constitute only a portion of her purchases. The rest she is having delivered directly to the hotel.

Something in the window at Diego Della Valle catches Hillary's eye. She was not in the market for new shoes, but, well, why not just have a peek? She ducks through the door for a closer look.

Half an hour later she is underway again, some very expensive Diego Della Valle footwear under her arm, another American Express slip in her purse.

Leland, too, is on his way back to the Ambassador. After that unsuccessful call to the Hancock suite, he decided he needed a bit of fresh air. If what you breathe on the island of Manhattan can be considered fresh air.

Leland crossed Fifth Avenue and entered Central Park. He walked up past the Wildlife Center and the ice skating rink. He made it as far as the Carousel before turning back. Now he's back on Fifth Avenue, heading south. He knows Hillary made reservations for some new Broadway extravaganza. Something loud and irritating and obnoxious, no doubt. Too much noisy music. Too many bad lyrics. Too many flaky and flashy dancers jumping around the stage like circus animals.

Yup, Leland's in one ornery mood. Too much scotch. Far too much scotch. He's going back to the hotel, take a handful of Bayer, and have a little snooze.

Clara has a Coke. She probably only drinks one Coke a year. And this is it. She bought it at the corner deli on Madison and Sixty-ninth.

When Clara left Will in Suite 1424, she did not really have a meeting across town with her partners in the new gallery. That was just a ruse, something to tell Will so she could get out of the room, leave him alone to mull things over. She was not about to stand around after that wonderful lovemaking and argue about whether or not she knew both John and Will were alive.

Now she walks quickly, carrying the shorts and shirts and new shoes for the boys she bought at the Ralph Lauren store up on Madison, headed back to the Ambassador. With her Ferragamo bag and her can of Coke.

Clara has no idea what her husbands will do, now that they know she knows. But she definitely knows what she will do: nothing. After all, she has been as much a part of their deception as they have. She really just wants them to know she knows, so their lives can be even better. Better than ever. More honest and relaxed.

Of course, Clara is not privy to certain information. She doesn't know about Frank or Zelda. Nor does she know Will has John locked in that root cellar. Clara thinks her husbands are great friends, the best of buddies.

Will also heads for the Ambassador. After Clara dropped her bombshell and left Suite 1424, Will, shell-shocked, just stood there in the bedroom for several minutes studying those photographs. He considered following her and trying to explain. But Will knew his wife would not be interested in explanations. Better, for the time being, to leave her alone.

So he's been walking and thinking, contemplating the situation. Earlier he walked right by his lover, Hillary Fisher, out there on Fifth Avenue. Passed within ten feet of her. But they didn't even see one another. He was too busy scheming. She was too busy shopping. Neither had the time or the state of mind for illicit love.

Will stops for a drink at a bar across from the public library on Forty-second Street. He stops for another one further uptown, at a bar near the Trump Tower. "Whiskey," he tells the bartender. "The cheapest, raunchiest rotgut whiskey you've got."

Will's feeling down and dirty, cornered, like he has just two options. Both options involve returning to Stockbridge. Today. This evening. Right now.

Option one: He returns to the bunker and kills John. Shoots him down like an old dog with that .38 Saturday night special and buries him out behind the barn. Clean and simple. Well, maybe not all that simple, but it gets the job done. Then he returns to New York and denies vehemently forevermore Clara's claims of duality. There will undoubtedly be some rocky times in the weeks and months ahead; but, eventually, she will let it pass.

Or will she? Will knows damn well she won't. Not Clara. No way. Will knows his wife is as tenacious as a terrier in pursuit of what she wants. And right now she wants her two husbands, front and center, at attention. Nothing less will do.

Which brings Will to option two. He goes back to the bunker, explains to John what has happened, then brings John back here to New York, where they deal with Clara together. As a team. Like in the old days. Two against one. Hancocks against the world.

But Will's not entirely out of touch with reality. He knows John might not be real keen on this particular option. Not after being attacked, beaten, drugged, and thrown in the dungeon.

"Son of a bitch," Will mumbles under his breath. He finishes that rotgut whiskey, throws some money on the bar, and heads back to the hotel.

Before he does anything else, he tells himself, he needs to have another little chat with his wife. See if he can find out how much Clara really knows. And exactly what she plans on doing with her knowledge.

THE BUNKER

Just over six hours John Hancock has been trapped inside this underground cell, but already he's going a little stir-crazy. An hour or so ago he bruised and bloodied his hands pounding on the door in an effort to escape. Then he splintered into kindling one of the two wooden chairs when he repeatedly used the chair as a battering ram against that same door. Neither assault caused the door even the slightest bit of damage.

John has checked every square inch of the room, every corner and crevice, and determined there is simply no way out. Short of starting a fire and burning the bunker down around him, he will have to remain here until Will, or someone, comes and lets him out. Until then, this room is his entire universe.

John feels confident his brother will come back. No way will Will leave him here in this cell.

Twenty by eighteen. John has paced it off. Six good strides in one direction. Not quite six in the other. A cheap piece of carpet covering the floor. A cheap sofa bed where he can sleep and sit. A table with a chair where he can work. A tiny kitchenette where he can eat. Not that Will left much food. Or drink. Two boxes of cereal. A loaf of bread. A bag of donuts. A dozen eggs. A stick of butter. A quart of orange juice. Half a gallon of milk. A gallon of water. On a normal day John eats and drinks this much before lunch. How long is he supposed to survive on this small stash? Two days? Three days? A week?

John does not have a single answer to any of his questions. He has only the hope that Will will come to his senses and remember that they are brothers.

John sits on the sofa and drops his head into his hands. This imprisonment, he decides, this banishment to the dark bowels of the earth, is merely the price he has to pay for the many wrongs he has done, the many sins he has committed. For his egotistical life of lies and deceptions. For what he did with those passports down on Caye Caulker. For robbing his brother of his identity. And for all the rest of it.

Ironic, he thinks, knowing that in the past few years he has come so far. Especially since the arrival of John junior and young Willy. He has matured. Grown up. Mended his selfish ways. Become a sensible and stable adult. A person who wants to give more than he takes. A first-class husband and a loving and devoted father. Ironic, all right. But then irony, John knows after so many years as a writer, is life's great equalizer.

He stands and paces. But he does not pace for long. His stomach rumbles. He's hungry now, ravenous. Before he can stop himself he consumes half that bag of donuts and at least a quart of milk.

Finally pausing to catch his breath, he slams his fist against the counter. "Dammit, Hancock, get hold of yourself! You could be here," he then mutters not much above a whisper, "for a long, long time."

His thoughts turn to Will. A deep and sudden hatred for his brother seeps into his soul. But he knows, just as suddenly, that his hatred is foolish. To hate Will is to hate himself.

But no, he tells himself, that's not true. I didn't lock myself down here; Will locked me down here. Made me his prisoner. Without warning. Without a trial.

"Damn you, Will!" he bellows.

WILL & DICKY

Dicky Cosgrove pulls the minivan into the underground parking garage beneath the Ambassador Hotel. The Gumshoe's dead body still occupies the floor in the back of the van, but Dicky's a little too preoccupied with his homicidal desires to worry about that little detail.

He parks next to a big BMW that looks exactly like the one he abandoned back at that McDonald's outside of New Haven. Same year. Same model. Same color.

Dicky grabs his belongings, locks up the minivan, and heads for the elevator. He ascends to the lobby of the hotel.

Dicky is acutely aware that at any moment he might come face to face with John Hancock. Or Will Hancock. This possibility causes his eyes to wander constantly in every direction. Quite a number of people mill around the lobby, but Dicky does not spot either one of the Hancocks.

Leland Fisher walks right by Dicky, but they have no reason to acknowledge one another. Neither do Hillary and Dicky, when Hillary swoops through the lobby a few minutes later.

At the front desk Dicky registers as Allen Brown of Brookline, Massachusetts. The clerk runs Al's Visa card through the credit card scanner for verification. No problem. Dicky signs on the dotted line. The clerk does not bother to compare Dicky's signature with the one on the back of the card. At the Ambassador they would never insult a guest paying in excess of four hundred dollars for a single night's lodging with such a crass and petty investigation.

"You'll be in Room fourteen seventy-two, Mr. Brown. That's a nonsmoking room with a nice view of the park. Please do not hesitate to let me know if we can be of service. Our staff is on call twenty-four hours a day."

Dicky stuffs the credit card and receipt into the pocket of his Gap khakis. "Right," he says. "Thanks."

"May I call a bellhop to assist with your luggage?"

"Luggage?" Dicky's eyes continue to wander around the lobby. Still no sign of Hancock. "No, I . . . I only have a few things."

"I understand, sir. Would you like someone to show you to your room?"

Dicky ignores the question. "Can you tell me what room Mr. Hancock is in? Mr. John Hancock . . . He and I have . . . some business."

"I'm sorry, Mr. Brown," replies the clerk, "all of our guests' room numbers are confidential. You understand. To protect your privacy."

Dicky nods. "Of course."

The clerk runs down his list of guests. "But I see I do have a Ms. Clara Dare Hancock registered. Would you like me to ring her room?"

Dicky shakes his head. "No. Thanks. I'll call later."

"Very good, sir."

Right on cue, Clara enters the lobby through the Sixty-third Street entrance carrying her Polo bag. She strolls right past Dicky. Their eyes even meet for a split second, but not a hint of familiarity registers with either of them. They have never laid eyes on one another until this moment.

Clara continues on, steps into the first available elevator, and pushes the button for the fourteenth floor.

Dicky's feeling a little confused right now, slightly off

his game. He walks in the direction of the Sixty-third Street entrance. Halfway across the lobby, he stops. And stares.

"Go up to the room," he mutters to himself. "Relax for a few minutes. Watch some TV. Take a hot shower."

Will Hancock's belly burns from the rotgut whiskey. Still, he decides to have one more quick one before going up to see Clara. He goes into The Chase and sits in a booth back in the shadows.

The waitress appears. The same one who served Leland all those ounces of Chivas Regal. "Yes, sir? What can I get for you?"

Will takes a look. Sweet face. Good body. "Whiskey," he tells her. "On the rocks."

"Any particular brand, sir?"

"The cheapest crud the bartender can find."

There's one the waitress hasn't heard before. Smiling, she heads over to the bar and repeats it verbatim to the bartender. They have a little laugh.

While Dicky, waiting for an elevator to transport him up to his room, peers into The Chase, eyes alert and searching for John or Will Hancock. Those eyes roam and soon zero in on the man seated at the back in the far booth. It has been over a decade, but Mad Dicky Cosgrove recognizes that face instantly. He has that face plastered like a billboard across his brain.

Dicky's first and furious instinct is to charge into the bar, pull out his straight-edge razor, and cut Hancock from ear to ear.

Will's whiskey arrives. He does not waste time with it. As soon as the waitress places it on the table, Will picks it up and tosses it down in one long swallow. The waitress just stands there and watches. She can't wait till her husband graduates from law school so she can quit this stupid job and they can move to the suburbs and start having children.

"Another one, sir?" she asks.

Will shakes his head. Time to go see Clara. Talk things

over. "No thanks. Just put it on my room tab. Suite fourteen twenty-four. Add a fiver for yourself."

"Thanks," says the waitress, who might just make it ten.

Will stands. Dicky watches. Will starts across The Chase. Dicky takes a step or two back. Will leaves the bar and heads for the bank of elevators out in the corridor. Dicky retreats, his brain racing through his options. An elevator opens. Will steps inside. Dicky darts right in behind him. The doors slide closed.

They both face forward. Will stands behind Dicky. Dicky longs to turn and slash, but tells himself to wait, to be patient.

Will does not have a clue that he is now trapped inside a six-by-six space with a homicidal psychopath who thinks Will murdered his sister.

"Floor?" asks Dicky.

"Fourteenth," answers Will.

Dicky, happy to have that knowledge, pushes the appropriate button. The elevator begins to ascend.

Dicky continues to think it would be nice to slit Hancock's throat right here. Right now. Yes, very nice indeed. But he decides it's too risky. Too messy. Better to follow him to his room. Get the murderous bastard good behind closed doors.

The trouble is, at least for Dicky, he is giving off some very bad vibes, some extremely hostile energy.

Will Hancock, who has traveled through some of the most hazardous places on the planet, has developed an instinct for danger. He can both sense and smell the insanity oozing out of this guy standing in front of him. So intense is this odor that Will actually takes a couple of small steps to his left in an effort to get a look at his fellow passenger's profile.

The face does not immediately look familiar. Then, in a flicker of eye contact, no longer than a fraction of a second, Will connects. Recognition flows instantly through his brain and spinal cord, right down to every artery, joint, and nerve ending in his body.

The elevator slows. Settles. And stops. It takes forever, but finally, the doors slide open.

Neither passenger moves. An eternity passes. The doors begin to close.

Will slips around his adversary, blocks the closing door with his foot, and steps out into the wide corridor. But he does not turn right in the direction of Suite 1424. No, he turns left. Away from his room. Away from Clara's room. It seems like the prudent thing to do.

Dicky steps out also. And follows.

Will's brain is not moving slowly. It's moving briskly, firing now on all cylinders, making thousands of tiny calculations and decisions every second. Does Mad Dicky have a gun? A knife? Some other kind of weapon? Should I make a run for it? But run to where? The sign indicated the emergency exits were back the other way.

Maybe thirty feet dead ahead Will sees the end of the corridor. He is rapidly running out of options. Only three or four more rooms remain. Soon there will be nowhere to go. He passes Room 1466, his old buddy Leland Fisher's room. Leland is, in fact, in there right now. Sleeping off the Chivas. But Will has no idea about all that.

Dicky, safe inside his psycho's cocoon, does not think for one second that he has been recognized or found out. He is merely following Hancock to determine exactly which room his sister's murderer occupies. The fact that Hancock appears to occupy a room right near his Dicky views as a small gift from the Almighty.

Dicky stops in front of the door leading to his own room. Room 1472. He can see there are only two more rooms before the end of the hall: 1474 and 1476.

Will, having finally decided upon a course of action, stops in front of 1474. He pulls his room card out of his pocket and sticks it in the slot. The card, of course, does not open the lock. Still, he makes a show of it. Twists it, wiggles it, tries to get it to work. He keeps hoping someone inside 1474 will hear him, open the door, save his hide. But no one comes.

So Will sighs, glances back down the hallway, shakes his

head, and says to the man standing in front of Room 1472, "Damn, this card doesn't work."

Dicky shrugs. "Sure you have the right room?"

Will nods. "Pretty sure. Fourteen seventy-four."

Dicky shrugs again.

"They must've given me the wrong card down at the front desk. Guess I'll have to go down and get the right one."

"Guess so," says Dicky. Dicky unlocks his own door and pushes it open. He steps over the threshold into the room.

Will immediately turns and heads back toward the elevators. He thinks about breaking into a sprint, making a run for it, but he does not wish to give himself away. As he approaches Room 1472 he fully expects Mad Dicky to grab him, pull him inside, slam the door closed.

"Excuse me?"

Will, now just a stride or two beyond the open door, stops dead in his tracks. The air whooshes out of his lungs. Very, very slowly he turns around. "Yes?"

"I don't mean to intrude upon your privacy, but are you by any chance the author, John Hancock?"

Will thinks about saying no, but he knows without question that Mad Dicky already knows the answer to his own question.

"Yes," Will answers, "I'm John Hancock."

"I love your work," says Dicky, who truly believes that Hancock does not know who he is, does not recognize him from Adam. "I've read every word you've written."

"Thank you," says Will, then gives his customary reply. "It's always good to know people are out there reading your work."

"I'm right in the middle of your new one now. *The Settlement*. It's excellent. I love it. Very suspenseful."

"Thank you."

Dicky says, "I have the book here in my room. Maybe you could come in, just for a second, and sign it for me."

"Well, I . . . I . . . I . . ."

No way is Will going into that room. Not under his own

power. Make an excuse, he orders himself. Tell him anything.

"It'll only take a minute," says Dicky.

"Yes, I'm sure, but—"

The door to Room 1476 opens. A man and a woman step out into the corridor. An older, well-dressed couple on their way to the opera.

They walk right between Will and Dicky.

"Good evening," says the gentleman, a big-bucks oil man from west Texas.

Dicky forces a smile.

Will takes the opportunity to put some space between himself and Room 1472. All the while, his brain keeps working.

As he moves away along the corridor with the oil man and his wife, he calls back to Dicky, "Sorry, I'm in a hurry right now. Why don't I stop by later this evening. We can talk about the books. Sign any copies you have."

Definitely, thinks Dicky, the idiot doesn't recognize me. "Sure," he says, not having much choice, "that would be great. Come back tonight. Or in the morning. Come back anytime."

"I will," Will assures him. "I'd enjoy that. Room fourteen seventy-two, right?"

"Right. Fourteen seventy-two. Right next to your room."

Will nods and waves and smiles, then he steps into the elevator with the Texas oil man and his spouse. Will decides it would be wise to stay away from Suite 1424, Clara's suite at the opposite end of the corridor. No good could come of leading Mad Dicky to that particular location.

Of course, what he should do is call the cops, sic them on Mad Dicky's hide, put a quick end to this potentially dangerous situation.

But no, there will be no call to the cops. Will has a better idea.

NAPPING

Clara misses all the action down at the far end of the fourteenth floor. The clock on the walnut stand beside the bed reads 6:17. That's 11:17 Paris time. Not all that late, but Clara has been up since the crack of dawn.

She wonders where her Hancock boys are. Maybe Will went to get John. She still cannot believe Will tried to deny the whole mess. Though she understands his denials were probably a pretty typical response under the circumstances. People who tell lies hate being confronted with the truth.

But Clara feels sure Will will come around. They both will. They'd better. She is not inclined to give them much choice.

She yawns again. Sits on the edge of the bed. Picks up the phone. Calls the house in Boston. No answer. Just the machine. Strange, she thinks. No one has been home all day. Not John or Nicky or Sylvia.

But at the moment Clara is too tired to think about it. So she leaves a short message for John to call her when he gets in, then she hangs up the phone. She stuffs some earplugs into her ears, slips between the sheets, and in no time at all falls sound asleep.

•   •   •

Down the hall, in Room 1466, Leland Fisher sleeps also.
He sleeps off the effects of all that afternoon scotch. Sleeps
and dreams. Dreams of bedding the lovely Clara Dare
Hancock while John and Hillary, in chains, watch without
recourse.

"Leland! Leland! Wake up!"

Leland's eyes snap open. He sees his wife, stark naked,
hair damp, motoring around the room.

"Christ," Hillary tells him, "you sound like you're
about to have a wet dream. Moaning and groaning up a
storm."

Leland says nothing. He wants to get back to it.

Not a chance.

"If you want to shower and shave," says his bride,
"you'd better get moving. The play starts at eight and you
know how I hate to be late."

Leland takes a look at his wife. She has some fine
breasts and an excellent set of hips. Too bad she's an unfaithful bitch with a big mouth.

Poor Lee. Torn between ravaging his bride and throwing her out the window.

A few doors down, Dicky Cosgrove's far too wired to
sleep. He lies on top of the bed, still in his Gap clothes and
his new tennis sneakers. The sneaks have been slightly
stained by the blood of Sylvia and Nicky, but they still
look pretty good.

Dicky wishes he could sleep, catch a few Z's, even just
relax for a little while. But he has a few too many things on
his mind. Like whether or not he should have followed
Hancock. Like whether or not Hancock recognized him.
Like whether or not he should have slit the bastard's throat
when he had the chance.

For right now anyway, he's decided to just wait it out.
Work on being patient. See if maybe Hancock actually
comes back. If he does, fine. And if he doesn't, well, Dicky

will just have to go next door and pay the son of a bitch a little visit.

Dicky picks up the phone, orders room service. Turkey club and chocolate shake.

"And maybe a couple beers," he adds before hanging up. "And what the hell? Bring me up a bottle of bourbon. Wild Turkey."

Dicky's not normally a drinker, but tonight he might have a little nip. Maybe it will calm his nerves, help him relax.

Rafe sleeps, his breathing soft and steady. He rests his head on Babe's shoulder while Babe gently rubs his neck. Babe has not rubbed a man's neck in quite some time.

Babe listens to the steady rumble of the Greyhound's engine and wonders if there might be some kind of chemistry between her and this nice-looking and very pleasant black man from Belize. She thinks maybe there is. In fact, she thinks maybe Rafe is the real reason she wound up on this cross-country Greyhound, now running east along Interstate 76 somewhere west of Pittsburgh, Pennsylvania.

Maybe this trip has nothing to do with the Hancocks. Maybe this journey is not about them at all, she tells herself. Maybe it is about me.

Go for it, Babe practically mutters right out loud. Take a chance. Don't be afraid of a little risk.

Rafe stirs, opens his eyes, looks up at her, and smiles. He's not really such a bad guy. Really just a boy who never grew up. Who has spent the better part of his manhood trying to act cool. Babe knows this. She can feel it. She understands Rafe very well, despite the fact that she has known him for less than a day.

She leans forward. Their lips touch.

SIBLINGS

Rush hour traffic had started to dissipate by the time Will left the Ambassador. Now he's back up on the Taconic State Parkway in his BMW 750il, traveling north, his speed hovering between seventy and eighty miles an hour.

He has a plan. A new plan. New and improved. He's driving, working out the details, going over all the possibilities. It makes sense. At least in his somewhat warped sense of reality it does. Really it's a pretty simple plan. Nothing much to it: Get John down to Manhattan. Into the Ambassador. Up to Clara's suite. Do some yakking. Listen to Clara lambaste them for their evil and deceptive deeds. Then send Johnny boy down the hall to Dicky's room. Where Dicky can do whatever his nasty little heart desires.

Will thinks he has a way to get John down to Dicky's room without making John suspicious. It'll demand a bit of finesse, but John won't have any reason to think he's walking into a trap.

Will exits the Taconic and heads up over the rolling hills into the state of Massachusetts. The much tougher part of the plan, Will knows, is just ahead. Going down into the bunker. Making his apologies. Trying to sound sincere. Keeping John from going ballistic.

Will thinks maybe he should take the gun with him. The same gun John brought back from Mexico all those many years ago. The same gun they were going to use to kill Hagstrom.

But no, maybe the gun's a bad idea. Maybe the gun will just annoy John. Provoke him. Make him obstinate and uncooperative. Will does not need any of those things. He needs John calm and feeling reasonably secure.

In the end Will decides to take the gun along, but keep it hidden. Tucked away in a pocket.

Will takes a few deep breaths. Time now to quit thinking and start acting. He feels confident he can pull this off. Con his brother into thinking all is well.

They may be brothers, but John is feeling extremely hostile. He sits on the edge of the one remaining wooden chair and pounds furiously on the computer keyboard. For an hour or more he has been trying to write a reply to Will's psychotic memo. Never in his life has John had so much trouble stringing together a few words.

> *Will,*
>   *You are one sick and psychotic son of a bitch for locking me down here. If I ever get my hands around*

John struggles to finish the sentence, but can't.

Finally, fed up, he stops. He stands and stretches. Paces. But there is nowhere to go. Nothing to do. No phone. No radio. No TV. No kids. No wife. Barely any goddamn food. No booze. Not even a beer. Not one stinking beer. And no books. The bastard didn't even leave me any books.

"I'll kill him!" John tells the four walls. "If I ever get my hands around his neck, I'll choke the life right out of him."

No, I won't, he tells himself a few seconds later. I'll yell and scream at him, maybe even bloody his lip or blacken his eye, but I won't kill him. He's my brother. My identical twin brother. My wife's husband. My boys' father.

If he had it all to do over again, he would not put his brother through this stressful ordeal. Will, he knows, was never really equipped to handle this kind of life-style. The guy did okay for a while, for several years even, but clearly he has been driven mad by the pressure. Hagstrom, Zelda, all the lies and secrecy, all the travel and solitude, and, of course, Clara. Will, John knows, needs to be with Clara all the time, every single day. He needs someone to take care of him, to love him and want him, make a fuss over him.

John sighs. Rubs his forehead. Feels the pain. Feels his brother's pain.

So, okay, what next? What am I supposed to do? How am I supposed to handle all this insanity? Am I supposed to be understanding? Forgive and forget? All that Christian bullshit?

Just step right up when—and if—Will comes back, and say, "No problem, Will, that you locked me down here like I'm some old and rabid dog. No problem at all. And the fact that you left me very little food and maybe enough water for a couple days? No sweat. I can handle that. And virtually nothing to stimulate me mentally or physically? Not a big deal. Really. Don't worry about it. The fact that you offered me no explanation whatsoever other than that sick fucking message on the computer? Perfectly reasonable. Absolutely understandable.

"Come here, little brother. Give me a hug. All is forgiven. After all, we're in this together."

At least, I thought we were.

THE HANCOCK BOYS

The key hits the lock. The dead bolts slide back.

John freezes.

Will pushes the door open and cautiously enters the bunker.

They stand, the Hancock boys, and look at one another. John and Will.

Will has the gun. He stopped at the farmhouse and took it from its hiding place in the bottom drawer of the bureau. He brought it, just in case. It's in the pocket of his suede jacket. Hidden. Out of view.

"Fuck you," says John.

"Right," says Will. "Fuck me."

"Feeling guilty?" John asks. "Is that why you came back?"

"No," answers Will, "that's not why I came back. I came back because I lost my head, and now I want to make things right."

"You want to make things right?"

Will nods. "I lost it for a second, but then I came to my senses."

"A second?" John glances at his Rolex. "Try eight hours, twenty-three minutes, and forty-seven seconds."

"John, listen to me. I was going crazy. I thought you
and Clara were in cahoots against me."

"What? Why did you think that?"

"Clara left a message on the Adventure Travel Enterprises line. She insinuated that she knew about the two of
us."

"About you and me?"

"Right."

"About both of us being alive?"

"Exactly."

John's eyes narrow. He needs a few seconds to think
this over. No way does he trust his brother. "So *that's* why
you clubbed me over the head, and locked me in this cell?"

Will does his best to look sincere. "Like I said, I lost my
head. I had to try to figure out what was going on. But
once I found out, I came right back. And now I think we
should try to get past this."

"Get past it, huh? Just like that? Forget it happened?"

"We have to."

"So are you here to let me out? Give me back my freedom?"

"Absolutely."

"For how long?"

"For forever."

"Why don't I believe you?"

Will feels the twitch of impatience. He'd like to club
John over the head again and just drag his complaining,
whining ass down to Manhattan. But he has to play it cool,
play it smart.

"I know how you feel, John. Really. And I'm incredibly
sorry. You'll see. I'll make it up to you."

"You'll make it up to me how?"

"How? I don't know. Any way you want me to."

"Maybe I want *you* to spend eight or nine hours locked
down here. Alone. Just to see how it feels."

Will looks around the room. But he doesn't really see
anything. Just like he doesn't feel much remorse for what
he's done. Really no remorse at all. What he really wants
to do is pull out that gun and empty the six-shooter into

John's chest. Put an end to all this stupid make-believe bullshit. And if John doesn't shut up, quit his crybaby routine, he might just do it.

"But locking you down here won't be the same, Will," continues John, "because you'll know I'm coming back."

Will tries a bit of levity. He laughs and says, "Come on, bro, you knew I was coming back."

"The hell I did."

"I could never leave you down here."

"I think you're sick, Will. I think you need help. Professional help."

Will sighs. He's not really in the mood for this. "Yeah, yeah, I need help. But it'll have to wait. Right now we have a situation."

"A situation? What kind of situation?"

"A couple of situations, actually."

Neither brother has moved more than an inch or two since Will walked into the bunker. They stand about ten feet apart, separated by nothing but empty space and that cheap piece of industrial carpet.

"You might say I have good news and bad news."

"I'm not real interested in your games, Will."

"Forget the games, John. Just tell me this: Would you be interested in seeing *The Settlement* as a major Hollywood movie?"

"Did our agent call? Did we get an offer?"

"No, we didn't a call from our agent. But we're definitely about to get an offer."

"From who?"

"From Mad Dicky Cosgrove," Will would like to say, but instead says, "First let me tell you the bad news."

John takes a couple steps to his right, sits on the arm of the sofa, and crosses his arms. "Go ahead."

Will does not waste time. "Like I said before, Clara knows. She knows everything."

"How do you know she knows?"

"Because she told me."

"When did she tell you?"

"Just a few hours ago."

"Where?"

"In New York, bro. At the Ambassador Hotel."

John frowns. "You saw her?"

"I sure did."

"How did you know she was at the Ambassador?"

"Like I told you, she left a message at Adventure Travel."

"She left a message saying what? That she would be at the Ambassador?"

"Look," says Will, "let's cut through the crap. The point here is this: Clara knows all about us."

John, dubious, asks, "How long has she known?"

Will shrugs. "I think she's known for a pretty long time. Years even. Maybe ever since we were first married."

"No way."

"Sorry, bro, but I'm afraid so. Sweet Clara has been playing us the same as we've been playing her."

John listens to this tale, but he is not at all sure he believes Will's spiel. It could just be more of his brother's sick game. But after all that has happened over the past few days, John figures it might be best to just go along, keep his options open.

"So what did she say?" he asks Will. "What does she want?"

"To tell you the truth, she didn't say too much. And I don't really think she wants anything."

"She must want something."

"She wants us to acknowledge the truth."

"And how, exactly, does she want us to do that? By making some kind of public announcement?"

"No, I don't think she's interested in going public. I just think she wants the whole business aboveboard."

"Among the three of us?"

"Right."

"But no other changes?"

Will shrugs. "All I know for sure is that she wants to see us. Both of us. At the same time. Together."

"Where?"

"Down in New York. At the Ambassador."

"We can't be seen together."

"We'll have to be careful. Go up to the room separately."

John takes a few seconds to think this over. It's possible what Will says is true. But it's just as possible the whole thing is a lie.

"I get it now," he says to his brother. "I see why you came back. Now that Clara knows, you can't just let me rot down here. She wants to see us together, so you had no choice but to come back and pretend like—"

"No," interrupts Will, "that's not true. For chrissakes, John, relax. That's not why I came back. I came back because you're my brother. I came back because I made a terrible mistake, because I—"

"You're such a goddamn liar, Will. I swear to God." John does some pacing, tries his best to ignore the dizziness swimming around in his head. Little by little, one small step at a time, he moves forward, closes the distance between himself and his brother.

"John," says Will, "I'm not lying. I'm telling you, I came back—"

"Why don't you tell me about the other situation. The one involving *The Settlement* as a major Hollywood movie. Maybe that piece of good news will help diffuse some of the tension around here."

Will nods. He's happy to spin the conversation in this direction. "It's a guy from DreamWorks. He's staying at the Ambassador. I talked to him this afternoon."

"From DreamWorks? Who is he? What's his name?"

"Allen Brown." (Before leaving for Stockbridge, Will paid a bellhop twenty bucks to find out the name of the guy staying in Room 1472. Will felt pretty sure Dicky was not registered under his own name.)

"What's his position?" asks John. "They have some heavy hitters at DreamWorks."

"Executive Vice President in charge of acquisitions. He has money in his pocket."

"And he wants to buy an option on *The Settlement*?"

"Forget the option, bro. This guy wants to go straight into script production."

John eyes his brother while moving another step closer. "Are you shitting me?"

"Absolutely not. I swear to God, this guy's the real thing."

"So why's he talking to you? Why didn't he contact our agent?"

"Look, John, don't get all worked up. This was like a chance meeting. I was at the hotel bar. Having a drink. He recognized me and came over. Christ, he had a copy of the book. We did some talking."

"So did you talk numbers?"

"He wanted to, but I cut him off. I knew I needed to talk to you first. But we have to get back to him ASAP. Even tonight, if possible. Or early tomorrow morning. He flies back to L.A. in the afternoon."

"Why don't we call him now?"

Will shakes his head. "No good. Better to keep this a face-to-face business. I think you should meet him. See how you like him."

"You're being awfully goddamn accommodating for a guy who earlier today bludgeoned and drugged me."

"Look, John, *The Settlement* is *our* novel, not *my* novel. So drop all the ulterior-motive stuff. You need to talk to this guy. Soon."

John, despite his suspicions, nods. He's always thought *The Settlement* would make an excellent motion picture. "If he's legit, you're right, I should talk to him."

"He's definitely legit."

"So then what's the deal?"

"The deal is we go back to the Ambassador, talk to Clara, calm her down, see what she has in mind, then you go and meet this guy Brown. See what you think. He's on the same floor as us at the hotel."

John's brain tries to suck it all in. "What was his name again?"

"Brown. Allen Brown. From DreamWorks."

"Right. Allen Brown. DreamWorks." John has always wanted one of their books made into a movie.

"He's waiting for us right now," Will tells him. "Waiting for you, actually. For John Hancock. In Room fourteen seventy-two of the Ambassador Hotel."

"Room fourteen seventy-two?"

"Right. Waiting even as we speak."

John moves to within six or eight feet of his brother. He continues to pace. Clara, DreamWorks, Allen Brown—he has no idea if there is even one kernel of truth in any of it. But he certainly intends to find out. And soon. On his own terms.

"So what do you say?" asks Will. "Are you ready to get out of here? Make the drive to New York?" He checks his own Rolex, exactly like John's. "It's getting late. Be closing in on midnight by the time we get back."

John decides the time has come. It's now or never.

He does not waste a second. Three or four quick steps and he's on his brother. He drives his head hard into Will's solar plexus. The wind whistles out of Will's lungs. John, his adrenaline flowing, drives Will all the way back against the wall. Will's head slams against the stone foundation.

A moment later, Will collapses to the floor.

John stands over him, heart racing, breath coming in short, frantic bursts.

Will does not move a muscle. He is out cold.

John cannot believe how fast it all happened. Trembling, he bends down, checks his brother's pulse. It feels strong and steady.

John reaches into the pockets of Will's trousers. He finds the keys to the BMW, the Mercedes, the bunker, the card for Suite 1424. Then, in the pocket of Will's suede jacket, he finds the gun, the Saturday night special he hauled across the Rio Grande all those years ago.

"Jesus Christ, Will," he says to his unconscious brother, "what were you going to do with this? Shoot me?" He sighs and shakes his head. Then he removes the bullets from the gun, shoves them into his own pocket, and drops the weapon to the floor.

Wondering how this mess can possibly work itself out, John crosses to the sofa and picks up a pillow. Pillow in hand, he stands over his brother. Several seconds pass. All kinds of fratricidal thoughts flash through John's brain.

But John does not act on any of these thoughts. No, he fluffs up the pillow and gently places it under his brother's head. He then stands and moves to the open door. "I'll be back, Will. You can count on that."

John turns and leaves the bunker, locking the door and securing the two dead bolts on his way out.

JOHN & LINDA

It is a warm late spring evening, calm and clear. A crescent moon hangs over the western sky. John feels pretty happy to see that moon. Less than an hour ago he had started to wonder if he would ever see the moon or the stars or the light of day again.

He glances over his shoulder, down those dark cellar stairs. The idea of locking his brother down there gives him no pleasure or satisfaction at all. But right now, under the circumstances, he does not know what else to do. The situation has become increasingly complex. How, he wonders, will I ever be able to trust Will again? And if I can't trust him, how can I set him free?

John sighs, crosses the yard, and enters the farmhouse. He goes directly to the answering machine and hits the play button. Nothing but a couple of messages from people looking for subscriptions to the ATE newsletter.

He picks up the receiver and dials the number of the town house in Boston. Three rings and the machine picks up.

Where, he wonders, are Nicky and Sylvia? As he punches in the code to replay any messages, he glances at his Rolex: 9:33. Strange, he thinks, for both of them to be out at this hour.

He listens to the six messages. Two from Clara. One from Linda Carson. Three others of no particular relevance. Though the times of the calls, dispersed throughout the day, make him think that Nicky and Sylvia have been gone since morning.

But he has no time to worry about that right now. He decides to call Clara and Linda from the road. So he goes outside. He spots the Benz and the Beamer sitting in the driveway. He decides to take the big BMW sedan. It offers a much plusher ride than the ML320.

A few minutes later he passes through Stockbridge. He dials Linda Carson's cell number on his brother's cellular. The call bounces around the Berkshires, then heads north for New Hampshire. It finally rings at a snug wooden cabin on the banks of a trout stream in the middle of the White Mountains.

Linda answers on the third ring. "Hello?" She speaks softly so as not to wake the boys asleep in the open loft overhead.

"Linda, hi. It's John. How are you?"

"Fine."

"And my sons?"

"Also fine."

The cellular connection is good, but not great. Kind of sparse and crackly.

"Sorry I took so long to call," says John. "I just got your message."

"That's okay."

"The boys having a good time?"

"Absolutely. We had a great day. Let's see. We went for a hike. Then we went fishing. Took a little swim. At least they did. Water's too cold for me. After dinner we played the author game."

"The old card game? With the pictures of the authors on the cards?"

"That's the one. The boys wanted to know why Dad wasn't in the deck."

"Maybe," says John, laughing, but really pretty choked up thinking about his little guys up there in the mountains, "I'll make the next edition."

"I'll tell them that."

"Maybe I could tell them."

"I'd have to wake them up. They're both zonked out."

"No," says Dad, "let them sleep. I'll call tomorrow."

"That would probably be better. They talked to their mother a little while ago."

"Clara called?"

"Yes."

"I'm on my way to New York right now to see her."

"She asked if I'd heard from you."

John wonders if Linda knows about him and Will? Clara, John knows, shares just about everything with her friend. He considers asking Linda, but decides against it. He will hear it straight from Clara soon enough.

So he tells Linda again that he will call the boys in the morning. Then he says good night and hangs up.

He does not call Clara. Better to talk to her in person.

JOHN & CLARA

Not long before midnight, weary from the long drive and this incredibly long day, John heads straight for the fourteenth floor of the Ambassador Hotel. All the way down from Stockbridge he has been wondering what he will say to Clara. How will he explain? How, if it is true she knows, will he justify the deception?

He unlocks the door of 1424 and enters quietly. A light is on in the sitting room.

John stands very still for several seconds, then he crosses to the bedroom door. He gently pushes it open. He sees Clara between the sheets, sound asleep, her breathing calm and steady.

For more than a minute John just stares at Clara. His thoughts and emotions are all frazzled and confused. But unlike his brother, John is not here to deny. John is here to face the truth.

He closes the door, throwing the room back into darkness. He takes off his pants and his cotton pullover. He drapes them over the back of a chair. Then, wearing nothing but a pair of silk boxers, he slips between the sheets and presses close against his wife.

Clara moans softly. "Hancock," she asks in a groggy whisper, "is that you?"

"Of course it's me."

Clara smiles, though the room is too dark for John to see her pretty lips part. "And which one of you is it?" she asks.

And John knows she knows. "It's John."

"Not Will?"

"No."

"Kiss me," she tells him. "That way I'll know for sure which one of you it is."

The whole insane way he has lived his life since leaving Belize slams directly into John's chest. Despite the pain, he does what she asks. He kisses his wife on the mouth.

Clara moans again, not quite so softly this time. "You told the truth."

"So you know it's me?"

"Of course I know it's you," she says. Then, "Do you two silly boys really think you kiss the same?"

"I guess I thought we did."

"You don't really do much of anything the same."

John tries to think of something to say. All he can come up with is, "Unbelievable."

Clara laughs, then yawns, then asks, "What time is it, John? It feels like the middle of the night."

"It's around midnight."

"No wonder I'm so sleepy. I've been up forever."

John is a long, long way from sleepy. "Clara," he says, "we need to talk."

"I know, but not now, lover. We'll talk tomorrow."

"Tomorrow?"

"After all these years tomorrow is soon enough."

John thinks about it for a second or two. "Okay," he says. "Tomorrow. In the morning. But I just want you to know I'm sorry. I'm sorry that I've been so incredibly selfish. I'm sorry I've been such a liar. I'm sorry I didn't tell you the truth years ago. I love you, Clara. I never wanted to hurt you or the boys. I just wanted—"

Clara reaches out and presses her index finger against

John's lips. "Shh. It's okay, baby. Believe me, I love you, too. I adore you."

"You do?"

"Of course I do. But tomorrow, Hancock. We'll discuss all this tomorrow. You and me and Will. Our funny, crazy little trio. We'll talk everything over. But I have to sleep now. You know how I need my sleep."

John leans over and kisses his wife. He knows kisses are far more important right now than words.

PART FIVE

JUNE 10, 1999

TIMES SQUARE

Just before dawn, that cross-country Greyhound pulls into New York's Port Authority Bus Terminal. Babe and Rafe are asleep in each other's arms when the long ride finally comes to an end. They slowly stir, rise, gather their belongings.

All night long Rafe has been thinking. Thoughts have been tumbling around in his head at an alarming rate. He has made a few decisions.

They find a coffee shop. It's pretty empty at this early hour. Just a few seedy types. They take a booth near the back. The waitress brings coffee.

"So where is it we're going?" asks Babe. "What hotel?"

"The Ambassador," answers Rafe. "Up by Central Park."

Babe sips her coffee. She looks dreamy. And kind of disheveled after her long journey east. "The Ambassador Hotel. Just the name sounds wonderful. Easy to imagine a hot bath and clean towels and a soft bed and ten or twelve hours of deep, deep sleep."

Rafe nods. "That does sound pretty good." He pours some sugar in his coffee and takes a sip. He hasn't told

Babe yet, but a few hours ago he decided not to go anywhere near the Ambassador Hotel. Being in possession of
less than half the quantity of cocaine he was hired to deliver could pose some very big problems. Nasty problems.
People, Rafe knows, get killed for delivering only half bags
of cocaine. Better to deliver no cocaine at all. Better to just
push straight through to Boston, put his extortion plan
into action.

All this is actually pretty good thinking. For a couple of
reasons. First of all there's Antonio Cuervo, a big-time
New York coke dealer. He's asleep right now in his Brooklyn garden apartment, but he has plans to be at the Ambassador today at noon for a pickup. But what Antonio
doesn't know is that several agents from the Drug Enforcement Agency will be there also. These agents, coworkers of
Matilda's, have been after Antonio for more than two
years. Today they plan on nabbing him. The second this
Rafe Paquita fellow from Belize hands over that bag of
cocaine, the DEA intends to swarm all over Antonio like
flies on scat.

"Listen," Rafe says to Babe, "I have to go make a few
calls. So why don't you just sit tight. Have some breakfast.
I'll be back in a little while."

"I'll be right here," Babe assures him.

"Right." Rafe stands, squeezes her hand, smiles, and
goes. He leaves his gear behind. Everything except for the
small duffel bag containing the diminished bag of coke. He
takes that with him.

Rafe leaves the bus depot, goes out into the hustle and
bustle of the big city. Only six A.M., but still plenty of
dudes and brothers sliding along the sidewalks looking for
action. Rafe doesn't really know how things work here. He
has no idea how easy it is to get into trouble.

Rafe is definitely not on Caye Caulker anymore.

Cruising the same territory where William Wilhelm
Hancock sold umbrellas forty years ago, Rafe starts
spreading the word among some of the brothers that he's
made a score and he wants to deal.

A tall, skinny black brother, not more than sixteen or seventeen and wearing a big gold hoop earring and laceless Air Jordans, saunters up to Rafe and asks, "Buying or selling?"

"Selling," says Rafe.

"Follow me," says the brother.

Rafe, seeing only the possibility of dollars, follows the brother down Eighth Avenue to Thirty-seventh Street. A tall wooden fence lines the sidewalk. The fence is a barricade for a big construction project taking place on the block. A fancy high-rise office building for the new millennium.

The skinny black brother squats and passes through a small hole in the fence. Rafe hesitates for just a second, then he goes through the hole in the fence, too. It's deserted back there behind the fence. Nothing but a couple of bulldozers and a backhoe and this huge hole in the earth. It's at least thirty feet deep. Looks kind of muddy and foul down on the bottom.

Rafe and the brother stand near the edge of the hole. A little closer than Rafe thinks they should be standing.

"So what do you got?" asks the brother.

"Coke."

"How much?"

"Maybe four, five ounces."

The brother points to the duffel. "In the bag?"

"Yeah. Wanna buy it? I'm selling it cheap."

"I first got to see what you got."

Rafe bends down and unzips the bag. "It's excellent shit," he tells his potential buyer.

But the brother doesn't hear. The brother is too busy picking up that two-by-four lying over in the dirt. He picks it up and cracks Rafe over the head with it. Down goes Rafe. Flat out without a whimper. The brother wallops him again. Right on the skull. No respect for human life at all.

The brother moves fast. He pulls loose Rafe's wallet, then, using his Air Jordans, he shoves Rafe's limp body over the edge of that hole. Rafe comes to rest along the edge of the muddy bottom.

The brother takes a look, flashes a satisfied smile, scoops up the duffel bag, and slips back through that hole in the fence. He has things to do, places to go, people to see, dope to peddle and snort.

DAWN

Across town at the Ambassador Hotel, a vast majority of the guests sleep right through Rafe's beating and mugging. It's still rather early, after all. Barely past dawn.

Leland and Hillary, up in Room 1466, sleep. They didn't even go to bed all that long ago. Last night they went to the theater, then out for a late dinner, then downtown to listen to some cool jazz at the Elbow Room. They got back to the hotel around two-thirty, had some lazy, alcohol-induced sex, made plans for an extended family vacation to Italy, and finally nodded off around four.

Right before he fell asleep, Leland said to himself, Okay, maybe my wife had a fling with Hancock. But if she did, that's the way it is. I can handle it. I love her. I'm going to be a better husband. Spend more time with her and the family. Do less drinking. I'm going to get it right this time.

Hillary fell asleep thinking about the handsome waiter who made a pass at her in the restaurant when Leland slipped away to use the facilities.

See, it doesn't really matter if Leland mends his ways or not. The guy could become the world's greatest husband. Hillary would still have a wandering eye and the moral fiber of an alley cat. Leland would do better to run for his

life. But closing in on fifty, scared and insecure, three di-
vorces already under his belt, it's unlikely he will be going
anywhere at all.

And so, nuzzled up against his bride's behind, he
dreams a dream wherein he kicks Hillary in the ass and
throws her unfaithful body out into the hallway. "My lawyer will be in touch with your lawyer," he tells her and
slams the door.

Just down the hall Mad Dicky, too, is still asleep. He has
been asleep for hours. Since before midnight when he consumed three beers and three shots of Kentucky sour mash.
The man was exhausted from the killing spree he went on
yesterday.

Last evening, after parting company with Will Hancock,
Dicky waited in his room for three or four hours. All that
killing and all those chocolate shakes had him pretty well
wired. So he eventually got up, went downstairs, hung
around the lobby, kept his eyes peeled for another glimpse
of Hancock. Around eleven he went back upstairs, stopped
by his room to get his razor. Then he went along the hall
and knocked on the door of Room 1476. Dicky had his
hand in his pocket, fingers around his straight-edge. But
Hancock did not answer his knock. Some fat guy did. Like,
three hundred pounds worth of fat guy. With nothing on
but a pair of enormous boxers covered with hearts and
roses. The fat guy did not look happy about being bothered at that hour. Especially after Dicky asked for John
Hancock.

"Wrong room," the fat guy grumbled before slamming
the door in Dicky's face.

So Dicky, perplexed and irritated, went back to his
room. Within just a few minutes he had consumed the
three beers and the three shots of bourbon. Soon after that,
shoes off but the rest of his clothes still on, Dicky stumbled
into bed and fell sound asleep.

All night long he dreamt. Silly dreams mostly. He and
Zelda and their mother and father in a big Vermont field

playing ring-around-the-rosy. He and Zelda flying in a hot-air balloon. He and Zelda crossing the ocean on a big sailboat. He and Zelda in rocking chairs growing old together. He and Zelda torturing the Hancock boys with cattle prods and razor blades.

Dicky misses Zelda. Every single day. Sure, Dicky's a nut case and a murderer and a full-blown psychopath, no question about any of that. But really, in many ways, the guy is a lot like all lonely people sliding through their lonely days.

In Suite 1424, down at the other end of the hall, Clara sleeps. She sleeps deeply. No dreams at all.

Beside her, however, John Hancock does not sleep. He did sleep for a while last night. But mostly he just lay there and thought about Clara. And Will. And the boys. And the new book. And this guy down the hall in Room 1472 who says he wants to make a movie out of *The Settlement*.

John thinks he might as well go see this guy, hear what he has to say. But first he wants to wash that root cellar out of his skin. And then some breakfast. Bacon and eggs. Home fries and buttered toast. Coffee and juice. The whole shebang. It will help drive the meager vittles down in the bunker deeper into the past.

He glances at the clock on the stand beside the bed: 6:41. Probably best not to bother the Hollywood tycoon for another hour or two. Still, John decides he's had enough lying around, thinking it all over. So he squeezes Clara's thigh and kisses her cheek. Then he slips out from between those silk sheets and silently steers for the bathroom.

Will does not have a bathroom. He has only an old brass chamber pot over in the corner. He wanted to put in a bathroom, run piping and plumbing into the bunker, but, well, he just never got around to it. And then, rather suddenly, push came to shove.

And now, through stupidity and neglect, Will finds himself where brother John should be.

He's not real happy about it.

Will hasn't slept a wink all night long. Over and over he has replayed that scene with John. He cannot believe he let John get the drop on him. And so easily. Even though he had the damn gun in his pocket.

Now the gun's resting on the table in front of the computer. Will's thinking about using it to blow his brains out, but no way will he do that. He doesn't have the guts or the stomach for suicide. Besides, John'll be back. And soon, too. Probably this morning. Or this afternoon. Tomorrow at the latest. Not a chance in hell John'll leave him down here. John is too much the goody-goody to do that. All mouth and no muscle. Talks a good game, but in the end, after all the bullshit has been spread, he can't get the job done. Never could.

Like the way he took the bullets out of the gun, but then left the gun behind. Not a real good move, considering that Will had another round of ammo in the other pocket of his suede jacket.

Will has spent the past ten hours reassuring himself about John's inevitable return. He knows John will let him loose. Give him his freedom. And then Will will be able to put his plan into action. His plan that calls for the elimination of John so that he can have their life and Clara and the kids all to himself. One way or another Will feels certain he will find a way to get what he wants.

Only one small problem. One not particularly insignificant little detail: Mad Dicky Cosgrove, a.k.a. Allen Brown, Hollywood mogul, occupant of Room 1472 of the Ambassador Hotel.

Will, assuming he would return to New York with John, told John all about Allen Brown, executive VP at DreamWorks. Will set John up. Set him up to walk straight into the lion's den. But if John goes into that den and winds up getting himself killed, there will be no one to let Will out of the bunker. No one else in the world will know where he is.

Will does his best not to think about this. During his long and sleepless night he simply erased the possibility from his brain.

Now, hungry, he again throws caution to the wind. He eats half a box of cereal and several slices of bread. He sucks the orange juice directly from the carton. One long swallow after another.

Unlike his brother, Will sees no reason to conserve his meager stash.

THE AMBASSADOR HOTEL

The Ambassador Hotel has been around a while, but so far as anyone can remember, no one has ever been murdered here. Beaten, raped, robbed, yes—but murdered, never.

Plenty of murders in New York, however. Several of them every day. An endless parade of victims. Although today, Rafe Paquita is not one of them.

Construction workers found Rafe down in that muddy hole not too long ago. He was rushed to Bellevue. Admitted as John Doe, since he had no identification on his person and was unconscious with a severe concussion. It will be weeks before he comes around, before he can tell anyone who is he or where he is or why he came to New York City.

In the meantime, Rafe's newfound friend, Babe Overton, is busy looking for him. She waited in the coffee shop at the Port Authority Bus Terminal for over an hour and a half. Then, after five cups of coffee, she gathered up their gear and began her search. No sign of Rafe in the bus station or outside along Eighth Avenue. Babe finally decided maybe Rafe went directly to the Ambassador. She asked a cop, and soon enough had directions to the hotel. It being a fine and pleasant morning, and having not had any exercise for several days, Babe decides to walk to the Ambassador.

While Babe walks, Clara and Hillary and Leland and Dicky sleep. John eats. And breezes through *The New York Times*. Nothing much in the paper today really catches his interest. The same stuff day after day, year after year: War and famine, winners and losers, births and deaths. Besides, Mr. Hancock is preoccupied this morning. With his own personal news stories and with the eggs Benedict filling the large plate in front of him.

He sits in the Café Ambassador. At a booth in front of a window with a nice view of Central Park. Maybe after breakfast he'll go for a little stroll through the park. Stretch his legs. Or maybe he'll just go straight back upstairs and meet with this Hollywood guy who wants to buy *The Settlement*. He hasn't decided yet. First things first. He picks up his knife and fork, slices off a chunk of poached egg smothered in Hollandaise, and slips the tasty treat into his mouth.

Delicious.

Babe enters the Fifth Avenue entrance of the Ambassador Hotel carrying her suitcase, her leather handbag, and Rafe's old surplus duffel. She right away starts looking for Rafe. She looks in the lobby. She looks in The Chase. She looks in the small kiosk selling gum and cigarettes and newspapers. No sign anywhere of her new friend.

Her feet hurt from the long walk. Her shoulders ache from carrying those bags. She takes a seat in the lobby. It feels good to set the bags down.

Then she gets an idea. She crosses to the front desk and asks if it would be possible to page someone. The clerk politely tells her no, but suggests she might want to take a look in the restaurant, the Café Ambassador.

Babe, thinking Rafe will surely be in the restaurant having a breakfast meeting, heads down the corridor for the café. She takes her large leather handbag, but leaves the suitcase and the duffel behind. Babe feels good this morning, as good as she has felt in years. And she knows she will feel even better as soon as she finds her friend.

Babe enters the restaurant. The hostess asks if she would like a table.

"No, thank you," says Babe. "I'm just looking for someone."

The hostess smiles and turns away to another piece of business.

Babe scans the room. She looks at every person sitting at every booth and every table. She does not see her friend. No sign of Rafe at all. In fact, she does not see a single black person. She sees an Indian. A couple of Asians. Plenty of Caucasians. Mostly of the male variety. In jackets and ties.

As Babe scans the room, her eyes keep crossing the path of a man sitting directly opposite, in a booth next to the window. Each time her gaze passes over him he begins to look more familiar. She cannot immediately place him, but for sure she has seen him before. Somewhere.

She makes her way across the restaurant for a closer view. A better angle. She wants to see him face-on.

And the second she does, it hits her. "My God!" Her hand instinctively comes up and covers her mouth.

She retreats. She does not want him to see her. Not yet.

Babe digs into her bag. She digs out the paperback novel she has been reading, slowly, since somewhere back in New Mexico. She finds the book lying in the bottom of her handbag, beside the small black pistol. Babe pulls out the novel and turns to the author photo on the inside back flap. She looks again at the man sitting in the booth. The air catches in her lungs.

She retreats even further. Out of the restaurant. Out into the long and deserted corridor leading back to the lobby. She suddenly feels nervous, edgy. What, she asks herself, should I do? Should I just go in there? Tell him I want to talk to him?

Babe takes several deep breaths. She cannot believe she has suddenly been delivered to this point in time. Here. In this hotel. Straight out of the blue. After all these years.

Her heart pounds. Her temples throb. She can feel the perspiration collecting along her brow and under her arms. A clear picture of her lover, Frank, Big Frank Hagstrom, fills her brain.

The gun, she thinks. I need the gun.

John Hancock finishes his breakfast and charges it to his room. He stands, folds his newspaper, tucks it under his arm, and heads for the exit. He has decided to take a little walk in the park, go up and check on Clara, then stop by and see this joker from Tinseltown.

"Good morning, Mr. Hancock."

John looks at the woman. He does not recognize her. He nevertheless smiles and returns the greeting. As a best-selling author and minor celebrity, John is used to being recognized in public places.

Babe tells herself to remain calm. She takes several deep breaths, exactly the way she learned back in acting school. Then, as though this is some kind of bad B movie, she says to John Hancock, "I have a gun. Do exactly as I say."

John's smile dissipates, replaced instantly with a frown. "Excuse me?" But an instant later his frown turns to fear when he catches a momentary glimpse of that snubnose pistol Babe has half hidden behind her handbag.

"I said," says Babe, in her best film noir voice, "I have a gun. Do exactly as I say."

"Who are you?" asks John. "What do you want?"

"I'm Babe Overton," she tells him. "You probably don't remember me."

John takes another look. His jaw drops. "Babe Overton! Jesus! How did you find me here?"

"Fate," answers Babe. "God sent me."

John does not like the sound of that. That kind of stuff

scares the bejesus out of him. He remembers his conversation a couple days ago with that shrink from L.A. What was her name? Gerdy something. *Potentially dangerous.* Wasn't that what Gerdy said about Babe? Definitely something like that.

"So," John asks, trying to stay cool with that pistol pointed at him, "how are you? It's been a long time. What can I do for you?"

"Then you do remember me?"

"I do. Yes. Of course."

"I want to talk to you," Babe tells him. "In private. Just the two of us. Are you staying here? Do you have a room?"

Stupidly, without thinking, John says, "Yes, I have a room, but—"

"I want to go there. Now."

"Why?"

"I want to talk."

"Talk?"

Babe nods, but then, thinking she should sound more threatening, adds, "If you cooperate, I won't shoot you."

"Please, Babe, don't shoot me," pleads John. "I have kids. Little ones. Sons. Just starting school."

"I won't shoot you. I promise. As long as you do what I say."

"We could talk here. In the restaurant. Over a cup of coffee."

Babe does not want any more coffee. "No, not here. In your room. And I want to talk to your brother, too."

My God, thinks John, Babe Overton knows? Seems like all of a sudden everyone knows. That shrink told him Babe had lost her way. That's looking pretty obvious. So what about the gun? Would she actually use it?

John turns, Babe follows close behind. They cross the lobby to the bank of elevators. The elevator doors open. John and Babe step inside. The doors close.

"What floor?" asks Babe.

"Why don't we just talk here? It's nice and private."

"What floor?" repeats Babe.

No way is John about to take her up to Suite 1424,

expose Clara to this lunatic. She might shoot both of them. She also might tell Clara about Big Frank. About Big Frank's hanging not being a suicide. That's not news John wants Clara to hear.

An idea pops into John's head. Not a great idea. But about all he can come up with on short notice.

"Fourteenth," he tells her. "Fourteenth floor."

Babe hits the appropriate button. The elevator begins to ascend.

"Look," says John, "I'm perfectly willing to talk to you. About anything you want to talk about. But I think it would be better if you put that gun away. Guns make me nervous."

"They make me nervous, too," says Babe. "But just to keep you honest, I'll keep it out for the time being."

John thinks, with a little luck, he could probably overpower her, but right at this moment he's not willing to take that chance. He has Clara to think about. And the boys. And his brother. Locked down in the bunker. Getting himself shot, and possibly killed, won't do anybody any good.

The elevator stops at the fourteenth. The doors open. John steps out first. There is no one in the corridor. Not a soul. John does not turn in the direction of Suite 1424. He sticks to his plan. Heads for Room 1472.

Babe, nerves frayed and jittery, perspiration flowing freely now, follows a step or two back. She cannot believe she is doing this. Holding a man at gunpoint.

Suddenly she blurts out, "Is your brother here at the hotel, too?"

"My brother," says John, without thinking, "is dead. Been dead almost twenty years."

"You lie," says Babe. "I know he's not dead."

You and everyone else, John wants to reply, but doesn't. "And why do you think that, Babe?" he asks.

The sound of her name uttered in that long and deserted corridor throws Babe off balance for an instant. Then, recovering, she announces, "Rafe told me."

Those three little words throw a jolt of electricity

through John's body. "*Rafe* told you! Jesus! How do you know Rafe?"

"How I know him is unimportant. It's what he told me that's important."

What Rafe told her is not very hard for John to imagine.

Babe sees they are nearing the end of the hallway. "Which room is yours?"

John stops in front of Room 1472. Okay, he tells himself, this is it. He has to decide. Should he knock on Allen Brown's door or not?

No, he quickly decides, knocking on this guy's door is not a good idea. It's a bad idea. I can't get this guy involved. *What the hell was I thinking?*

Struggling to find an alternative, John reaches into the pocket of his trousers. He searches for his room card. His make-believe room card.

"What is it?" Babe demands. She's getting shaky now. Just about ready to lose it.

"I can't find my room card."

"What! Where is it? I want that door open. We need to get out of this hallway. We need to get out of this hallway now."

John sighs and pats his pants. "I know, Babe, but I don't have the card. I must've left it downstairs in the restaurant."

"In the restaurant?" Babe thinks she might just have to flee.

John, aware of her annoyance, shrugs. "Sorry. I probably left it on the table. It's a bad habit I have."

Babe, flustered and frustrated, steps forward. "No one's in the room?"

John shakes his head vigorously. "No," he insists, afraid at any moment she might begin pounding on the door, "no one. No one at all."

But at that very moment, the door swings open. A man stands there in wrinkled khakis and a rumpled blue button-down shirt. He looks bleary-eyed, like he just woke up. His face is kind of puffy, his hair sticks out in a hundred different directions.

John and Babe freeze.

The man, scowling, demands, "What the hell's going on out here? What's all the noise about?"

John remembers that he is supposed to know this disgruntled gentleman. He says, in as cheery a voice as he can muster, "Mr. Brown. Good morning. It's John Hancock."

Mad Dicky Cosgrove hears this and freezes, too.

"I thought," John continues, "we might be able to discuss further the movie rights for *The Settlement*."

Dicky shakes himself awake. He cannot believe Hancock has returned. Walked right up to his door. Paranoid by nature, Dicky wonders if it might be a trap. Who's the bitch? What's she doing here? Is it Hancock's wife? Doesn't look like his wife. Not that it matters. Whoever it is, Dicky will slit her throat, too.

But for now, he musters a little smile. "Yes, right, *The Settlement*. Come in."

So in walks John Hancock. Straight into the lion's lair. Followed closely by Babe Overton.

It's dark in the room. The heavy drapes are drawn.

John looks for a light switch.

Babe does not know what to do. Any control she had has been snatched away.

Dicky turns and heads for the other side of the bed. "Let me get those books for you to sign."

John is immediately confused by this, but figures Will must have agreed to sign some copies of their books. "Sure," he says. "Right."

Babe pushes the door closed.

Dicky picks up the plastic bag containing a copy of each and every John Hancock novel. From the floor beside the bed, he also scoops up the straight-edge razor. This particular item he slips into his pocket.

John finally finds the light switch and flips it on. The lamps on either side of the bed light up, illuminating the room. But still John does not get a good look at Dicky. Dicky has his face turned away.

"So," says John, wanting to get the conversation going

in order to keep Babe distracted, "I've been thinking more about a movie version of *The Settlement*. With some subtle changes in the plot, I think it could make one hell of an action thriller."

Babe has absolutely no idea what is happening. Nor does she possess the strength of character to take charge of this quickly deteriorating situation. She is having a difficult time even getting her mouth open.

Dicky has no choice. The time has come to turn around. But he figures Hancock didn't recognize him last night, and he didn't recognize him at the door a minute ago. And in a couple minutes it won't matter if Hancock recognizes him or not. In a couple minutes Hancock will be a sliced and bloody mess.

Too bad Mad Dicky's wrong about Hancock's powers of recognition. Yesterday, on the elevator, Will recognized Dicky the instant he got a good look at him. And now, the second Dicky straightens up and turns around, John gets a clean look, too. A fraction of a second after that John's eyes widen. Two little words spill from his mouth. "Holy shit!"

Unlike brother Will, who last night kept his cool inside that elevator, John comes immediately unglued.

Mad Dicky swings instantly into action. He pulls out that straight-edge, scrambles across the bed. He waves his weapon through the air, driving both John and Babe away from the door, into the center of the room.

John grabs Babe's arm. "Quick! Babe! Give me the gun. Now! Give it to me."

Dicky hears the word *gun* and slows up. He glances at the woman. And, much to his amazement, she does indeed have a weapon. Just a little pea-shooter, but plenty big enough to cause some serious damage.

The woman does not, however, give the gun to Hancock.

In fact, to Dicky's confusion, she pushes Hancock away. Shoves him aside, revolver at the ready.

Babe may not have a clue what is going on, but no way

is she giving up the gun. She instinctively knows without the gun she will be completely powerless.

John, caught between these two psychos, cannot believe this is happening. This is like some bizarre scene out of one of his novels. Which, he thinks, might just be the point. So many ironies he can hardly keep them all straight.

And then it dawns on him—Will sent him here. Straight to Mad Dicky's lair. That whole bit about the Hollywood mogul from DreamWorks was bullshit. Pure bullshit. Will set me up. The bastard set me up. My own brother.

Dicky powers forward, grabs John by the arm, and swings him around. "Time to say bye-bye, Hancock." Dicky presses the single-edge blade against John's throat. "Drop the gun, sister," Dicky tells Babe.

"Why should I?" Babe asks Dicky.

"Because otherwise I slit your boyfriend's throat."

"That's not my boyfriend," Babe tells him. "That's John Hancock. Or maybe it's Will Hancock. I don't know. But he killed my man. Either him or his brother."

"No shit!" says Dicky. "They killed my sister."

Babe shakes her head. "I wonder how many others they've killed?"

John decides the time has come to put his plan into motion. Or at least into words. "I didn't kill anyone," he says softly, not wanting to work his Adam's apple too hard for fear that blade might slice open his jugular. "I swear to God, I haven't killed anyone. Not Frank and not Zelda. My brother killed them. Will did it. He's a very sick individual."

Dicky presses the blade against John's throat. "Shut your filthy fucking mouth, you lying piece of shit."

"But I mean it. Will—"

"I said, shut——the——fuck——up." And to prove he means it, Dicky nicks a neat little gash across John's throat. Not a deep cut, but deep enough to draw blood.

Babe, who hates the sight of blood and loathes violence, points the gun at Dicky's face and says, "That's enough of that. Put the blade down."

"Screw you, sister."

"I said," repeats Babe, "put it down. Put the blade down and let him go. I don't want him hurt. I'm here to find out what really happened to my Frank. I'm not here to just start killing innocent people."

"Now you're talking, Babe," says John. "Let's be sensible."

Too bad Mad Dicky does not have a sensible bone in his body. "You don't have the guts to use that gun, sister. So put the pea-shooter down, or after I slice up this son of a bitch, I'll slice and dice you into little pieces."

Babe does not put the gun down. She holds her ground. Keeps the gun pointed directly at Dicky. Too bad John stands between them. So in reality, the gun points primarily at Hancock.

Dicky says to John, "Tell me where your brother is and I won't kill you."

Oh, yeah, sure, thinks John, and I know the formula to turn iron into gold. Still, he's desperate to buy some time. "Will's here," he answers. "In the hotel."

"Where?"

"Put away the blade and I'll tell you."

Dicky doesn't think so. And to demonstrate his convictions, he makes another incision across John's jugular. This one goes deeper than the last one. The blood flows freely from the wound. John tries to shut off the flow with his fingertips. He suddenly realizes if Mad Dicky cuts his head off with that blade, he'll die in the same gory and gruesome way his parents did out on the San Diego Freeway.

And then Babe says, "I told you not to do that." And to prove that she, too, means business, she decides to fire the gun. Not really at anyone, but just to make a point. So she pulls the trigger. But nothing happens. Just a soft little click. She pulls the trigger a second time. Same soft click.

Dicky laughs.

The laughter irritates Babe. So she points the gun at Dicky and pulls the trigger a third time. This time the gun goes off. The bullet slams into John Hancock's shoulder. He cries out in pain and slips from Dicky's grasp.

Dicky lurches forward, slashing at the air in front of Babe's face.

Babe keeps pulling the trigger. The bullets flow freely and quickly now, one after another. Dicky takes one in the chest; another one grazes his cheek. This one deflects off the bone and hits Hancock. The final bullet penetrates the skull, arbitrarily destroying brain matter.

Just a few doors down the hall in Room 1466, Leland Fisher lies on the floor doing sit-ups in a vain effort to get rid of some of his midriff flab. But the second he hears those gunshots, he's on his feet and moving for the door.

He opens the door and cautiously sticks his head out. He peers up and down the corridor. He hears nothing, sees no one. The shots have stopped.

But then, suddenly, he hears a woman screaming. A high-pitched howl. Seconds later a door opens and the screaming woman comes rushing down the corridor. Leland thinks about closing his door, minding his own business, maybe going back to bed and pulling the covers up over his head.

But before he can decide what to do, the woman descends upon him. She's still screaming. Arms flailing, she is completely out of control.

"I shot them!" she screeches. "I shot them both!"

"Calm down," Leland tries to tell her. "Who? Where? What happened?"

And then Hillary's up and out of bed, throwing on a robe. "Leland, what the hell is going on?" She turns to the hysterical woman. "Who the hell are you? Leland, who is this woman?"

Leland shrugs.

The woman grabs his arm and begins pulling him down the hallway.

"Christ!" pronounces Hillary. "What kind of an insane asylum is this?"

One look into Room 1472 and they all find out.

There's the gun, now empty, lying in the doorway. There's the straight-edge razor, dripping with blood, lying on the pale white carpet. There's Mad Dicky Cosgrove, a bullet lodged in his brain, lying against the bed. And there's—

"My God! Leland," hollers Hillary, "look! The one against the wall. It's Hancock. John Hancock!"

"Christ Almighty!" shouts Leland. "You're right. It is."

Leland steps into the room. Hillary watches from the threshold. Out in the hallway, Babe whimpers. Others have started to join the melee. The corridor is beginning to fill with the curious.

Leland steps over Dicky and crosses to his best-selling author.

"Is he dead?" asks Hillary, thinking if Hancock is dead, the bastard probably deserves it.

Leland, extremely squeamish about this kind of thing, mutters, "I'll check." He puts his hand against Hancock's chest. He cannot find a heartbeat. But Leland is definitely no doctor. He does, however, have this thought: Looks like old John won't be tooling my wife anymore.

Clara, having heard the commotion, is now out in the hallway. She spots Leland Fisher's wife. At first she cannot recall the repulsive woman's name. But then it comes to her. "Hillary! Hi. It's Clara Hancock. What's going on?" Clara calls above the growing din of the milling crowd. "What's all the excitement?"

"It's John," Hillary tells her. "He's been shot."

"John? *My* John?"

Hillary nods.

Clara pushes her way forward. She reaches the doorway and spots her husband.

"We think he's dead," Hillary announces above the hubbub.

"Bullshit," replies Clara. "John's not dead."

She steps over the dead body of Dicky Cosgrove and bends down to her husband. She ignores the blood oozing from his neck and pulsing out of his shoulder. She presses her ear against John's chest. For at least thirty seconds she remains there, motionless.

Leland gives her plenty of room.

Finally, she looks up and meets Leland's eyes. "Call an ambulance," she orders him. "And please—tell them to hurry."

PANIC

Several minutes ago, when Dicky first cut John, Will, miles away, instinctively grabbed his throat. It was a primal move on Will's part, something that can easily be traced back to the twins' shared days in Lenore's womb.

Will grabbed his throat. And held it. And knew, without a doubt, that his brother was dead. That Mad Dicky Cosgrove had slit John's throat.

And now, being brutally honest with himself, Will realizes that with John dead, he, too, will soon be dead. John's death was short and relatively painless. But his own death, Will knows, will be slow and agonizing. First the food and then the water will run out. He will fade from starvation, then die of dehydration.

His prospects look grim.

He picks up the Saturday night special that John brought home from Mexico. He has replaced the six bullets that brother John removed last night.

No, Will does not intend to kill himself. He thinks maybe he can blow the lock off the door. Shoot his way out of the bunker. Blast his way to freedom.

Will positions himself about ten feet from the door. He takes careful aim at the old massive steel knob and gently pulls the trigger. An instant later the first bullet slams into the door and lodges itself in the wood an inch or so above the knob. It does nothing to enhance Will's chances for escape.

The second bullet hits just below the knob. Does little or no damage. Will pulls the trigger again. The third bullet strikes the knob, but glances off.

"Goddammit!" announces Will Hancock, the first word he has uttered aloud since being imprisoned in this underground cell.

He steps even closer to the door, now just a few feet away. He raises the gun, takes careful aim. With his arm stretched out, the barrel is only inches from the steel knob.

Will fires. The bullet strikes the door knob dead on. Then ricochets straight back. Still traveling at an excessive speed, the bullet rips a hole in Will's throat.

He tries to cry out, in pain and for help, but nothing more than a low guttural moan seeps from his mouth.

Blood spills from the wound.

Will drops the gun and plugs up the bullet hole with his index finger. The pain is terrible.

He stumbles back to the sofa, collapses onto the cushions. The blood trickles out from around his finger. He pulls off his cotton pullover. Rips it in two. The momentary exertion causes the wound to pump out even more blood.

Will takes the torn pullover and ties it around his neck in an effort to control the bleeding. He ties it as tight as he can stand it. Ties it so tight he can hardly breathe.

But the bleeding stops. At least it slows to a gentle ooze.

Will lies back. Tells himself to relax. Take it easy. John, he feels certain, will return any second now. Any minute.

No, he won't, Will reminds himself. John is dead. I as good as killed him myself.

In the end, Will knows, every man suffers, and eventually dies, from the life he leads.

EPILOGUE

THE END

Will Hancock took that bullet in the throat at approxi-
mately 8:33 on Thursday morning. It's now just after 7:30
Friday night.

Clara drives the big BMW sedan. John sits beside her.
His neck is wrapped in gauze and his right shoulder is
bandaged, arm hanging in a sling. Considering how bad
things looked for a while back there in Room 1472, John
feels pretty good.

The ambulance rushed him from the hotel to New York
Presbyterian Hospital. The doctors soon enough discovered his wounds were definitely not life-threatening. Still,
they kept him in overnight for observation.

John's biggest problem was that he could not talk. Well,
he could talk, but only with difficulty and barely at a
whisper. Dicky had done some damage with his straight-
edge razor. But a specialist was called in and he quickly
assured the Hancocks that in a week or two John's speech
would return without impairment. Until then he was to use
his voice as little as possible. No talking unless absolutely
necessary.

So for now John and Clara ride along in silence. Clara
has a thousand questions, a million questions, but it's just

too much trouble to ask them and then wait for John to write down the answers.

Now Clara, who has played a pivotal role in this whole insane scenario, will have to wait to have the rest of her questions answered. She will have to wait to hear about the late Richard Cosgrove. And about Babe Overton, whom the police have arrested for murder and attempted murder. And about the dead body of one Allen Brown, discovered late last night by hotel security in his minivan down in the parking garage. This Brown fellow, Clara learned, is somehow connected to Richard Cosgrove. Who seemed hellbent on killing her husband, slitting his throat.

Yes, Clara will have to wait to find out about all this. She's feeling rather rattled and bewildered by the whole mess. Not a comfortable situation for a woman who prides herself on being in control.

The situation, of course, will get much worse before it has even a prayer of getting any better. Clara hasn't arrived at the bunker yet. She hasn't seen Will. Nor does she yet know what she will find when she finally gets back to the Beacon Hill town house. That terrible carnage still awaits her discovery.

But she is certain her sons are safe. She called Linda just before leaving New York to drive north. She said nothing about what had happened at the Ambassador, but she felt much better after hearing all was well up in the White Mountains of New Hampshire.

Clara and John drive through Stockbridge. Past the Norman Rockwell Museum and the Red Lion Inn. North out of town.

One of the longest days of the year, they still have another hour or so before night falls. It is a beautiful evening: warm and clear and dry, the onset of summer. John points and Clara turns. Up into the hills and finally down the gravel drive.

As they approach the old stone farmhouse, Clara spots her ML320. "How did that get here?" she asks.

John shrugs painfully, rolls his eyes, and points to himself.

"You drove it?"

He nods.

Clara parks the BMW directly behind the Mercedes. She turns off the engine and looks around at the grounds and the garden. "This is lovely. You own this, right? You and Will?"

John nods again. That's about all he can do: nod, shake, and shrug.

"The boys would like it here," says Clara.

And smile. He can still smile. John nods and smiles. The idea of having his boys running around the farm gives him enormous pleasure.

Clara heads for the front door. "Will must be inside."

John grabs her arm, shakes his head.

"He's not inside?"

Again John shakes his head. Then he takes his wife's hand and starts across the lawn.

"How do you know he's out here?"

John shrugs.

They approach the old root cellar. John steers Clara around to the back. Off to the west, the sun, huge and bloodred, hangs over the blue Berkshires.

John has so many things he would like to say to Clara. So many explanations he would like to make. But right now he must set Will free. He cannot for one more minute leave Will locked down in the bunker. And then he has to begin to set the record straight. The three of them have to begin dealing with the past, and preparing for the future.

John motions for Clara to start down the concrete ramp.

"You think he's down there?" she asks, confused.

John nods.

Clara sees the two thick deadbolts on the large wooden door. "It's locked."

John reaches up and pulls back the higher bolt.

"Why is it locked?" Clara looks not only confused now, but a little bit afraid. "Is Will locked in there?"

John sighs and pushes back the lower deadbolt. He pulls the key out of his pocket and unlocks the door.

Clara is more rattled and bewildered than ever. She is not at all sure what to say. Or what to think. The dead body back in Room 1472 was pretty bad. But this does not look very good either.

John slowly pushes the door open. The last light of another day flows into that underground prison.

John steps in first. Clara comes in right behind him. Their eyes need a few seconds to adjust to the dim light.

Will lies on the sofa. Stark naked. In the past thirty-six hours he has used every stitch of clothing on his person to try to stop every last drop of blood from draining out of the puncture wound in his throat. Right now he has his left pant leg wrapped around his neck. It is soaked through, as red as that setting sun.

Will has been off the sofa only once since yesterday morning. Sometime last night he rolled onto the floor and crawled over to where he had dropped that Saturday night special. He picked it up and crawled back to the sofa, thinking very soon he would use the last bullet in the gun to put himself out of his own misery. Several times he has held the gun against his temple, but pulling the trigger has proven impossible. At present the gun lies down between the cushions, under his right elbow.

John stands there, gaping at the gore. Consumed by his brother's condition, he is unable to move.

Clara looks back and forth between her two husbands. There is blood everywhere. Will, dead or dying, lies on the sofa in a pool of blood. John just stands there, doing nothing. John had Will locked in here. In this dungeon. My God, she thinks, John must have shot him. Shot him or cut his throat!

Clara does not at the moment have the ability to reason all this insanity out. "Do something!" she screams. More at herself than at John.

John shakes his head. He does not understand what could have happened. "I took the bullets," he mutters in a low and practically inaudible voice. "I took the bullets from the gun."

"The gun!" repeats Clara. "What gun?"

But John does not respond. He crosses to Will, leans over the sofa, and whispers in his brother's ear. "Christ, Will, what the hell happened?"

Will does not answer. He cannot answer.

"Is he dead?" screams Clara. "Did you kill him?"

John turns. He looks agonizingly at his wife. He shakes his head, tries with all his strength to tell her that he did not do this. Never in his life would he do this. Not to anyone. Certainly not to his own brother. His identical twin brother. But John cannot turn his thoughts into spoken words. Nothing comes out of his mouth at all. Nothing but soft, useless whimpers.

"You shot him!" shouts Clara. "You shot him, then locked him in this . . . in this hole."

John wildly shakes his head. Blood seeps through the gauze around his throat.

He leans down again, puts his ear right against his brother's heart. It's still beating. Not very much, not with any great enthusiasm, but there is still a faint and occasional rhythm.

John whispers very softly in his brother's ear, "Tell her, Will. Tell her I didn't do this. If it's the last thing you ever do, please, tell Clara I didn't do this to you."

Will does not move a muscle or make a sound.

"Please, Will, tell Clara what you've done. You must tell her it was you and not me who started all this. I love her, Will. I love her so much. Her and the boys. I'll take good care of them when you're gone. No one on earth will be better cared for or more loved than Clara and John junior and little Willy. No one. I promise. So tell her, Will. Please. Tell her."

But still Will does not mutter a sound.

"My God," cries Clara, the whole history of this bizarre trinity flashing through her mind. "What have we done?"

John begins to cry. For himself. And for his brother. "Tell her," he continues to beg, shaking Will's bloody body. "Tell her, please."

"Leave him be!" shouts Clara. "If he's not dead already, let him die in peace."

But Will cannot die in peace unless he takes his brother with him.

And so, using the last miniscule scrap of strength left in his almost dead body, Will reaches under those cushions and pulls out the Saturday night special that John brought home from Mexico all those years ago.

Before anyone can say or do anything else, Will sticks the barrel of that gun against his brother's temple.

And pulls the trigger.

THE HANCOCK BOYS

Saturday afternoon. The White Mountains. The Hancock boys, worms on their hooks, fish for trout in the cold, fast-moving stream.

The sun is up now, high and hot.

"Can we go swimming?" John junior asks Aunt Linda.

"Yeah," says young Willy, "I'm sick of fishing. I want to go swimming."

Linda sits behind them on the bank, reading. She closes her book, a best-selling novel written by their fathers. "Swimming? Sure, you can go swimming."

"You come, too."

"No," says Linda, "not me. The water's way too cold for me."

"Just for a minute," pleads John junior

"Yeah," urges Willy, "just for a minute."

Linda sets the book down in the grass and stands. "Come on," she says. "We'll go down around the bend to the swimming hole. The water's deeper there."

The Hancock boys happily follow Linda along the path beneath the old white oaks to the swimming hole. They take one look and jump straight into the cold water. Linda has to work her way in more gradually. An inch or two at a time. The boys paddle around her like a couple of puppies.

"It's freezing!" she shouts, the water now almost up to her waist.

"Want to play the shark game?" John junior asks.

"Yeah," says young Willy. "The shark game! The shark game!"

"What's the shark game?" asks Linda.

"It's where I swim around under the water and grab your leg and pretend to bite it like a shark."

"That sounds terrible," says Linda.

"The shark game!" shouts Willy. "The shark game!"

"Dad taught us," John junior tells Linda. "He used to play it with his brother when they were kids."

John junior slides beneath the surface, disappearing in the cold dark water. Ten or twelve seconds pass.

Linda does not like this game. She is going to tell the boys they cannot play. She is going to tell them they have to get out of the water. It must be time for lunch. Or almost time.

And still no sign of John.

"John!" Linda shouts.

"Where is he?" asks Willy.

"I don't know," answers Linda. "But I wish he would come up for air. I don't like this at all."

Something grabs Willy's leg. The youngster screams.

John junior pops up out of the water. "Gotcha!" he yells at his brother.

Willy punches John junior on the shoulder.

Linda breathes a sigh of relief.

"My turn to be the shark," says Willy.

But before Willy can take his turn, they hear someone coming down the path through the canopy of trees.

"It's Mom and Dad!" shouts young Willy. "I'll bet you a million dollars it's Mom and Dad."

But it's not Mom and Dad. It's just Mom, the weight of her lost and broken world heavy upon her shoulders.

"Mom!" the boys shout. And they paddle to shore, climb out of the water, and race to their mother's side.

Clara hugs them close. Her boys. The Hancock boys.

ABOUT THE AUTHOR

THOMAS WILLIAM SIMPSON is the author of five previous novels, including *The Caretaker* and *This Way Madness Lies,* which has been optioned by Paramount Pictures.

Mr. Simpson lives in New Jersey, where he is at work on his next novel, *The Editor.*